Praise for *Laptop of the Gods*

'Peter Chippindale's [*Laptop of the Gods*] is Terry Pratchett before he became unreadable' *Sunday Telegraph*

'[*Laptop of the Gods*] is a promising start to a projected series' *The Times*

'As a light-hearted satire on the Western obsession with flickering screens, this will appeal to Pratchett and Monty Python fans alike' *Guardian*

'This prudently timed novel is a fun read which casts much cynicism on the millennium bug hype'
The Express

'One of the most original and funny stories I have read in a long time' *New Insight Magazine*

'A very witty novel from a very talented and funny writer' *Black Tears*

Peter Chippindale was born in 1945. He began writing seriously as a front page investigative journalist on the *Guardian*. He then went on to make documentaries for London Weekend Television before leaving to concentrate on his writing. He is the author or co-author of more than a dozen non-fiction books, including the critically acclaimed trilogy on the media industry — *Disaster!*, *Dished!* and *Stick It Up Your Punter!* — the latter recently republished.

Laptop of the Gods is Peter's second work of fiction following his anthropomorphic novel *Mink*, described as '*Watership Down* with claws, confidence and panache' by *The Times*.

He has three young children and lives with his wife Susie near the sea in Cornwall and is currently at work on a sequel to *Laptop of the Gods*.

LAPTOP OF THE GODS

A Millennial Fable

Peter Chippindale

POCKET
B O O K S

LONDON · SYDNEY · NEW YORK · TOKYO · SINGAPORE · TORONTO

First published in Great Britain by Simon & Schuster, 1998
This edition first published by Pocket Books, 1999
An imprint of Simon & Schuster UK Ltd
A Viacom Company

1 3 5 7 9 10 8 6 4 2

Simon & Schuster Ltd
Africa House
64-78 Kingsway
London WC2B 6AH

Simon & Schuster Australia
Sydney

A CIP catalogue record for this book is available from the British Library

ISBN 0-671-85568-9

Typeset in Goudy Modern 14.5/15.5pt by
Palimpsest Book Production Limited, Polmont, Stirlingshire
Printed and bound in Great Britain by
Caledonian International Book Manufacturing Ltd, Glagow

Acknowledgements

I owe special thanks to my wife, Susie, and my friend, Roger Michell, for their encouragement and support, along with Ray Bowler, Charlie Dancey, David Leigh, Helen Wood and Steve Dooley, who also helped with the manuscript in their individual ways.

Grateful thanks in addition to my agents, Carole Blake and Julian Friedmann, and my editor, Gillian Holmes.

Above all, though, my greatest thanks go to Nick Webb, both for having faith in this publication and for making it possible.

for my son, Jon Peter

Contents

PART 2

PART 3

Prologue

The Factory was roaring. And Jupiter loved it. The buzz. The crack. The sheer exhilaration of being here in the Planet Earth control room in the land of the gods while the earthlings approached such an epic moment in their history. The energy he and his fellow gods and goddesses were pumping out to help them! He could picture the outside of the Factory's glass pyramid, high on its hill overlooking Godsville, positively vibrating with its power.

And now more than energy. As the digital calendar hanging over the rows of workstations flicked on to 03.31.00/21.07.1969, GMT, Earth Time, anticipation was surging through the enormous room.

The American space mission to end them all was nearing its climax.

'We have an affirmative.' Mercury whacked SEND and jumped up from his terminal, punching the air in exultation. 'All systems are go!' he yelled. 'Looking good, fellow deities!'

All raised their heads briefly from their screens to

cheer. Then they hunched back over their clattering keyboards, continuing to input furiously to the central computer of GOD.

'Thanks to my baby!' yelled Apollo, the golden young god of light for whom the earthlings' capsule had been named.

'Borne on my wings,' came an answering croak from Saturn, the ancient god of time, his name emblazoned on the mighty rocket that had blasted off from Cape Canaveral.

'Yet controlled by me from the Land of the Gods.'

As god of communications, Mercury was determined to remain in charge.

'It's not just down to you,' Jupiter roared to appreciative cheers and whistles. Where would the American astronauts be now, for example, if he hadn't continuously sent them blasts of good fortune? 'It's all of us together.'

'I'll drink to that!' With a crack like a bullet, Bacchus, the god of vines, let loose a champagne cork at the ceiling.

It rebounded downwards, only for Mars, the fiery god of war, to lunge deftly over his monitor and grab it.

'To boldly go!' he cried, hurling it at Venus.

'Love conquers all!' she laughed, capturing it with a flick of her slim wrist and lobbing it on to Flora.

'And nature rules!' the goddess of flowers shouted happily, throwing it to Cupid, who squealed with delight and aimed it fair and square at Terminus, the dour god of boundaries.

Jupiter rose from his seat and surveyed the enormous room.

Everywhere he could see gods and goddesses pouring

into the aisles to join the fun. As the Highest of the High Order (Greco-Roman Deities) he should assert his control by setting them back to work. Why bother though? Each had done their job magnificently. Another few minutes and they would all be raising their glasses to another triumph in concert with the earthlings.

Never forgetting the central computer of GOD, of course.

Jupiter leapt forward and wrested away the magnum before Bacchus could empty it down his throat.

'All for one and one for all!' he roared, taking a giant swig and tossing it over to Vulcan, who sucked on it greedily.

'One?' Bacchus pushed aside his retinue of giggling nymphs and rummaged in the cooler under his desk. 'There's enough here for an entire army of gods.'

He thrust bottles into eagerly outstretched hands.

'All ranks stand by to celebrate!' Mars was shouting above the fusillade of popping corks, when Juno broke away from the scrum and jumped onto her desk.

'To the moon!' she cried, raising her bottle high.

For a nanosecond Jupiter hesitated. As a sun god he could never — would never — forswear his allegiance to the fiery ball that ruled his immortality. Yet who was he to deny his consort, his beloved moon goddess, the glory of her moment?

'To the moon!' he joined the thundering chorus.

'And all who sail on her!' Neptune's gruff voice was adding to more cheers, when Cupid gave a piercing scream.

'Look out!'

They turned to the giant wall screens encircling the room and Jupiter joined the gasps as he saw the rough, boulder-filled crater looming up. He should have known. Nothing was ever simple with the earthlings' adventures. They always teetered like this, between triumph and disaster. Yet wasn't that the whole, wondrous cusp they and their gods continuously balanced on? The zest? The essence? Not just of earthling mortality, but their own immortality?

'Fuel low. Fuel low,' a mechanical voice began repeating.

They froze, mesmerised by the red light winking urgently on Mercury's control panel.

'Come on, baby.' His fingers skittered across the keyboard. 'You can do it.'

SEND, he punched again, and there was a communal sigh of relief as, with a lurch, the crater was replaced by a vista of a soft, powdery dust.

The hush resumed while the capsule inched down.

'Altitude fifty feet and counting,' the mechanical voice relayed.

'Just one tiny blast, my little beauty,' Mercury crooned, making Juno smile. He was sounding more like an earthling mother than a techno-king! 'One teeny-weeny correction, my lovely.'

SEND, he punched for the last time, and let out a whoop as the vista rocked, then settled.

'Houston. Tranquillity Base. The Eagle has landed,' the wall screens boomed to ecstatic cheers.

The eagle, Jupiter thought proudly whilst they waited breathlessly for the great moment.

His symbol.

'That's one small step for a man, one giant leap for mankind.'

'And one massive bound for its gods!' Jupiter yelled, glancing at the digital clock as the control room erupted.

03.56 Greenwich Mean Time on Planet Earth. Or 'Gods Meridian Time', as they joked.

Then they were dancing in the aisles, hugging each other in ecstasy, while Mars and Vulcan hoisted a rapturous Mercury onto their shoulders for a triumphant tour of the room.

'So, is it down to us, or GOD?'

Juno broke off from the daisy chain she was absentmindedly making and glanced up automatically at the searingly precise geometry of the Factory pyramid. It might only be the outstation linking them to GOD's mainframe on the edge of Godsville. Yet the computer's very spirit seemed to permeate every inch of its glass sides, glowing in the liquid light of dawn, as pinkly, she smiled to herself, as a baby's bottom.

They were lying, blown out, on the grassy bank in front of the vast central atrium, where they had spent the remains of the night in a riot of Bacchanalia, returning occasionally to the Earth control room to share the thrill of the astronauts bouncing weirdly across the lunar surface and looking back in wonder at their planet home.

'Him and us.' As the hero of the hour, Mercury was being uncharacteristically modest. 'Symbiosis,' he added airily. 'GOD's the hardware — the basic DOS running anything from the carbon cycle to natural reproduction. The things that don't alter. Just keep going round and round.

'The solid state,' he added, immensely proud of this new phrase, so much more up to date than 'transistor'.

'In other words' — he gave an ostentatious yawn — 'the boring bits. It's our input, through our terminals, which is the software that separates the earthlings from mere beasts.' He spat the last word with deep contempt. 'Because when we and GOD are working like this in a seamless interface, you've got what it's all about — progress!'

He gave a proud clenched-fist salute to the pyramid.

Juno frowned. She wasn't the only goddess suspicious of this all-embracing catchword that GOD had foisted on the earthlings.

'Progress or not progress, it's never worked as well as this before,' she sidestepped.

'Because we never had techno like this to work with on Planet Earth before.'

Mercury, back to being supercool, donned his Ray-Bans in tribute to the rising sun.

'Neither did the earthlings,' Cupid interrupted shrilly. Why did the adult gods always leave them out of the equation? 'We must never forget the part they play. After all, without them we wouldn't even exist, would we?'

Jupiter turned back from watching Godsville emerge through the morning mist.

Would there ever be a day they didn't talk shop? Yet who could blame them? Juno was right. It had never worked like this before. Both for the earthlings and themselves as their gods. Which wasn't just Mercury's doing. All the assorted gods and goddesses lying around him had been responsible, in their own ways, for the recent dizzying changes on Planet Earth.

Today, admittedly, was Mercury's day.

Yet the Americans landing the first men on the moon was only the latest in the long string of extraordinary events when others had led the show — Flora, Juno, Vulcan, Neptune, Venus, himself. Not just Higher

Order members either. The most minor and regional deities had pumped their energy into GOD to help raise the earthlings to these new heights.

'We're on a roll,' he commented unnecessarily.

A roll! More like an awesome, gut-wrenching, roller coaster of a ride that had transformed their immortalities!

Only the other day Apollo had led them on their GOD-granted Earth tickets to matter-transfer across space and join the quarter of a million earthlings gathered at the Rolling Stones' free concert in London's Hyde Park. How they had revelled in immersing themselves in the new era of sex and drugs and rock and roll!

Except for Mars, sulking at seeing so many young earthlings celebrating making love, not war.

'I am the little red planet!' he had belted out angrily, before getting so far out of it they had eventually had to matter-transfer him, comatose, back to the Land of the Gods.

'I can't get no godly action!' Venus, the personification of youthful beauty with all its power and passion, had transfixed the earthlings as she stripped to the waist and stood grinding her hips, whilst her son Cupid shot round pinging everyone in sight.

'Love is love and I'll make it stay!' he had shrieked happily.

Meanwhile, Flora, suitably bedecked, had refused to let her invention of flower power be eclipsed.

'If you come to sunny Godsville,' she had sung happily, 'Be sure to wear some flowers in your hair . . .'

Because not just London was swinging. This new spirit of freedom had swept the entire western hemisphere, which was their responsibility as gods. San Francisco, LA, Paris, Munich, Rome, Oslo, Copenhagen.

And with it had come this elation, this optimism, this grandeur. You couldn't dismiss it as mere style. Or cliché. The earthlings weren't simply dedicated followers of fashion. Of course there were the clothes, the music, the parties.

Underneath, though, was something much more fundamental.

One day, a load of sad old gits would doubtless sit around on Planet Earth, saying things like 'Amazing, man!' and 'Far out!' whilst they farted on about how wonderful it had been for everyone.

Yet, seeing it in the here and now, Jupiter certainly didn't think it that wonderful for the vast majority of earthlings, even in the pampered West. However much you were for the new age, you had to admit it was largely the province of the young, the educated, the beautiful people from the middle classes with the time to enjoy just being hippies and swingers. Of whom, of course, you also had to recognise a fair proportion were absolute shits. Especially those reared by Britain's public-school system.

Jupiter knew that when he laid down the law, as he was prone to do, about how he saw the earthlings' position many gods thought his attitude didactic. Puritan even. Yet they couldn't deny that for many earthlings life was as grindingly sterile as ever. For the males long lifetimes spent in mind-numbing, hazardous and health-destroying work in heavy industries like mining, steel and factories. Equally hard and monotonous work for the females, along with the additional burden of bringing up children, while all the time treated by most males as inferiors.

Who could disagree, Jupiter would demand in ringing tones, that there were still as many wrongs to be righted? As many oppressions to be dealt with? As many things that didn't work?

Take the United Nations, which he personally spent so much time and energy trying to crank up. How many times had he bust a gut to get everyone in agreement, only to find some stupid buggers like the Brits pompously exercising their veto and bringing everything he had worked for crashing to the ground?

Meanwhile, not just he, but all of them, had to face the fact that a lot of the new wave, far from being 'groovy', was just plain silly. Naive froth scathingly, and accurately, dismissed by more 'sensible' earthlings, as they called themselves, as ludicrously impractical.

Yet this new irreverence for authority had brought such a breath of fresh air. Slain so many sacred cows. You could criticise it for being childish, irresponsible, tacky, commercial, hyped. Be as negative as you liked.

In the end, though, you had to admit it added up to a positive.

But still a tender plant, as Flora always put it. A germinated seed, sprouting its first tentative shoots. The fledgling leaves that they were nurturing, often in the face of a hostile and chilly climate.

'And it only takes one sharp frost . . .' she would warn ominously.

Yet, if they could only raise it to successful fruition . . .

Because they weren't wrong.

Something was poking its head skywards down there. Something wonderful. Something worth believing in. Something which, under the froth, contained a strongly spiritual side. Often misguided, maybe, but spiritual nonetheless. And, as spirituality was what all gods fed on, it had woken them up, like spirits from the dead.

Never had Earth tickets been so popular.

Now, with Mercury's latest moon success, things seemed set to continue on the same path, right to the end of this amazing decade of the sixties.

Jupiter jerked himself out of his reverie.

'Still on the same roll,' he added, even more unnecessarily.

'How long since it was last like this?' Vesta's perfect brow delicately and deliciously furrowed.

Jupiter sighed and turned back to look out over Godsville.

The goddess of hearth and home could be so remarkably pedantic. What was time, when you were immortal? Apart from Saturn, strapped by it as his speciality, it was meaningless after you had spent two thousand odd years struggling to raise the earthlings above mere animal existence. If it *was* two thousand odd. It might as well be two million for all any of them could remember, thanks to PML, the Progressive Memory Loss, which afflicted all immortals, causing the past to fade into a confused blur.

Like so many other things, PML was a factor in the Land of the Gods outside your control. You could regard it as benevolent, vindictive, or − probably most accurately − both. You never quite knew where you were with the central computer of GOD. Yet they all understood how necessary it was. How else could they clear space in their heads to do their job of concentrating on the present?

Not that there wasn't a downside. Because PML also meant, of course, that GOD, with his multiple memory banks and faultless logic, held all the correct answers. Which, in turn, was the major key to his power . . .

Gods, Oracles and Deities, Jupiter mouthed, nodding in mock obeisance towards the shining pyramid.

Their mentor. Their taskmaster. Their controller.

Because, for all that Vesta's question was pedantic, it still raised a valid point. Despite PML, they were all certain Planet Earth had had a Golden Age like this before. A time, way back in the mists, when they had been as plugged in, as connected, as right in there. Which only made the current sequence of events even more mind-bogglingly, thrillingly exciting. They were back! And it was all coming right again!

The good old earthlings were a decent lot after all. Not just brave, but absolutely correct, to renew their faith that there was someone out there with their welfare at heart. Because there was: themselves, working their tits and balls off to help Planet Earth be so wonderfully, refreshingly — above all innocently — reborn.

'How long is it?' Jupiter appealed to Saturn.

The venerable old god, sitting in his flowing white robe, stroked his white beard and raised his sickle.

'How many times must a god look down

'Before he sees Planet Earth?

'Yes, 'n' how many times must his lightning bolts fly

'Before he's secure in his birth?

'The answer, my deity, is in the Land of the Gods,

'The answer's in the Land of the Gods . . .'

His sickle swept in a hissing arc.

'Amazing gods,' Juno interrupted in her sweet contralto, giving Jupiter a loving smile.

'What power they have

'To save earthling . . .'

'All you need are gods . . .' Venus, spectacular in a

diaphanous purple robe, rose to her feet, strawberry-
blonde locks tumbling down her back.

'Dum de de diddy dum!' they roared at the tops of
their voices. They loved this bit!

'All you need are gods, gods!'

'Gods are all you need.'

'All you need, all you need . . .'

Now they were really getting down to it.

'I went and pinged those California girls,' Cupid
trilled excitedly.

'Dum de dum de, dum de dum de, dum de dum de,
dum de dum de!'

The chorus swayed ecstatically from side to side.

'I'm the ping-ball wizard

'And I want you to know,' Cupid was switching
tracks when Apollo rode over to him.

'Earthlings try to put us down.' His air guitar
stuttered like an earthling machine gun.

'Just because we're all around,

'Things we do look awful old,

'Yet immortals are always bold . . .

Breathlessly, they waited for the chorus.

'Talkin' 'bout my v-v-v-veneration,' they pounded
out,

'My veneration, earthlings,

'My veneration . . .'

'We all live in Neptune's godmarine.'

The salty old seagod hoisted his trident.

'Neptune's godmarine. Neptune's godmarine . . .'

Jupiter grinned. He had never seen them so happy.
Maybe Neptune was right. They didn't really live in
the Land of the Gods after all, but some bizarre subaqua
machine. With what GOD was capable of dreaming up,
stranger things had happened.

But who cared? It was so much easier letting everything roll into the songs. They said as much as any debate. If not more.

He jumped up off the grass, bursting with the joy of being immortal.

'You say you want a godly evolution,' he boomed out, Godsville, now clearly visible, laid out below him.

'Well you know, we all want to change Planet Earth,

'We know we have a new solution . . .'

'Don't you know it's gonna be, all gods!' everyone belted out:

'It's gonna be, all gods . . .'

'Goodness, gracious, great god of fire!' came a horribly tuneless shout.

Vulcan, gobs of spittle spraying into his air microphone, writhed horribly as he attempted the splits.

'Well it's one for the planet,

'One immortal show,

'You'd better be with us,

''cos its go gods go . . .'

With Vulcan's crony Mars cranking up his Elvis impersonation, Jupiter knew what was coming. Technically, Elvis might not be a god. Yet they all afforded him equal status when it came to partying.

'They say our love is GODly-sent,' he sang softly to Juno, nodding towards the car park.

He had to get away before the thrash began again.

Maybe it was because GOD — or whoever ran GOD — had saddled him with eternal middle age. Yet Jupiter suspected not. They had all become so locked into their work at his Factory they were utterly drained. Their private lives abandoned, all they did these days was eat, sleep and dream Planet Earth. As well as party, of course. You had to, to banish the adrenaline coursing round your system. In reality, though, if they would but admit it, every single one of them, god, goddess – even little Cupid, for all his energy – was terminally exhausted.

Not yet fucked, by a long chalk. But getting that way.

'Sorry, but I'm knackered,' he apologised to Juno as he gunned the red Ferrari 250 GTO out of the car park.

Jupiter was aware cars weren't as popular on Planet Earth as they once had been. Yet he couldn't help liking his a lot. He'd never had a better model from Maranello.

Flooring the throttle, he snatched third and whacked the back end out, putting them into a classic four-wheel drift which sent them howling round the ramp leading onto the expressway.

'Quite honestly,' he shouted over the roar of the six Weber carburettors as he hit 6,500 r.p.m., 'I don't know how much longer I can keep this up. Any of us can.'

'Us, or the car?' Juno shouted back. 'The car's fine. Minerva's message for us, though, is "Not much longer".'

Jupiter snorted as he settled the Ferrari down at a steady 130 m.p.h. in the fast lane.

The females were always raving about the reclusive goddess of wisdom as the fount of all knowledge. Yet even he could see the warning signs. Which way did you want it? was today's question. Sink another bottle of Scotch? Empty the brandy? Slam down the tequila? Break out the rum? Vodka, comrade? Another G and T, darling?

Or the alternatives?

Smoke another joint? Eat a few more magic mushrooms? Take a tab? Cram in the speed? Pop an upper? A downer? Snort a line? Get the needle out?

Or why not go the whole hog and stick both sides of the equation together?

It was like the earthling football pools Jupiter, as god of fortune, so enjoyed fiddling with. What had he slipped in last Saturday? Barnsley 6, Wrexham 6 (Third Division North), followed by Forfar Athletic 5, Berwick Rangers 5 (Scottish League Division 2).

That must have caused a few earthling heart attacks!

There were as many possible permutations with the drugs and alcohol. They should know. Like the earthlings, they'd tried virtually every single one. And, as the drugs became harder, the excesses were becoming more pronounced. It had to blow sooner or later — in the Land of the Gods as well as on Planet Earth. They might not have reached it yet, but even gods and goddesses had to have breaking points.

Jupiter cursed, his chain of thought abruptly broken.

They had reached the section of expressway running on raised legs over the inner-city slums, inhabited by a nightmare collection of deities and spirits going back to the beginning of earthling time. Whenever he looked down on the ragbag of crumbling roofs and, even more, the twisted forests and primordial swamps bordering the Stygian river which bisected Godsville, Jupiter always wondered how they stood being so packed together in their vile, smelly ghettos.

As well as where GOD had got all of them from, so many were entirely weird. Like this Dark Age tree spirit, gnarled, hairy, covered in moss and with a face like wrinkled bark, which had somehow managed to break out of the coned-off monster lane to blunder clumsily about in their path.

Jupiter hit the horn, dropped two gears and swerved to take it on the inside, receiving a look of pondering wonder in return.

To think, some earthlings had once worshipped that!

'It does make you wonder, doesn't it?' he remarked absent-mindedly.

'You're always wondering, J. That's what you do.'

Jupiter tried to suppress his irritation.

'This time I'm right to, though, Juno. You know that. Do you really think Planet Earth's getting any better? Or are we just trying to convince ourselves it's all working?'

'You think it's an illusion, don't you, my dear?' she enquired gently. 'A bubble that'll burst to send us and the earthlings hurtling back into the past?'

'It's just that a lot of the stuff down there seems too good to be true,' he replied lamely. 'What about the other side, Juno?'

How could anyone suppress feelings of deep anxiety with events like the Sharpeville massacre in South Africa? Hungary, Czechoslovakia, both ground again under the Russian heel? The South American military juntas? The torture and brutality practised daily by terrorists, death squads, lone assassins — government-employed or otherwise? President Kennedy? Martin Luther King?

The political murders had severely depressed him.

'What's that song Flora always sings when she's down?'

'Where have all the worshippers gone, aeons passing?' Juno sang back. 'When will earthlings ever learn? When will earthlings ever learn?'

'That's the one. So when will they?' he demanded, blaring the air horns savagely at a minor deity in a Ford Anglia who had strayed across into their lane. 'Take this Vietnam business Mars is stoking up. It's getting really ugly.'

Yet, now they were out into the suburbs and slowing for their exit, he couldn't prevent his spirits lifting. Junction 14, he thought proudly. Everyone wanted to be seen leaving by it. So much so that some Lower Order gods, like the jerk in the Anglia behind them, used it, even though it wasn't their correct turn-off, in a vain attempt to convince others of their higher status.

'Shh!' Juno chided, reaching over to put a placating finger to his lips. 'When will you ever learn, my dear god, just to go with the flow? That there's nothing else to do?'

'Hippie talk,' he mocked affectionately as they approached the familiar entrance to Arcadia Close. 'Is it all fab down there, then? Gear, even?'

'Well, why go with the flow, when you can be a proper god and take control?'

Without warning he snatched first gear and sent them screaming up the Close. At the last second, he spun the wheel, yanked on the handbrake and slewed to a screeching stop in a flurry of gravel, inches from the bumper of Juno's yellow Lotus Elan.

He grinned as he saw her wince, before they both sat, listening to the tick of hot metal whilst they sniffed the pungent smell of scorched brake pads.

'Boys and their toys.' She blew out her cheeks.

'And why not?' Jupiter asked, entirely unabashed. 'As for there being nothing else to do, how about this?'

Before she could move he had leapt out, run round, opened her door and scooped her up in his arms.

Ducking under her hanging baskets, he kicked open the front door of number 31 and carried her giggling upstairs.

What if all this stuff on Planet Earth was an illusion? he thought as he whisked her in and out of the shafts of sunlight pouring through the windows. If so, as Minerva's wisdom kept reminding them, as with any illusion it was bound to end in tears.

Yet Juno was still right. Like the brave earthlings possessed of the same courage, they should go with it while they could. Pump in the passion, the energy, the commitment.

Both sides would just have to cope with the crash when it came.

'Immortal,

'Us gods are immortal,

'Us gods are immortal,

'Here every day . . .' he boomed, giving his consort, his beloved moon goddess, his hugest smile.

How much he loved her! Not just her, but everything and everyone, both here in the Land of the Gods and on Planet Earth. Even GOD, although loving a crotchety, slave-driving computer wasn't always easy. For the most brilliant thing about this roll they were on was how it was uniting them, suppressing even their giant individual egos as each recognised the part the others were playing in creating the whole, mad, driving shooting match.

They were working, as they should, as a team.

Alongside, of course, the earthlings in their tender charge.

'We're computer GOD's Immortal Spirits Band,' he sang joyfully,

'We know you do enjoy our show!

'We're computer GOD's Immortal Spirits Band,
'Relax and let your psyche flow . . .
'I like little Cupid,' he couldn't help breaking off
to add. 'For such a junior god, he's got a good point.
Because we must never forget the part the earthlings
play, must we? A lot of them are being heroes, just as
much as us.'

'Or heroines,' Juno ticked him off sternly.

If there was one point on which she found him
sometimes lacking it was his attitude to the young
earthling females determined to throw off the inferior
role that male domination had confined them to. Juno
had put a lot of her weight behind the burning of bras
to demonstrate the new-found equality.

'Or heroines,' he grinned apologetically as they
reached the bedroom door. 'Sorry, Juno.'

She smiled back forgivingly, knowing how difficult
it was for all gods to adapt to such a fundamental change.

At which point they both switched the earthlings
off.

For the next few hours, at least as far as they were
concerned, astronauts or not, they would have to look
after themselves.

PART I

Chapter I

Fired Up

Jupiter opened a piercing blue eye and stared balefully at his glowing digital alarm clock. 06.31/15.12.1999. Why had he woken so early? His and Juno's pattern these days was a late start, with breakfast taken at their leisure. Which was par for the course in the Land of the Gods, where nothing usually happened until mid-morning. If anything happened at all, Jupiter thought bitterly.

Not that, a recent stern GOD e-mail had reminded them, any of them had a right to be bitter.

Rather, it had decreed, they were extremely fortunate.

Especially Jupiter, being god of fortune.

'I will not tolerate any more negative grumbling,' it had warned. 'Merciful I may be, yet I am also infinitely mighty. Which means I can be as vengeful and wrathful as I choose. Got it?'

To ram home his point, he had then switched on his public broadcasting system and bombarded Arcadia Close with the greatest hits of Status Quo.

For twelve solid hours.

'No more!' they had begged, sinking to their knees as he threatened them further with a continuous Monkees medley, interspersed with 'Simon Says' on auto-repeat. 'We agree. We are incredibly, enormously, hugely fortunate!'

Yet still not always.

For now Jupiter was wide awake. Which was unfortunate, whatever GOD might decree.

He lay listening to Juno's regular breathing whilst he pondered his options. He could always go downstairs and watch GODS TV's 'good news agenda' about Planet Earth. Once, he vaguely remembered, this had been compulsive viewing. Everyone had used to leap up, eager to see the results of their Herculean struggles on behalf of the earthlings.

Now, of course, there were no longer any struggles to be interested in.

But there had been a further change which sent Jupiter into paroxysms of rage. The format of GODS TV had been revamped to 'infotainment', rendering it a mishmash of lightweight chatter, zany graphics and snippets of 'lifestyle'.

The Lower Order gods might love this jokey new bit culture.

But not Jupiter.

And that wasn't, he kept informing them, simply because he was the Highest God of the High Order.

'It's not snobbery saying things have gone downhill,' he would boom. 'It's just plain fact.'

Not that they listened, of course. But that was the Lower Orders for you.

Also gone downhill, in Jupiter's opinion, was Jeffrey Archer, whose latest effort was currently lying next to the alarm clock. Ye gods! GOD might insist they had to absorb this mush in order to stay in touch with popular culture on Planet Earth. Yet there were times, like when GODmail delivered yet another CD of some lookalike girlie group, along with both fanzine and poster . . .

Jupiter shook his head. Something more important than earthling business was nagging at his mind.

He looked back at the alarm clock.

06.35/15.12.1999.

Then it registered.

This was his big day!

Throwing back the covers, he bounded to the window and flung back the curtains to reveal the silent rooftops, sparkling with morning dew.

'Fellow residents of Arcadia Close,' he thundered, 'today you are to witness a magnificent victory for the rights of the property owner . . .'

As a loud blaring suddenly drowned him out, he peered down, fuming.

There was his enemy, Vulcan, silhouetted on top of the revolting heap of metal that adorned the garden of number 29!

The god of fire, spotting him at the window, gave an ostentatious finger, then went back to winding the handle of the antique-looking siren he was holding up.

Jupiter bellowed with rage and pointed a thick forefinger to zap him with a lightning bolt. Not just one, either, but a whole coruscating battery of the things. Or what would have been a coruscating battery, had GOD not disempowered him for 'safety reasons'.

All he could muster these days was this feeble blue flame, which was now flickering politely, accompanied by the most discreet rumble of thunder you ever heard.

Cursing, Jupiter shook his fist as a substitute. Would he never learn to break the habit? Then suddenly Juno was by his side, as naked as himself.

'I thought we vowed to play this by the book,' she shouted, slamming down the window and driving him backwards with a series of furious prods to his chest.

'I'm sorry,' he replied meekly as his back thudded into the wall. 'It's just that he winds me up so much.'

'That's what he's aiming to do.'

Jupiter dropped his eyes penitently to the carpet. He knew the feud with Vulcan had become so obsessive it was in danger of harming his and Juno's relationship. Yet that was the way things seemed to be in the Land of the Gods, at this grim fag end of this earthling century.

'You're a moon goddess, Juno.' He tried to excuse himself for the thousandth time. 'You've got a more balanced temperament. Us sun gods are much more excitable. Every time I clap eyes on him I just see red.'

'How do you think I feel, with his attitude towards goddesses?' she was shouting back, when the blaring outside abruptly stopped, to be replaced by the angry cries of gods and goddesses hurling abuse, at both Vulcan and each other.

Jupiter slumped against the wall, his spirit hit by an overwhelming melancholy.

What had GOD's bullshit pack labelled Arcadia Close, here in the leafy suburbs of Godsville?

'A post-modern version of the pastoral dream.'

Jupiter snorted.

Superficially it might look that — the neat twin row of palatial villas with their 'marble-style' Corinthian columns, the turning circle at the end, where number 31 occupied a commanding view, the sculptured lawns, specimen trees, vista of the Elysian fields. Beyond, the Sylvan glades, the green meadows dotted with fleecy sheep and milk-white cows, the fields of rich brown earth, recently cleaved by Ceres' curvèd plough . . .

'A model community,' GOD had decreed. And exactly what he programmed every hard-working earthling executive to aspire to.

Just scratch the surface, though, Jupiter thought grimly, and you uncovered such a seething mass of hatred, mean-mindedness and back-biting jealousy it made the soaps on GODS TV look like kindergarten. Even more so in the rougher areas of the Eurogods' suburb, like the gross Lower Orders' estate and the nightmare Valhalla Villas housing the Nordic and Teutonic deities.

Which wasn't their fault, every god and goddess agreed. GOD could bang on as much as he liked about their being 'extremely fortunate'. In reality, though, as they endlessly moaned, he had dumped them here, like chickens in a coop, to stew.

And, when you left gods to stew, they did it in a way befitting such awesome beings.

A big way.

'Go and see Jupiter,' Vulcan's coarse voice cut over the babble outside. 'It's all down to him.'

There was the sound of running feet.

'Ignore them, J,' Juno instructed, pinioning him with her green eyes whilst loud drumming began on the front door and the bell ding-donged crazily.

How typically male to have triggered this latest spat!

Yet her heart was still going out to him. Way back in time, she could dimly remember them both behaving so badly they had sparked enormous ructions between them. But, as goddess of conjugal love, she had long since repaired the damage. Now they saw themselves as locked together for ever — or 'better or worse', as GOD put it.

And worse it had certainly become. So bad that recently she had needed every ounce of her considerable strength.

'I wish I'd never started it,' J had fallen into the habit of remarking during his increasingly prevalent dark moods.

'Except, of course, I didn't,' he would promptly contradict himself, while she wondered if she should have egged him on as she had.

How could she have known such a trivial-seeming matter as this boundary dispute with Vulcan would drag on for so long, spin through so many loops, maybe — dare she think it — even get out of control?

'You know what immortality feels like, Juno?' He looked utterly defeated. 'Like every morning you wake up, only for GOD to dump a bucket of shit on your head.'

'He did design our immortality to mirror the lives of the earthlings,' she reminded him, running her fingers through his grey chest hair whilst she fought to stay calm. 'Remember his e-mail when he piped in Sky TV? "Just keeping your fingers on their pulses," it said.'

Jupiter ignored the opportunity for the corny joke about their getting Sky TV because they lived in the sky.

'Bugger their puny pulses, Juno,' he protested. 'We're not earthlings. We're immortal deities.'

'But the earthlings' immortal deities, J. That's the point. GOD's told us the same thing a million times: "What they get, we get".'

She spoke the phrase like a mantra, trying to stabilise herself as much as him.

Only to find that she had provoked the opposite reaction.

'Which is where half the bloody trouble lies, isn't it?' he was now thundering at the top of his voice. 'Because GOD's not even being honest, is he? "What they get, we get" indeed!'

His piercing blue eyes bored into hers.

'What about what we don't get, Juno?' he demanded. 'The things in the big picture. Like death, for a start. I don't mean ordinary death, either – passing away peacefully, surrounded by loved ones, after a fulfilling and worthwhile life.

'No. I mean ghastly, agonising, excruciating death – and existence – caused by the jolly diseases GOD's thought up to inflict on the earthlings. Cancer, spina bifida, Alzheimer's, autism, childhood leukaemia, paranoid schizophrenia. Never mind his latest wheezes of AIDS and BSE.

'Why, Juno? I mean, what do any of them prove?'

She said nothing. Having sparked his standard rant, she would now endure it.

'You know what an earthling once said about life?' he demanded further. 'It's solitary, poor, nasty, brutish and short. And with some reason! How would any of us like to be cut off in our prime — worse, never even be allowed to achieve it — by something as horrible as any of those? How would we like the pain, the misery, the affliction of something about which we'd been given no choice? Over which we had no control?'

He paused, the hurt showing in his eyes.

'Anyhow, if we do get what the earthlings get, aren't we supposed to be what they call "major players" down there these days? Big cheeses? Bosses?

'So why are we stuck in this dead shithole, bored out of our brains, like those idiot earthlings who somehow think they've risen above their fellows and "made it"?

'Made it!' he sneered with deep loathing. 'Made it to their bloody epilogues, more like!

'As for the rest, it's like some mad bloody recipe, isn't it?'

He gave a hollow laugh.

'Here's what you do,' he intoned in a passable parody of GODS TV. 'First, take a good collection of gory civil wars and mix with loads of overpopulation until everyone's fighting for space.

'Then pour in assorted pollution — oil slicks, carbon dioxide, acid rain, deadly chemicals, lead in the atmosphere. All that sort of thing.

'Now, add a good pinch of mass starvation. Throw in a selection of weapons of mass destruction. Cover with a thick layer of natural disasters, from famine to droughts to floods.

'Finally, make a nice big hole in the ozone layer.

'Place in a pot, stir the whole mess until it's well and truly boiling, and serve piping hot to an ego-led race which you've carefully designed to specialise in murder, torture, cruelty and mayhem, then further equipped with an appetite for nasty and fatuous ideological conflict beyond anything anybody sane could possibly imagine.'

Juno thought she saw her chance.

'We're sane, though, J,' she jumped in.

Too soon.

He hadn't finished.

'Now, the sweet course,' he boomed, overriding her. 'Something nice and light from the trolley, Juno? A plate of bullshit? Dollop of mass consumerism? Melange of marketing? Piece of presentation? Assortment of financial services? Spot of advertising? Slice of spin-doctoring?

'How trivial, insignificant, phoney, is life down there to become?

'Because, no matter what anyone says, I still maintain that underneath it all most earthlings are basically decent. Which is why I'm absolutely sure this isn't what GOD originally intended for them.

'I mean, what could anyone possibly have done to deserve a fate like that?'

He stopped and stared at her, looking utterly defeated again.

'It's sick, Juno. Not just sick, but sad,' he added brokenly.

She looked back at him fondly.

These things needed saying. Which was why she had let him have his head.

Not every day, by everyone. But some days, by someone.

At times like this she recalled the image of a crouched earthling, the weight of the whole planet on his back. Was this the load J was imposing on himself? No. That wasn't fair. As the greatest god, it was the one he had been loaded with. Further, one he had not shirked his duty and responsibility to, thereby earning her eternal respect.

If he could only lighten up a bit, though. Not be so entirely heavy about it!

Except, of course, there was no getting round the fact.

It was a heavy subject.

Right now, though, she needed to hoick him out of it. Bring him back to the different reality, in many ways so much more germane, of what was actually happening in their own immortalities.

'Remember where this Vulcan business started,' she reminded him. 'OK, it's only a boundary dispute. Low-grade, minor, nothing to do with our stewardship of the earthlings.

'Yet we agreed there was a principle involved, didn't we? That we would use it to determine how much shit's dumped by GOD, and how much we're dumping on ourselves?

'Only then, we decided, could we do something about it.'

Outside she could hear the mob going back to berating Vulcan.

'Which is why, for the hundred thousandth time, we decided to make a stand.'

A glint came into her eye as her hand ended its downward journey.

'And that's something you could do right now,' she smiled, despite the disappointing flaccidity of his mighty member. 'You're still every inch a god, you know.' She gave it an affectionate tweak. 'You're just stressed out.'

But at that point she lost him.

'Stressed out!' he thundered, shoving her roughly out of the way. 'Stress is just another bloody modern GOD invention, Juno!

'Was I stressed out when I was indulging in heroic quests?' Furious, he flung on his dressing gown. 'When I was slaying monsters? Forging earthling destinies?

'So I'm hardly likely to be stressed out by a scumbag like fucking Vulcan, am I?

'Especially,' he boomed in a final sally from the landing, 'when I'm just about to nail the bastard to the wall.'

Chapter 2

Doom! Doom!

Juno fought back the tears as she sat at her dressing table, brushing her short curly hair. It wasn't her consort rejecting her advances, horny though she'd been. Her psyche wasn't that fragile. Anyway, she always had her GOD-given vibrator to fall back on in emergencies.

No, it was the rest of it, currently being brought home by the ongoing row from next door.

What had happened to those halcyon days she dimly remembered? Those days ushered in by the fabulous kingfisher, from which they derived their name?

'Days of calm and quietude? Lovely days, loving days, days of generosity and warmth of spirit?' she had unexpectedly found herself asking everyone at a recent barbecue Apollo had put on at number 17, her nostalgia sparked off by the song on the sensurround player.

'When a god loves the earthlings,
'It gives him peace of mind;
'He tries to deliver
'All the goods things that they need . . .'
'Days when the whole universe seemed in bloom,'
Flora had sadly agreed.

'All was sweetness and light.' Apollo had looked
gravely up at the stars.

'Planet Earth was your oyster,' Neptune had chipped
in mournfully.

'An oyster for romantics!' Venus's eyes had shone.
'One with the grit to produce the shining pearl!'

'Only thanks to my pinging!' Cupid had squeaked
self-importantly, breaking the spell by making them
laugh.

Except that it wasn't funny.

Through the haze of Progressive Memory Loss, they
knew deep inside themselves that long, long ago, there
had been halcyon days. Days when their immortalities
had been wonderful. When they had been loved,
worshipped, feared even, by the earthlings in their
charge. And not just long ago either. What about the
more recent period, when they were equally certain
they had recaptured the same old exuberance? The
same passion. The same power.

'. . . He gives up his immortality,
'To help them through their lives . . .'

Why did the old songs always bring the feeling back?
Was it myth? Reality?

'Or just a GOD-inspired whimsy?' she had mused
out loud as the heart-tugging ballad came to an end.
Percy Sledge. What a name! 'A conceit, a caprice, sent
to torment us?'

Not that she was exactly sure what a caprice was.

It sounded right, though. Like a flight of fancy, as if no one cared.

But then J had stepped in and shattered the mood by delivering his standard diatribe about giving up on their responsibility to the earthlings. After which the debate had run through its normal muddled stages until, as always, it petered out.

The truth was that PML had reduced the past to such a jumble of telescoped time, lost sequences and fuddled reminiscences, none of them knew the answer. Yet the question remained. If it had been like that, especially recently, who had changed? Themselves? The earthlings? GOD?

Because something, somewhere, was responsible for reducing them to this level of the Lowest of the Low, rather than Highest of the High.

Like this stupid, pathetic boundary dispute with Vulcan she and J had locked themselves into. Somehow it summed everything up: it was so infinitely boring yet horribly fascinating. Juno couldn't conceive of anything more petty in the entire universe. Yet J had poured all his energy into it, all the time knowing GOD had arranged about the biggest thing in their entire immortalities for that very evening. From the way J talked about that, though – or rather didn't talk about it – you'd think he'd forgotten it completely.

OK, the fence business was bound to arouse strong passions precisely because it was so entirely minuscule, so irritatingly infuriating. Yet it was still a typically male mistake to accord it the massive significance that J had.

But the reality, as Juno knew full well, was that he was using it to block out his really important responsibilities.

To be fair, though, he was an honourable god, unlike so many these days. Goddesses as well, she was forced to admit. He still retained his spirit of self-sacrifice, cared for the earthlings, worked his fingers to the bone at his terminal on their behalf, exhausted himself dealing with their endless committees and selfish vested inter-ests, the fudgers, deadheads, time-servers, corrupt . . .

Which she had to admire him for. Yet at the same time, like his standard rant, where did earthling business get you, compared to the things that were actually happening, or about to happen, in your own immortality?

Such as her dream in the night, which she hadn't dared mention, in case she upset him at such a cru-cial time.

In the mirror she saw her hairbrush begin to shake.

The dream that was resurfacing!

Not again, she pleaded with a sudden flash of fear.

Juno didn't have dreams that often, and hardly ever nightmares like this had been. Neither had she ever attached much significance to them, treating them as interesting, but nothing to particularly dwell on. So why her feeling that this one was different? A portent? A sign she must take notice of? A negative sign, filling her with foreboding, yet giving her no way forward? Nothing tangible to do, no line to follow?

And a dream she was now powerless to prevent taking over her mind again, transporting her back to her beloved pomegranate orchard. The orchard that, not only for her, but the earthlings, symbolised conjugal love and always brought thoughts of it flooding into her mind.

She went there regularly, using it as a resource, a private place, which J respected. A place where she could recharge her batteries, reaffirm her faith. As now, with the feeling she was recapturing the halcyon days. Winter stripped away, fruits swelling on the branches, dancing leaves providing welcome dappled shade so that she floated, cocooned in a bubble of happiness at having such a warm and wonderful kinship with her surroundings.

Such all-embracing love. Such a deep, deep sense of being at one. Of belonging.

Yet already she could see the wind approaching. Like a wall. A dry, arid wind, stirring up the dust into menacing eddies, which then grew into towering dark columns that blotted out the sun.

As they drew nearer, she could hear the cackling glee of the voice contained within them.

'Doom! Doom! The earthlings are all doomed!'

'Not I, but the wind blowing through me,' she found herself inexplicably protesting, rising to her feet in alarm and dread as the wall hit her.

Now she was battling to stay upright, her long tunic, flapping madly behind her, tugging her off balance. Dry grit was being flung in her face, stinging her eyes and forcing its way down her throat, so she could no longer breathe.

She tried to turn her back, but no matter how much she ducked and weaved, the wind moved round with her.

There was to be no escape. Nowhere to hide.

For her, or her precious pomegranates.

All round, the branches, whipped and thrashed with supernatural ferocity, were shedding their unripe fruits.

'My babies!' she cried as they thudded to the ground round her.

So tenderly nursed since budding infancy, now being plucked too early!

She rushed about, frantically trying to gather them into her tunic. She had to put them back, reattach them to the life force!

Yet they bumped and bowled infuriatingly away from her, as if possessed of a life of their own. Teased her by staying quiveringly stationary. Then jumped, just as she reached for them.

She went down on her knees and flung herself on top of them, reaching below her to grab their hard bumps. Only to recoil in horror as each she touched instantly putrefied into a vile, loathsome slime which clung to her hands.

She beat at it furiously.

Yet the more she touched it, the more it adhered, until it had coalesced into a stinking mass, now being covered in turn by a layer of leaves, withered to brown crisps.

She looked up.

The bare branches had formed into a ghastly face with glowing red eyes.

'Doom! Doom! The earthlings are all doomed!' it hissed gloatingly, revealing nasty pointed yellow fangs, whilst snaking tendrils reached out to first grip, then pinion her.

She was trapped. Her arms, legs, body, hair, face — all being buried under the mass of vile slime, while it grew darker and darker, until all she could make out was that wicked luminous grin.

'Doom! Doom! The earthlings are all doomed!' the dreadful voice cackled again.

Suddenly the solid earth underneath her feet was whisked away.

The vortex had opened!

She was in freefall, nothing for her windmilling arms to grasp. Nothing to stop her plunging helplessly into the maelstrom of whirling chaos from which she had emanated. Ever deeper, ever deeper, lumps of slime breaking off to fall eerily beside her.

She was coming to pieces. Breaking up. Disintegrating.

She was dying . . .

With a clatter, she dropped her hairbrush onto the dressing table.

An awful feeling of malevolence, of hope gone for ever, had chilled her to the core, penetrating so deep into her very soul she knew she had been deprived of her orchard resource for ever.

Some balance had changed, which was not to change back again.

Never, despite now being back in her much-loved home surroundings, had she felt so achingly, awfully alone.

'Doom! Doom! The earthlings are all doomed!'

She shuddered. That ghastly face. The red eyes. The eerie cackle. The chilling prophecy.

What did it mean? Where was it taking them?

Determined to calm down, she picked up her hairbrush, meanwhile regarding herself gravely in the mirror. Her neck and jawline were still firm, the crows' feet round her eyes no deeper than before. Yet the downturn in her mouth, which she thought made her look sad, seemed to be becoming a permanent feature.

She gave herself a brave smile. She should consign her dream to the past, where it properly belonged. There were enough real negatives about already. Stupid to load in further fears from her imagination.

She'd better watch it, or she'd be getting as intro-
spective as J!

She glanced at the alarm clock.

07.13.

Plenty of time before the showdown over the boundary dispute J was already so worked up about. After
which he would have no further excuses for avoiding
the hugely significant event GOD had arranged for that
evening.

Was it ironic, or deliberate, she mused, to have both
the micro and the macro happening on the same day?

She simply didn't know.

Right now, though, she would take a shower. As
much to wash away the vestiges of vile slime still
clinging in her mind as anything else.

Then, if only for a little while, she would take her
opportunity and escape into her GOD-sent Catherine
Cookson.

J might sneer at her taste. Yet she wasn't ashamed.
Undemanding it might be, but at least it took her into
a world so infinitely more homely.

And comforting.

Chapter 3

Ghost-U-Like

Ignoring the twee details of the replica Tuscan kitchen GOD had imposed on them, Jupiter strode up to the ambrosia dispenser on the wall and stabbed BLACKCURRANT. Why had he gone off Piedmont cherry? he wondered as the thick liquid oozed into its carton with a series of mechanical clicks. It had always been his favourite, yet now he couldn't stand it.

Probably another scumbag Vulcan trick, he thought savagely, plucking a ripe fig from the wicker basket on the worktop and biting into it.

He swore, spat out a spray of bits and scrutinised it more closely. It wasn't real, but made of bloody wax! This was one of the troubles with living in the Land of the Gods. GOD was constantly making changes to your personal immortality to keep you poised on what he called the 'cutting edge' of earthling life. A few might be announced in e-mails, but usually objects appeared and disappeared without warning or explanation.

This inanity, presumably, must be the latest accoutre-ment he had inflicted on the earthlings.

Jupiter dropped the remains on the floor and ground them under his heel, meanwhile taking a gulp of blackcurrant ambrosia to rid himself of the taste. His fury at the injustices of earthling life had now been replaced by the massive irritation he always felt when he examined his and Juno's surroundings.

Why did the earthlings spend so much time and energy trying to recreate a past they had long since left behind? If it had ever even existed. Look at this ludicrous pastiche of rural simplicity! Crude 'country' earthenware, as thick as the peasants it presumed to mimic, meaningless and impractical 'craft' objects littering every surface, 'hand-crafted' wall tiles, sup-posedly 'more authentic' because they failed to butt together properly.

Yet each a cover for a gigantic fraud, as every gadget and labour-saving device known to earthling had been surreptitiously installed alongside them. Juno might complain he took it all too seriously, but that didn't mean he was wrong. It was so outrageously dishonest — the province of the sad, twisted bastards who dominated so much of the western world on Planet Earth these days.

Jupiter had much preferred the kind of loony honesty of the previous craze for shiny, hi-tech environments to celebrate the 'progress' concept GOD had hooked the earthlings into.

Only the other day, while rooting though a kitchen drawer, he had unearthed an old manual which had had him roaring with delight.

'Remember the electric carving knife?' he had shouted to Juno.

'What I do remember is your taking it as a personal insult,' she had laughed back, before imitating his grave voice. '"The implication, Juno, has to be that I have neither the strength nor the expertise to do the job without power assistance . . ."

'And when you tried it!'

'You said the dining room sounded like a cross between an abattoir and Vulcan's shed,' Jupiter had roared. 'Until you upended your wineglass over it.'

They had both fallen about as they recalled it shorting out with a satisfying bang and cloud of black smoke.

Jupiter jerked himself back the present. Juno was right. He shouldn't get so worked up about these minor matters. Why couldn't he adopt her method of coping and simply screen them out?

He picked the ghost delivery menu off the beech-block worktop.

'THE BIG GOD'S BREAKFAST™,' he read out in a sneering voice. 'TWO RASHERS OF SUCCU-LENT, PIG-U-GONNA-LIKE BACON, raised on our own caring farm ("It's so oinkingly organic we hate to leave!" says Perky Pig), then smoked over individually selected hickory logs (Please note: we only use trees from sustainable forests, whilst, in the further interests of ecology, planting a suitable replacement), accompanied by TWO DELECTABLY FRESH EGGS, gifted this very morning by our happy free-range hens just to you (COCK-A-DOODLE-DO-YOU-LIKE-'EM!), done any way you like and topped off with—'

Jupiter flung the menu into the bin.

'A kilo of smoked salmon. French bread. Fresh

orange juice. Two litres of black coffee,' he barked into the ghost tube.

He broke the connection before he was engaged in a conversation of a 'Fish-U-Like' nature and voice-activated the weather forecast onto the wall screen. Rain later, but a dry morning, GOD was decreeing. Which was Jupiter's first bit of good fortune today. He was insisting Terminus make the all-important pronouncement that would blow Vulcan out of the water *in situ*, outside.

Out of habit, he zapped to GODS TV.

'It's Day Sixteen on the millennium countdown and here at London Zoo they're right on the ball!' an excited voice shrieked over shots of bored-looking seals balancing balls with '16' stencilled on them.

Jupiter killed the machinery with a peremptory 'Off'.

Day 16, like this evening's GOD event, was too uncomfortably close to think about.

He drummed his fingers impatiently on the 'farm-house' table, wincing at the feel of its distressed 'antiqued' surface. GOD's ghost service operation, which all gods relied on, was hard to fault in theory. It began with earthlings spending their lives trying to get to Heaven, Nirvana, the Happy Hunting Ground, or whatever destination GOD had put into their heads.

Only to find, when they died, they had been imported to the Land of the Gods to do all the work. Which was entirely necessary. Gods, and goddesses, had better things to occupy their time than menial tasks.

The ghosts still appeared over the moon, which indeed they were. Not just over it, but in a different dimension, which rendered the Land of the Gods invisible to prying eyes from Planet Earth. Desperately anxious to please the gods they had been brought to serve, they slaved away as assiduously as they could.

Which was where, unfortunately, GOD's theory broke down in practice. For, whatever criteria he used to select them, efficiency certainly wasn't one. Apart from being appallingly slow, time and again they made such a mess of things you ended up wishing you'd done them yourself.

As the breakfast that had now materialised was horribly demonstrating.

Jupiter had ordered 'French bread'. Not this limp, sliced crap, importantly labelled 'fresh bread'. Meanwhile, a note pinned to the tray was informing him, they had run out of orange juice yet again. Would he be kind enough to turn this temporary shortage to his advantage by accepting as a substitute today's special of *'jus de la poire au naturelle'*?

In other words, normal bloody pear juice, Jupiter scowled.

Apparently not, however, he read on. This pear juice was 'made from *poires* exclusively and organically grown in our unspoilt orchards, then picked by certified virgins in order to preserve the essential purity lying at the heart of every fruit.'

'And then squeezed between their pristine thighs?' Jupiter snorted as he fished with his finger to remove what looked suspiciously like supporting evidence of a blonde pubic hair floating on top.

He didn't like pear juice, *au naturelle* or *non naturelle*, or *au pubic* or *non-pubic*.

He should tear the delivery ghosts off a strip.

If they were still here, of course.

Like all gods, Jupiter normally immortalised in G-mode, which screened out all but his fellow gods.

Now, though, he switched to the alternative EG-mode, which also revealed ghosts.

And found it was as he had guessed.

Rather than hovering about as they were supposed to, the delivery ghosts had already cleared off. Probably quite rightly anticipating his displeasure. Instead, all he was revealing was the normal complement of scrubbers, painstakingly removing every speck of dust and dirt.

And there was no point in addressing them. They always smiled politely and explained that unfortunately they were in a different ghost union. Delivery, as opposed to cleaning up afterwards, was not their responsibility, they were sorry to have to say.

Ghost union! Jupiter harrumphed to himself. Why did GOD feel it so necessary to reproduce every nonsense he visited on Planet Earth?

Jupiter's only other course was to make an official complaint. Yet he had long since given up filling in the necessary forms in triplicate. All they got you were apologies of such a grovelling nature you felt quite sick, whilst nothing practical was ever done.

Anyhow, he didn't have time. With his big Vulcan occasion looming, he needed to get on with the prov-erbial three S's. Or two in his case, being a bearded god, before getting dressed.

He gave out an ear-splitting groan, making the ghosts jump, as he remembered.

Overriding his vociferous protests, Juno was insisting he wear not just a suit but, ignominy of all ignominies, a tie and even — he couldn't believe it — cufflinks.

'Cufflinks!' he had cried in horror. 'Nobody in the Land of the Gods wears cufflinks!'

'Well *you* are,' she had ordered him tersely. 'You know what a stickler Terminus is for protocol.'

Protocol, Jupiter sighed, sipping his *poire au naturelle pubic* with a sour face.

After seeing the results of that on Planet Earth, he had long since decided it was another GOD affliction he could do without.

Chapter 4

Fenced In

The same kinds of thoughts about the god of boundaries were meanwhile occurring to Vulcan as he stumbled around the chaotic interior of number 29, his euphoria about the siren now subsided.

He had known it would get everyone on his back, but considered that worth it, not just to silence Jupiter, but to test out his latest creation. Which, to his huge satisfaction, had performed perfectly, although the subtleties of his craftmanship had obviously gone clean over the others' heads.

'Stuff you all!' he had finally shouted, slamming the door on them. 'I'm telling you — Jupiter started it. Just like he started this whole sodding business.'

But he had seen they didn't believe him.

'The conniving bastard,' he muttered, rummaging through a rich-smelling pile of discarded clothes. 'Why

didn't I call in the ghost laundry service? Oh, I know
– to launder what?'

The same point had cropped up once when he had
been laying down the law to Venus.

'Being a god, you stupid female, is not about having
anything you want,' he had shouted in what had proved
to be the culmination of their various rows. 'It's about not
having anything you *don't* want. And I'm not a fashion
victim. So I don't want posh clothes. Or any of that
designer crap with bloody logos plastered all over it.

'And because a god can also do anything he likes,
whenever he likes, wherever he likes, I can carry on
keeping my welding torch in the kitchen. And my lathe
in the front room.

'Furthermore, I don't have to do anything I don't feel
like doing. So I don't have to brush my teeth. Or cut my
nails, never mind clean them. Or shave. Or wash. Or
clean out between my toes. Or even, come to think of
it, rid myself of my smegma.'

Which, he had realised afterwards, must have been
one remark too far.

For at that point, whilst not openly disagreeing, she
had simply left him.

Not that that had been a problem.

When it came down to it, goddesses were good for
only one thing. If he fancied a bit he just had to attend
a Bacchus rave, borrow an Apollo groupie or simply
grab a passing nymph. And if he got absolutely, totally
desperate there was always some rough stuff hanging
around the Lower Orders' estate.

Meanwhile, with no female to clutter up the house,
he could import his workshop in from the shed. Which
he had done, to the extent that the two were now
indistinguishable.

'You should be proud to be associated with a hands-on god,' he would endlessly retort to the stream of fellow deities trailing round to complain about horrible smells, clouds of smoke and loud banging day and night. 'Not like some, afraid to roll their sleeves up and get stuck in.'

He would delight in watching them cringe as he lit a roll-up with his torch and blew acrid fumes in their faces. 'As the god of fire,' he would proclaim in ringing tones, 'my job is to heat the forge, pour the glowing crucible, hammer the anvil and generally metal-bash.

'I'm not ashamed of that. And I'm not going to stop doing it for anyone.'

As for the hate e-mail that poured into his terminal, he simply wiped it.

Now, though, he was paying the price.

Vulcan had always secretly envied Jupiter's imposing figure and air of *gravitas*. On top of which, how to match the immaculate suit and pristinely ironed shirt Juno would equip her consort with? He could see her now, inspecting him like a soldier going on parade, adjusting his collar, straightening his tie . . .

A tie, Vulcan thought with a sudden stab of alarm, pushing over an old oil drum and sending a pack of rats squeaking for cover.

Did he even own one?

'"Remember, J,"' he mimicked in a high-pitched voice, '"a place for everything and everything in it's place."

'The stuck-up clench-arse is obsessed with appearances, that's her problem,' he muttered, flailing about in what he laughingly called his wardrobe.

Suddenly he froze as he was struck by a brain wave.

'I know,' he grinned craftily. 'I'll play it the other way — wear my normal work clothes! Not shower, brush my hair, or do anything special. So I've got filthy hands? Black fingernails? Well, I've got warts, too, haven't I? And I won't be afraid to show them off, either.

'That'll spite her. Spite all of them!'

What had he thrown on when he dashed out to deal with Jupiter? Some old T-shirt and tatty pair of black trousers.

Perfect!

'Now, socks.' He peered round in vain.

'But why should I wear any?' he asked himself, prising his horny feet into his favourite boots with their dented steel toecaps. 'At least I won't be putting on a hypocritical show. And if a god can't be himself in the Land of the Gods, where in the universe can he be?'

He scrutinised himself in the smeared mirror.

Excellent!

So why this sudden bout of nerves?

He gave a huge sigh as he remembered. His conver-sation yesterday with Mars.

'It's bad enough Jupiter calling in Terminus in the first place,' he had angrily explained. 'Boundary disputes should be settled god to god — not by some busybody who only exists to poke his nose into the affairs of others.

'I told Jupiter: don't blame me for your bloody pumpkin dying. As a working god I've a right to empty my sump oil wherever I please on my own property. Is it my fault if your stupid vegetable chooses to spread its roots onto my land?'

Mars had nodded back sympathetically. Everyone knew how proud Jupiter was of his vegetable garden, and above all the pumpkin he grew each year for the harvest festival, then magnanimously donated to the gruesome inhabitants of downtown Witchway for their Hallowe'en ceremony.

After this year's had so unexpectedly perished, every-one had been agog to see what retaliation would be offered.

'I wasn't ogling Juno when she was sunbathing,' Vulcan had grumbled on. 'I told him: if I wanted to see a pair of soggy old melons, I just had to look in his veggie patch.

'Which was when she weighed in. Accused me of being a chauvinist boor. You won't believe what she called my fine metal sculptures: "ugly piles of rusting scrap"!' He had shaken his head in wonder. 'How dare she, when they're what I do — my very meaning as a god? I told her: if you knew anything about art, you'd feel privileged you can view them so easily.

'And what about your bloody peacocks, I asked her, shrieking all the time and shitting everywhere?

'So, you see, there was never any need to put up the stupid fence in the first place. But moving it across and erecting it on my land was the last bloody straw. For that meant they were claiming the fucking pumpkin roots were on their land as well.

'Which simply wasn't true. And gave me the right, as I told them, to do what I liked with it. Including chucking it in my furnace.

'Of course that was when old High and Mighty sneaked behind my back and called in Terminus.' Vulcan had sucked angrily on his roll-up. 'All pious he was: "In the circumstances, Vulcan, I'm afraid that both Juno and I consider that matters have reached the point where it is necessary to duly inform the correct authority."

'Some worthy crap like that. You know what a pompous git he is.'

Mars, dark eyes glittering beneath his tousled black hair, had nodded again. He knew what Vulcan meant about Jupiter, as well as having heard this justification a dozen times. Yet in Arcadia Close it was mandatory to listen to other gods' moans so that they, in turn, would then listen to yours.

'Absolutely,' he had agreed. 'None of us want prats like Terminus strutting round telling us what to do.'

'Well don't you worry about that!' Flicking his dog-end into the sink, Vulcan had rubbed his hands with glee. 'Because when the bureaucratic bastard does issue his judgment, everyone'll see how old High and Mighty's plan has blown up in his face!'

'Great!' Mars had agreed enthusiastically. 'There's nothing I like more than a fucking huge explosion!'

Secretly, though, he hadn't been so sure. Vulcan might be a good mate. But pieces of paper, and especially legal niceties, were hardly his forte.

'I'm sure it'll be a piece of piss,' he had added soothingly, doing his best to keep the disbelief out of his voice.

Only to see from Vulcan's sudden look of uncertainty how he had picked up on it.

'Anyhow, whatever Terminus's judgment, it'll be a load of irrelevant bollocks that won't solve anything,' Mars had then gone on in a clumsy attempt to undo the damage. 'So fuck him, eh?

'I mean, it's only a boundary dispute, isn't it?

'Not as if we were talking about thermonuclear war,' he had added an even more unwise afterthought.

'Only a boundary dispute!' Vulcan had screamed back, aghast. 'You're saying, firstly, that it's not important? And, secondly, that I might lose?

'Whose fucking side are you on, you pillock?'

With a huge effort, Mars had restrained the anger that had flared up at this insult.

'Yours, of course, Vulcan. It's just that . . .'

But it had been too late. They had ended up having a flaming row.

Vulcan now tried to put his resurfaced doubts behind him by hitting the PIEDMONT CHERRY button on his ambrosia dispenser. The action cheered him up. That particular little trick should have got through to Jupiter by now!

'Fire! be be boom, be boom boom,' he sang loudly to raise his spirits as he watched the machine disgorge its glutinous contents. 'I am the god of fire, be be boom, be boom boom . . .'

He picked up the brimming carton and raised it in a toast.

'To justice — after which old buggerlugs can get another pumpkin and stuff it up where it belongs.'

He gulped down his elixir in one hit.

'Her too,' he muttered in an afterthought. 'Back and front.'

Chapter 5

Terminal Error

As he crunched up number 31's gravel drive, Terminus kept his eyes down, his entire attention focused on not marking his gleaming black shoes. Reaching the front door, he rubbed them on the back of his trousers to make doubly sure, hefted his leather briefcase, made a final adjustment to his tie, then reached for the bell.

Under the cover of its chimes he cleared his throat, meanwhile avoiding looking at the spy hole by pretending to admire Juno's hanging baskets. Arcadia Close had been suspiciously quiet as he made his clipped way along from number 11, giving him the uncomfortable feeling that dozens of eyes were drilling into him from behind the nets.

For now, near his moment of truth, he was having to confess to an attack of the jitters.

'Tut tut, Terminus,' he reprimanded himself. 'You are here to do a job, so a job you will do.'

Yet that in itself was already an admission of defeat. After retiring from earthling affairs, the god of boundaries had vowed to avoid all further conflict. No matter how many gods and goddesses came hammering on his door, he flatly refused to be drawn into their acrimonious disputes.

'Sort it out between yourselves,' he dismissed them all, while knowing full well that they couldn't.

'You see, you don't need just knowledge, but experience,' he remembered pontificating to Jupiter after the greatest god had dropped in unexpectedly, carrying a welcome bottle of Chianti Classico. 'Because, no matter what your status or speciality as a god, nothing is more important than your boundaries.

'I, for example, pride myself on being an exemplary neighbour. I live neatly and quietly, never interfere in other gods' affairs and, most important of all, utterly respect their boundary lines.'

Jupiter had nodded gravely, whilst thinking disputes were hardly likely when Terminus had the equally correct Janus, the god of doorways, on one side, and Sylvanus, the mild god of trees, on the other.

'The definition of a boundary, you see,' Terminus had gone on, fuelled by generous pourings of Chianti, 'is "that which serves to indicate the limit of anything".

'In other words, the fixed lines which enclose us, the parameters around which we revolve, and which provide the stability both gods and earthlings need to function correctly.

'No respect for boundaries, and our immortal lives, never mind the lives of mere mortals on Earth, become something without edges. Then where are we? Why, adrift on a sea of nothing!'

He had got to his feet and begun striding up and down the living room.

'Ask Mars how earthling wars start,' he had continued, raising his index finger dramatically. 'One nation nibbles at another's boundary. The other knows if it gives an inch it'll lose a mile. One crosses the line . . .

'Both sides, you see, know that a boundary is a principle. A principle applying equally to gods as to earthlings. For, without anything to show them where their limits lie, how can either ever be free?'

Temporarily exhausted by his own rhetoric, he had come to a stop, head spinning with the unaccustomed alcohol.

'I couldn't agree more wholeheartedly, Terminus,' the god of thunder had said, immediately springing the trap. 'Which is why I am now commanding you to enforce that all-important principle — in practice.'

'But Jupiter, I thought none of us had to do our thing any more?' Terminus had wailed. 'Aren't we all retired?'

'Not all of us.'

Terminus had flinched before those piercing blue eyes.

'It's all very well hiding behind this lot,' Jupiter had continued, waving at the maps and law books covering the walls and heaped up on the floor. 'But you know as well as I do how this feuding's eating up everyone's energy.

'Look at this latest spat between Bacchus and Neptune. OK, keeping great white sharks in his outdoor pool could be a problem. Yet they still haven't patched up their row about the leak which Bacchus claims destroyed his vines and his wacky baccy plants.

'It's the same everywhere you look. Vesta complaining about the noise from Bacchus's raves. Him trying to close down Venus's sex parties because he's jealous at being upstaged. Her complaining about Pan's noisy pipes. Him demanding Flora stop using her stinking fertiliser . . .'

He looked Terminus straight in the eye.

'Juno's persuaded me. It's time to draw a line. You're the line-drawer. So I'm commanding you to go into action over this fence business.'

'It's not just your pumpkin then?' Terminus had asked, surprised at his own temerity.

'No, it's bloody well not!' Jupiter had roared back. 'You said it yourself — it's the principle.'

'But Jupiter, if I adjudicate in your case, I'll have to in everyone else's,' Terminus had pleaded. 'Then how will I ever get a moment's peace?'

'You won't,' Jupiter had replied shortly. 'But what sort of peace are any of us getting, with things as they are?'

Terminus had wriggled for another hour before capitulating.

'It'll open up a can of worms,' he had then grumbled unhappily.

'You're not denying it's your duty, though, are you?' Jupiter had replied gently. 'And I've always trusted that, like me, in your heart you remain a dutiful god.'

'I do,' Terminus had replied sincerely.

'And for that reason,' he had continued, a firm note entering his voice, 'I hereby give due warning that: one, my authority is final; two: it's more than my job's worth to come up with anything other than an entirely correct result.' Now it had been his turn to look Jupiter squarely in the eye. 'And I trust you to understand precisely what I mean by that.'

It had been his last hope that the god of thunder would withdraw.

Instead Jupiter had just smiled knowingly, as he was doing now whilst he opened the front door.

'My dear chap, do come in!'

Terminus sprang to attention, heartened by the immaculate pinstripe and the tie with its impressive forked-lightning motif. Cufflinks even! And Juno, behind him, was wearing a grey business suit which was the pinnacle of decorum.

At least one side was treating his proceedings with the respect they deserved!

Not the other, though, he realised after being ushered through the conservatory into the formal Italian garden. Juno must have been out here for days, he thought, nodding approvingly. Or the ghost gardeners had been working overtime.

He had never seen the low box hedges so immaculately clipped, the lawn beyond so perfectly mown. And, though the flower beds had largely died down, every remaining leaf was precisely in place, just as he specified to the ghost gardeners at number 11.

Then he had spotted Vulcan and gasped in disbelief. The god of fire must have deliberately dressed to flout his authority! Peeringly, he deciphered the wording on the disgusting T-shirt: WELDERS DO IT BY TORCHLIGHT. He shuddered. And Vulcan's trousers! They were so caked in grease they were actually gleaming in the bright sunlight! Those dreadful old work boots. With nothing in between, Terminus then realised. No socks at all — not even dirty ones!

It wasn't just his clothes, either. From head to toe his actual person was utterly, entirely filthy!

Just as bad, what were all these others doing, many equally disrespectfully attired?

The lawn was jam-packed, and not just with Lower Order tiddlers. There was Mercury, tapping away on his laptop, Saturn leaning on his sickle, Apollo tuned into his Walkgod, Mars, Flora, Vesta — even that brat Cupid, rudely sticking out his tongue.

As for his mother! Not only was Venus pretty much in a state of dishabille, but Terminus had never seen her looking so rough. Which didn't entirely surprise him. Although, naturally, a strict abstainer from the pleasures of the flesh himself, he had been unable to shut out the lurid tales circulating on Bacchus's grapevine.

'Gang-bangs with phalanxes of primeval tree spirits,' the Lower Order gossips had been delightedly whispering. 'Big phalanxes too, from the look of her. She's positively bandy-legged.

'And it's only last week she was being stuffed by that voodoo chicken lot!'

There was Bacchus himself, openly swigging from a bottle! While, judging by the giggles, the motley collection of nymphs and satyrs round him were high as kites.

Raucous cheers were now greeting his appearance

'Come on, you old line-drawer,' came a slurred shout. 'Show us your ruler!'

'Yeah — get 'em off, Termy!'

Desperately trying to ignore them, Terminus walked stiffly across the lawn and through the gap in the hedge screening the vegetable garden.

Only to find, to his dismay, the motley mob following.

'I thought we agreed these proceedings were to be
strictly *in camera*,' he hissed at Jupiter.

The greatest god pointed a rigid forefinger at the
putrescent, slug-eaten pile he had deliberately left lying
by the fence as evidence.

'What's *in camera* about that? Nobody's talking
about anything else.'

Which Terminus knew simply wasn't true.

Never mind Venus's shenanigans, there would now
be the question of who had been doing what to whom at
Bacchus's last night. As well as the arguments provoked
by the 'dum dum dum' of the rave beat going on until
nearly dawn.

But that was gods for you, Terminus sighed. So
vain, nothing else mattered except their particular
obsession.

There was no point in even trying to argue.

Yet, as he put down his briefcase and reverentially knelt to extract the key document, he could
not suppress a burst of pride. He held it up, demonstrating how he had painstakingly written it out
by hand. On parchment even. They might jeer at
him for being so old-fashioned, but he didn't care.
How could a computer printout be an adequate substitute when exercising such grave, and legal, responsibilities?

Extracting his half-moon glasses from their silver
case, he drew himself up to his full height, which
was not great.

'I, Terminus, by the authority vested in me as god
of boundaries, hereby do pronounce . . .'

The boos he could ignore. But not the glowering

figure of Vulcan, standing in front of him, breathing heavily. And not about to be happy with what he heard.

Yet Terminus was now drawing strength, not just from his authority, but from being so absolutely clear in his own mind. He had accessed GOD in infinite detail and pored over countless deeds and maps, ignoring the grumbles about how long he was taking, before reaching his definitive conclusion.

Jupiter was in the right — although almost certainly not in the way he had foreseen.

Both sides had come to him brandishing maps and insisting theirs was the oldest. But in GOD's deepest bowels Terminus had succeeded in accessing two even more ancient — the first for Vulcan, the second against. And the latter dated back to 400 BC, the start of the original settlement that was now Arcadia Close. Before that there were no records on disk.

'I therefore find in favour of the owners of number 31, Jupiter Zeus and Juno Hera,' he concluded, 'and by the authority vested in me order the fence remain *in situ*.

'That means, where it already is,' he added for the benefit of the Lower Orders, removing his spectacles and looking up, blinking.

Jupiter, whooping with elation, was punching the air like an earthling sports winner, whilst Juno wrapped herself round him in adoring congratulation.

But Vulcan's face had contorted with rage.

'It's a fix!' he screamed, running over and delivering the sad remnants a mighty kick with his steel toecap.

As they splattered against the fence in gobbets of stinking mush, Jupiter thrust Juno to one side, ran across and jumped onto the god of fire's back. While the crowd cheered and hooted with delight, the pair toppled to the ground and rolled around, wrestling clumsily, before tearing up cabbages and Brussels-sprout plants to press into service as makeshift weapons.

Terminus shrank back, clutching his parchment in horror, as the pair then crashed into the row of runner-bean poles and went sprawling.

Whatever had happened to Jupiter's talk of principles? They were both as bad as each other. Why, oh why, had he allowed himself to be talked into this fiasco?

'You're not fit to be gods any more,' he screamed. 'You're worse than . . .' — he struggled for the final insult — 'earthlings!'

Whipping round, he saw Juno standing alone, looking shocked.

'I resign,' he cried, ostentatiously ripping his precious parchment to shreds and hurling it to the ground.

He spun on his heel and marched off towards the gap in the hedge.

Only to freeze in his tracks as a blinding white light filled the sky, whilst a choir of angels suffused Arcadia Close with ringing tones:

'Oh GOD our help in ages past,
'Our hope for years to come,
'Our shelter from the stormy blast . . .'

Disaster! Terminus realised. He had been intending to ram home his point by being the first to leave. Now he was finding himself knocked to the ground, briefcase torn from his hand.

Not just the boundary dispute, but he himself had been swept to one side as, with one accord, everyone ran in mad panic to access their dedicated system terminals.

Chapter 6

Me First

Naturally, GOD was the most powerful mainframe computer in the universe. Or 'server', as Mercury insisted on calling him.

'Precisely how powerful, even I don't know,' the god of communications had been saying the other day, bending everyone's ear. 'Massive BPS — that's Baud Communication Speed,' he had explained with a condescending smile. 'Even more astonishing FLOPS — Floating Operations Per Second,' he had added with a superior smirk. 'As for his capacity, it's so beyond earthling limitations, it can't be measured in mega-, giga-, or even terabytes! Only godobytes! Teragodobytes by now, I shouldn't wonder!

'Exponential growth, you see,' he had concluded, nodding emphatically and sucking his teeth in awe.

Jupiter had pointedly avoided stepping into the trap

of asking what exponential growth was. Mercury would never get him to share his enthusiasm for techno.

Yet, like everyone else, Jupiter could see the result. More e-mails.

GOD's massive output concerning Planet Earth poured onto their terminals in a hundred forms — mission statements, rules, regulations, reports, policy pronouncements, think-tank proposals, changes in direction, new ways forward, manifestos, consultative documents, spreadsheets, analyses by the billion, statistics by the trillion, news flashes updated every second . . .

The constant flood either reduced you to your knees, pleading 'Information overload!', or froze you at the controls, your mind pulped to a blank.

Yet still the flood continued, every second of every minute of every hour of every day. You could organise, prioritise, definitise, try any sort of '-ise' you liked. In the end sheer self-protection dictated there was only one answer.

You pressed DELETE.

Only for the flood to keep on coming.

Even with the limitations imposed by Progressive Memory Loss, the gods intuitively knew it hadn't always been this bad. Once Planet Earth had been a simpler place, where any self-respecting deity prepared to put the hours in had been able to keep abreast of their speciality.

Yet, as GOD grew ever more bureaucratic, and Planet Earth more complicated, what had once been urgent, vital work you threw your whole being into had degenerated into just stuff which you had somehow to get through.

Which was why GOD had introduced hymns — or 'mes', as he called them.

A 'me', broadcast over his public address system, signalled that his latest missive was no ordinary e-mail, but what he labelled an 'imperative'. To make sure they all read it he would continue to broadcast the 'me' until every single god had signed the 'imperative' off. Which, the gods had to admit, worked, as everyone dreaded being last and therefore universally slagged off as responsible for the dreadful din continuing.

Jupiter, only having to extricate himself from Vulcan's embrace and the runner-bean poles and sprint in from the garden, might even be first, he congratulated himself as he whacked into his leather swivel chair.

Which, or course, entirely befitted his station, not only as the greatest god, but now also the clear winner in the boundary stakes.

Smiling smugly, he pressed ACCESS and began reading.

Only for his good mood to vanish.

```
E-mail

mail to: all Gods and Goddesses (Greco-
Roman), Higher Order, Lower Order, Major,
Minor, Regional and Local. Also Denizens,
Indigenes, Nymphs, Satyrs, Cherubs,
Amorphettes etc. I.E. EVERYONE

09.31.00/15.12.1999 ET

From: GOD [Gods, Oracles and Deities]

Blessings on you all.

Y2K technology situation report 493771/665
```

As per previous notifications, as of
00.00.01/01.01.2000 I will be updating from
my current system of Universe 7.8.9 aka.05
retake 2, to my new system, Megaverse 2000,
now rock-steady and ready to ship.

To remind you, this op.sys.update (the first
for over 200 years) has been necessitated
by the earthlings being in the process of
developing an electronic communications
and technology infrastructure similar to
the one you enjoy here in the Land of the
Gods. This is already leading to rapid and
far-reaching modifications to mortal life,
not all, as I am sure you are aware despite
your limited contact these days, of an
advantageous nature.

Especially in view of the poor response to
my previous communications, I therefore
absolutely command each and every one of
you to attend the emergency meeting I have
instructed Jupiter to call in the Forum
tonight, starting at 19.30. At this I am
requiring you all to vote on your joint
input to this vital update and your desired
future participation within it.

So as not to influence your decision, I
myself shall not be taking part. As I have
warned you many times (see updates 235
through 639), it is not my future which
is at stake, but yours. Please note also
that in view of the extreme importance of
this event, although I shall be opening
Retroland™ at 10.00 as usual, I will be
suspending it at noon. It will not reopen
until further notice.

Therefore, if you do choose to take up a

```
position, you are advised to start closing
it down appropriately.

Have a good day.
.sig

Personal PS for Jupiter: As previously
discussed in principle. Relying on you to
get them there.


E-mail ends
```

Jupiter signed off the missive and sat back in his chair, waiting for Juno to finish. With the boundary dispute over, and this on his plate, he could no longer avoid what was coming.

'Bloody GOD,' he grumbled as she emerged from her personal computer room. 'He could have given us a bit of time to celebrate.'

'Celebrate what?' Her voice was icy.

'Our victory of course!'

'After that exhibition?'

She bit her lip. She had felt like punching Vulcan in the face herself. Or, more satisfactorily, kneeing him in the balls. Yet it was her consort who had devalued much of what they had worked for.

Mind you, they had still won.

'We got a good result,' she said, summoning up an affectionate grin. 'Wasn't the suit worth it?'

'And got what it richly deserved!'

Proudly, Jupiter looked down at the damage. Never mind the ground-in earth, even the invisible mending ghosts could never repair the rips in the sleeves and lapels. And he'd succeeded in losing not just one cufflink, but both!

Then he frowned as he put his hand up gingerly to his face. What he wasn't happy about was what felt suspiciously like the beginnings of a black eye.

'Who's ever going to believe it was a beanpole, rather than scumbag Vulcan?' he asked plaintively.

Juno laughed, not sure whether to take his word for it. Except that his absolute honesty — more like naiveté on some occasions — was his most endearing, and reliable, trait.

'Me, for one,' she laughed reassuringly.

They both fell silent, staring into each other's eyes as their thoughts moved separately to GOD's meeting.

'I'd better get on with the round-up.' He rose heavily from his chair.

'Your charm offensive, you mean,' she grimaced sympathetically. Why had GOD loaded the onus of getting a full house onto his back, broad though it might be? 'Still trying to convert them to your way of thinking?'

'Bloody right I am!'

'Do you have to, J?' she asked, knowing she must tread carefully. 'All GOD's requiring is you ensure they attend. How they vote's up to them, surely?'

'Not if I've anything to do with it.'

Juno didn't press the point.

'I'll see the goddesses. Their attendance is just as crucial.'

'Are they acknowledging that?'

'Not really.'

'Neither are the gods. "It's only a bloody GOD meeting, nothing to do with us," they keep whining.' He wheeled round in his chair, harrumphing in disgust, whilst Juno marvelled at his male ability to switch from micro to macro without even a blink. 'Only the most important decision they've had to make this whole earthling century, more like — if not their entire immortalities.'

'Try to go a bit easy on them, J,' she pleaded, knowing how his pompous attitude put everyone's back up. 'Even deities find it hard to take responsibility for deciding their own futures. It's so much easier to pretend there's nothing you can do. Especially as they're all short-term thinkers these days.'

'Even when they're faced with the longest-term decision they'll probably ever have to make?' Jupiter appealed.

'Even more so, I'm afraid.'

He stared at her, recognising they were setting off round an old loop.

'I'm going to change,' he announced, striding towards the stairs.

'*Nil carborundum*, J!' she called after him.

'*Nil carborundum* indeed!' he muttered to himself as he walked into the bedroom struggling to loosen the forked-lightning tie, which Vulcan had pulled into a knot as hard as iron.

Right now Jupiter was feeling well and truly car-borundummed.

What about this terminal guilt he was feeling for Terminus? Poor sod, pressurised into doing his bit, only to see his authority degenerate into such a pathetic fisticuffs. He was such a stuffy bugger — Jupiter knew the boundary-line way of imposing order on Arcadia Close was now dead.

Yet it was he, not Terminus, who had blown it.

And what about the ignominy of him and Vulcan huffing and puffing away in such an unseemly fashion? Like two old farts on an earthling housing estate. From the look of hatred in the god of fire's eyes, Jupiter wasn't even sure it was over.

What had Minerva counselled Juno? 'Don't get drawn into things like that – they just waste your immortality.'

They were all wasting it, mouldering away in this dump.

Jupiter dropped the remains of his suit gloomily onto the floor and flicked through his wardrobe, looking for something looser, yet still with a stamp of authority. How much lower could they go? he wondered, selecting his 'old fogey' tweed jacket, as Juno called it.

A long way, he had a horrible suspicion. Starting with this evening's meeting which, now he was really thinking about it, was shaping up to be the biggest downward step it was possible for them to take.

Which was also why, with now only fifteen full days left until the millennium, he had been doing everything he could to avoid having to think about it.

For not only were its possible implications shattering.

They would also last for all eternity.

Chapter 7

The Red Baron

As Jupiter walked round the side of Mars's villa, the mere sight of the virtual-reality capsule was enough to set his blood pressure rising. Inside the white geodesic dome, he knew, the god of war would already have escaped the present by fleeing for a last blast into Retroland™. Not that he would be alone. These days it was the focus of most gods' and goddesses' immortalities.

Jupiter had warned that would happen the moment GOD had introduced it.

'Can't you see it'll destroy our society?' he had ranted to anyone who would listen. 'Turn us into pathetic morons like today's earthlings? Divert us from our true purpose? Stop us being proper gods?'

Which, to be fair, it made no bones about doing. Due to GOD's policy of linking them to the tyranny of mortal time, Retroland™ participants were restricted to re-enacting events in the earthling twentieth century.

And then only as earthlings, rather than gods.

Yet Jupiter's one-god campaign had got him nowhere, he grimly recalled as he ploughed across the unkempt lawn, skirting the mini-craters caused by Mars's weapons practice. Everyone else had thought escaping from being a real god was Retroland™'s greatest attraction. Why continue with that responsibility, when GOD was offering the alternative of their playing at being any irresponsible earthling they chose?

Mercury, proudly announcing he had 'come out' as a 'techie', had led the charge for the opposition.

'Where do you think you're coming from?' he had challenged Jupiter with a nerve that rendered the god of thunder speechless. 'Real reality, virtual reality — what's the difference, man? We're electronic now. Digital. On the leading edge. Pursuing excellence. Just like the earthlings will be when they follow in our footsteps.

'I can understand crumblies like Saturn not being able to hack it. But I'd never rated you as just another techno-fear old fart.

'Until now.'

At which point his laptop had bleeped and he had rushed off in his normal butterfly fashion, little wings on his feet whirring frantically.

Getting the same reaction, if more muted, from everyone, Jupiter had hit the Scotch. Especially when he discovered even Juno was on the other side.

'You're being too hard on them, J. As well as yourself.' He remembered her sitting on the edge of his armchair, kneading his neck whilst he stared moodily into the fire. 'Immortality's like everything else. It shouldn't be all work and no play. You can see where that's got us. We've worn ourselves out.'

'I haven't,' he had thundered back.

'You mean you just won't acknowledge it,' she had replied sharply. 'You need somewhere to escape to more than anyone. You know how you can never relax. GOD's right — Retroland™'s ideal.

'Harmless enough, too. Providing it's kept under control.'

'It's already *out* of control, Juno!' Jupiter had riposted, upsetting his drink in his agitation. 'The Factory's nearly deserted. No one's interested in working on behalf of the earthlings any more. Especially the Lower Orders — and that includes goddesses as much as gods.

'They're so obsessed, they're in there every second it's running.'

Which was from ten to ten, each day of the week. Except Sunday, when GOD switched it off entirely.

Yet Jupiter had not even elicited sympathy, never mind support.

'Of course they're obsessed,' she had countered sternly. 'Are you trying to deny their fundamental natures? And who can blame them for wanting to be somewhere else?

'What is there left to be here for?'

Jupiter had to admit it was a good question. Only the other day he had come across an old earthling phrase which had stuck in his mind.

'What's happened to the ghost of old eagerness?' he had repeated to Juno. 'The pumping energy? The excitement?'

'They've done it all, J,' she had replied gently. 'Got the T-shirts. Not once, but a million times.'

Yet Jupiter still wouldn't give in.

'All I know,' he had replied defiantly, 'is that something within me rebels against it so strongly I'm going to demand GOD remove my personal capsule.'

Which, somewhat to Jupiter's surprise, he had done.

After which, feeling oddly deprived, Jupiter had hated Retroland™ even more, until today he saw it as a major cause of their troubles. And to his relief, Juno was slowly coming round to his point of view. As they now agreed, if gods and goddesses didn't even live in the present most of the time, how could they possibly make a good job of it?

Reaching Mars's capsule and ignoring the red light, Jupiter ripped open the door. What a positive pleasure to break into the god of war's current fantasy! Except that he was so engrossed at the controls of his stripped-down, matt-black timesurfer he didn't even notice when Jupiter took the seat next to him and slapped on the sensors.

As he had already half guessed, he was immediately pitched into Mars's current obsession with the Second World War. He had transmogrified into a British fighter pilot, Hurricane pitched in a semi-suicidal dive, wings juddering, Merlin engine screaming. Through the scratched perspex the Messerschmidt 109 stood out below him, its overland camouflage useless in breaking up its outline against the deep blue of the English channel.

In the din and vibration of the crude cockpit he was being fired with adrenaline as heady as the 101 leaded octane he was burning. He had been handed a copybook attack. The 109, having turned tail for home, was wave-hopping for safety. Probably low on fuel. Maybe even out of ammo.

Jupiter strained on the joystick to level out behind it, feeling almost sorry for such a sitting duck. But, he reminded himself, this was no garden party. This was war, with no quarter given or taken. Even by an English gentleman.

As the French coast rushed towards them he lined up his victim in his sights. YAMMER YAMMER YAMMER went the .303 machine guns, and immediately smoke poured from the Messerschmidt's engine. The plane dipped, caught the white horse of a surging wave and rose again, only to catch another.

This time it spun into a crazy cartwheel which ripped off both wings while the fuselage, propeller still uncannily rotating at full speed, jumped high in the air like a leaping fish, before driving itself down into the wall of water.

Jupiter peeled off, bursting with pride. Another kill to be added to the nine already stencilled on the Hurricane's nose. If he could get the CO to accept it, of course. He was on his own, with no chums present to verify.

'Hitler has only got one ball,' he sang as he banked round,

'Goering has two, but very small . . .'

The Hun was on the run. They were winning the Battle of Britain. Everything was right in his world.

His thoughts moved on to old dear Biggin Hill — Susie waiting anxiously, the wild ride in the MG, the watery beer at the village pub, bawdy singing round the piano, creeping surreptitiously upstairs at his digs, stifling Susie's giggles . . .The other chaps could claim what they liked. Speaking for himself, he couldn't do it in an MG.

'Himmler is very sim'lar,

'But poor old Goebbels
'Has no balls at all.'
A sign flashed up:
> YOU HAVE REACHED EXIT POINT 6. PRESS
RETURN IF YOU DO NOT WISH TO CONTINUE <
Reluctantly, Jupiter stabbed the keyboard.

Mars, who had no choice but to come out after being destroyed, beamed in delight as they both ripped off their sensors and threw them down on the desk.

'Thanks for killing me,' he laughed, white teeth flashing in his eager dark face. 'It's the ultimate buzz, you know. Wham! Bam! Then you're gone for ever! Talk about wipe-out!' He gave Jupiter a playful, but hard, nudge in the ribs. 'I never guessed it was you, though. Told you you wouldn't be able to stay out for ever!'

Jupiter grinned. Whatever their current differences, Mars's boyish enthusiasm, which wound him up, Jupiter always thought, like a coiled spring, was still hugely infectious.

He had a point, too. Jupiter had stuck rigidly to his famous 'no Retro' stance except for brief immersions like this, when he could make an excuse to himself. Yet these only confirmed his convictions that this was dangerously pleasurable stuff. He must stay out if he was not to be swept away like all the others.

'By the authority vested in me as god of war,' Mars was now intoning, right arm raised in a mock Nazi salute, 'I hereby award you the Retroland™ Iron Cross, First Class.'

'Honoured, I'm sure.' Jupiter bowed stiffly.

'Ve vill now switch wars,' Mars further announced in an atrocious German accent, holding out the sensors. 'I, ze red planet, am now ze Red Baron, fighting ace of World War Ein. I challenge you to a duel, English schweinhundt. Fighters at dawn, over ze trenches!'

Instead Jupiter grasped his wrist in a steely embrace.

'First, about tonight.'

The god of war (and agriculture, as he occasionally reminded everyone) heard him out. Yet Jupiter could see he was listening with only half an ear. All the time his black eyes were sliding back to the giant wraparound screen.

'You're an addict, aren't you?' Jupiter regarded him pityingly. 'Narrowed your immortality down to your next fix, haven't you?'

Mars wriggled furiously. But although GOD had coded him with a permanently younger body, Jupiter had the all-important weight advantage.

Inexorably he arm-wrestled him down onto the desk.

'GOD may peddle the line "Retroland™ takes you back in time",' he hissed, face inches away while Mars looked daggers. 'But it's just pastiche. Comic-book stuff.' He released his grip slightly. 'You think being a fighter pilot's the greatest, don't you?'

'Absolutely!' Mars responded eagerly. 'I tried being a general, an admiral, an air marshal. They were all the same. In-tray jammed, reports to be written, phone going mad. Flak from the politicians at one end, the ranks at the other.

'The biggest battle was getting anyone to fight in the first place. Otherwise it was all office politics. The bloody meetings! Just like tonight's going to be, I suppose. Yak yak yak yak yak!'

He pulled a sour face.

'War today's no good either. All techno. Just pressing buttons. I'm interested in heroism, glory, something which brings out the best in individual earthlings, causes them to rise above themselves, show valour, courage.'

He gave a big grin.

'Which is why I go back to when you really had to fly by the seat of your pants. Those were the days!'

'Really fly?' Jupiter cut across grimly. 'You weren't really flying. As for courage, you weren't really dying either. Otherwise you wouldn't be here, would you?

'Can't you see, it's all crap? Boys and toys? Games? There's absolutely no way you can say it's real.'

'So what is — life in Arcadia Close?' Mars's eyes blazed.

'Well, at least it's what us gods are actually doing,' Jupiter replied feebly, annoyed at himself for getting so wound up.

He was supposed to be getting Mars's support, and vote, for tonight.

'Red Baron,' he joked woodenly, completely releasing his grip, 'as god of fortune, I hereby award you the Distinguished Banner of Good Luck, First Class.' He gave a friendly smile. 'Only, though, if you'll vote with me against more Retroland™.'

But Mars, scowling whilst he rubbed his bruised wrist, was already reaching for the sensors.

'Well?' Jupiter demanded, losing patience.

'Forget it,' the god of war snapped back. 'I'll come to the meeting, but as far as voting's concerned, you're on your own.'

As Mars began throwing switches Jupiter stepped hurriedly out of the capsule.

Yet, at least for once, GOD was on his side, he thought as he made his way back across the pockmarked lawn. Not long now and Retroland™ would be closed down and the Red Baron grounded.

He emerged back out onto the Close, his spirits lifting at the prospect of his next visit. As he vaguely under-stood it, Saturn Chronos was his father. Yet PML had intervened to the extent that Jupiter couldn't think of himself as his son. It would be such a pleasure, though, to relax amidst the ticking of the dozens of clocks which, Jupiter had discovered to his astonishment, the old god painstakingly wound himself, eschewing the ghost maintenance service.

Many, like Mercury, might spurn him as a miserable old git, so ancient as to be hopelessly out of touch. But not Jupiter. He respected his slowness and taciturn manner, knowing the god of time never pronounced on any subject without suitably reflecting.

'My teaching can be hard,' he had once explained, 'but it is always just. Which is why I carry the scythe of death for the earthlings.' He had indicated the wickedly sharp blade shining from its hook in the hall. 'My job, you see, is to clear away the old and useless.

'And that applies just as much to ideas and mindsets as physical bodies.'

Jupiter smiled as he pushed the doorbell and heard the three concentric planetary rings fade away. Was it Mercury who had said the old bugger wouldn't know a joke if it hit him in the face!

Yet, when Jupiter re-emerged, just as Retroland™ had been closed down amidst angry shouts, the smile had been completely wiped off his face.

Chapter 8

Teatime Blues

After seeing Jupiter off on his 'charm offensive', Juno briefly considered stepping into Retroland™ for a bit of r and r. She could access her favourite location, the pretty cottage hospital where she became an earthling midwife bringing a new little person into the world. It never failed to settle her: it was such a joyous and happy thing to do, whilst also carrying its own edge of danger and suspense.

Yet there wasn't really time before the tea ceremony at Vesta's. Instead she would use this extraordinarily balmy day, at least for mid-December, for a tour of her garden. After all the work she had put in she should enjoy its sights and smells whilst she could, meanwhile girding her loins, as J would say, for tonight.

Juno sat staring into the flames whilst one of the goddess

of hearth and home's six Virgins poked discreetly at the sacred fire. As GOD had long ago updated it to a modern flickering gas effect, this was an essentially meaningless gesture. Yet, as Vesta resignedly pointed out, force of habit was hard to break, whilst a bit of tidying up never did any harm.

Juno always found Vesta's inner sanctuary immensely soothing. And never more so than now. Maybe it was the isolation of the one window, so high up it showed only the sky, the bare whitewashed walls, the simple cushions on the tiled floor, the beeswax candles.

Or possibly even Vesta herself — her shining beauty, so pure and bright it was like the flame that was her symbol. Once Juno could remember feeling positively sick that even a goddess could remain so unsullied. Until she came to understand that, although Vesta's strong feminine centre might be extraordinarily stabilising, it was achieved only at the cost of a limited outlook.

Nonetheless, though, the magic still worked, triggering off deep feelings Juno normally suppressed. She hadn't been intending to unburden her dream onto the others. Now she had, though, her sense of foreboding had receded.

Flora and Minerva sat equally silently on the floor round the low table, digesting the import.

'What do you read into it, Juno?' Vesta eventually asked.

'I don't know, V. Or maybe I just don't want to know,' she added, more honestly. 'None of us do these days.'

'No. All our boxes are full.' Vesta looked pensive.

Their 'don't-want-to know boxes', they called them. Those places in your head where you hid the unpleasant and uncomfortable things you'd rather not have to

think about. The things you wanted to avoid. Like
J, blocking out GOD's forthcoming meeting with the
boundary dispute.

Vesta took a sip of her tea and screwed up her
face.

'Fucking ghosts,' she apologised, whilst Juno smiled
at this coarse reminder that she wasn't perfect. 'I
ordered Earl Grey as usual. But they're so excited
about GOD's latest tetrahedal tea bags they refuse to
send anything else.

'"After many years of extensive testing and exhaustive rescarch,"' she read off the menu, '"we proudly
announce that TEATIME WILL NEVER BE THE
SAME AGAIN! For, thanks to our latest refinements,
now brought exclusively to your table, never has tea
contained within the first platonic solid released such
a FULL AND FULSOME FLAVOUR!

'"Why not TAKE OUR TIP'?" . . .'

Vesta was irrationally annoyed at this spoiling of
the precision of their quaint tea ceremony. They had
been holding it so long, they only vaguely remembered
starting it to help kick the booze-and-drugs habits
which had got so out of hand.

Originally the formality had been a jokey protest at
GOD's continuing to peddle this hoary myth of normal
female activity. Giggling, they had even made sure they
stuck their little fingers out when delicately sipping,
just like the old ladies on Planet Earth.

On a practical level the idea had worked, providing a framework that had whittled down the
drug-taking until it became, as now, strictly recrea-
tional and under control. Yet the ceremony had lingered,
to grow into a solemn, and settling, ritual. Which was
why Vesta always went to such enormous lengths to

ensure everything was entirely correct, right down to the fine bone china and equally translucent slices of lemon.

Knowing the gods scoffed at their activity only made it even more important in reinforcing their belief that goddesses represented the more contemplative side of earthling life. The strict formality of the tea ceremony, they would constantly fire back, didn't mean their being archaic, or boring, as the gods constantly guffawed.

Rather, its quiet simplicity, and the way it locked them into a time span, reaffirmed their conviction that goddesses, unlike gods, didn't have to roar round all the time doing things to prove they had the power.

Their role, as the more subtle and complex side of the gender equation, was, like the moon, to sway the greater tides. The powerful, underlying fundamental ebb and flow that was the real stuff of earthling life.

Compared with them, the gods were as but froth on a cappuccino.

'Still waters run deeper,' as Minerva summarised it.

But maybe sometimes a bit too deep, Juno had been thinking recently. It was all very well looking to the goddess of wisdom for her clarity to cut through things. Yet that didn't mean you always had to agree with her.

Were they in danger, Juno had been wondering, of becoming out of tune with the increasingly feisty female attitude back on Earth? The way the females down there, confident of their own role, were no longer afraid to set their own agenda?

The thought displaced her dream, which she could see anyhow they were avoiding discussing. Their 'don't-want-to-know' boxes again.

'When did any of you last go to the Factory?' she asked.

They looked guiltily down into their cups.

'Take an Earth ticket?'

They stared down even harder.

'I did think the thrill of that journey across the starry firmament would never pall,' Flora admitted. 'Remember the charge when you mind-entered an earthling?'

'The power!' Juno cheered up. 'I remember once mind-entering an earthling wife being battered by her husband.' She laughed. It seemed funny now. 'He was a real pig. So I turned her head round and she simply threw the bacon on the floor, before laying him out with the frying pan!'

It had been a minor incident. A cliché even. But not only were Earth tickets vital in keeping them closely involved by enabling them to be there, taking the temperature, feeling the reality, but they gave the huge pleasure of being able to rectify wrongs on a personal basis.

It all went back to the shit dumped on everyone every morning, on Planet Earth just as much as the Land of the Gods. Out on their tickets, they could erect little umbrellas which made things better, if only for a few individuals. It might not be much, but it made you feel involved, very one to one with the particular earthling whose life you had chosen to change.

'When I turned that farmer's field brown. He was a real see-you-next-Tuesday. The stuff he put on his land!' Flora hated chemical fertilisers. 'Then purple, then yellow, then stripes, until in the end I faded it to black. He simply couldn't believe his eyes.

'It worked too. When I checked him out later he'd gone totally organic.'

'The way we slaved at our terminals.' Juno dragged them back to the subject. 'Doesn't it seem madness now?'

Earth tickets had been holidays compared with the gruelling work in the Factory where they oversaw bigger events and shaped collective destinies. Attended to 'the big picture', as J always called it.

'Remember how we got so excited? Thought it such a change from being eternally bored?' Vesta asked rhetorically. 'Until it got like the drugs. Couldn't stop, could we?'

'Then the earthlings changed.'

'Retroland™ came along.'

'And we realised we'd worn ourselves to shadows.'

With the spin imparted by Progressive Memory Loss, no one was any longer sure which had come first.

Juno pictured the Factory in her head.

'Our terminals must be still there, gathering dust.'

'Dust to dust.' Minerva raised her head from her cloak and looked at them with smouldering black eyes.

'Ashes to ashes,' Juno responded automatically, her thoughts tracked back to her dream.

There was a long silence while Vesta, lips pursed, handed round the butterfly cakes. Normally she regarded herself as sanguine, both about the state of the earthlings and themselves. Her task was simply to keep the home flame burning. Yet, after taking a rare trip out to attend the pumpkin meeting, her thoughts had been troubled, even before Juno recounted her dream.

'We must have caught a dose of PMT,' she laughed gaily.

The others didn't respond as she was hoping. With

only just over two weeks to go, pre-millennium tension was no longer a joke. Especially with tonight's meeting now weighing so heavily on all their minds.

'I'm sure we'll feel better when GOD's moved to Megaverse 2000,' Vesta tried again. 'Remember, we won't just be getting a new system, but we'll all be allowed to access the Energy Pool.'

Again, PML intervened. Yet they could still feel how this event, which came with every major system update, would put a new spring back in their steps, help them slough off the weariness wearing away their very beings.

'It's been so long since our last recharge we're simply shagged out,' Vesta added brightly.

'Venus certainly is.'

Juno didn't approve of the way the goddess of love, conspicuous by her absence, had let herself go so badly. She wasn't the only one who didn't attend the tea ceremony these days. Juno particularly missed Diana, the aggressive goddess of hunting. Yet nobody could pull her out of her terminal sulk at the way GOD was canning her speciality on Planet Earth. These days she either spent all her time in Retroland™ or hiding away, grumpily polishing her weapons.

'Will we feel any better, though?' Flora asked, stroking the white lily she had brought from her hothouse to grace the low table. 'With more genetic engineering? Supercrops? FI hybrids?'

'It does feel less warm down there,' said Vesta, joining the downer. 'Almost as if a flame's gone out.'

She stared mournfully into the artificial fire.

'Say that at tonight's meeting,' Juno urged.

'I think not.' Vesta smiled self-deprecatingly. 'I'm not afraid to admit I'm a bit shy in public.'

'But the gods will all be banging on about how the place is absolutely fine,' Juno protested.

They'd gone through it many times. The way gods were so much better at screening out reality and substituting the picture they preferred to see. It was because they were more focused, the goddesses had decided. But only in a narrow way, which made it easier to distort everything to fit. If they would only recognise this as a fault, rather than ruthlessly exploiting the edge it gave them, as they were bound to do tonight.

'Anyhow, GOD will already have determined the outcome.'

'That's defeatist, Vesta.'

Juno knew her protest sounded half-hearted.

'I know. But I'm not apologising,' Vesta replied firmly. 'I'm prepared to let him decide. Quite honestly, I've lost my spark. Like everyone else, I suppose, I find Retroland™ so much easier.'

She smiled as she thought back to the idyllic simulated evening she had just spent round a camp fire in the Rocky Mountains. The sweet tang of burning pine, smoke rising lazily in the air, murmured conversations, snatches of guitar music, all round the peace of nature. Retroland™ was so predictably corny. Which was why she loved it so much. It made the great things come true.

'What seems easy is hard, and what seems hard is easy.'

As Minerva lapsed back into silence, Vesta jerked herself back to the present.

'Anyhow,' she addressed Juno, 'won't Jupiter be telling them?'

'I'm sure he will,' Juno replied loyally, frowning.

This had been supposed to be a dynamic pre-meeting to gear them up for tonight. Not an exercise in moody and futile soul-searching.

'What's the matter with us?' she demanded. 'Have we turned into wimps, mere victims of the gods' activity?'

'No,' Vesta replied sharply, stung by the accusation. 'But, as goddesses, we've always been more realistic. So if we see it like this, who's to deny we're right?'

It was a good point, Juno had to concede. If that was the way it was, it took more courage to recognise it than pretend otherwise.

Her thoughts were dragged back to her dream.

'Doom! Doom! The earthlings are all doomed!'

'We are a gloomy lot today, aren't we?' Vesta smiled brightly, trying to lighten the atmosphere.

It was no use.

'Maybe with good reason,' Juno couldn't help remarking.

After which the four of them sat for a long time, staring silently into the fire.

Yet not even Minerva, for all her wisdom, could find any answer, or even solace, in GOD's flickering gas effect.

Chapter 9

Stretching It

J upiter grimaced as he eased the stretch limo over the speed bumps standing guard at the entrance to Arcadia Close. Even gods had to admit there were some things they couldn't do, one of which was synchronising such a massive wheel base with such alarmingly soggy suspension. The result was always this series of sickening lurches.

Not like his latest Alfa Romeo. That treated these GOD-installed objects with the robustness they deserved.

Yet Juno had insisted he use the stretcher.

'You gods need to travel together to mend your fences,' she had smiled acidly.

'You goddesses?' he had countered.

'We'll be in my gods' carrier. Not that we've the same fences to mend.'

'Just different ones,' he had muttered.

Still shaky after her dream, she had let the remark pass.

Jupiter gritted his teeth as Neptune's voice came from the back. 'A life on the ocean wave, a life on the rolling deep . . .'

With a final bounce, he cleared the last hump, gained the entry ramp and eased them onto the expressway.

Engaging the cruise control, he glanced across at Vulcan, who had bagged the front seat and was now fiddling annoyingly with the aircon. His rank, goatlike odour proved conclusively he still hadn't washed, or changed. In the aftermath of the vegetable-patch fight he now looked rougher than ever. Yet Jupiter couldn't help feeling vaguely jealous of such independence of spirit. He himself had been re-equipped by Juno with a replacement suit, a fresh forked-lightning tie and a white shirt with a collar so stiff it was biting viciously into his broad neck.

He looked in the rear-view mirror. Saturn, Mars and Neptune were staring fixedly ahead, while Apollo, Bacchus and Mercury, backs to him in the jump seats, appeared equally rigid.

How to break the ice? he wondered, looking round for inspiration. They had reached the section of the expressway raised on high legs which largely shielded them from the reality below. Meanwhile the aircon, although defeated by the all-pervading Vulcan, was working overtime to filter the worst smells from outside. Yet there was no getting away from how awful it looked down there, especially in the dank, wintry drizzle which had descended like a clammy hand.

'If GOD's insisting on a hundred per cent turn-out he could have sent better weather,' he tried, switching on the clunking wipers and peering through the smeared

screen. 'There are times I wonder if he even controls it.'

Nobody rose to the bait.

'I know we've had our differences lately,' he ploughed
on, 'but can we now start pulling together?'

More silence.

Jupiter increased the speed of the wipers and cast
around for a fresh subject, his lip curling at the sight
of the horrors making their disparate ways along the
coned-off monster lane. What had they got this evening?
Some warty weirdo, bloatedly hopping along like a
giant earthling toad. A groaning celestial cow, being
led by a gruesome twelve-headed beast with six legs.
A pack of slithering serpents, hissing and snapping at
each other. A scaly, hawk-headed horror with a vicious
twisted beak . . .

'A time for every thing, and every thing for its time,'
Saturn croaked from the back.

Jupiter grunted in recognition. It was a shortened
version of what the old god had said that morning
during his homily about time maybe running out, which
had so shaken Jupiter.

'To every thing there is a season, and a time to every
purpose under the heaven:

'A time to be born, and a time to die . . .' he had
intoned, fixing Jupiter with the gravest look he had
ever seen.

Maybe the motley crew whose homes lay underneath
them had to inhabit reconstructions of the periods when
they had the power. Yet did their dwellings have to
remain so basic and crude? So deeply unsophisticated?
It would take so little effort to improve their circumstances, Jupiter always thought on the rare occasions
he braved their ghettos. Like his annual pilgrimage to

deliver his pumpkin to the hags and crones populating Witchway, who, to his surprise, still held vestigial influence on Planet Earth.

As the thought rekindled the memory of this year's disaster, he just prevented himself from bopping Vulcan, turning his punch into a passable imitation of moving to adjust the aircon. Which was anyhow entirely necessary. No doubt purposefully, the god of fire had turned the interior into a roaring furnace which was roasting Jupiter inside his suit.

'It's all the monsters deserve.' Mercury's high voice unexpectedly cut in from the back, picking up Jupiter's thread of thought. 'If they'd only get online to the Internet . . .'

'Can't we let them be themselves tonight?' Jupiter pleaded. 'We must get things straight between us.

'I was thinking, if we all voted together, that would give a lead the others might well follow . . .'

They had already stopped listening.

Approaching the centre of Godsville, the road was becoming increasingly crowded with the vehicles of both gods and earthling ghosts, most of the latter returning home after their day's work on outlying service operations. Jupiter held a steady course in the middle lane. They were in good time. Anyhow, it was pointless to even think of carving anyone up in this lumbering heap.

'It's bad enough having to see the monsters,' Mercury cut in again. 'But you could at least give the ghosts the magic boot. Do we have to put up with their crappy presence?'

'Yes.'

Jupiter's gravelly voice was firm, even though he knew he was being a hypocrite. Normally, like them all, he would never think of travelling in anything but G-mode. Yet tonight he had purposefully switched to EG-mode to make the ghosts visible.

'We're about to decide our future relationship with the earthlings,' he elaborated in what he hoped was a chummy tone, 'so "their crappy presence", as Mercury puts it, is precisely what we need to remind us why we're here.

'Take a good look, everybody. There goes your reason for immortality.'

There was more silence as they reverted to staring gloomily out of the rain-streaked windows.

Jupiter glanced in the mirror and saw a battered Volvo coming up fast behind. His instinct that they were being targeted was confirmed when it drew abreast and slowed. In the hushed interior of the limo he continued looking straight ahead, while wild faces leered madly out of the Volvo's side windows, followed by two hairy, shit-stained bottoms.

Even with the limo's windows sealed, they could hear the coarse singing.

'I luff to go a'deitin',
'Along ze godly treck!
'Und as I go I luff to sing,
'My leptop on my beck!
'Valderee! Valdera! Valderee! Valdera-a-a-a-a-a-a-aaaargh!
'My leptop on my beck!'

'I'll delete them with my new red-eye zapper,' Mercury cried, reaching into his pocket. 'Watch this — it'll blow their engine to pieces!'

'No,' Jupiter thundered. 'Just pretend they're not there.'

It was the only way to deal with the Valhalla

Villas lot when they were in this mood. Which was often enough.

Jupiter winced as the Volvo surged ahead, before cutting in viciously. He should have anticipated that. Now he had no option but to slam on the featherlight power brakes, pitching everyone forward to a despairing shriek from the tyres. Vulcan sniffed appreciatively at the blast of burning rubber sucked in by the aircon as more mad faces mouthed insults through the Volvo's rear window.

Then, in a cloud of smoke, it had accelerated hard and gone jinking through the traffic, lager cans flying out of the back.

Followed by a larger object, which began bouncing, as if in slow motion, across their path.

Jupiter slammed hard on the brakes again and it passed harmlessly in front of them, only to smash into the windscreen of an ancient lorry trundling along the slow lane. As this veered abruptly towards them, Jupiter hit horn, brakes and steering wheel all at once, sending the stretcher into a violent skid on the greasy surface. He spun the wheel and just managed to recover the back end, catching a glimpse of startled dusky faces as the limo scraped past by a whisker.

Watching in the rear-view mirror, he saw multiple arms windmill out of the windows while the lorry changed course violently, leapt the monster lane cones, bounced off an unyielding Stone Age deity and crashed onto its side.

Jupiter kept his eyes riveted on the scene, feeling as though he had just received a blow in the solar plexus. There could be no doubt about his identification of the object splattered across the lorry's screen.

It was, or rather had been, a pumpkin.

'Look out,' Mercury yelled.

Jupiter jerked his attention back to the road and saw he was about to ram the back of a tatty Fiat Panda, which must have been doing all of twenty miles an hour. He spun the wheel and again just scraped by, recognising the family of minor agricultural gods who had berated him on his round-up earlier in the day.

As they shook their fists and furiously tooted the horn, he could only hope the others had missed the pumpkin in the fresh confusion.

Until Vulcan let out an explosive laugh.

'Pumpkin pie, anyone?' the god of fire roared, slapping his knee and turning exultantly to the back seats. Good old Thor! He'd known he could count on him.

'Nice one, Vulcan,' Jupiter managed to growl, swallowing hard.

After which he concluded it would be politic to conduct the rest of the journey in silence, even when they passed the glass pyramid of the Factory, lights blazing like a beacon, despite its being empty.

Or like an accusing forefinger, Jupiter thought grimly. But one pointing at them?

Best, he quickly decided, not to even attempt to discuss it.

As Juno had forecast, the goddesses' journey was more harmonious, apart from an incident when a leering Lower Order yob tried to carve them up in his RS Escort, only for Juno to throw the wheel over and slam the door on him so comprehensively he ended up buried in the monster lane cones.

'Isn't it amazing how gods still think male values rule the road?' she commented. 'No wonder they're the ones who suffer from road rage.'

With which they had all heartily concurred.

Otherwise, everyone was equally subdued, even though, like Jupiter, Juno tried various stabs at conversation, only to find them petering out in a similar fashion as everyone stared gloomily through the windows.

The blazing Factory lights did, however, spark a brief discussion.

'I nearly took the turn-off,' Juno laughed, swerving back onto the main carriageway at the last second. It had been so like driving into work in the old days, she had been temporarily lulled into assuming that was their destination. 'Maybe I should have,' she added. 'We could have gone in and got on with it, just like we used to!'

'I went in the other day,' Minerva volunteered out of the blue.

Juno was so astonished she jumped a lane, narrowly missing a ghost refuse lorry.

'Why didn't you tell us that earlier?' she asked, thinking back to the subdued tea ceremony.

'None of you asked,' Minerva replied coolly.

'So what was it like?'

'Much as before. Everything working. Empty of course — bar the ghosts and Mercury.'

'Why go in the first place, though?'

'Just following a thought.'

'What thought?'

'A thought, that's all.' Minerva's voice was cold. 'I'm entitled to them, aren't I?'

They reverted to silence until they hit the heavy traffic close to the Forum, when Vesta suddenly spoke up.

'I haven't changed my mind, in case you're wondering,' she announced. 'I'm taking it as read the gods will be doing all the talking. And I'm not afraid to say I'm going to let them.'

'Those who speak do not know,' Minerva chimed in. 'Whilst those who know do not speak.

'At least, not yet.'

Juno scrutinised the goddess of wisdom in the mirror. Her little sayings lately had either been unbearably trite or exceedingly meaningful. Juno preferred to think the latter. Because, when it came down to it, Vesta was right. By its very nature, the meeting was bound to be gods-dominated.

It was not that the goddesses were so cowed by their male counterparts, they were simply content to let them lead them by the nose. Yet, even though they were confident in their own sexuality, Juno knew tonight would be an occasion for male bluster. The goddesses would have to use other ways, and occasions, to exert their full, underlying influence.

'You are all still going to abstain, though, aren't you?' she enquired, receiving firm nods in confirmation.

It had been the best compromise she could achieve.

Yet what, she was now wondering, was Minerva saying she knew, but was not yet speaking?

Chapter 10

Tempus Fugit

J upiter looked down from the platform on the multitude assembled between the soaring, fluted columns of the Basilica.

'Silence!' he commanded over the babble. 'GOD didn't summon us here to have a chat.

'Let me remind you all how crucial this moment is in our immortalities. The only opportunity he is ever going to give us to forge our destinies when he moves to System Megaverse 2000.'

'Who says he'll take any notice?' came an irreverent cry.

'That's right! He's not interested in us!'

Jupiter hammered with his fist on the marble table. It said a lot about the state they'd reached that the Lower Orders had the temerity to heckle at all, never mind peddle their negative line. If only he had his thunderbolt back, he'd zap the lot of them.

It was so terminally disappointing.

He had begun the meeting in an enormously positive frame of mind, already charged up by simply wending through the bustle of the city centre, the stretcher reduced to a crawl while it nudged multifarious gods spilling off the narrow pavements of the restaurant quarter.

At last, some energy! he had thought, picking up on the buzz as they sat aloof, whilst curious faces peered in at them through the smoked glass.

He had been given a further boost by the huge crowd waiting at their destination. Except that, as they were stepping out of the stretcher, with a deafening clap of thunder the skies had opened. Hurriedly, they had abandoned the roofless Forum and crammed themselves in here, whilst Jupiter struggled to recover from the shock.

He was the god of thunder. So what had that been? A GODsent omen? Some sort of warning shot? Or just more weather incontinence?

He had cheered up again as he greeted everybody heartily and was reminded what a plethora of minor, regional and local GrecoRoman deities existed. Some, like Aurora, the goddess of dawn, glowing in an appropriately pink gown, were unforgettable. But Jupiter could barely recollect dozens of others. Never mind the hordes of nymphs (wood and sea), satyrs, amorphettes, cherubs, zephyrs, sirens and general celestial hangerson. Even a herd of centaurs, accompanied by Pegasus the horse, wings politely furled.

Also, of course, the Nordic and Teutonic residents of Valhalla Villas, now forming a noisy bloc at the side, next to the moody-looking and silent collection of Celtic gods, whose assorted low brows said it all. Not even Jupiter knew them, so seldom did they emerge from their isolated, inward-looking Edgetown, way past the city limits.

'Lovely, isn't it?' he had whispered to Juno, basking in the warm glow of having fulfilled his promise to GOD. The brilliant turn-out had banished his worst-case scenario, in which pretended indifference — i.e. evasion of responsibility — had been so widespread no one had even turned up. 'Like a family reunion.'

She had smiled back noncommittally. What an old softy he could be!

'Lovely' was the word he'd often used in the past as he rushed round creating this jolly sort of atmosphere. Like an eager puppy, she had always thought affectionately. Until Retroland™ had shrunk public events to nothing. When even video-conferencing failed to save the regular meetings about Planet Earth, Juno hadn't been happy. Unlike her consort, though, she had accepted it as the way it was. As Mercury kept emphasising, it would be the same on Planet Earth when Megaverse 2000 came online.

But as soon as the meeting started Jupiter's high had evaporated. The fact of the matter, he was instantly forced to acknowledge, was that they weren't the slightest bit concerned for the earthlings.

Only for themselves.

'You can't wriggle out of it by saying GOD's not interested or won't take any notice of us.' He thumped the table again. 'All change on Planet Earth means all change for us too. So get this into your thick heads. Under Megaverse 2000, GOD's going to reprofile us all, whether we like it or not.'

He glared at them angrily.

'Which is why he's called us here to answer his question. What do we want? he requires to know. A return to the old days? More involvement with Planet Earth? Working again on our Factory terminals? Taking Earth tickets?

'Or the alternative — nothing but more Retroland™?'

He groaned as the cry he was expecting went up. Why did he bother? He had known he was wasting his time when he was out on his round-up. There might be a modicum of debate on Arcadia Close. But not on the Lower Orders' estate.

'You arrogant bastards think you run this place,' the family of minor agricultural gods he had nearly creamed on the expressway had shouted over the massive wall screen pumping out GODS TV.

Jupiter had sat resignedly on the black and orange sofa, staring at the swirling pattern on the blue carpet while he let it wash over him. At least they'd let him in. Other doors had simply been slammed in his face.

'Only come down from the Close when you want something,' the tirade had continued. 'Like that randy sod Bacchus. That filthy Vulcan. Or that nympho Venus. Bloody child molesters, all of them.

'Well, now you're here you can listen to us for once. We're not interested in the earthling wankers any more, got it? We prefer Retroland™. So would you, if you were stuck in this dump, rather than poncing about in your posh villa.'

Jupiter, tired of skirting dead cars, broken glass and dog shit, had seen their point. Yet he had persevered until he extracted a surly promise they would attend.

'No trying to trick us with clever talk, mind,' they

had shouted in a final sally as he struggled to close
the sagging garden gate. 'You Higher Order lot don't
dictate to us any more, right? These days we run our
own show.'

Recalling this gloomy episode, Jupiter glanced at
Juno. Before they had set off she had impressed how
he would gain nothing by opposing the overall will.

'No, J,' she mouthed, shaking her head emphatically.

He glared back at her equally emphatically. Rightly
or wrongly, he simply couldn't accept such a crucial
decision being made without the pros and cons even
being considered.

'Have you no humanity left?' he berated the floor.
'I'm not saying the earthlings are the greatest beings
in the universe. But some of them are doing their best.
Don't you feel responsible for their fate any more? Or
is it just me, me, and more bloody me?' He swept his
eyes over them, shaking his head sadly.

'Who invented the ego, eh?'

To his surprise, they either looked at each other
shiftily or stared guiltily — at least he hoped it was
guiltily — at the floor.

'What will Megaverse 2000 do for the earthlings,
anyhow?'

Jupiter suspected the questioner was playing for time.
Yet he still had to go through the motions.

'The original System 7.0 ushered in the Industrial
Revolution, in concert with the Age of Revolution,' he
intoned wearily. 'That in turn introduced the concept
of progress to the Western world, thereby changing
earthling life for ever.

'You all know this,' he burst out, trying to inject
some dynamism into his voice. 'As Megaverse 2000 takes

Planet Earth into the Information Age the Western world will once again be in the vanguard.'

He paused before playing the trump card he had prepared. 'You know the consequences of the computer technology we have here in the Land of the Gods only too well.

'I trust you're happy with them.'

He glared down triumphantly. That should have done it! Roll out all the grumbles! Now we'll see what they really think about what's coming the earth-lings' way!

Yet, to his immense chagrin, no one picked up the gauntlet.

The bastards are either too clever or too dumb, he thought grimly.

Or both.

'Never mind the earthlings, what's in store for us?'

'The whole point,' Jupiter yelled, struggling to keep his temper, 'is that that entirely depends on how we vote now.'

'Says Mr. High and Mighty!'

'God of Know-it-all!'

One more remark like that . . . Jupiter thought.

But now Mars had sprung to his feet, his small, intense figure instantly stealing the spotlight.

'Why should we bother with the earthlings any more? The only thing they worship these days is money!'

There were huge cheers.

'That's right! Sock it to 'em, Marsy boy!'

'And the market.' Apollo, now also on his feet, sounded equally bitter.

'All shopping, isn't it?' Vulcan sneered in support, sparking off the chant.

'Shopping-oh! Shopping-oh! Shopping-oh!' the floor began singing,

'Shopping-oh! Shopping-oh! Shopping-o-oh!'

Jupiter calmed down and temporarily let them have their head.

The same complaints were always trotted out as the standard excuses. But with justification, Jupiter had to admit. Even before GOD introduced Retroland™, changes on Planet Earth had caused a massive drop-off in interest.

For the one crucial difference between Planet Earth and the Land of the Gods was the absence of money. Which was a difference for which every god and goddess was profoundly grateful. Earthlings might have to demean themselves by thinking about ackers, beans, gelt, shekels, nickers, greenbacks, bars, smackers, bucks, readies, pieces of eight, wedges, wads, rolls, piles, packets, stacks, heaps, dimes, quids, ponies, monkeys, grands, spondulicks, lucre, dough, loot, brass, bread, cabbage, lettuce, dosh, lolly, mazuma, moolah, macaroni, wonga, scratch, payola, gravy, folding stuff, the wherewithal, the necessary — the very proliferation of earthling terms said it all.

But not gods.

How could you possibly be a god, or goddess, if your mind was polluted, ruled even, like so many Western mortals, by such base material?

'Never contributed anything useful to the earthling race, and never will,' Jupiter remembered telling Juno after returning from New York on one of his last Earth tickets. 'Yet everyone I mind-entered was obsessed by it. They must be crazy, Juno. Just when so many can begin to relax about it, all they're interested in is acquiring more.

'Plain greed, I call it. Not just on Wall Street, either. Everywhere, from the earthlings in suits at the top, down to the thieves and muggers at the bottom, it's the same.

'The language! Bottom lines, tax breaks, investment opportunities, currency futures, traded options, venture capitalism, junk bonds, leveraged buy-outs . . . I couldn't understand a word of it.

'The upshot's clear enough though,' he had crisply summarised. 'The only purpose they're interested in now is one they can add up on a calculator.'

'What can you do?' Juno had sighed.

'I'll tell you what I did, Juno,' he had replied, rubbing his hands with savage satisfaction. 'Crashed the Dow Jones index! Just to make them aware that fortune can cut both ways.

'But do you know what the bastards did?' He had shaken his head incredulously. 'Saw it as a buying opportunity and just piled in for more!'

'It's not only shopping and money,' came a coarse Lower Orders shout. 'The wankers have turned Terminus into a bus station.'

'End of the line now, Termy!'

'All passengers please disembark!'

'Mercury into a logo.'

'Trying to connect you! Trying to connect you!'

'How's the rubber-goods business, Vulcan?'

'Safe sex, eh?'

'Give us a light, Vesta!'

'Anyone for a Mars Bar?'

'Flora spreads easily, don't you, eh?'

The goddess of flowers blushed at the ribald guffaws.

'Worst of all, the wankers have forgotten us Teutonics

entirely!' Thor was on his feet, red beard flying, hammer swinging wildly round his head.

'So stop whining on about them,' he addressed Jupiter directly. 'Or shall I come and match you up?'

Jupiter, acutely conscious of the purple swelling disfiguring one side of his face, fought to restrain himself. He could handle his own Greco-Roman lot. But the Valhalla Villas' mob was different. Especially now he had a personal axe to grind after seeing Vulcan give Thor a sly thumbs-up.

'Make my day, punk!' he shouted melodramatically, hatred in his heart.

There had been a time he had respected Thor as the very apotheosis of a warrior, heroically tireless in his readiness to face combat and danger. Yet nowadays he could only think of him as thick — or 'rudely simple', as the Nordic god would openly boast himself.

And now, as Jupiter had feared, he had opened the Lower Orders' floodgates.

'The earthlings are doing brilliantly!'

'Controlling their own destinies!'

'Got McDonald's!'

'Coca-Cola!'

'And Pepsi!'

'Disneyland!'

'Five hundred channels of TV!'

'Live sport all the time!'

'Best of all, for the Brits — the lottery!'

Jupiter swallowed hard.

He had always considered Britain more civilised than its raucous transatlantic counterpart, where it was sometimes hard avoiding the conclusion that every birth was another disaster for Planet Earth.

So when a GOD e-mail had announced his lottery plan for the island inhabitants, Jupiter had fired back angrily.

'Good fortune is one thing,' he had laboriously typed into the system with two fingers. 'But dangling such vast sums, when the chance of winning is so remote, is not only cruel, but merely increases the money obsession.

'In addition, as you may not have realised, instead of accepting personal responsibility, individual earthlings will use failing to win it as their excuse for not changing their lives,' he had ended.

Somewhat convolutedly, he had felt, wondering how he could improve his phraseology. He always had difficulty getting things down on screen in a simple way. Yet after various laborious reworkings had only made it seem worse, in the end he had sent it anyhow.

GOD's response had been so furious even Jupiter had been taken aback.

'How dare you lecture me like this, you pompous god?' an e-mail had shot back. 'Who exactly do you think you are?

'Get off your high horse and do your job. Which is not to oppose my will, but follow my command by picking out the winning numbers.'

Surlily, Jupiter had complied, taking a few Earth tickets to half-heartedly point the finger and announce: 'It's you.'

Finally, nauseated by the climate of avarice he was helping to promote, he had spent a whole day tapping winning numbers into the computer, first for months, then years, in advance, all the time waiting for GOD to remonstrate with him.

Yet, to his surprise, his entries had been accepted without question. After which he had managed to salvage some pride by taking a perverse delight in visiting misfortune on the winners.

Now it was Mercury's turn to spring to his feet, his lengthy toilet beforehand making him appear the very apotheosis of a modern god — eternally young, thrusting, vigorous, gelled blond hair, Armani suit shrieking the height of fashion.

'Not long now, fellow gods, and the earthlings are to have the amazing Age of Information, ushered in on the Super Highway by the Internet!' His eyes shone with messianic fervour. 'Awaiting Planet Earth is a glorious age, an age when earthling can share knowledge with earthling, free and unencumbered, around the globe.

'An age when, for the first time, all earthlings can, and will, communicate!

'It doesn't end there,' he shouted over the roars of approval. 'Like us, they are also to enter Cyberspace through Virtual Reality! I don't need to tell you that is the greatest thing coming their way.' He raised his arms dramatically above his head. 'No longer just boring, old-fashioned, stick-in-the-mud Real Life. Like us, they are to be given the gift of Virtual Life!

'How lucky can they be? Because soon they'll be joining us in fabulous, realler-than-real Retroland™!'

'Which means there's nothing for us to do,' Thor roared in support from the floor. 'Because we'll be meeting them there anyhow!'

Jupiter felt himself being engulfed by a wave of depression.

'Techno's no answer to Earth's problems,' he thundered in response, seizing the god of communications by the shoulder pad and shoving him to one side. 'Can't you see that in many ways things down there are getting worse? Spiritually bereft, selfish, heartless? Values crumbling? Standards going out of the window?'

He turned in heartfelt appeal to Juno.

'Tell them.'

Juno immediately abandoned her previous decision not to speak.

'Jupiter's right!' she cried. 'And you know one of the main reasons? The continuing domination of male values. Planet Earth needs more female input . . .'

An angry hail of boos and sexist cries drowned her out, bringing home the reality of Vesta's gloomy prediction about the gods dominating the meeting. Should she aggressively ride over them, hammer home the validity of her statement in the face of such a vacuous, yet confrontational, male consensus? As she had told Jupiter, they must bow to the overall will.

'You're a load of useless male bastards!' she shouted witheringly instead, sitting down and dismissing them with a contemptuous shrug of her shoulders.

Jupiter gave her a nod to show he appreciated her trying, then scanned the rest of the top table in despair. All the others — even Minerva — seemed determined to stay out of it. Now what?

He felt a sudden ray of hope as Saturn rose creakingly to his feet.

'You will listen to me,' the ancient god intoned, his authority bringing an instant hush. 'And you will hear what I say.' His sickle cut through the air with a menacing hiss, light bouncing off it blindingly. 'For gods you may be now, but gods you may not necessarily remain.'

This is more like it, Jupiter thought, cheering up. The backup he had been promised earlier by this traditional god of the old school — long beard, white robe, the works. He may not frighten them, Jupiter grinned to himself, but by GOD he frightens me.

'For time, like an ever-rolling stream, sweeps away all that is old, useless and decayed.'

Hiss!

'Mark my words, all of you — like the earthlings, time is all we have.'

Hiss!

'Therefore it behoves each and every one of us to remember — *tempus fugit*.'

Abruptly he sat down.

Jupiter stared at him, gobsmacked. What had that all been about? He could see the audience looking equally mystified.

Until Bacchus broke the spell.

'Come in, Planet Six!' he guffawed. 'Your time's up!'

'Very funny,' Jupiter glared.

'Glad you like it,' Bacchus leered back, openly squeezing the breast of the smiling nymph refilling his wine cup.

Jupiter saw the Valhalla Villas mob convulse with merriment.

'Think it's funny too, do you?' he challenged.

'Not him, you thick bugger,' a low-browed Nordic yelled back. 'Her! See you outside, love!'

He was cut short by a thwack across the chops from a gigantic female with blonde plaits.

Jupiter looked around, puzzled.

'And don't bother to put them back on again!'

Thwack!

'Unless you fancy them being ripped off!'

Thwack!

Jupiter's eye settled on Venus, wearing a little black dress and a wide grin. Suddenly it clicked. She must be up to her old trick of not wearing any. Which, raised up as she was on the platform, must be giving a fairly stunning view.

'Party time, darling!' Bacchus lunged along the table, upsetting his wine cup into Vesta's lap.

'Sit bloody down!' Jupiter bellowed at the swaying god of vines.

He'd had quite enough of this. All he wanted to do now was get it over as fast as possible.

'Right you lot, that's it,' he announced to his truculent audience. 'Now, to answer GOD's questions.

'First, who wants to reinvolve themselves with Planet Earth, go back to work in the Factory, take Earth tickets, just as we used to?'

He stuck up his hand.

Mercury's followed eagerly, then, more slowly, Juno's.

That was it.

Except for, of all gods, little Cupid.

'And who just wants more Retroland™ to play in?'

The sarcasm was wasted. A forest of hands had gone up.

He glared at them, bottom lip curled.

'Democracy,' he pronounced slowly, 'is a flawed concept.'

The only answer was more boos, this time accompanied by a rain of empty lager cans from the Teutonic direction.

'Abstentions?'

There was some consolation in the number of raised hands, especially all the ones at the top table, much as Juno had predicted. At least they weren't voting headlong for what Jupiter was sure was total disaster. Just passing the buck to GOD. Which, he supposed with a resigned sigh, he must accept. In a way, it was where it correctly stopped.

At the top table, he had seen only Mars vote actively for Retroland™.

What about Bacchus, though?

Jupiter noticed the empty chair.

The god of vines was no longer at the table, but underneath it.

As the nymph smiled helplessly, he gave a con-temptuous gesture of dismissal and turned to fire his parting shot.

'Now you've voted to switch off the earthlings entirely, let's hope for your sakes that GOD switches Retroland™ back on again.'

There was a shocked silence.

'He wouldn't dare not.' Mars was on his feet again.

'He's dared suspend it for the moment though, hasn't he?' Jupiter shouted triumphantly. 'How does the Red Baron feel about being grounded?'

He was about to add 'Meeting closed', when there was a shrill shriek.

'We can't turn our backs on the earthlings, just when they're heading for terrible trouble and need us most!

'It's simply not fair!'

Jupiter glared down at the small head of curly hair now poking above the tabletop.

'Not fair, Cupid?' he thundered. 'And who, precisely, ever decreed that earthling life, or immortality, should be fair?'

Chapter II

Bowing Out

'I am a proper god,' Cupid always insisted to every-one, though there were times he wondered if even the giggling cherubs believed him. 'I've got a very important job.'

Not as important of course, as his hero, Jupiter. Jupiter was cool. Not too laid back, maybe, but, as the greatest god, not sniffy about Cupid's activities, like so many adults. As well as being so friendly and, above all, so awesome, yet really interested in the earthlings.

When he refused to disappear into Retroland™, Cupid faithfully followed his lead. Not just, as he cheerfully admitted to his mentor, because he loved the earthlings so much.

'Retroland™'s OK, but it's only a game, isn't it? There'll never be anything there I enjoy more than pinging. That moment when my arrow strikes home!

It's so zingy! So real!' His voice had gone squeaky
with excitement. 'Got to be the essence of immortality,
hasn't it?

'The earthlings think it's just as wonderful, don't
they, Jupiter? Falling in love, they say — brilliant!
The best! Some responsibility I've been given, eh?
Wicked!'

'Conducted just as responsibly?' Jupiter had smiled
back, making him redden.

Yet how could you turn down the opportunities for
mischief when love-matching? The way, like no other
god, you could turn earthlings' lives upside down? The
pranks you could play? No wonder they said love was
blind! Their weaknesses and foibles never ceased to
amaze and delight him. Adult gods might dismiss his
activity as infantile, but Cupid didn't care. As far as he
was concerned immortality was for doing things. And
if he was having fun, immortalising spontaneously for
the moment, then he was doing what he was there for
— spicing up otherwise dull earthling lives.

Always, of course, in concert with Venus. Romance,
with all its heady excitement, was one thing, but even
Cupid knew true love, or at least the enduring kind,
involved more than just that.

He was also aware, eternally trapped as he was on
the awkward cusp of adolescence, that his knowledge
of sex had to be patchy. Yet he'd come to terms with
this in what he thought a tremendously adult way.

'I know the earthlings I ping don't just gaze into each
other's eyes,' he had confided to his hero. 'Shagging's
only part of it, though, isn't it? Getting your kit off and
all that stuff? So I've decided the less I know about the
details, the better.

'Then I won't get muddled up with lust, will I?'

'Which would be the most terrible thing, Cupid, wouldn't it?' the greatest god had smiled down, making Cupid wonder for a moment if he was secretly laughing at him. But it had just been teasing. Jupiter had followed through with the endorsement Cupid had been seeking.

'I remember Juno once saying there should be a separate goddess of leg-overs,' he had recalled, grinning. 'Because you're righter than you know, Cupid. Being able to distinguish between love and lust is what it's all about.'

Yet it was precisely that distinction which had led to the massive falling out with his mother that Cupid was still struggling to come to terms with.

It had begun with his ears burning at hearing other adults openly describe Venus as a 'shag bag', with even cherub chums flinging 'naughty lady' taunts. Nonetheless Cupid had defended her loyally, until the fateful afternoon he had found her little black book lying on the dresser, almost as if it had been left there to tempt him.

He had taken what he promised himself would be just a quick peek. Only to become immersed in an eye-popping trawl from cover to cover.

On page after page were references to multiple sexual liaisons and bizarre practices he didn't even know existed. Albeit in tantalising note form, which somehow made them thrillingly worse. As did the participants, mostly drawn from the weird ranks of the downtown monsters.

What in the Land of the Gods was 'Chicken Voodooloo', described as 'finger-licking good' and rating 8.5 out of 10? 'Succulent swamp sucking' (9)? 'Egyptian Ra-ra romps – sunshine all the way' (7)? Cupid did

know enough to blush to his roots at 'Shiva's lingam —
never mind the quality feel the width!' (8), along with
'Stepping the Giants' Causeway!', followed by a list of
extraordinary lengths (9.5!).

He had just been trying to puzzle out 'Best broom-
stick ride ever — shame about the spell' (6), when Venus
had unexpectedly walked in.

'I can't believe this, Mother,' he had exclaimed. 'It's
completely gross! You're falling apart.'

'I'm the goddess of love, Cupid,' she had snapped
back, angrily snatching the book from his hand and
stuffing it down the front of her dress. 'So I can love
who I want, how I want.'

'That's not love, Mother,' Cupid had protested,
remembering what he had agreed with Jupiter. 'It's
lust. You always taught me that was love's enemy!'

'Think you're so clever, don't you?' she had fired
back. 'Never mind what I used to teach you. Don't you
realise things change, even for immortals? Not that I'm
saying that I'm proud of anything in there,' she had
added, indicating her bosom.

'It doesn't seem that way to me,' Cupid had accused
primly.

At which she had blown her top.

'While you, I suppose, are now proud of being a little
sneak prying into his mother's secrets?'

'It wasn't my fault,' Cupid had wailed. 'You shouldn't
have left it lying there.'

But it had been too late.

A barrier had been thrown up between them and
she had reverted to treating him as a child, not old
enough to understand anything serious. In response he
had withdrawn and the intimacy between them had
been lost.

'And the earthlings say your relationship with your mother is the hardest in your life,' he had confided ruefully to Jupiter. 'They think they've got problems! Why is she acting like this, never mind giving up on the earthlings like all the others?'

'It's not entirely her fault, Cupid. Or theirs.'

Jupiter had felt an annoying need to excuse his fellow adults in the face of such juvenile directness. Oh that he had such essential purity of heart, such an unsullied ability to retain clear thinking!

'Just be thankful you're young enough not to understand burn-out,' he had counselled, feeling tremendously old and tired by it all. 'Or cynicism. I don't know which is worse, really. Yet even I find it hard to muster much sympathy for the earthlings these days. You must have noticed how things down there have changed.'

'There does seem less fun about,' Cupid had reluctantly agreed.

Being younger, he related to younger earthlings and these days came across more and more lost, frightened, even in despair, at the state of their precious planet. Hence the drugs, which he himself largely stayed away from. He retained enough boyish enthusiasm not to need them.

'Planet Earth's still a wonderful place, though, Jupiter, isn't it?' he had asked, worried.

'In some ways, Cupid.' Jupiter had sounded extremely grave, which hadn't helped. 'Grown-up matters are always more complicated than they appear.

'So why not forget about the rest and just concentrate on enjoying yourself?'

Which, after such reassurance, Cupid had managed to do.

Until just the other day, when he had received the shock of his immortality.

Cupid was fully aware he was not allowed to hack into the parts of GOD that were strictly off limits. Yet he was equally certain other gods must have been up to the same thing in the past, even though they might not be bothering with their terminals any more. Wouldn't any god or goddess with a bit of spirit?

Not that they ever talked about it openly – or at least in front of him. It was no good trying to swap notes with the cherubs either. They weren't even allowed to touch the terminals.

So he had carried on secretly hacking on his own. Not all the time. Just when the mood took him. He never got very far, or learnt much new. Yet there was always the challenge of beating the techno barriers GOD placed in the way, along with the thrill of the unknown. A bit like those metal-detector things some earthlings got so excited about. Most of what you found was dead boring, but you were always egged on by the hope something amazing might be round the corner.

What you didn't expect to find was something that scared the absolute shit out of you.

Which was what had happened to Cupid.

If it had really happened.

It had been so weird and spooky, he had since been doubting his senses. Could he really, in GOD's darkest recesses, have learnt that bad things were about to happen to the earthlings? That they were in big trouble? Maybe even doomed?

He had no proof. Only his word. But how could he possibly give that, or even explain to anybody, without disclosing his hacking? Which had to land him in all sorts of trouble, even with Jupiter, understanding though he might normally be.

More alarmingly still, maybe with GOD himself. His terminal might be withdrawn!

But there was an even worse side to it. What he had seen had been inside GOD, so presumably must be part of him. Yet it couldn't be, if he really was looking after the earthlings alongside them.

Or rather, now the other gods had withdrawn, virtually on his own.

And that, of course — Cupid gulped at the thought — gave him a free hand . . .

After endlessly racking himself with tangled thoughts and dreadful imaginings, Cupid had finally pinned his hopes on the meeting. If others came to his aid by raising the same thing, he would be off the hook. Maybe even able to confess his hacking, thereby supplying real, and horrible, confirmation.

Except that, as he sat listening to the superficial debate, he had to accept he was not going to be handed this easy way out. The meeting was nearly over. If he didn't say something now, no one would.

Yet as soon as he opened his mouth, he knew he had got it wrong. They thought that 'fair' was a child word!

'I don't mean not fair,' he tried correcting himself. 'I mean not right.'

He had never spoken at a meeting before. It was scary seeing all the heads turned in his direction, especially as none looked the slightest bit pleased. Venus, whose creamy thighs had closed with an audible slap, appeared the most disapproving of all.

'Not right?' Jupiter was now glowering down.

Cupid felt his cheeks change from rosy to scarlet. But he had put himself on the spot. He must carry on.

'Yes, not right,' he appealed to his hero. 'Giving up on the earthlings so totally, just when they need us to save them.'

'Am I hearing you right?' Jupiter's great brow had clouded over.

'I can't hear anything,' Neptune chipped in, ostentatiously cupping his hand to his ear.

There were roars of laughter. Everyone knew the salty sea god's habit of not hearing things that didn't suit him, always claiming the noise of his watery kingdom had blotted them out.

'Maybe I did hear something.' He pretended to listen with rapt attention. 'A dolphin squeaking, I think!'

Cupid's cheeks moved along the colour spectrum to crimson.

'Perhaps you could tell us exactly what we need to save the earthlings from?' Jupiter enquired after the laughter had died down.

Cupid hopped up and down in agitation. How to explain, without giving away his hacking?

'I don't know exactly what, Jupiter. Just that bad things are going to happen.'

'And how, precisely, do you know that?'

Cupid's eyes dropped to the floor. He couldn't bring himself to tell them.

'I just know,' he pouted sulkily. 'Anyway, aren't we supposed to work with them, help them be their greatest, whether trouble's coming their way or not?'

That had to be safer ground. What Venus, Jupiter – all of them – had always taught him. Except they didn't seem to mention it any more.

'Now you're telling us our purpose?' Jupiter rumbled ominously.

He was feeling somewhat betrayed. He liked his private chats with Cupid and the way he could help him along. But, if he did know something, why hadn't he revealed it in confidence?

Because what Jupiter absolutely could not allow was this lecturing in public. To no purpose, anyhow, now the Retroland™ decision had been taken.

'You know the saying "Little gods should be seen, but not heard"?' he addressed the bent head. 'These matters are far too complex for you to understand. You must leave them to your elders and betters.'

Elders and betters! he thought to himself. What a hypocrite!

Although the admonishment was delivered in a kindly enough tone, Cupid detected the hard line underneath. He looked up into the steely-blue eyes, knowing he was being given a chance to withdraw gracefully. Yet, although his legs were quaking and he felt he might wet himself any second, he couldn't stop.

He simply had to warn everybody!

'Please! Please!' he cried shrilly. 'I'm not joking. It's really serious. We can't leave the earthlings to face the future with just GOD.'

'It's you who should be leaving, you little dickhead. Right now.'

Mars had lunged across the table, grabbed his bow and begun flexing it dangerously above his head.

'Give me it back,' Cupid wailed. 'It's my best one. You'll break it.'

The god of war carried on holding it tantalisingly out of reach, whilst the audience jeered at Cupid's discomfort.

'Only when you get the message, fuckwit, that you're not here to tell us what to do.'

Venus, frowning, was about to intervene when there was a loud crack.

Mars lowered the bow and looked at it dumbly. Only its string now held it together.

'Fuck off out of here, will you?' he shouted, now angry with himself.

Knowing how much it meant to Cupid, he hadn't been intending to break it.

'Listen to me!' Jupiter thundered before Cupid could move.

The greatest god had been reconsidering his decision. The vote might have been taken, but he should still pursue the line Cupid had opened up. What the lad was talking about, never mind where he'd got it from, Jupiter didn't know.

Yet he had raised a valid point. It had been a mistake to let the meeting proceed on the assumption — true or false — that the earthlings' future was rosy. What if Cupid, or he, could now persuade them otherwise? Mightn't that cause a change of heart, at least in some of them?

It had to be worth a try.

'I hereby order we carefully consider what Cupid has just said,' he announced, rising sharply to his feet.

Too sharply, he realised as he felt his shin come into vicious contact with the table leg.

So vicious he couldn't prevent tears welling up in his eyes.

Desperately, he hopped about the platform, the tears running down his face, his black eye pulsating.

'It's your boss you should be saving, you daft little bugger, not the earthlings,' he could hear Thor shouting at Cupid, while the laughter swelled all around.

Cupid hovered uncertainly. The last thing he had been intending was this humiliation of his hero. Even if it hadn't been entirely his fault.

At least, though, the plight of the earthlings would now be raised.

Except that Jupiter's control had snapped. Whatever happened next, he simply wasn't bothered any more.

'You're not gods, but fools!' he berated them. 'Blind, arrogant fools! Will you ever learn to take anything seriously?'

Apparently not, was the answer.

Seeing the chair so completely lose his dignity had obviously been the final fillip they had been seeking.

'Bye-bye, boss,' they were crying as they streamed out of the Basilica. 'See you in Retroland™ along with the earthlings one day, eh?'

Chapter 12

Retroland™ Rules

As a sweetener for the meeting, Jupiter had suggested everyone repair afterwards to Neptune's Trattoria Tridentia, which had been such a focus of their immortalities when they had been full-time in the Factory. Against his better judgment, he had further acceded to demands from the Lower Orders that he revive the karaoke which had then been all the rage.

Now, as the last tittering figures drifted out of the Basilica, he informed Juno flatly, 'I'm going straight home.'

'You'll lose even more face if they see you can't accept defeat gracefully,' she replied, triggering a hollow laugh.

'Anyway,' he objected further, 'I have to report back to GOD.'

'After all the work you've done, GOD can wait.'

Still grumbling, Jupiter had reluctantly conceded.

Only to conclude, the moment he walked into the restaurant, that Juno had pushed him into a mistake. Neptune might be enormously proud of playing mine host, but his and Jupiter's tastes had long diverged. Jupiter had been a great fan when the sea god had started the trattoria with the neat concept of a trendy, yet intimate, little number, such as you found in the best places on Planet Earth. But he had expanded it so wildly he had now ended up with this riotous mishmash of singalong pub, yuppie wine bar and pizza joint. Complete with sawdust, and a lot worse, on the floor.

Even copious amounts of frascati weren't enabling Jupiter to come to terms with the worst aspect — the appalling din. Saturn was grinding out 'I Was Born a Wanderin' Planet' from one giant wall screen, a scratch band led by Apollo and Pan bashing away on another whilst GODS TV blasted inanely from the third. Only the fourth, a huge sheet of glass, remained silent as it showed off the menu, lugubriously cruising the outdoor sea-water tank.

That was just the background.

Overlaid was a deafening hubbub of shouted conversations, drunken laughter and crashing crockery, underpinned by the rumble of Neptune's latest innovation of ghost waiters careering around on roller skates.

Jupiter's ankle, black eye and head were throbbing, while he was also suspicious he was being set up for yet more humiliation. He had already muttered to Saturn how performing had to be the ultimate embarrassment, only for the ancient god to chastise him as a spoilsport.

'If you had the mindset of my age,' he had chuckled, 'nothing could embarrass you. After all, what have you got to lose?'

Only my dignity, Jupiter now thought, seeing the sly grins being exchanged whilst the god of time groaned blithely on. The impromptu rap sessions at the Factory had been one thing. But this was just tacky crap.

And meanwhile, here at the High Table, the tensions underlying the meeting were bubbling over again.

'You should never have allowed the little prick to even be there,' Mars was yelling at Venus. 'Never mind open his stupid mouth.'

Still angry over breaking Cupid's bow, the god of war was now in an even fouler mood. He had challenged Vulcan to an oyster-opening competition and not only lost, but cut his finger so badly it was pouring blood. The wound would heal. But the embarrassment was infinitely more painful.

'Can't you control him, or what?' he demanded, flinging the plate of oysters across the table at her.

Venus regarded him disdainfully from under lowered lids.

Slowly and deliberately, she fished around with her long fingers until she found the plumpest and most blood-soaked oyster. Holding Mars's eye, she arched her delicate neck and slid the juicy mollusc lasciviously down her throat.

'Next?' she smiled, running her tongue round her lips. 'I always swallow, you know.'

'You filthy tart!' Mars, beside himself, switched targets by jerking his head in Jupiter's direction. 'Your little dickhead is as bad as him — lecturing us as if he was GOD bloody almighty.'

'Enough.' Jupiter gave a warning growl.

'Enough? After the bollocks you laid on us back there?'

Jupiter stared back at him venomously.

More even than Thor, for him the once-noble god of war was coming to symbolise the way the Land of the Gods was degenerating. The language was just an outward sign of the coarseness running like a dark thread through all their immortalities. Try to explain that, though. Get him — and the rest — to acknowledge it. Never mind do something to halt the slide.

Jupiter looked at Mars's face, made ugly by rage.

Forget it.

'I was just doing my job,' he shouted instead above the racket.

'Another jobsworth now, are we?' Mars sneered, waving derisively at Terminus down at the end of the table, in a world of his own as he nervously rehearsed the verses of 'I Draw The Line'.

A cheer suddenly went up.

Neptune had plunged into the outdoor tank and appeared at the glass, grinning whilst he pointed towards a plump sea bass, before giving chase. It was his party trick and he did it well, running triumphantly back into the restaurant, his writhing quarry speared on the prongs of his trident.

He marched up to the High Table and dropped it, dripping and flapping, in front of Jupiter.

'For you,' he announced proudly.

Jupiter, suspicious again, was trying to work out whether this was a set-up, when Mars dived in.

'There's something real,' he scoffed. 'Let's see you get your teeth into it.'

Without thinking, Jupiter seized the fish.

Holding Mars's eye in the same way as Venus had,

he slowly raised his victim to his mouth, inserted its head, then, in one hard jerk, bit it clean off.

He ran his tongue round his lips, again like Venus, before noisily spitting the head onto the table, aiming so it came to a slithering stop by Mars's plate.

'I always ejaculate, you know,' he sneered.

The god of war glared at the two piercing blue eyes, then at the baleful fish eye staring accusingly up from the table.

Reaching forward, he picked up the head and flung it into Jupiter's face.

At which point the greatest god pushed over his chair with a resounding crash and they were both on their feet.

Immediately Neptune lowered his trident.

'Outside, both of you,' he commanded, prodding them firmly in the direction of the exit. 'You know the rules.'

Everyone tensed in the comparative quiet as Saturn groaned to a full stop. Neptune might boast about the 'friendly atmosphere' of his restaurant which, roughly translated, meant being allowed to do more or less what you liked. Including shagging on the tables and food fights, which he often started himself.

Not real fights, though. They wrecked everything. And everyone could see this pair were way beyond the bread-rolls stage.

As he retreated Jupiter could feel the waves of resentment being beamed towards him. Was there no justice? he thought incredibly. It had been bad enough being castigated for his role at the meeting. But now to be cast as party-pooper, when the restaurant had been his idea in the first place!

Gently, he pushed Neptune's trident to one side.

'I was leaving anyway,' he announced stiffly to the silent room. 'I didn't come to spoil things.'

He meant it too. He sincerely wanted them to have a great time, if only to remind themselves what fun their immortalities had once been.

'Let's leave it that we choose to disagree,' he added equally stiffly to Mars and felt the tension evaporate as the god of war nodded grudgingly back.

'You stay,' he further instructed Juno, unable to prevent himself glaring at her as if to say this was all her fault.

'Enjoy yourselves,' he addressed the rest of the room. 'No hard feelings, eh?'

Sensing the answer might not be entirely in agreement, he quickly walked out, reeling as the crisp night air hit his face.

At least he had escaped becoming personally involved in the karaoke horror, as well as the inevitable finale of 'We Are the Champions.'

Instead, as he had originally intended, he could motor back in the stretcher and get on with the more urgent business of his report back to GOD.

'Fight the good fight
    'With all thy might
    'GOD is thy strength
    'And GOD thy right . . .'

Jupiter hammered on the steering wheel in frustration whilst he crashed the stretcher cruelly over the speed bumps. He had known he was too late the moment he saw the blinding white light hanging over a deserted Arcadia Close.

If only he'd followed his instinct! At least he would have got his oar in first.

He ran inside and flicked up the screen.

mail to: all Gods/Goddesses

22.31.00/15.12.1999

from: GOD

PLEASE NOTE: IN PREPARATION FOR MEGAVERSE
2000, AND AS AN ESSENTIAL COMPONENT OF
THE RE-IMAGING EXERCISE CONDUCTED BY MY
PRESENTATIONAL AGENCY, I HEREBY ANNOUNCE
THAT HENCEFORTH I SHALL NO LONGER BE
OPERATING AS 'GODS, ORACLES AND DEITIES',
BUT UNDER MY NEW CORPORATE IDENTITY OF
'GLOBAL ONLINE DIVINITY'.
    HOWEVER, AS YOU WILL NO DOUBT NOTE, THIS
DOES MEAN MY RETAINING THE ACRONYM WITH
WHICH YOU ARE ALL SO FAMILIAR.

Technology situation report 493771/667

Hi!

Congratulations, my favourite gods and
goddesses, on such a brilliant meeting!

I know you appreciate I had to let you decide
for yourselves. And you didn't let me down!
It was great seeing you so focused and
knowing exactly where you were coming from.
Even better, not being afraid to say, in no
uncertain terms, exactly where you want to
go! It's not just I who knows what's good for
you, eh?

Now, I have to make a confession – something
I know you're not accustomed to my doing

often! I must admit things haven't been
too hot for you recently under System 7.8.9
aka.05 retake 2. But what could I do? As time
passed, it transpired it had developed such
multiple bugs and viruses even I could not
rectify them.

However, I can assure you these will be
entirely eradicated under System Megaverse
2000. So next millennium you can leave that
tedious business of running Planet Earth to
me and get on with enjoying yourselves!

Because I've now got some even greater news!

Tomorrow I'll be reinstating Retroland™.
Not boring, old-fashioned 7.8.9 aka.05
retake 2 Retroland™ though! No, in a
special sneak preview, new, improved mega-
wide, mega-deep, mega-high, mega-super-
fantastic Megaverse 2000 MEGA-RETROLAND™!

Even better, you lucky goddies, as of
00.00.01/01.01.2000 MEGA-RETROLAND™ won't
be operating on the previous restricted
timescale which was such a meaningless
hangover from the past. It's going to be
open 24 hours a day, seven days a week,
meaning you'll never have to take part in
Real Immortality again!

Just think – your eternal opportunity to
run all your old favourites, whenever you
like, as long as you like! Never mind all the
new goodies I'll be introducing later! It's
going to be fun, fun all the way, especially
as you'll have accessed the Energy Pool and
have all your old zing back!

You voted for the brave new world of
Megaverse 2000 Mega-Retroland™, goddies!

```
Now's your chance to go for it!

Who do you want to be today?

.sig
```

There was another personal PS:

```
Many, many congratulations on the excellent
turnout - in line with my highest
expectations! Well done, too, for carrying
out your duty to put the other side with
such flair!
```

Jupiter sat rereading as he let it sink in.

Mega-Retroland™ he might have guessed. What he hadn't anticipated was the presentational agency's 'Global Online Divinity'. He instantly disliked its style. The fake bonhomie. Smarmy insincerity. It was too matey, too much like — he cast around in his mind — GODS TV, of all things! And whatever Gods, Oracles and Deities' other faults, Jupiter would never have accused him of that.

The changes under Megaverse 2000 were obviously going to be, in a favourite GOD word, manifold. As well as being implemented without a pretext at further consultation. And although the prospect of any change, even if Jupiter didn't like it, was suddenly hugely stimulating, he still couldn't let this pass without comment.

He stabbed at the keys with thick fingers, thinking how Global Online Divinity might make changes to the password system. BIG BOY indeed! It might be better than its predecessor, GERONIMO, yet he still felt it had the same sarcastic edge. GOD couldn't be taking the piss, surely?

Not that Jupiter could compare notes with anyone to find out, even Juno. 'In the interests of security', as GOD justified it, their minds were programmed so they were incapable of repeating their passwords to each other.

> REDUNDANT PASSWORD. INPUT REPLACE-
MENT <

Jupiter blinked.

> NO REPLACEMENT ISSUED < he typed back clumsily.

> ACCESS THEREFORE DENIED <

> BIG BOY < he tried again.

> REDUNDANT PASSWORD. INPUT REPLACE-
MENT <

> GERONIMO <

> REDUNDANT PASSWORD. INPUT REPLACE-
MENT <

Jupiter compressed his lips and straightened his chair.

Dawn was lightening the sky when he slumped in his seat and forced himself to admit defeat. He had tried every way he knew, first keeping his cool, then finally ending up crashing his huge fist onto the keyboard.

He, the greatest god, defeated by a poxy machine! How he hated techno. It gave GOD so much control.

He glared at the screen.

> ERROR CODE <

> DRIVE NOT READY <

> INPUT REPLACEMENT <

> ACCESS DENIED <

> ACCESS DENIED <

> ACCESS DENIED <

He turned away and kneaded his brow, trying to alleviate the headache brought on by a combination of the frascati, working at the screen and the continuous broadcasting of 'Fight the Good Fight'.

Rubbing his eyes, he looked back, to see a new message:

> RETROLAND™ IS NOW THE REAL THING <

He shook his head in disbelief. The real thing was being here, trapped as always in GOD's web, wasn't it?

> BIG BOY < he was typing in frantically when Juno walked in, bleary-eyed.

'Look at this!'

'Can't you ever take a break?' she snapped.

'But Juno,' he pleaded, 'either my terminal's gone haywire or GOD — Global Online Divinity or whatever he now calls himself — has gone mad. I've been shut out.'

'What do you mean?' she asked, giving him a peculiar look.

'Locked out, kicked off the system, deleted as a user.'

'Hang on.'

She rushed to her own terminal, gritted her teeth and typed in > RED HOT MOMMA <

> REDUNDANT PASSWORD. INPUT REPLACEMENT <

Gritting her teeth harder, she input her previous password.

> SEXY KNICKERS <

> REDUNDANT PASSWORD. INPUT REPLACEMENT <

> RED HOT MOMMA <

> REDUNDANT PASSWORD. INPUT REPLACEMENT <

> SEXY KNICKERS <

> REDUNDANT PASSWORD. INPUT REPLACE-
MENT <
> LET ME IN YOU BASTARD <
> INVALID INSTRUCTION. INPUT PASSWORD <
She ran back to Jupiter's room.

'My password's been rejected.'

'That makes two of us.'

Jupiter blew out his cheeks. There was some relief in not being singled out.

'Maybe more than two,' Juno replied slowly. 'What if it's not just us, but everyone?'

PART 2

Chapter 13

Bread of Heaven

As he walked up the gravel drive to Jupiter's front door, Cupid told himself he had absolutely grown up. He had no choice, he had decided, following his brief, but definitive, conversation with his mother.

'I'll get your bow mended, Cupid. But I don't want to hear another word about your "earthlings in trouble" nonsense. I know how you're always imagining things. And if you've been naughty as well, that's your problem, not mine.'

Naughty was a child word! Cupid had snorted to himself. But if she did suspect his hacking . . .

Hastily, he had left the matter there.

Yet his knowledge was burning such a hole in his head he had to share it with someone. And that had to be Jupiter. Why hadn't Cupid had the courage to tell him before the meeting? Quite apart from admiring

him, the logic was simple. As the greatest god, he had
to be the correct one to inform.

'I need to talk to Jupiter right now,' he blurted as
Juno opened the door.

'That urgent, Cupid?' she smiled, ushering him into
the kitchen. 'Well I'm afraid I'm going to have to
disappoint you. You see, he's disappeared.' She jerked
her thumb at the window. 'Into that.'

Cupid looked out and saw the roof of a massive
Virtual Immortality capsule, topped by a glowing red
light, poking above the hedge.

'It's the first Mega-Retroland™,' Juno explained.
'He said he was just going to give it a quick test run.
The trouble is, he hasn't come out. It's self-contained,
with all amenities, so he doesn't have to until he
feels like it.

'Quite honestly, I don't know when I'm going to see
him again.'

Cupid gawped at her uncomprehendingly, the bottom
just dropped out of his world.

Jupiter, trapped in Virtual Reality, after holding out
for so long?

It wasn't possible.

'But . . .'

'Don't judge him too harshly.' Feeling for Cupid,
Juno tried to cushion the impact. 'He's not being weak,
if that's what you're thinking. He's simply recognised,
as we all should, how things have changed.

'You know J – never does things by halves!' She
grinned with fierce affection. 'He sent me an e-mail
telling me he'd sampled being Kennedy, making the
Russians climb down over the Cuban missile crisis, and
he was just going to dip into being Churchill winning
World War Two. It wouldn't take long.

'That was yesterday. I e-mailed him back, but there's been no reply. And of course his mobile's switched off.'

Cupid sat at the kitchen table, trying to take it in. He had invested all his faith in Jupiter precisely because he believed him to be so constant and reliable. Yet now Juno was saying his mentor had abandoned all his principles! And at the very point the earthlings, never mind Cupid, needed him most!

'Don't feel betrayed,' Juno added softly. 'It's a hard lesson, but one we all have to learn sooner or later — it takes more than one god to change the universe.

'Right now, he's like any newcomer to Retroland™. Wants to play the big boys. So I'm letting him have his fun. After all his work, he deserves it.'

Cupid looked at her imploringly. Now it was all being explained away in the name of fun!

'Come and have a look,' she suggested helpfully. 'It really is quite something.'

Reluctantly Cupid followed her through the gap in the hedge, then gasped in astonishment at the size of the capsule, sitting gleaming on a freshly laid bed of concrete where the putrescent pumpkin had previously been.

'Almost twice as big as a System 7,' he remarked wonderingly while they circumvented its huge girth, interested despite himself. 'Why so huge?'

'I don't know, Cupid. He hasn't let me see inside. The upgraded facilities, I suppose. Whatever they may be.'

They had reached the sealed entrance door.

DO NOT DISTURB: GOD AT PLAY, a red sign glowed menacingly.

'I'll try him. What shall I say you want?'

'Just to see him,' Cupid mumbled, no longer quite sure whether he still did.

She tried the handle.

'Sorry. Still mindlocked.'

Back in the kitchen, she handed him a glass of home-made ginger beer. One of the curiosities of immortality was how crazes came round again and again. She was already tired of the plant in the cellar, with its exploding bottles. It was time GOD replaced it with some new fad.

'Something else is troubling you, isn't it, Cupid?' she enquired sympathetically. 'It's funny you should call, you know. After what you said at the meeting, J told me he planned a little chat with you.

'Until he got carried away, of course,' she added, playing her card carefully.

'Maybe I can help instead?' she suggested, sounding casually unconcerned.

Cupid took a sip of his drink to play for time.

He had always liked Juno and was being touched by her warmth. So unlike the hard face Venus showed him these days. And it was so cosy in here. That delicious smell of baking bread!

With a start, he realised he felt more at home than he did in his real one.

'Or is it gods' business, and not for goddesses?' Juno followed through, a twinkle in her eye.

'It's not that,' Cupid replied hastily. How could she have read his mind so accurately?

He stared down at the distressed table top.

'A bit personal, that's all,' he mumbled.

'Something you've done?' Juno enquired shrewdly. 'I won't be cross, promise. I don't give away secrets, either. Except to J, of course. We share everything. So telling me is really just the same as telling him, isn't it?'

Except that they both knew it wasn't.

Picking up the gloves, she opened the oven, while Cupid looked on, astonished. He had never seen Venus do any real cooking. At home everything was delivered by the ghosts.

'Some of us still enjoy doing things, you know,' Juno smiled, tipping the steaming loaves out of their tins onto the table in front of him. 'J's veggie garden's the same. They're only gestures, but they keep us in touch with the earth.'

Laughing, she began singing one of GOD's favourite 'mes'.

'Bread of Heaven
'Bread of Heaven
'Feed me now and ever more . . .
'Like some?'

'Yes please.' Cupid's mouth was watering.

'Careful, it's still hot,' she warned, placing a slice, thickly spread with butter, in front of him and watching with pleasure while he tucked in.

'This "gods' business" of yours,' she grinned conspiratorially. 'Give me a clue.'

For a second Cupid was tempted to spill it out.

But it was too big a step.

'It's something inside GOD,' he hedged, his voice muffled by the bread.

'A computer matter?' Juno brightened up. 'Well, if you feel you can't wait for J, and yet you can't tell me, why not try Mercury? He's probably the best anyway. You know J and techno.'

And me, she thought to herself. Not without reason

did the gods think of it as a male preserve. Its logic suited their more rigid minds.

Cupid took another bite, feeling torn. Looked at one way, it was a computer matter. But not if looked at the other. Yet how to explain, without revealing the hacking business?

'Tell you what,' Juno suggested, her instinct telling her not to press him further. 'I'll e-mail J, then get in touch the moment I hear back. Not that I can make any promise about when that'll be.'

Cupid stopped chewing and looked at her thoughtfully. The same idea about Mercury had already occurred to him. With Juno's endorsement, it now made even more sense.

'Fine,' he agreed, getting down from the table.

'You're welcome any time, little god,' Juno smiled as she let him out of the front door. 'Not that I can always promise bread from the oven. But there's loads more ginger beer.'

'They were delicious,' Cupid smiled appreciatively.

Juno was watching him go down the drive, when she was hit by a sudden doubt. Mercury might be the most competent god to decipher a computer secret. Yet he was so fanatical about techno, there were times Juno couldn't help wondering whose side he was on.

Should she call Cupid back? Have another try at prising something out of him? Maybe she had been too oblique, not blunt enough. It might turn out to be nothing in the end, of course. Yet a gut feeling was telling her it could be extremely serious.

She was about to shout out, when Vulcan hurtled out of his front door and began transparently pretending to examine the tyres on his pick-up.

Hurriedly, Juno went in and slammed the door.

The last thing she needed was him sticking his nose into this.

She picked up her laptop.

'Mail to: Jupiter. Priority urgentest,' she voiced in.

Not that she held out much hope.

But what else could she do?

Chapter 14

Hacked Off

W hen Mercury didn't reply to his doorbell immediately Cupid nearly gave him a miss. Suddenly
desperate to get his secret off his chest, he had walked
straight across to number 19 without thinking further.

His resolution was just faltering when the door-
answering machine made the decision for him.

'Can't you see I've a thousand things to do?' Mercury,
relayed direct onto the screen, looked frantic.

What's new? Cupid thought. The god of communications was always shooting from one self-imposed
drama to another.

'I have to see you, Mercury. It's very important.'
Cupid tried to place the banks of computer equipment
in the background. 'Where are you?'

'In the Factory, of course. If it really can't wait, you'll
have to come here. Otherwise, e-mail me. Got to go.'

The screen blanked.

Cupid thought allocating him a Honda C 90 Cub,
when grown-up gods had four wheels, a sick GOD
joke. Especially after he discovered it was the favoured
vehicle of pizza-delivery drivers on Planet Earth. Not
that Cupid, like anyone, could wrap his head round
the computer's sense of humour. Except that it must
have one. Why else had it invented boustrophedons —
one of Cupid's favourite words! — those snaking queues
at earthling theme parks he found equally hilarious and
perfect for pinging activity.

Mind you, he thought the same about the parks
themselves. GOD must have some idea of a joke to
be putting more and more earthlings through loops
like those!

Cupid had complained about the Honda allocation,
only for GOD to fire back a blizzard of bureaucracy
about his not being old enough to hold a full licence. Old
enough, when you were immortal! Cupid had snorted.
Maintaining the comparative status of the others, more
like! But when GOD further warned that, if he moaned
any more he would be demoted to a tricycle, he had had
the sense to shut up.

GOD could have been compassionate enough to adjust
the weather to suit, though, he thought as he buzzed
along the expressway. Winter had returned with a
vengeance and the bitter easterly was buffeting him
across lanes, provoking much hooting and fist-waving
from minor deities creeping along in their highly polished Protons and Metros.

Not that Cupid was the only one having trouble.
Two misshapen Dark Age giants who had ignored the
flashing signs advising high-sided gods not to proceed

had been blown over, causing a monster pile-up across all four lanes. Threading his way through the traffic jam and past the ghost accident squad struggling to jack the unfortunate victims back upright, for once Cupid had occasion to give thanks for the Honda.

Yet he was still freezing by the time he ran into the Factory. He tore off his outdoor gear in the glittering foyer and went into the central atrium, bathing in the rush of warmth whilst he rubbed his hands and legs to restore the circulation.

Without any expectation, he automatically put out his palm to test the invisible force field that now barred them from the Curtain, behind which lay the docking booth they had used to enter to be propelled outwards, destination Planet Earth. How sad and forlorn it now looked, its ticket machine draped in cloth to signify how Earth tickets had been withdrawn.

Would they ever go through it again? Cupid thought glumly, flicking from G- to EG-mode.

Immediately the previously deserted space filled with the normal complement of ghosts, futilely polishing surfaces already polished and tidying areas already tidy. Cupid felt a sudden burst of anger at GOD. Why did he keep them working away like mechanical toys, when their mundane tasks were currently so redundant? Couldn't he give them a break?

Cupid felt so sorry for them he went back into the foyer and deliberately scattered his gear all over the floor, just to give them something to do. Then he set off down the corridor to the Planet Earth control room.

It was Mercury who had discovered that, although their home terminals had been barred, their individual ones at the Factory were remaining live. Not that

that news had particularly excited anyone. The promised sneak preview of Mega-Retroland™ had caused
interest in Planet Earth to plummet to minus zero,
meanwhile sparking a clever-clever adult joke Cupid
did not really understand – 'For ACCESS DENIED,
read IN DENIAL!'

He had still come in and tried a regular stint at
his terminal, but found some vital element missing.
Maybe it was his worry about the earthlings, but he
had soon left Mercury to pitch in on his own, as he
was doing now.

Approaching the god of communications' work-
station, Cupid sensed he must not interrupt. Mercury's
fingers were flying round the keyboard, whilst he
simultaneously voiced in a battery of instructions.
Finally, after piling layer upon layer of code, he
typed EXECUTE, hit RETURN, and swivelled round,
punching the air.

'Oh, it's you,' he exclaimed. 'See that? Talk about
close encounters! Wow!'

'Really?' Cupid asked politely.

'You bet!' Mercury replied excitedly. 'You can't
believe the strain Y2K's throwing on Planet Earth's
techno resources. It's the millennium bug, you know.
I'm getting crash after potential crash to deal with.
Clock this.'

He tapped a key and the screen in front of him
erupted in a riot of red lights.

'Got the picture? The earthlings need me like mega!
So, whatever you want, make it snappy.'

'It's amazing how quickly you work.' Cupid's admir-
ation was genuine.

'Some of us have the gift,' Mercury smirked, smoothing his gelled blond locks.

Cupid sensed he mustn't overdo the flattery. As well as get on with what he was here for. Mercury's attention span was notoriously short. Yet seeing him in his element like this brought back flickering memories of the glory days, when the Factory had been roaring. Then the god of communications had been a constant inspiration, zooming about aiding the technologically challenged. As programmer, operator, teacher even, everyone had agreed — no one could touch him.

'None like you, Mercury,' Cupid added, meaning it.

He took a deep breath. He might as well plunge in at the deep end.

'I hope you don't mind me asking, Mercury, but have you ever tried to hack into the parts of GOD we're barred from?'

He had been intending the question to sound casual, but to his annoyance it had emerged as a worried squeak.

'Absolutely not.' Mercury appeared deeply shocked.

'Anyhow, GOD wouldn't allow it,' he added dismissively, quickly turning back to his screen in order to hide his face.

He had always feared this coming up one day. But through Cupid, of all gods! Not that he was even a proper god.

And why now, of all times, after what Mercury had just uncovered?

He counted silently to ten to stabilise himself, then swung back violently.

'You have, though, haven't you?'

Bullseye! he thought as he saw the telltale blush rising.

'Just fooling around,' Cupid mumbled unhappily.

'Fooling around?'

Mercury felt the prominent vein on his forehead begin to throb. Why had GOD ever allowed this irresponsible brat to access him, even if only in a limited way? He was so childish, and his falling-in-love speciality so irritatingly illogical. He should have been barred, like the cherubs. Then this would never have happened.

But it was too late for that now.

'Have you any idea what you've been fooling around with?' he began browbeating the little figure. 'GOD is work, if you didn't know. Deadly serious work at that. Mega-radical stuff.'

'I didn't mean any harm, Mercury,' Cupid stuttered, dismayed.

'Never mind what you meant,' Mercury snapped back harshly. 'What did you actually do?'

'It was more what I saw,' Cupid wailed.

This was all going too fast. Why hadn't he waited for Jupiter? Even confided in Juno? 'It doesn't matter,' he mumbled, turning to leave.

'Oh yes it does.'

Mercury grabbed his elbow in a vicelike grip.

'What did you see?' he hissed through clenched teeth.

'Well it all started when I hit ALT by mistake,' Cupid confessed miserably. 'Then I tried CONTROL and OPTION and one thing sort of led to another. I got lost — ow, you're hurting! — so I tried HELP. Then I just kept pressing keys until I came across a file called PASSWORDS MASTER.

'I opened it and found I could go anywhere I wanted . . .'

He faltered to a stop.

He wasn't explaining very well.

Mercury's nimble brain spun through the connotations. You did get occasional leakages, especially with the system's current glitchy state. 7.8.9 aka.05 retake 2 said it all! Cupid could well have hit a crossover.

But accessing PASSWORDS MASTER! That had to be the key to the entire system! Even Mercury's own assiduous hacking had never got him near it.

So where had the little bastard been? More importantly, what had he uncovered?

'I chose NOSTRADAMUS,' Cupid added unexpectedly.

Mercury gave a jerk.

'Why?'

'It just sounded funny.'

Cupid stared at the carpet. It didn't sound funny any more. Merely ridiculous.

Yet, for some reason, Mercury's face had gone chalk-white.

'What happened?' he was now demanding to know.

'I got into all these directories about bad things happening on Planet Earth.' Cupid shuddered as he felt the familiar chill run up his spine. 'I had a feeling of a presence in there — something huge and dark. The screen gradually began blacking. Like an eclipse of the moon.'

He paused. The chill was stronger.

'Then?'

'The ghosting started. I thought the screen might be failing, so I boosted the contrast.

'Which was when I saw the face.'

Mercury twisted his arm viciously.

'Face?'

'A horrible, hairy face.' Despite himself, Cupid's bottom lip began to tremble. 'Half earthling, half animal, Mercury,' he went on tearfully. 'No body. Just a face. With slitty red eyes that glowed like coals and seemed to look right inside my head. There was this awful chant: "Doom! Doom! The earthlings are all doomed!".'

He shuddered.

The terror.

'Then?' Mercury's narrowed eyes were as hard as flints.

'The face gave this dreadful slavering laugh, showing horrid pointy teeth. I felt it entering my mind. And that's when I knew I was looking into the eyes of the Beast.'

'Beast? Who told you that?' Mercury's voice cracked like a whip, whilst he bent Cupid's arm so hard he was forced to his knees, shrieking with the pain.

'Tell me, you little toerag, or I'll make your balls drop.'

'Nobody told me, Mercury! I just knew. Like you know things, you know. Aaaargh! You're breaking my arm!'

'You haven't told anyone else? Not Jupiter?'

'No,' Cupid cried in fresh shock. How could Mercury know what he'd been planning? 'You're the first. Honest! Cross my heart and hope not to live for ever!'

Mercury slackened his grip slightly whilst he did a quick calculation. Cupid couldn't possibly have got in so deep! Down through so many levels. Yet, clearly, somehow he had.

There was no time to waste on speculating how, though. One way or another, he had to be silenced before he blabbed to anyone else.

'"Knew it was the Beast",' he repeated scathingly. 'You can't have a "beast" inside a computer. Even

GOD, though he is the biggest server in the universe. Apart from anything else, he occupies a hermetically sealed environment.'

Not that Mercury knew that for certain. GOD might make no secret of being located inside the giant rock that dominated the outskirts of Godsville, yet nobody had ever entered him.

But it would be sacrilege to think he existed in any other conditions.

'I know it doesn't make any sense, Mercury,' Cupid sniffled, feeling the pressure coming off slightly. 'All I know is what I saw. And felt.'

'You sound just like one of the goddesses,' Mercury replied with withering scorn. 'I'm always having to tell them — you don't "know" or "feel" with a computer.

'How can you non-techies ever appreciate the precision of GOD's machinery, the perfection of his circuitry, the symmetry of his logic? It's so entirely unscientific to jumble him up with "knowing" and "feeling" — it's an insult to his artificial intelligence.'

Seeing Cupid's hangdog look, he decided to take a chance.

'Anyhow, if you had really seen something — a rogue digital image, say — you would have taken a hard copy.' He glared down triumphantly. 'So where is it?'

'There wasn't time,' Cupid cried, choosing not to admit he had frozen at the controls. Only afterwards had he cursed his lack of foresight. 'The face faded away, until only the grin was left. Then that disappeared as well.'

'You never saw it again?' Mercury demanded.

'I never found PASSWORDS MASTER again.'

That wasn't a proper lie, Cupid told himself. Just half a truth.

'Red eyes! Pointy teeth! "Doom! Doom! The earthlings are all doomed!".' Mercury, his confidence now restored, moved in for the kill.

'It's a joke, isn't it?' he hammered the little figure. 'Another of your stupid pranks?' He leant down and put his face inches away. 'You know what you should have taken a hard copy of?' he hissed. 'The inside of your head.

'Because that's the only place your so-called "Beast" existed — in your stupid, boring, infantile, idiot imagination.'

'But, Mercury,' Cupid pleaded, flinching, 'there are other things I haven't told you about yet!'

'And never will,' Mercury replied decisively, rounding off the scotching process. 'Neither will you ever repeat a word of this to anyone.

'You think it's funny, don't you?' he further accused. 'Well, you're wrong. It isn't. It's dangerous. You know how Pre-Millennium Tension is growing. This kind of crap could trigger all kinds of wild rumours. Maybe even cause some gods — or goddesses, more likely — to lose faith.

'You wouldn't want to carry the can for that, would you?'

'Of course not, Mercury,' Cupid replied, distraught. 'You must believe me, though. The poor earthlings are in terrible trouble, I just know. Something bad's about to happen down there!'

'Shut up!'

'Sorry.'

Mercury saw the tear splash onto the floor.

First job done.

Now, to plant something in his head to divert the little fool.

'You know Seekers™?' he enquired casually, loosening his grip further.

'Of course, Mercury.'

Cupid was surprised by the question. Everyone knew the complex GOD sent the ghosts to after they had served their time in the service operations, so they could choose their personal belief system for their return to Planet Earth.

Apart from anything, its massive dome was almost as prominent a landmark on the outskirts of Godsville as GOD himself.

'If I was as worried as you about what's in store for the earthlings, I'd go there,' Mercury pronounced.

'Seekers™ is strictly for ghosts,' Cupid protested.

'Precisely,' Mercury riposted. 'Which is why you need to go. Establish the ghosts' most popular belief system and you'll have a good idea what's going to happen on Planet Earth in the future.'

He put his head back and studied Cupid closely, as if he was a simpleton.

'Surely, even a little god like you can understand that?'

Cupid felt stung. He could see what Mercury was driving at.

But what about the problem?

'Gods aren't allowed to enter Seekers™, Mercury,' he protested again.

'That's because they don't normally seek!' Mercury grinned down at the worried-looking face. It was working! 'In case you've forgotten,' he went on sarcastically, 'a god's job is providing the answers.

'But if you're now asking the questions, you've

become a seeker instead. Which means you'll be able to go in, won't you?' He put on his most contemptuous sneer. 'I know the real reason — you're scared!'

'I'm not.'

'Bet you are.'

'Not.'

'Dare you!'

'Accepted!' Cupid shot back defiantly. 'Dare and double-dare!'

'You have to bring back some proof.'

'No problem.'

'That's a deal then.'

Mercury let go of his arm and swung back to face the screenful of red lights.

Cupid stood uncertainly, rubbing his sore arm while he stared at the pyramid on Mercury's desk which he had constructed out of the tetrahedal tea bags provided by the ghost service. Then he aimlessly read and reread the 'CYBERSURFERS DO IT DIGITALLY' sign, before finally deciding Mercury was so locked back in he must have forgotten him entirely.

For a moment he thought of going to boot up his own terminal. Not that he would be hacking again, after that encounter.

Yet, with the millennium so close, and the earthlings obviously in so much techno trouble, what other problems might they urgently need help with?

Already, though, he was preoccupied with the Seekers™ challenge. Mercury was right. It could well provide an answer.

The trouble was, Cupid hadn't the faintest idea how he would manage it.

'You couldn't give me a clue how to get in, could you?' he addressed the bent back.

When there was no reply, he set off disconsolately back down the corridor.

Mercury continued staring fixedly at his monitor until he was absolutely sure Cupid had disappeared. Then he got up and strolled over to the window, bursting out laughing as he pulled back the curtain to reveal the crestfallen little figure skirting his silver Porsche Boxster and heaving its stupid moped off its stand. Children were so easy to fool! Cupid would never get into Seekers™ if he tried for the rest of his immortality.

Which was precisely what Mercury planned on making him do.

Then, from nowhere, as occasionally happened with his mercurial temperament, he was swamped by one of his savage depressions. He rushed back to his desk, looked furtively round in EG-mode to make sure no ghosts were present, then mind-unlocked his confidential drawer.

Extracting the black file, he laid it reverentially on the desktop and stared yet again at the printout. He had tried every way to computer-enhance it, yet it remained tantalisingly faint, even though that was technically impossible. Even so, there was still no mistaking the half-human, half-animal face, the red eyes, the pointy teeth . . .

Mercury had always known that to remain a successful god of communications he must maintain absolute faith in technology. A rock-solid, unshakable belief that it was working for the good of the earthlings, rather than their detriment.

When he had first uncovered the face on one of his hacking missions, he had mentally blanked it by categorising it as a machine error. As he had continued to do with other ominous oddities he had come across.

Until yesterday, when he had been rooting about in the system in much the same way as Cupid must have been doing.

Mercury put the printout of the face to one side and once again examined the hard copy of the document he had unearthed, even though by now he knew it by heart.

```
mail to: all Gods/Goddesses

21.31.00/15.12.1999

From: Gods, Oracles and Deities


Y2K technology situation report 493771/666


I have always taught you that patience is a
virtue. Unfortunately for you, after so many
centuries, mine has finally run out. I am
therefore hereby officially informing you
that your decision at the meeting has given
me no choice.

I have reminded you often enough, 'as ye
sow, so shall ye reap'. Now you must learn to
live, or rather not live, with the manifold
consequences of your action.

As of 00.00.01/01.01.2000, therefore,
with the withdrawal of Universe System
7.8.9 aka .05 retake 2 and the introduction
of System Megaverse 2000, you are all to
be . . .
```

Mercury lifted his head and stared unseeingly at

the red lights peppering his screen, panicky thoughts running round in his head.

Then he pulled himself together, replaced the black folder in the drawer, and turned back to the keyboard.

After rattling out a complex series of commands, he typed in > NOSTRADAMUS < and hit SEARCH ALL. Even with GOD's awesome godobyte power, executing such a universal command would take some considerable time.

Not that he was even necessarily expecting a result.

But if it took the rest of his immortality — and he gulped at the new thought that spun in — he would find a reassuring explanation.

There absolutely had to be one, somewhere on GOD's vast system.

Chapter 15

Seek and Ye Shall Find

The trouble with adult gods, Cupid thought as he secreted his moped behind a fence near the entrance to Seekers™, was that they were too clever. Why had he been stupid enough to accept Mercury's dare?

He stared up at the massive dome, whose smooth round curve was such a contrast to the sharp lines of the Factory pyramid. It reminded him of an enormous mushroom, strangely old-fashioned — or at least timeless — in contrast to the Factory's modern cutting edges. But then Mercury was always preaching how softer roundness was much more '90s. Meanwhile its gigantic size paid suitable homage to the unchanged earthling mania for the onward march of techno.

Right now, though, it just felt horribly intimidating, especially with its recent new signs of THE DOME IS IT!, WELCOME TO THE MILLENNIUM and Y2K RULES!

For what Cupid had not revealed to Mercury was that he had tried to get in before. His motive had been simple curiosity, coupled with the thought that his pinging might work on the ghosts inside. What fun to preordain their fates by making them fall in love, even before they returned to Planet Earth!

But he had found himself firmly rejected.

'Genuine seekers only,' one of the posse of the heavy-looking angels at the gate had proclaimed, lifting him up by the collar. 'The confused, good. Can't make their minds up, very welcome. Don't knows, absolutely. Lost sheep, perfect. The meek, they're the business. But no time-wasters, dabblers, or rubberneckers.

'And by the way, it doesn't work in there.'

Since when, shocked at having his mind read, Cupid had stayed away.

Now he could see the angels at the entrance had been replaced by a row of modernly impersonal booths, numbered 1–31. Cupid wasn't surprised. GOD had been delegating more and more power to machinery in the Land of the Gods, just as much as on Planet Earth.

It might even be easier to beat, he thought hopefully as he sized up the disparate gods passing by along the road. He didn't want any to see him going in. At the very least that could lead to embarrassing questions. At worst, a first-hand report back to Venus.

He hovered about until the coast was clear, then dived into booth 31, for no particular reason except that its green entry light was on and, being at the end, it felt more private.

The soothing music faded as the door closed, sealing him into the softly lit interior.

'Sit down, please,' a warm, yet somehow mechanical, voice instructed.

Cupid parked himself on the only chair. He was wearing casual clothes, similar to the ghosts', but had made no particular effort to disguise himself, conceding that his true identity was bound to be uncovered.

'To obtain entry to Seekers™ you must submit to the sincerityometer. Press "yes" if you are willing so to do.'

Cupid pressed the yellow button.

'You must now answer the first question: "How much do you truly seek?"'

'Place your hand, palm downwards, on the square marked "verify".'

Cupid obeyed, thinking how small and chubby it looked on the glass plate covering the spinning metal disc.

There was a loud hum and a series of clicks.

> 62% < a readout flashed up.

'Excellent!' the voice intoned. 'Your previous angel assessment was a mere three per cent.'

'You know who I am?' Cupid asked apprehensively.

'Of course.'

'You're not ejecting me?'

'Not necessarily. Everyone genuinely seeking is equal in the eyes of Seekers™.'

Eat your heart out, Mercury! It looked as if he was going to get in!

'My last assessment can't have been that low,' he protested shrilly, recovering his nerve.

'As we are infallible, we do not make mistakes,' the voice replied sternly. 'Next question: "How much are you seeking for the sake of Planet Earth?"'

'Place your hand on the square marked "General Sincerity".'

This was hardly user-friendly, Cupid frowned, whilst

still obeying. Presumably, genuine seekers were so desperate, or humble, they put up with any humiliation.

> 31% < the readout indicated.

Cupid sat mortified.

'Now place your hand on "Personal Sincerity".
This gauges how much you are only interested in
yourself.'

Cupid shifted his hand.

> 69% <

'That can't be right,' he burst out, shocked. 'I'm on
a mission.'

'They all say that.'

Remembering Mercury's dare, Cupid flushed.

'Congratulations, nonetheless, on achieving the highest general score since October thirty-first!' the voice
added unexpectedly, sounding so genuinely pleased that
Cupid recovered his composure.

He obviously wasn't doing that badly.

Mind you, he had another thought: he was only
being compared to ghosts.

'The last question: "What, pray, have you come
to seek?"'

'The truth about what's going to happen to Planet
Earth in the next millennium,' Cupid mumbled, suddenly shy.

Did he hear a hollow laugh?

'And you,' the voice reminded him.

Recalling his 'Personal Sincerity' rating, Cupid was
blushing again, when he felt a surge of elation.

The voice was signing him off!

'On behalf of the management and staff of Seekers™,
I would formally like to wish you good luck on
your quest.

'Please take the directory with you.'

Cupid picked up the heavy tome that had materialised in front of him as the wall rolled back, to reveal
a huge lobby where hundreds of ghosts were milling
around. It reminded him of the airport waiting areas
he occasionally visited on Earth tickets for a spot of
international pinging.

Sitting down on one of the benches, he leafed
through the thousands of directory entries. He could
work out from the map at the back that the complex
was divided into different earthling ages and geographi-
cal areas. Otherwise, though, there was such a surfeit
of everything he was completely baffled.

There was only one way.

Follow the herd.

He stepped out alongside the rest through the auto-
matic doors, then stopped, gobsmacked by the scale.
Enclosed within the vast area of the dome was a
massive representation of a human figure, surrounded
by rows and rows of units and display areas, which
stretched both into the far distance and away on
both sides.

Yet all boarded up.

And why was the scurrying crowd ignoring them? As
if they were in a ghost town, he was just managing to
joke to himself, when his eye was caught by the huge
ELEMENTARY sign. Of course! They were still in the
age when the earthlings had worshipped the various,
and varied, downtown monsters. No wonder the ghosts
weren't stopping!

Cupid felt a rush of anticipation as he rejoined the
throng and moved into PANTHEISTIC [EUROPEAN], his
heart giving a further lurch as he saw the faded sign
loom up: GRECIAN AND ROMAN DEITIES.

'*Veni Vidi Vici*', a small subhead announced.

Stepping to one side, he examined the decrepit front-age sadly. It would be so easy to spruce up. A few licks of paint, a bright young female ghost up front, comfy chairs, espresso and cappuccino on tap, Chianti round the back . . .

Then recalling Juno's remark about it taking more than one god to change the universe, he reluctantly moved on, seeing the crowd slow and split as it reached the brightly lit MONOTHEISTIC area.

Not, Cupid soon realised, that this was all good cheer, despite the fervent evangelists singing and clapping in noisily competing groups. Wandering off the main thoroughfare, he found himself in a miserable side alley manned by dour representatives of outfits such as DOOM AND GLOOM ENTERPRISES ('Abandon hope all ye who enter here') and WRATHFUL AND VENGEFUL ('Mighty Is His sword').

He was just nudging between REPENT YE SINNERS THE END IS NIGH! and a group of Seventh Day Adventists loudly proclaiming the same message, when he was abruptly pinned to the wall.

'Just a little chat about the meaning of it all.' He saw the JEHOVAH'S WITNESSES sign above the posse of ghosts now expertly blocking his every exit.

'We're recruiting bright young fellows like you to go back and spread the word on Planet Earth.' Their broad smiles looked as though they had been glued on. 'Naturally, we'll be equipping you with a pair of stout shoes, as well as putting you through our exclusive door-opening course.'

'You'll also no doubt be fascinated to know,' another picked up the thread, 'that our image-makers will be implementing an exciting new strategy for Y2K. In future, on the doorstep, we're going to be starting with some other topic — weather, football, price of fish — anything will do.

'Only when we've got them chatting will we be working round to religion.'

'Except we'll be dropping that word too.' An earnest female, glasses flashing in the overhead lighting, butted in. 'You see, our surveys indicate it now has nega-tive connotations, attitude-wise. Especially amongst the young.

'A real no-no, we're told. Deeply unradical. Not at all hip. Coolness rating zero.' She gave a bright smile. 'You must know all about that!'

Cupid looked round desperately. How to escape signing the ominous-looking document they were brandishing under his nose? They were so determinedly pushy. Hadn't they heard of invading a god's territorial space?

Of course! They didn't know he was a god!

'I have to inform you all,' he got through at the third attempt, 'that GOD has empowered me to cause earthlings to fall in love.'

His persecutors fell back nervously.

'You don't mean indulge in the sins of the flesh?' one was asking tremulously, when a newcomer leapt between them.

SAY NO TO CONTRACEPTION. Cupid read the headline as the lurid leaflet was skilfully inserted into his hand.

'Dat fornification is a terrible t'ing,' the leafleteer chanted. 'Praise the Lord for chastity!'

'You enjoy shagging, though,' Cupid protested, seeing his chance. 'Some of you are quick enough off the mark, if you didn't know. My best time so far is eye contact to bed in less than thirty seconds!'

They backed further away, whispering to each other.

'Perhaps, on reflection, you're not exactly who we had in mind,' one eventually came forward to announce. 'May we suggest, brother, you study your texts more closely? After that, we're quite sure, you'll begin to see the light.

'In the meantime, please rest assured, we shall be praying for you.'

Thanks for nothing, Cupid thought, leaping out before they could regroup.

That couldn't be Planet Earth's future surely? he was thinking, when he spotted the discreet brass plaque: KINGDOM OF HEAVEN RELIGIOUS BROKERS – ALL DENOMINATIONS CATERED FOR.

'Seek and ye shall find,' a subhead encouraged in flowery lowercase.

This looked better. Hopefully a chance to sweep the whole spectrum at once!

Cupid walked in through the open door, only to find he had entered a huge cathedral. It had the same reverent atmosphere as the one on Earth, where he had once mischievously pinged a bishop and arch-bishop, thereby elevating them into becoming leading activists for gay clergy. Similar massive stone pillars, rendered multicoloured by light filtering through the stained-glass windows, soared up to the vaulted roof, whilst his footsteps on the huge flagstones had the same ringing tone.

In the middle of this echoing emptiness hung a large sign reading IMMIGRATION. Underneath, an angel in an all-enveloping white garment, rendered dazzling by a strategically placed shaft of sunlight, sat at a solitary desk.

As Cupid approached, he saw he was scratching at an illuminated manuscript.

'We like to keep up the old ways when we can,' the angel beamed, carefully replacing his feather quill in the inkpot. 'How can I help you?'

'Could you tell me which particular belief ghosts are currently signing for?' Cupid asked clumsily.

'Judging from the number we're attracting, most of them don't believe in anything any more.' The angel smiled wearily. 'But there's no point in dwelling on that, is there?' He rubbed his hands together briskly. 'Allow me to explain our line of business.

'We are licensed to operate under the umbrella of GOD's UBS — that's Universal Belief System. I presume you're familiar with the three letter acronym, or "TLA", as they say on Earth today.' He smiled wryly. 'Also that it contains many myriad factions, some doing quite well, others — how can I put it? — not quite so fashionable.

'Which is where we come in, by tailoring your particular requirements to the one most appropriate to you.

'Like to take a few brochures, to mull over at your leisure?'

'No thanks.'

Cupid wasn't going to be fobbed off that easily.

'See the video?'

A screen slid out of the floor.

'Is this building real?' Cupid asked, looking round the huge interior.

How could he have missed something so enormous from the outside?

'What is real these days?' the angel smiled wanly. 'Put it like this, it's as real as you think it is.' He frowned and flicked a switch on the desktop. 'Maybe it would be simplest if you talked direct.'

'Admissions and admin.'

A bearded figure, wearing a similar dazzling white garment and jangling a bunch of keys, had appeared on the screen. In the background Cupid could see angels piled high with files running back and forth. In the occasional lull between bellowed commands, harps played a soothing melody.

'Hello,' Cupid said politely. 'I'm just trying to find out which branch of your belief system is most popular at present.'

'General enquiry, eh? Nothing specific?' the figure barked crossly. 'I simply don't have time to discuss basics.

'We're being computerised for Y2K, in case you hadn't heard. You've no idea how much paperwork's piled up over the ages. There's a right old mess to sort out, I can tell you.

'How many popes do you think there've been, for a start?' He glared at Cupid fiercely. 'Never mind edicts.'

'I'm sorry, I didn't mean to interrupt,' Cupid apologised.

The figure appeared to relent.

'I'll have to take a few details first,' he announced gruffly. 'Name?'

'Cupid,' Cupid replied disingenuously. He hadn't thought to prepare an alias.

'Palmprint.'

Cupid leant forward and placed his hand on the glass covering the spinning disc on the desktop.

'Good, the new system's working,' the figure on the screen muttered, clicking away on a laptop. 'Here we are: "male/heathen/adolescent god/irreverent/speciality love-matching/for full list of associates access Greco-Roman Deities".'

He looked up.

'Not one of us, eh? Nothing we can do for you, then.'

What an attitude, Cupid sighed.

'Surely you can show me where to start?'

'The overall requirements?' The figure sounded surprised. 'Have faith, truly believe, love thy neighbour as thyself, keep thine own counsel, hold fast to that which is good, obey the Ten Commandments, above all honour the collection box . . .' He broke off, looking even crosser. 'You must know all this, surely?'

'Not really.'

'Heavens above, boy! After the massive investment we've made in raising earthling consciousness? The brainwashing over so many centuries. The miracles, advertising, promotions, special offers. Saints' days, holy days, festivals. To say nothing of our regular communions and services.' He shook his head sadly. 'What's the world coming to, eh?'

'That's exactly what I'm trying to find out,' Cupid replied eagerly, hoping he wasn't sounding too clever.

But the figure had shot off at a tangent.

'Not gay, by any chance, are you?' he was asking, peering at Cupid suspiciously.

'No,' Cupid replied, surprised.

He did gay pinging, of course. But it was only a sideshow. Bestiality even more so. Although the figure wasn't expressing any interest in that.

'Shame,' he was remarking. 'We're actively recruiting in that neck of the woods. New market and all that. Women too. Know any who might be interested in joining the priesthood?'

Cupid snorted inwardly at the thought of putting Venus's name forward.

'Not really, I'm afraid. All I want is a few facts and figures.'

'With all this going on?' the figure exploded. 'Next you'll be wanting to know how many angels can dance on the head of a pin, or some such tomfoolery.

'Well I just work here, right? Any more questions, ask at the desk.'

The screen blacked and slid back into the floor.

'Sorry about that.' The desk angel leant forward conspiratorially. 'To be perfectly honest, we're a bit passé here, for want of a better word. Things are a shade – how shall I put it? – difficult.

'I'm sure they'll settle down after we've rejigged.' He brightened up again. 'There's even talk of church attendance going up!

'Meanwhile, though, I don't want to waste your time – or mine.' He gestured at the illuminated manuscript. 'Why not take my tip?' he whispered furtively. 'Try the millennium section.

'Meanwhile, please accept this bible with my compliments.'

Cupid took the proffered volume and weighed it in his hand. It might not answer his quest, but it was smaller and lighter than the directory. He could take it back as the proof Mercury required.

'Would you sign it for me, please?' he asked politely.

'With pleasure.'

'To Cupid. Blessings on you, Archangel Gabriel,' Cupid read upside down as the quill scratched wet ink across the flyleaf.

'Thanks, Gabriel.'

'The blessing of GOD almighty . . .'

Cupid slipped the bible into his pocket and made for

the exit, where he was immediately caught up in a mass
of ghosts surging excitedly towards the sparkling sign
beckoning from the distance: MILLENNIUM ENTERPRISES
ARE HERE!

Along with everyone else, he quickened his pace.
His quest, it appeared, was nearly over.

Chapter 16

Challenged

No wonder Gabriel had pointed him in this direction, Cupid thought as he saw the glittering array
of hi-tech units stretching out in front of him to the
outer limit of the dome's vast curve.

Everything up to now appeared hopelessly old-
fashioned as he was swept along, dazed and buffeted
by the cacophony all round him. Everywhere hysterical
ghosts were scrabbling to clamber aboard the different
organisations competing through screaming signs —
THE GET-RICH-QUICK CORPORATION, INSTANT GRATI-
FICATION ENTERPRISES, FEELGOOD FACTORS, GO FOR
IT INC., HAVE IT ALL NOW PLC, THE HAPPY COMPANY.

And towering above them all, way, way up in the
dome, the huge illuminated display: DON'T JUST GET A
LIFE! GET A STRATEGY FOR THAT LIFE!

Strategy? Cupid frowned uncomprehendingly.

Quite apart from which, faced with such a plethora of bewildering varieties, where did you start?

The answer immediately became apparent.

You didn't start on them.

They started on you.

'Hello, sir! I know your one desire on your return to Earth is to be mega-rich.' A sharp-suited ghost had accosted him with a determination fully matching the Jehovah's Witnesses. 'Well, lucky sir, your search is over! For here at the Mammon Corporation we can offer you not just that, but much, much more!

'You must have heard of the fabulous wealth generated by the exclusive services we provide for our members — best share tips, winning lottery numbers, racing results in advance — a zillion opportunities to cash in without lifting a finger?

'Just name your preferred activity and leave the rest to us. Everything's included, minimum commission, no-frills dealing, instant settlement . . .' The salesghost beamed with pride. 'But I must warn you, sir, to profit even further, you'll have to hurry. Because right now we're running the never-to-be-repeated promotion of a free Mercedes for life!

'Just sign here' — he jammed his clipboard under Cupid's nose — 'indicating choice of model and colour. Although I must emphasise the latter cannot be entirely guaranteed . . .'

'Can I trade in a Honda C 90 Cub?' Cupid asked wonderingly.

'Escaping from being disadvantaged, eh, squire?' The besuited ghost tapped his nose knowingly. 'Of course! We'll trade anything! Meanwhile, though, a little bird tells me that maybe you're more the BMW type? Like a goer, eh?' He winked archly and nudged

Cupid in the ribs. 'Well, sir, it's truly your lucky day! Because it just so happens that I have one — one only — accidentally overlooked during our last promotion . . .'

A burly ghost shouldered Cupid roughly aside, grabbed the clipboard out of the salesghost's hand and scribbled his signature on the bottom.

After congratulating his latest recruit, the sharp-suited ghost turned back to Cupid apologetically.

'So sorry you lost that one, sir. Maybe you're unfamiliar with modern Earth? Well, sir, if you don't mind me saying so, let that be a lesson to you. These days it's first come, first served down there. No room for those who can't hack it.

'I'm afraid you'll have to wise up, sir, if you don't want to become a loser.'

'If I do?' Cupid asked boldly.

'Thinking of joining the spirituals?' The ghost pulled a sour face. 'So superficially appealing, eh? All that spurning materialism, dropping out of the rat race, accessing the true meaning of life . . .

'Believe me, sir, everyone comes round to our view in the end. So do yourself a favour — cap the oil well, seize the window!' He stood back, sucking his teeth. 'Maybe, though, you're considering being a techie?

'If so, I'm afraid the same applies. More so, when you look at the price of the equipment you'll be programmed to desire.'

'Is that how it works?' Cupid asked wonderingly.

'Beginner, aren't you?' The ghost shook his head pityingly. 'In a nutshell, you make your choice, we reprogramme your DNA to give you suitable genes, then place you on Earth with a background commensurate to achieving your stated desire.'

'I'm not sure what that is yet,' Cupid replied, sincerely.

'Determined to learn the hard way, sir?' The ghost had clearly lost patience. 'In that case, on your own head be it. Nerd City to your left. Assorted spirituals to your right. And assorted they certainly are.'

'Straight on?' Cupid enquired.

'More money. Not pure, though, like here,' the ghost sneered. 'Dressed up in consumer loops – SHOP TILL YOU DROP, McWORLD, LOGO LOVERS, GETTALIFESTYLE – hundreds of them. All adding up to the same bottom line though.

'That's today's lesson on Planet Earth, sir – nothing else counts.'

Finding a relatively quiet corner, Cupid paused for a breather. Mercury would just love this, he thought, gazing out over the piles of electronics and crude versions of Virtual Reality, all being puffed in a welter of technobabble.

'Forgive me being personal sir!' A salesghost was pushing through the press of anoraked ghosts animatedly examining shiny catalogues. 'But after all, that's what we're here for, isn't it?'

He flashed a broad smile, revealing teeth so perfect and white Cupid wondered how they could possibly be real.

'Tell me, sir,' he continued eagerly, 'in your past life did you feel unfulfilled, lonely, that somehow you were missing out?' Without pausing, he answered his own question. 'Not any more, sir! For today technology is here to make you a king!'

'Everyone can't be a king,' Cupid protested.

'Why not, sir? Just choose your castle, get online, and you're a winner!'

'Surely, for every winner, there has to be a loser?' Cupid pointed out.

'Not if they're both communicating,' the salesghost beamed.

'What's the purpose in communicating if you've got nothing to communicate?' Cupid tried again.

'Why, to gain more information, sir.'

The salesghost was now looking puzzled. Or pretending to. Cupid reminded himself you could never tell with salesghosts.

'Information about what?' he asked, mystified.

'Anything you like, sir. Plus, of course, your big, big bonus that every day, every way, you'll be just love, love, loving your equipment!'

'What, more than my fellow earthlings?' Cupid felt vaguely threatened.

'Why, of course, sir! Once we've programmed you for a lifelong love affair with techno, who, or what, else could you possibly need?'

'Someone or something,' Cupid replied grimly, pushing past him and negotiating his way out of the hi-tech bedlam by using the standard brush-off of 'Just surfing'.

The answer, he was now convinced, must lie with the spirituals – an impression instantly confirmed as he entered the comparative peace of their section. Soft music, tinkling wind chimes, natural colours – everything spoke of something more laid back, as well as deeper.

Or did it?

For money appeared to have subtly permeated this area as well. Everywhere fame and fortune were on offer – through crystals, tarot cards, the I Ching. Most of all, though, astrological versions of his fellow gods.

Cupid had always been jealous at not having a planet named after him like so many of the adult gods.

Until now.

'You write my birth chart according to my specifications,' he repeated back unbelievingly, 'then when I return to Earth everything follows without my doing anything whatsoever?'

He had foolishly paused to see if his mother was in the ascendant, only to be pounced on by a female salesghost in a flowing orange robe.

'Absolutely!' she breathed with a beatific smile. 'You see, the secret lies in recognising we are all in the grip of cosmic forces. As everything is therefore predetermined, we simply programme you to go with the flow and take the trip!'

'What — just lie back and think of Godsville?' Cupid asked, outraged at this supine suggestion.

As for taking the trip — what in the Land of the Gods did she think he was doing right now? He might be here on a mission, yet he was feeling vaguely jealous of the ghosts round him. They were all so determined — or predestined — to make commitments for a lifetime. In contrast, he was feeling disengaged, like the Honda when its gears weren't meshing properly.

Yet, more than anything, he was so dearly wishing the ghosts to make the right choices. Ones speaking of better times to come on Planet Earth. Surely, somewhere in this morass of high-pressure salesghostship, someone must be delivering the spiritual goods?

He perked up as he fell in with a stream of ghosts following signposts labelled PERSONAL DEVELOPMENT.

This looked more promising, as well as popular.

Then he reached the first unit and his eyes boggled, before he started giggling.

VOA, a huge acronym was announcing, above, in smaller letters, its full version: VANISH UP YOUR OWN ARSEHOLE.

How could any belief system possibly have the nerve to give itself such a crude label? Cupid thought wonderingly.

Even if it was accurate.

'Feel free to sample the rest.' The smooth salesghost lounging at the desk did not even deign to rise off his chair. 'I guarantee, though, sir, you'll return to us in the end.

'Because you see, here at VOA, we don't believe in conspiracies, or hiding the truth. Just in being honest. Which is why, rather than fudge the issue, we took the decision to award ourselves such a direct title.

'Not too blunt for you, sir, I trust? Because, I must agree, subtle it certainly ain't!' The salesghost laughed cheerily. 'But it's proving very, very popular indeed, I can assure you.

'Cynics, of course, dismiss it as a gimmick. But more discerning ghosts, of which I am sure you are one, can see the tremendous breakthrough we've made.

'Put simply, sir, we've cut out that confusing middle element of a belief system. With us, all you believe in is your personal life-journey. We programme you with your crisis and send you back to Earth to live it.

'No materialist sideshow, no idle trappings that soon pall, no being strapped with a belief system you'll only lose faith in.' He smiled wolfishly. 'With every earthling looking for something more fulfilling for the millennium, what better than being entirely preoccupied with yourself?'

'What about everyone else?' Cupid asked weakly.

'That's the whole beauty of it, sir!' The salesghost, ecstatic, leapt to his feet and approached Cupid eagerly.

'You'll join millions of others just as dedicated to the same thing.' He clapped him on the shoulder as if they were old buddies. 'I'm not OK! You're not OK! So we're all not OK! OK, sir?'

He glanced shiftily to both sides then leant closer.

'The trouble is rather a lot of ghosts are, how shall I say it, a bit slow,' he stage-whispered, tapping the side of his head knowingly. 'Takes a bit of time for the message to sink in. Fortunately for them, though, they usually get here in the end.'

'Well back on Earth I'd rather CIA than VOA,' Cupid said loudly, then started backwards as the salesghost nearly jumped out of his skin.

If a ghost *could* jump out of its skin, Cupid then thought wonderingly. He had gone completely white and was shaking like a leaf. What could have provoked such an extreme reaction?

'CIA?' the salesghost hissed urgently, cringing as various potential ghost customers looked round curiously. 'You mean, you know?'

Know what? Cupid thought. Had he hit on something?

'CIA – Compassion Is All,' he explained impatiently. What was the matter with the fellow? Now he was looking like a ghost who had seen a ghost.

'My philosophy for when I'm in my new life,' he explained further. 'At least CIA would mean I was actually living it as a member of the earthling race, rather than just selfishly VOAing.'

The salesghost stared at him open-mouthed.

'Compassion?' he gasped uncomprehendingly.

'Yes, compassion,' Cupid reaffirmed. 'Because I, for one, happen to know there's a lot more to earthling life than just your VOA stuff.

'What about gods, eh?'

'Gods?' the salesghost spat back disparagingly. 'We gave up gods ages ago!

'There's no mileage in them these days,' he sneered, rapidly recovering his poise. 'No market.'

'Hence better to VOA?' Cupid enquired.

'Absolutely!' the salesghost beamed, fully restored to his former urbane self. 'Good one, sir! You gave me quite a fright for a moment! Yet I knew the moment I saw you you were one of us.

'Of course not only we recognise it,' he added, suitably candidly. 'But you're always better off with number one and all surveys prove that we're comfortably outselling our main rivals, Gazing at Your Own Navel Inc., even on a like-for-like basis!'

Cupid automatically looked down towards his before pulling himself together.

'Why don't you just FO?' he replied crudely, attempting to fight fire with fire.

He moved on rapidly, only to find himself in BIOTECH and yet more technology. Transplants, implants, bypasses, artificial replacements, nose jobs, breast jobs, freezing for the future, cloning . . .

'Have you ever stopped to consider, sir, what it would be like to live for ever?' a salesghost said, buttonholing him.

Cupid grinned back fiercely.

At last his chance for revenge!

'Been there! Done that! Got the T-shirt!' he replied triumphantly, turning away.

He had achieved his mini-triumph. Anyway, he couldn't absorb any more of this stuff.

Half closing his eyes, he passed rapidly through SPORT'S THE ANSWER!, heading for the exit.

Only to find, as he might have guessed, the sting in the tail.

TAKE THE CHALLENGE WITH YOU, a huge display was now confronting him, with no way round the wall-to-wall salesghosts.

He made for the prettiest.

'What challenge?' he enquired wearily.

'Why, whatever you choose to be challenged at,' she trilled encouragingly. 'Socially, physically, academically, aurally, sexually . . . We've as many "alleys" as you like.' She gave a tinkling little laugh. 'In addition, we offer two distinct services.

'Advisory, under which we help you compose your own problem portfolio. Or discretionary, when we compose it for you.

'Which, of course, is perfect for those choosing to be terminally challenged!' The tinkling little laugh again. 'Either way, you will be in the hands of a fully experienced life executive . . .'

'Why should I want to be challenged?' Cupid interrupted, baffled.

She scrutinised him suspiciously.

'Are you sure you haven't signed up with us already, sir?'

'No,' Cupid replied indignantly. Was he appearing mentally challenged? 'It's just that this is all news to me.'

'I do apologise, sir,' she laughed, apparently happy again. 'Allow me to explain. Once suitably challenged, back on Earth you're free to do anything you like, because no one can hold you responsible!'

She didn't seem challenged in any way herself, Cupid frowned, equipped as she was with such DD breasts they were in danger of giving him an erection.

'It's absolutely the way forward for Y2K,' she was now gushing enthusiastically. 'And to enable you to fully exploit your victim status, we're currently offering free legal aid for life. Let's face it, you can't get far on Planet Earth these days without a good lawyer!'

'We'll start by equipping you with an overarching disadvantage.' She ticked some boxes on her clipboard. 'Membership of a minority group, I think.' She looked up brightly. 'How about being a Native American? Or Scottish? Many of our customers find that just as good. Though I must admit numbers have dropped off since they've decided to devolve.' She looked disappointed. 'Can't blame the Sassenachs for everything any more, you see.

'Getting the picture, sir?'

Cupid was. And feeling depressed by it.

'Now, a suitable life crisis. Number one at present is sexual abuse by one of your parents. Both, if you want to spice things up a bit. Single mothers are still popular though.' She smiled brightly again. 'As well as being orphaned. We recommend an air or car crash for the full trauma quotient.

'Lastly, something specific. Such as being vertically challenged.' She put her hand to her mouth. 'So sorry, sir! Of course you could go the whole hog by being a dwarf!

'Tell you what, let me introduce you to you to one of our life executives. Then you can sign the forms and be on your way tomorrow. With a ready excuse for everything, you're going to be made!'

'Not me, I'm afraid,' Cupid replied gently. He didn't want to upset her, she seemed so utterly sincere. 'I suppose I must be perceptively challenged,' he joked weakly, squeezing his way past her magnificent front age, while she stared at him blankly.

Nearly out.

He stopped as he saw the lines of ghosts queuing in the departure lounge.

His attitude to these future earthlings, he realised, had already changed. What a venal, selfish lot they now seemed. Setting off on their crappy life-journeys, to no purpose apart from looking after number one.

Was Planet Earth in trouble if this lot were about to populate it!

Shuddering, he threaded his way through until he reached a similar row of booths to the entrance. Again choosing number 31 without any particular thought, he sat down and waited until the door closed.

'Please state why you have failed to make a choice,' the mechanical voice demanded.

'I did not locate anything precisely suiting my requirements,' Cupid replied stiffly.

'I notice you're carrying one of GOD's most successful publications, the Bible,' the voice commented. 'Has that not answered your quest?'

Cupid jumped. He had quite forgotten slipping it into his pocket.

'Just a souvenir.'

'Really?' The voice sounded unconvinced.

There was an awkward pause before the standard questioning resumed.

'Please indicate, out of ten, how helpful you found Seekers™.'

'Six', Cupid replied gratefully.

'Enjoyment rating?'

'Six again.'

'Facilities?'

Cupid kept on answering six until the flow of questions dried up.

'You have answered 666-666-666,' the voice concluded. 'Thank you for your time and may I be the first to congratulate you?'

'On what?' Cupid asked, mystified.

'Here at Seekers™ we pride ourselves on our unique service for those whose fundamental nature is to seek.' The voice gave a warm chuckle. 'Which is why you have achieved such success. You see, finding the correct answer is a disaster for any seeker, as it then negates their primary motivation, which is to seek.'

Cupid frowned. This was all getting too clever for him.

'So there is a correct answer?' he ventured.

'To each their own,' the voice sidestepped. 'You will see our philosophy written over the exit as you leave.

'Meanwhile, have a nice day and we look forward to your next visit.'

The street door opened.

As he hurried round the curve of the massive dome to retrieve the Honda, Cupid looked back.

IT IS BETTER TO TRAVEL HOPEFULLY THAN ARRIVE, a large sign read.

Cupid grimaced as he pressed the electric start.

Maybe it wasn't just better, but of paramount importance, the earthlings never arrived at the places most seemed headed for.

Especially if there were any plans that their gods should go there with them.

Chapter 17

Crashed

After his Seekers™ visit Cupid shyly avoided the other gods and goddesses. Yet although he constantly checked his e-mail, there was no communication from Juno. And when he peeked over the back fence of number 31, it was only to see the red light still glowing.

Although the cherub gang kept pestering him to join their games in the Sylvan glades, he couldn't relax in such childish company. Instead he retreated to his secret den in the summerhouse at the bottom of the garden, where he always went to chill out. Apart from him, only Venus knew it even existed. And as the only access was a convoluted tunnel through the tangle of trees and bushes, he could rest there, confident he would not be stumbled on by accident.

At least he had his best bow back, although his

mother had fended off his questions by telling him to just be thankful it had been restored to one piece. But it was doing nothing to quieten the confused thoughts whirling round in his head. Where did he fit in the next millennium? Venus too? He had found no trace of romantic love in Seekers™, or even love and beauty in general.

Meanwhile, of course, he was bursting to present Gabriel's autographed bible to Mercury. That would show him! Yet, otherwise, Cupid had a horrid suspicion the god of communications would very much approve of the Planet Earth of the future. All those techies enslaved to their machinery!

What Cupid needed was someone more sympathetic, to soothe his apprehensions. Or at least share his fears. Wistfully, he considered Juno, as well as more ginger beer. But he had made his commitment. He must sit tight and wait for Jupiter.

Yet, after a night spent tossing and turning, he had had enough. He was failing to chill out, whilst Jupiter was remaining locked in. Over his breakfast peaches delivered by the ghost service — 'they're so positively, particularly plumptious!' — he decided he couldn't just sit here for the rest of his immortality.

Instead he would compromise. Visit the Factory and present the bible to Mercury, thereby earning the respect he was due. But then leave without getting involved in any conversation that might complicate things or further increase his worries about Planet Earth.

Cheered up by doing something, he managerd to filch the Honda out of the garage and endured another chilly expressway journey, only to find Mercury's Porsche conspicuously missing from the Factory car park.

He went in just the same, discarding his outdoor gear in the foyer as before, and made his way to the Planet Earth control room. There, to his relief, he found Mercury's seat at his terminal still warm. Meanwhile the god of communications obviously had no shortage of work. His screen was so lit up with techno disasters it resembled one of the red-light districts Cupid occasionally visited on Earth tickets for a bit of fun pinging.

Mercury must have just popped out.

He would wait.

Except that waiting soon became as boring as sitting in the summerhouse, whilst all the time his own terminal was drawing him like a magnet. With his new-found knowledge from Seekers™, he might find something in the system to either confirm or scotch his fears.

Anyhow, there would be no harm in a quick look. Better still, with Mercury absent, a quick hack.

> PING PONG < he logged on. Like the Honda, he suspected his current password to be another tasteless GOD joke. As well as its predecessor > LOVERBOY <

> GOOD MORNING, CUPID < the screen greeted him. > NICE TO HAVE YOU BACK. WHAT WORK SHALL WE DO TO HELP THE EARTHLINGS TODAY? <

Cupid smiled happily. What a wonderfully warm feeling being back in the saddle! Like donning the old motorbike gloves which fitted him so perfectly. Nothing would ever give him more pleasure than the familiar routines through which he tried to raise the earthlings' lives above the mere mundane. How much he still loved them, despite what he had found in Seekers™!

Not just loved, but cared about them, feared for
them, now more than ever.

Not that Cupid pretended to have a complete picture
of everything happening on Planet Earth. No god or
goddess did. They could all browse generally, but the
real nitty-gritty — the very stuff of earthling life — was
hidden in the detailed directories each could access only
according to their speciality.

Through these Cupid, for example, could monitor
and input romantic love to Earth in a thousand different
ways — pinging individuals, or groups, creating con-
ducive situations, carrying out case studies, increasing
and decreasing its level locally and generally . . .

Like everyone though, he had to accept overall
control rested with the computer. The bottom line, like
the badgering salesghosts in Seekers™, was constantly
keeping his end up in GOD's overall scheme of things.
But if he chose to put more energy in, it went a lot
further.

As his screen was now indicating.

> MORE ROMANTIC SUNSETS, CUPID? OR
DO WE AGREE THEY'VE BEEN SOMEWHAT
OVERDONE OF LATE? <

Cupid laughed out loud. The 'golden sunset' campaign he had persuaded GOD to run had produced so
many, of such unmitigating glory, they had attracted
excited comment in the earthling media.

Cupid had grinned even further when he saw them
apportioning blame to pollution in the atmosphere.

> AGREED < he typed back. > RUN ROMANTIC
POETRY PROFILE INSTEAD <

As he was expecting, the graph had tailed off. You
needed to pay constant attention if your initiatives
weren't to be left to drift.

> WHY NOT BRING BYRON BACK INTO FASHION? < he suggested.

> WORDSWORTH YES, BYRON NO. <

Cupid frowned. Hadn't they done Wordsworth? Anyhow, Cupid thought him stuffy.

> COLERIDGE? < he countered.

> 'WATER, WATER EVERYWHERE,

AND ALL THE BOARDS DID SHRINK;

WATER, WATER EVERYWHERE,

NOR ANY DROP TO DRINK'.

AGREED <

> 'YEA, SLIMY THINGS DID CRAWL WITH LEGS

UPON THE SLIMY SEA' < Cupid typed back, smiling at this success.

He paused and sat back.

Should he input his latest idea, inspired by his Seekers™ visit, which had come to him in the summer-house? It was certainly mischievous, which was great. Yet not entirely so, which was even greater. Laying it out fully would need a long memo, but what if he could persuade GOD to empower him to ping earthlings electronically through the Internet? After all, that would be fully in line with Global Online Divinity!

The new breed of computer nerds' love affairs with techno were both aberrant and unnatural, he would submit. Yet the vast number visiting porno web sites, as well as indulging in cybersex, showed where their true interests lay. They might not yet appreciate their Internet in romantic terms, but Cupid, naturally, could see the huge potential — different cultures, vast distances, the ability to be intimate, yet private at the same time, take any part you liked, explore any fantasy . . .

Why didn't GOD empower him to ping Net nerds,

causing them to meet in person? Think of the boon to those sad anoraks, suffering such low self-esteem! Admittedly, if the romances were not to be primarily gay, more females needed bringing online. But that was just part of the whole new field waiting to be opened up . . .

Cupid snapped out of his daydream. Never mind working. To really find out what was happening, he must hack.

He knew he had got into PASSWORDS MAS-TER only by a fluke he could never repeat. Fortunately, though, as it had turned out, Mercury had cut him short before he could reveal an equally significant piece of information. He hadn't just found the NOSTRADAMUS password. Still imprinted on his memory were all the others, which the computer program had further informed him he could access by preceding them with the > SUA < code − >SUPER USER ACCESS <

Which belonged to which god or goddess, Cupid had no idea. Yet each would reveal a different aspect of life on Planet Earth. So, the more he accessed, the fuller the picture he would build up.

Which to start with, though, had to be a guess.

He flicked through them in his head.

BIG BOY tickled his fancy, yet he was somehow wary, as though it might reveal more than he really wanted to know. What about the intriguing BT, though? He had spent hours in the summerhouse trying, and failing, to work out what the initials might stand for.

> PING PONG/SUA/BT < he typed in.

He rocked back in his chair in a mixture of fear and excitement.

> WELCOME MERCURY < the screen was reading.

He was into the god of communications' files!

> UNLOCK CODED SECTION < he commanded.

> FOR MY EYES ONLY < a fresh message flashed up.

He was in Mercury's confidential files!

With a guilty start, he rushed to the window. But the Porsche was still missing. He could go in a bit deeper. Where, though? Scrolling through the multitude of Mercury's directories was reminding him of that earthling phrase about looking for a needle in a haystack.

Except that he didn't even know what a needle looked like.

Or did he?

> SEARCH BEAST < he tried tentatively, then felt a thrill like an electric shock.

Three separate directories had come up: > BEAST GEN./BEAST SPEC./BEAST THOUGHTS <

Hand shaking, he clicked on BEAST GEN.

Two subdirectories appeared.

The first > L FILES < meant nothing.

The second > BEAST ACCESS < made his heart thud.

Mouth dry, he clicked again.

And there it was.

Pages and pages of commands, adding up to a program way beyond his level of comprehension. Yet the overall strap was clear enough:

> CURRENT SITUATION REPORT: FURTHER REFINEMENT NEEDED BUT ACCESS SUCCESS RATE NOW RAISED TO 83%. FUTURE ACTION: INVESTIGATE PRECEDING PRESENT ENTRY

CODE WITH 666 TO ESTABLISH MISSING CROSS-
REF. AND TIE-IN WITH L FILES, VIZ.: 666/BT/
BEAST MANIFEST/AUTH. GOD/REF. TECHNO./
Y2K/FUTURE DIRECT. NEG. <

Cupid typed it all in.

> DO IT < he commanded before he lost his
nerve.

He quailed backwards as, with a mighty roar, the
Beast's face sprang onto the screen. Immediately he
was overwhelmed by the same awful dread. He could
hear himself screaming. Yet, held in thrall by those
red eyes, he was powerless to stop. And all the time
the grinning mouth, with its pointy yellow fangs, was
drilling the same Doom! Doom! chant into the heart of
his very being.

Or was it the same?

No! It had changed!

'Doom! Doom! YOU'RE all doomed,' it was now
repeating, not 'THE EARTHLINGS are all doomed'.

Who's you? Cupid thought in panic as he hammered
EXIT.

To no avail.

The Beast's grin just grew more wicked.

'Want exit, do you?' it suddenly hissed. 'Well, you've
got it. Not just you, either. All you gods and goddesses.
Not just for now either. For ever. You've meddled in
my affairs far too long.

'So, so long, suckers.'

With an electronic sizzle, the screen blacked.

Cupid slumped in his seat, drained.

Then hit by a sudden thought, he ran across to
Mercury's terminal. The earthling red lights had been
extinguished! Mercury's screen had blacked as well!

He ran down the aisle, looking frantically from

side to side. They'd all blacked! Every single terminal was down!

'What in the Land of the Gods is going on?' Mercury's voice suddenly screamed and, to his instant shame, Cupid wet himself.

Desperately, he ducked below the nearest desk, finding himself jammed up against Bacchus's wine cooler.

Too late.

He had been spotted.

'You bloody little fool!' the god of communications was shrieking in his direction while he stabbed frenziedly at his keyboard. 'You've crashed the fucking system. Cut us off from GOD. Put Planet Earth in deadly peril. Maybe even begun its destruction.

'How will the earthlings ever survive their Y2K techno-disasters now?' He sounded in utter despair.

'It wasn't me that did it, honest, Mercury,' Cupid cried from under the desk. 'I just opened BEAST ACCESS . . .'

He stopped, horrified.

'You opened what?' Mercury yelled unbelievingly. 'Come here, you little shit.'

Cupid popped his head out and saw the god of communications running down the aisle towards him.

He scrabbled forwards, managed to evade the wild lunge and streaked down the corridor into the foyer. He must retrieve his outdoor gear! The precious bible was still in its pocket. Yet, with Mercury so hard on his heels, there was no time!

Instead he ran out into the car park, hit the Honda at full tilt and wrenched it off its stand.

He buzzed down the road, throttle wide and not daring to look back, yet still certain he could hear the angry growl of the Porsche's boxer engine coming

up fast behind him. As a furious blast of air horns
confirmed his fears, he glanced despairingly around.
With such disparate horsepowers he didn't stand a
chance on the road.

There was only one way.

He stood up in the saddle, crashed over the kerb
and careered down the grassy bank, swerving to avoid
the saplings GOD had recently planted as part of his
inner-city beautification scheme. Pizza-delivery drivers
on Planet Earth might not do this kind of thing, but if
he could hit that grassy knoll at the bottom just right,
whilst yanking on the handlebars hard enough, with
the momentum imparted by the slope he should just
clear the metal fence screening off the expressway.

He landed in a pool of sticky mud by the side of the
monster lane, which sent him skidding sideways, yet
fortunately broke his fall.

He had made it by the skin of his teeth, he thought
as he lay, head ringing.

Then he heard the loud crash from the other side
of the fence.

The Porsche, clearly, hadn't.

Chapter 18

Cuddled

Venus was pleased to hear the Honda draw up outside. Although out a lot, she had noticed her son's restless vigil in his den. When pressurising Mars to mend his bow hadn't appeared to lift his depression, she had worried she had been too hard on him. Here was her chance to make amends, as well as getting to the bottom of what was troubling him.

Yet, as the door flew back, these thoughts were instantly swept away by the sight confronting her. Cupid, covered in mud, looked generally as though he had been dragged through a hedge backwards. And he was wearing only his indoor clothes! No wonder he was shivering so violently. He must be absolutely frozen!

'My poor boy.' She rushed to comfort him. 'What's happened?'

He drew back, staring like a cornered animal.

'He's coming to get me, Mum! He says he's going to make my balls drop!'

He gestured frantically towards the Close.

'Terminus?' Venus asked incredulously, looking out of the window and seeing the god of boundaries making his clipped way along the otherwise deserted pavement.

'No, Mercury, Mum! He'll be here any minute!'

Venus took quick stock. How could Cupid have outdistanced a Porsche?

'Upstairs,' she ordered nonetheless. 'Put on your dressing gown and anything warm you can find. Then hide under my bed. And, whatever happens, don't make a sound.'

He shot her a grateful glance before turning, frantic again.

'He'll see my bike, Mum!'

'I'll deal with it.'

Outside she had a fresh shock. The Honda, uncharacteristically thrown down, was covered in mud as well, whilst even her untrained mechanical eye could see the frame and wheels had been twisted by some violent impact. It was a wonder Cupid had been able to ride it at all. Had he run into Mercury's car? The god of communications was so inordinately proud of it, Venus could imagine the ructions that would cause. Where had the mud come from, though?

As she wheeled the moped lurchingly into the garage, she briefly and pithily cursed GOD. She had always worried about Cupid being on two wheels.

She pushed the machine into a corner behind her Mazda MX 5, threw a sheet over it and went back inside. After satisfying herself no noise was coming from upstairs, she sat down to wait, beside her, on the kitchen table, the can of mace she always carried.

And wasn't afraid to use either, when monster games threatened to get out of hand.

As they frequently did.

Wasn't it odd, she thought, staring out of the window, how focusing like this threw everyday immortality into such sharp relief? Watching Juno go into Vesta's across the way, she realised she had never noticed before the slightly crabby way in which she walked. Now Minerva and Flora were following, deep in conversation.

What were they up to? she wondered, then gave a self-deprecating snort.

She was getting as bad as Vulcan!

She stiffened and rose from her chair as a ghost taxi drew up outside and Mercury clambered out of the passenger seat. As he started up the drive, she could see he was limping. Meanwhile his forehead was plastered with blood and his normally immaculate suit crumpled and torn.

She opened the door to forestall him.

'Where's your car?' she asked, fearing the worst.

'Written off,' Mercury replied grimly. 'And your son's to blame. Where is he?'

'What's he done?'

How could Cupid possibly have written off a car?

'It's not just my injuries, or my bloody car.' Mercury peered past her into the house. 'He's only wrecked the whole fucking shooting match, hasn't he? Crashed GOD. Maybe even written off Planet Earth.

'I must find out exactly what he did so I can unscramble the damage before it's too late. Providing the little bastard hasn't already screwed things beyond repair, that is.'

'I'm sorry to hear this,' Venus replied, continuing to bar the door with her arm. 'He's not here, though.'

'You're covering up for him,' Mercury accused, glaring at her wildly. 'Bloody non-techies like you will never understand how incredibly serious this is, will you? Or that there's absolutely no time to lose?'

Cupid had obviously been up to something, Venus thought with a sinking heart. But a mother's first loyalty was to her son.

'If he was here, I'd tell you,' she lied.

'So where did that come from?' Mercury yelled, his eyes alighting on a distinctly fresh lump of mud where Cupid had thrown down the Honda.

'I've been gardening.' Venus struggled not to look to see if a telltale trail led to the garage door. 'Anyway, you can't come in. I've got visitors.'

The carefully placed innuendo paid off.

'You're disgusting!'

Mercury regarded her with unconcealed loathing. Once he remembered her being so absolutely gorgeous just gazing on her had sent him into paroxysms of love and lust, even though he didn't usually bother with that sort of thing.

These days, though, he saw her only as a slag.

'I don't care if you're fucking an entire Greek chorus in there,' he riposted angrily. 'I'm still coming in.'

Venus took two steps backwards and picked the can of mace off the table.

'You wouldn't!' Mercury breathed, the hatred in his eyes betraying that he knew she would.

'You'll really regret this when you discover what the little arsehole's done,' he spat while she reversed him down the drive. 'I know he's in there. I'll have him, one way or another.'

Venus, watching him limp back up the Close, waited until the door of number 19 closed. Then she hurried back inside.

'Out, Cupid,' she sternly addressed the snivelling from under the bed.

As he emerged, the snivels degenerated into deep racking sobs. He had put on his dressing gown and a pair of sweaters as instructed. Yet, the mud on his face now scored by the tracks of his tears, he only contrived to look more pitiful.

'My baby,' she cried, holding out her arms.

With a heart-rending wail, he buried himself deep into her bosom.

He lay there for what seemed an age, enfolded in a bubble of protectiveness which gradually made all the pain, the shock, the confusion in his mind go away. He was floating in a land of eternal reassurance, where everyone was secure that someone cared for them, no matter what their faults or what they had done.

Finally he had been in the sanctuary long enough.

He stirred and blinked as the outside world swam back into focus.

'Thanks, Mum.'

'Everyone needs a proper cuddle sometimes, Cupid, no matter how old they are.'

She gazing lovingly into his eyes while she continued to hold his hands, surprised at herself. How long since they had last communicated at this level?

To her surprise, he only let out a fresh wail of distress and buried his face back between her breasts.

She sat on the bed, rocking him patiently. He had to find his own way out of this.

'It's not just me that needs a cuddle, Mum,' he sniffled eventually. 'It's everyone, here and on Planet Earth. You see, the Beast's coming to get us!'

'He's not that bad, surely?'

'Not Mercury, Mum! The real Beast!'

'Why not tell me all about it, Cupid?' She stroked his hair soothingly. 'Right from the beginning.'

It wasn't long before she had to admit she was completely out of her depth. She could now understand why Mercury was so beside himself. Cupid had crashed his car, if only in a roundabout way, had been into Seekers™ and, worst of all, had hacked into GOD, causing GOD only knew what havoc. But this Beast and 'Doom! Doom!' business which was so terrifying him. His imagination? Or something terribly, terribly important?

She thought about her fellow goddesses, gathered across the street at Vesta's.

She didn't dare leave the house for fear of Mercury returning. She was also aware how deeply unpopular she was these days. Yet, if she called up, at least Juno, as the most senior goddess, might come across.

'It's so unlike J,' Juno was complaining. 'I feel he's forgotten me entirely.'

'I'm sure he hasn't,' Vesta was comforting her, when Flora cut in.

'Can't you see he's just proving GOD's 667 e-mail?' she said excitedly. 'OK, he might be infatuated after resisting Retroland™ for so long. But GOD said that, with twenty-four-hour-a-day Mega-Retroland™, none of us would ever have to live in Real Immortality again.'

'What the eye does not see . . .' Minerva muttered.

They had been talking about how cutting off their home terminals had already distanced them further from Planet Earth.

'You mean there's a danger of us saying goodbye to it for ever?' Juno was brooding, when her mobile rang.

'Maybe J!' she whispered hopefully.

Unconvinced, the others carried on talking.

Until Juno started so violently she nearly dropped the phone.

'Let me repeat that — "Doom! Doom! You're all doomed!"'? Wait there. We'll be right over.'

There was a flurry from the other end.

'Bugger Mercury,' Juno replied crisply.

Chapter 19

Crashed Again

'We were just saying we'd like a word with you,' Juno announced coolly, opening the door to Venus's kitchen before Mercury could knock. Not that that was quite true. So far she had had no time to talk to Cupid direct, but only received a brief summary from Venus.

'While *I* want a word with *him*.'

The god of communications barged past and headed for the stairs, only to find his path blocked by Venus, brandishing the can of mace.

'I won't hurt him, promise.' He held up his hands in mock surrender. 'But I absolutely have to talk to him.'

'Only after you've talked to us.' Juno's voice was icy.

'Fire away,' Mercury replied, to all their surprise.

'Anything I can do to help,' he added, smilingly pulling a seat up to the kitchen table.

Venus stared at him critically. He had changed his suit and appeared to have lost his limp, though there was no missing the large bandage on his forehead. Yet why was he suddenly being so compliant?

Mercury gazed back at her levelly. After calming down, he had decided on his next move. This would be his best chance ever to reverse the previous equation by explaining the fears he had been keeping to himself, the evidence he had gathered. Then, with Cupid's help, they could all compare notes to build as comprehensive a picture as was possible. A picture which, Mercury was more and more having to accept, looked like being the truth.

Not yet, though, he had finally concluded.

He might have some evidence, but it wasn't the totally conclusive proof which he required. Now Cupid also had seen the Beast, it must really be there. Yet surely the little tosser couldn't have found anything else that could materially add to Mercury's knowledge? In which case, what would bringing everything out gain him?

Rather, letting others into the secret — especially goddesses — would only muddy the waters. Worse still, start a wholesale panic.

Better to steer a middle course. Admit nothing, whilst rubbishing Cupid's story so comprehensively they swung round to believing — as they must anyhow be predisposed to do — that the little fool had made it all up. At the very least, convince them he had mistakenly put two and two together to come up with five.

Done cleverly enough, that would give Mercury the best of both worlds — the answer to the crucial question of how Cupid had crashed the system, whilst allowing him to remain the only one with the full picture, and therefore control.

At which point Mercury had had a stomach lurching moment of panic. Control! In a situation like this?

Yes, control, he had then reminded himself firmly. Or at least more control than if others were involved. Because if he could only get GOD's system up and running again, go back in, follow the track he had been on . . .

At the very least, there would still be hope.

He gave Venus a friendly smile as he carefully placed the plastic bag that was his key between his legs, then sat coolly whilst they ran him through the hacking, the Seekers™ dare, the Gabriel bible . . .

At which point, secure in the knowledge that this was mindlocked in his confidential drawer at the Factory, he pounced.

'So where is this supposed bible?' he asked, contriving to sound amused.

'That's the trouble,' Juno confessed. 'Cupid says he left it in his motorbike jacket at the Factory. Which was your fault for frightening him by saying you were going to make his balls drop, then chasing him like a mad earthling.'

Mercury ducked below the table, delved into his plastic bag and produced the garment with the triumphant air of an inner-city magician pulling a rabbit out of a hat.

'Nothing in there I can feel,' he said innocently, patting the pockets.

He thrust it at Juno, noting how they were now glancing at each other uncertainly.

'See for yourself,' he suggested amicably. 'Better

still, why not call him down? I'm sure he'll have an explanation.'

But he had struck too soon.

Juno hadn't finished.

'What does "Doom! Doom! You're all doomed!" mean to you?' she demanded.

'Nothing,' Mercury replied, genuinely surprised. '"Doom! Doom! THE EARTHLINGS are all doomed!" – Cupid told me about that nonsense. But not "YOU'RE all doomed". Unless I heard him wrong. Or he's got mixed up. You know what he's like.

'Really, we should have him down,' he urged further. 'Then we could go through his Beast bollocks as well.'

He saw the shock register on their faces, Venus's in particular.

'Red eyes, grinning mouth, pointy teeth, correct?' Mercury rushed to ram home his advantage. 'I got sick of him going on about it. How many times did I tell him not to fiddle around with graphics packages he didn't understand? You never know what you're going to get into.'

'You haven't seen this Beast, then?' Juno's voice was clinically cool.

'Possibly something like it,' Mercury replied with an airy wave of his hand. 'You get so many weird images thrown up you can't possibly remember them all.'

Juno hesitated. This had the feeling of a cat-and-mouse game, with neither side revealing its full hand, when she had a feeling everyone involved should be putting their cards on the table.

Yet if Mercury wasn't playing it that way . . .

Changing her mind about bringing up her own dream in the pomegranate orchard, she tried for the kill.

'What are the L files, Mercury?'

The god of communications managed to keep his face straight. Yet he could do nothing to prevent the telltale vein on his forehead starting to throb. If only he'd covered it with the bandage!

'L files?' he repeated dumbly, playing for time.

Nobody could get into anyone else's confidential files. This had to be a weird coincidence. At the very most a shot in the dark. Nonetheless, it was a bloody good shot. For if Cupid had been into the L files, how could Mercury possibly sustain his cover-up any longer?

'They mean nothing to you?' he heard Juno demanding, as if in a dream, and looked up to see them staring at him as dispassionately as if he was an insect under a microscope. Was their bloody feminine intuition telling them this was the cusp moment? The point at which he must jump one way or the other, with no going back afterwards?

'Never heard of them,' he replied firmly, then went onto the offensive. 'Look, I'm sure you all mean well. But your son' — he addressed himself directly to Venus — 'has acted incredibly irresponsibly.

'Why interrogate me, when the central fact — as I'm sure he's admitted to you — is that he's crashed GOD? Can't you see I absolutely have to get to the bottom of how he did it? Right now?'

Juno stared at him with cold green eyes.

'Let's get this right,' she summarised. 'You admit you dared him to go into Seekers™, and chased him in your car. But there's no bible, no Beast — at least as far as you can remember — no Doom! Doom! And you've never heard of the L files?'

'Correct,' Mercury replied briskly, the throbbing on his forehead subsiding now he had committed himself.

'And now I've answered your questions, it's time for Cupid to answer mine.'

'He's too upset at present,' Juno replied decisively. She had to interrogate him first. 'You'll have to wait until he's feeling better.'

At which point Mercury exploded. And, as he rec-ognised afterwards, lost it.

'You mean had a chance to make up some better lies!' he yelled. 'This isn't one of your stupid tea parties!' He glared wildly round the table. 'You're all in this together, aren't you? Playing your bloody female games, keeping him under wraps, when what you should be saying is, "Fuck me stiff! How can we help undo the damage the little cunt's caused?"'

'Don't use that word!'

Mercury spluttered in disbelief. Venus, the inner-city shag bag, telling him to moderate his language!

Juno was now looking at him in some amazement. Everyone knew he had a mercurial temperament, but she had never seen him get so worked up. Or so quickly. His face was quite crimson, whilst flecks of white foam had now appeared at the corners of his mouth.

'Those whom GOD wishes to destroy he first makes mad.'

For a second, Juno thought Mercury was going to hit Minerva. But the power of her hooded eyes stopped him dead.

'It's you who're all mad!' he bellowed at them instead. 'Hiding the little bastard behind your skirts whilst you hope all this will go away.'

'Hope exactly all what will go away, Mercury?' Juno demanded fiercely. Had she finally got him cornered?

Then Venus intervened and the moment was lost.

'You're the one who's going away,' the goddess of love had announced, picking up the can of mace.

Mercury backed away from the table and retreated through the door.

'You are mad! Wait until I tell the other gods,' he shouted as Venus slammed it in his face.

'Then it won't be just me who'll be back,' he shrieked from the other side. 'It'll be all of us!'

It took a nanosecond to decide they would have to move Cupid. Mercury might not be wildly popular, but he would still be able to get up a posse, if only by playing on the old male–female divide.

'I know where they'll never find him,' Venus announced confidently. Even if it would be a mite chilly.

'Where's that?'

'Better no one knows but me, Vesta.' Venus smiled patiently. 'Then there'll be no chance of them giving the game away, will there? I absolutely guarantee you he'll be totally safe. After all, I am his mother.'

Her voice carried such pride and warmth they glanced at each other in surprise. Something had changed about her. She was like a lioness, Juno thought, first neglecting her young, then rushing to the rescue when danger threatened.

She gave a friendly smile.

'I'll need to talk to him first. You must be present, of course. We don't want him feeling intimidated, do we?'

'What if Mercury brings the others back?' Venus asked.

'It's too late now,' Juno declared confidently. 'They'll all be stuck in at Bacchus's. I'm prepared to take the chance no one will be here until morning.

'By which time I'll have finished and you'll have tucked him safely away, won't you?'

'I certainly will,' Venus promised fervently.

It was past 3 a.m. when Juno let herself into number 31, poured a stiff Armagnac and sank back into her chair. The Bacchus rave, continuing even now, had given her the opportunity to go through everything with Cupid until they were both exhausted.

Admittedly, his story was peppered with oddities, holes and confusions. And on the Gabriel bible, the one point he claimed to have had solid evidence, he just kept insisting Mercury must have filched it. Which, if correct, meant the god of communications was lying – or 'telling a load of porkies', as Cupid had kept putting it.

Why, though?

Because Juno was certain he was lying. The real clincher had not come from anything he had said, but the 'Doom! Doom!' of her own dream, which Cupid had now repeated. How could the little god possibly have made that up? The dream that had brought the arid wind, the stripped orchard, the vile slime, the vortex, the dying . . .

And, she now knew, the Beast.

Yet there was still a confusion.

'YOU'RE all doomed!' Cupid had insisted the Beast had said. Not 'THE EARTHLINGS are all doomed!', as she had heard herself, and Mercury had confirmed.

So was the little god correct? Fond as she was of him, Juno couldn't be sure. And even if he was, who was 'you' anyhow?

What Juno did know was that her intuition had never screamed such dire warnings. How she needed J!

Not because she was a weak female, incapable of action. But the other gods would side with Mercury as a matter of course. Another male was needed to bang some sense into them. Unless, of course, the others were all part of the plot.

Juno wasn't normally one for conspiracy theories. But there was always a first time . . .

She picked up her laptop.

'Mail to Jupiter,' she voiced in furiously. 'Come out, you bastard. This has gone on long enough.'

She pressed E-MAIL SEND, followed by AUTO REPEAT.

Why was he letting her down when she needed him most? Usually his innate sense of good timing was one of their strongest bonds. The futility of male ego trips, she thought bitterly. And who better to demonstrate that than Winston Spencer bloody Churchill?

'I have nothing to offer but blood, toil, tears and sweat,' she intoned in a mock deep voice, hurling her empty Armagnac glass into the fireplace and watching it explode into a thousand shards.

Chapter 20

Dungeons and Dragons

Cupid sat in his den feeling utterly miserable. As well as cold. Talk about chilling out! He felt more as if he had been consigned to an isolation ward. How much longer before Venus decided it was safe to let him emerge? Since she had smuggled him down here in the dead of night, he had been left entirely alone.

Or had he?

Suddenly experiencing an uncanny feeling someone else was present, he looked out through the glass door. Why were those dead leaves at the edge of the clearing moving about, when the air was completely still? As if an invisible hand was whirling them upwards?

There they went again.

Cupid switched to EG-mode and felt the shock as he revealed a ghost operative — number 31, according to

the stencil on the back of his blue uniform — at work
with a rake.

'You!' he shouted angrily. 'Don't you know my
mother has issued strict instructions this area is to
be left entirely wild.'

'No harm in giving nature a helping hand, is there?'
the figure asked mildly, turning towards him.

At which point Cupid saw he was very, very old.
Slow, bent back, and with such an extraordinarily
wizened face he made Saturn look like a teenager.
Immediately Cupid felt churlish. It must be a genuine
mistake. For, whatever Venus might have ordered,
the ghost was right. The clearing could do with
tidying up.

As he put down the rake and slowly approached,
Cupid saw him peering in a way that suggested his
eyes were also failing. Until Cupid saw the vital, fierce
sparkle in their depths.

'Anyhow,' the ghost remarked further, 'what exactly
is wild these days?'

There was a loud rustling as the trees and bushes
began writhing round each other, until they had
reformed into a fantastic primeval forest. Panic surged
up inside Cupid as an awful malevolence bit into
his core. Was that the Beast's face he could see
materialising in the branches? Was he hearing the
same cackling glee?

Equally suddenly, everything reverted to comforting normality. Except that, for a nanosecond, Cupid
thought he saw the figure wearing a pointed hat,
covered in stars.

'You're no ghost,' he accused wonderingly. 'You're
a magician.'

Cupid had never really met one before. They did

emerge occasionally from their inner-city ghetto to entertain at cherubs' parties, but for Cupid their charm had faded after he had discovered you could learn to do most of their tricks yourself.

Grown-ups like Mercury didn't help by dismissing magic as 'BS' — the god of communications' word for 'bullshit'.

But now Cupid had one to himself, he could pose the question he had always wanted to ask.

'Could you please tell me,' he enquired politely, 'if there are really such things as dragons?'

'Say yes,' he breathed to himself, crossing his fingers. Venus always ridiculed them as fairy-story stuff, but he desperately wanted to believe in them.

Smiling knowingly, the magician mumbled something Cupid didn't catch.

From nowhere, a rhinoceros materialised in the middle of the clearing, peered about myopically, then charged the nearest tree.

Equally abruptly, in mid-charge, it vanished.

'Sorry. A bit rusty,' the magician apologised, jabbering again.

This time a beautiful insect with shimmering gossamer wings appeared and circled Cupid like a miniature helicopter.

'Tsk! Tsk!' The magician grimaced. 'Wrong way round!'

He jabbered for a third time, then broke into a satisfied grin as a huge, scaly creature materialised in front of them.

It belched a tongue of fire, incinerating a small bush, scratched its ear absent-mindedly and lay down, wagging its tail.

'It can't be real,' Cupid gasped.

'It!' the magician ticked him off. 'He, you mean. Give him a stroke. Don't worry — he won't flame you.'

Cupid approached the vast bulk and gingerly touched a scale.

It felt real enough.

'Harder,' the magician urged.

Cupid pressed more vigorously, at which the dragon nudged him with its head and rolled onto its back.

'He wants a tummy rub,' the magician explained helpfully.

Feeling slightly ridiculous, Cupid rubbed up and down the softer underbelly.

'Very good,' the magician praised over the dragon's little groans of pleasure. 'Most gods are as bad as earthlings. Can't cope with anything that doesn't fit scientific principles. Eh, Dennis?'

The dragon grinned and gave a loud upside-down belch, blasting a scorch mark through the grass.

'Sorry about that. He's been suffering from wind lately. Probably eaten too many knights in armour.' The magician looked at Cupid with a twinkle in his eye. 'You don't, by any chance, believe in troons as well?'

'Troons?' Cupid repeated, bemused.

'Troons — those tiny little dots with hairy faces, twenty-two legs and long tubes for mouths. You know, the other galactic beings who conjured up Planet Earth as a game to fill in the time before tea. Now they're so bored with it, they're going to trash it as soon as their food's served. Which, in Earth time, will be precisely the first second of the millennium.'

'That's silly. There aren't such things as troons,' Cupid protested.

'Try telling that to Dennis,' the magician replied

infuriatingly, while the dragon let loose another flaming belch.

Cupid stood listening to the grass crackling.

'You're pulling my leg,' he accused uncertainly.

'Only up to a point.' The magician smiled broadly,
giving a glimpse of toothless gums. 'Allow me to
introduce myself. I'm M. And let's just say that I'm
connected to different forces.'

'Still to GOD though,' Cupid reminded him, trying
to re-establish his bearings. 'So you must know he's
cut off all access. That everyone's terminals are down
– even at the Factory.'

He chose not to complicate matters by explaining his
particular role in this event.

'There are other modes,' the magician replied mysteriously.

Cupid had a sudden thought.

'Would you mind telling me,' he asked nervously, 'if
there is such a thing as a Beast inside GOD?'

Let the answer be no, he wished silently.

'Why not go and find out for yourself?' the magician
smiled craftily. 'Dennis'll take you. He's dying for a fly.
Aren't you, Dennis?'

As the dragon's tail thumped the ground Cupid
felt a deep thrill well up inside him. A ride on a
real dragon!

Yet the magician obviously wasn't aware of the
problems.

'What about the guardian angels, though?'

'Dennis will fly you past them.'

Which was fair enough. Cupid knew they weren't
impregnable. Once, in concert with the cherub gang,
he had succeeded in slipping past them. Only for them
all to run into an invisible force field, which had so

discomfited the cherubs they had run away. But then cherubs could never handle anything really heavy.

'How can he fly through GOD's forcefield though?'

'Just sprinkle some of this down his nostril,' the magician grinned, handing Cupid a small transparent packet. 'Angel dust,' he explained further.

Cupid held the packet up to examine its glittering contents, at which Dennis sprang eagerly to his feet, nostrils flared and a silly grin plastered across his face.

'Later, Dennis,' the magician promised soothingly.

But Cupid still wasn't entirely reassured. How could Dennis possibly help with the third, and greatest, problem?

'The real trouble is that I don't know the password.'

'You do give up easily, don't you?' M ticked him off mildly. 'There is no password as such. It's like everything else. To get the right answer you simply have to ask the right question.'

'Which is?' Cupid demanded.

But M's face had suddenly gone vacant.

There was a long silence whilst he stared unseeingly into space.

He's lost his focus, Cupid thought bitterly. Just like all the old ghetto spirits. Odd flashes of lucidity, maybe, but never long enough to add up to anything.

As if to confirm this thinking, Dennis now vanished into thin air.

Cupid shook his head. The small bush was still incinerated, the scorch marks remaining there in the grass.

M's frail figure gave a sudden jerk.

'What's for tea?' he demanded.

Cupid felt a stab of disappointment as sharp as a knife.

That was a question he understood only too well. Venus was always ramming home how he must help her pander to the ghost staff's every wish and fancy. It was so hard getting anyone reliable these days, she kept emphasising. If you didn't give them the perks they demanded, they were bound to be poached by another god or goddess.

'What would you like?' he sighed.

'Cream tea, please. With damson jam.'

Cupid groaned. Last time, the ghost service had been out of that and Venus had promptly lost her best gardener to Flora.

'Raspberry?' he countered hopefully.

'Damson,' M repeated. 'Care to join me?'

There was an awkward silence whilst they both waited for the ghost delivery service to get its act together.

Yet when the tea did finally materialise, to Cupid's pleasure and surprise, the jam was damson.

'No stones, eh?' M mumbled, chewing away on his scone.

'Not any more,' Cupid replied proudly. 'We insisted that the ghosts take them out.'

'Progress, I suppose.' M looked amused. 'More's the pity. You'll learn one day.'

What was the old fool rabbiting on about now? Cupid thought.

But he had reverted to his noisy masticating.

'Scrumptious,' he finally pronounced, smacking his lips and brushing the crumbs off his work uniform. 'Any time you want Dennis back, just close your eyes and vision him up.

'Meanwhile, take good care of that angel dust.'

With that he, too, disappeared.

Left alone in his den, Cupid practised the banana trick.

I bet I can't think of a banana for thirty seconds, he promised himself. Only to find he could think of nothing else. Not that that produced a real one. But when he tried as hard as he could not to think of a dragon, no sooner had one come into his mind's eye than Dennis manifested himself in all his bulk.

And this time equipped with both reins and a saddle.

Cupid mounted him without further thought. Whatever happened next, this had to be worth it.

He flung his arms round the dragon's neck as Dennis set off in a loping run across the clearing. Then they had achieved lift-off, soared over the trees and were climbing hard. Overwhelmed by a mixture of elation and terror, Cupid clung tightly to the edges of the hard scales, trying to take comfort in the reassuring normality of Godsville below — Arcadia Close, the ribbon of the expressway running into town, the multicoloured roofs of the ghetto, the dark, turgid river, the Factory on its hill, afternoon sun bouncing blindingly off its glass sides, the prominent dome of Seekers™ looming up . . .

Everything as normal.

Except that, all round them in the ethereal blue, other dragons were whistling past, some giving Dennis smoke-puffs of greeting, which then created small white clouds. Were they in dragon mode? Cupid was beginning to panic, when Dennis began his descent towards the all too familiar symbol containing GOD.

As he saw the guardian angels pouring out of their

encampment to rise in an avenging host, Cupid dug his heels into the dragon's side. Only to get no response. Then he remembered. The angel dust! He fished desper-ately in his pocket whilst Dennis, obviously anticipating what was coming, turned his head to present a large pink nostril, so conveniently flared Cupid was able to sprinkle in a glittering handful as easily as dropping it into a funnel.

The effect was electric.

Dennis sucked the dust down in one huge snort, let out a strangled cry of 'Yeehaaargh!', then bounded forward as if turbo-charged.

As the angels vanished into dots on the horizon, Cupid shut his eyes and braced himself. They were going to be splattered against the invisible surface of the force field as surely as a bird crashing into a window pane!

Feeling a hard jolt, he braced himself harder. Here it came!

After a long, long pause he finally risked a quick peek. Only to discover, to his chagrin and surprise, that Dennis had already landed. And also that M had meant exactly what he had said.

For they had come down slap outside the entrance to GOD!

Not only that, but Dennis was now rolling onto his side, easing Cupid off his back, whilst some unseen power was propelling him inexorably towards the terrifyingly ornate gold entrance door.

Chapter 21

It's All Aura Now

All the gods thought it fitting GOD housed himself in Ayers Rock. Even if it didn't look as imposing on the edge of Godsville as its earthling replica, so splendidly isolated in the flat wastes of the Australian desert. It was such a practical shape to house a giant mainframe, yet also so naturally beautiful with its warm red stone, which turned spectacularly purple at the end of the day.

The ornate gold door, with its exquisitely wrought 3-D panels, was even more impressive at close quarters than when Cupid had seen it at a distance on his abortive cherub visit, although the signature he could now read — 'Ghiberti' — meant nothing to him.

More to the point, though, was the wall screen.

> WELCOME TO GOD < it read. > PLEASE LOG IN USING PASSWORD CODE <

Cupid's stomach turned over. But M had said there wasn't a password!

He whipped round as he heard a loud groan behind him, only to realise it was Dennis. He clearly had no worries. He had fallen fast asleep.

> PING PONG < Cupid typed tentatively onto the keyboard below the screen.

> INCORRECT PASSWORD CODE <

Hearing another noise, Cupid looked round again and saw the host of guardian angels waving angrily from behind the force field.

This didn't look good at all.

> BIG BOY < he tried.

> INCORRECT PASSWORD CODE <

> NOSTRADAMUS <

> INCORRECT PASSWORD CODE <

> BT <

> INCORRECT PASSWORD CODE <

> RED HOT MOMMA <

> INCORRECT PASSWORD CODE <

Methodically, Cupid exhausted the entire stock he had memorised from the SUPER USER ACCESS file.

None worked.

Worse, a new message now appeared on the screen:

> YOU HAVE USED UP ALL YOUR ALLOTTED ENTRY OPPORTUNITIES BAR ONE. YOU ARE HEREBY WARNED THAT INPUTTING A FURTHER INCORRECT PASSWORD CODE WILL LEAD TO ACCESS BEING DENIED FOR A PERIOD OF 24 HOURS <

Cupid felt the panic rise. He couldn't spend an entire day and a night marooned here!

Remembering Mercury, he struggled to stay cool and approach the problem rationally. There was something

odd about these screen messages. They weren't asking
for just > PASSWORD < but > PASSWORD CODE <,
which was different. Meanwhile M, whom he had to
trust, had said there wasn't a password, but that to
get the right answer you simply had to ask the right
question.

So, was asking the right question the answer? And,
if so, what was the right question?

Cupid had a sudden inspiration. It was ridiculously
cheeky, especially bearing in mind who he was addressing. Yet it had a weird sort of logic. Until now he had
presumed when he had asked M what the correct question was, the old magician had simply gone vacant.

What if he hadn't?

Minerva's face suddenly flashed up as Cupid recalled
an occasion she had been chatting to Venus in the
kitchen and deliberately turned to bring him into the
conversation.

'Always remember, above all else, Cupid, that a wise
god, or goddess, never presumes,' she had impressed
on him with her solemn power. 'You will need to
remember that one day.'

So had he really seen a vacant expression on M's face,
as he had presumed until now? Or had it been one of
deep significance? Anyhow, what had he got to lose?
He had exhausted all his SUA passwords and, if he was
going to be stuck here, at least he might gain himself a
plate of his favourite Florentines.

'What's for tea?' he demanded out loud.

The screen stared back at him blankly and for a
moment he felt stumped.

Then he remembered himself.

> WHAT'S FOR TEA? < he typed onto the key-
board.

> WARNING – THIS IS YOUR LAST ALLOW-
ABLE COMMUNICATION ATTEMPT. ARE YOU
CERTAIN YOU WISH TO CONTINUE? <

> YES <

He was in it now.

> WHAT WOULD YOU LIKE? <

> CREAM TEA, PLEASE < Cupid typed in with
mounting excitement. > WITH DAMSON JAM. <

> PLEASE COME IN < the screen stated.

With a heavy rumble the door swung back on
its hinges.

A small yellow buggy powered silently out and drew
to a stop beside him.

'Do embark,' a deep voice said in such a profoundly welcoming tone that Cupid obeyed automatically.

Then, before he could touch the controls, the buggy
set off smartly into the interior.

Something that often led to rowdy arguments amongst
the gods was exactly how big GOD was.

'He may have been enormous once,' Mercury would
always maintain, 'but, as we techies know, computers
are becoming smaller and smaller, whilst exponentially
increasing in power. So, although GOD may now have
to be measured in terateragodobytes, he's so far ahead
of anything anywhere else he may only be the size of
an earthling matchbox!'

Many gods and goddesses, however – including
Jupiter and Cupid himself – found this thesis insulting.
Not just to GOD, but themselves. Surely he had to be
hugely, massively, gigantic to control all the functions
he did? It was one thing for Mercury to argue back
that equating size with strength was adolescent, but

how could you possibly respect something that was matchbox-sized?

Anyhow, if GOD was so small, why then did he inhabit such a vast edifice?

At which point the argument would come the full circle.

'He may have been enormous once . . .' Mercury would begin again.

Now, as the buggy glided into the hollowed-out rock, with a deep thrill Cupid congratulated himself on being right. Righter than his wildest imaginings! So Mercury didn't know everything, after all! It felt like entering the cathedral in Seekers™, yet on a much vaster scale. The roughly hewn rock of the ceiling appeared higher than a cloud in the sky.

Even more impressively, the interior contained neither gloomy heights nor depths. As far as Cupid could see, the entire area was illuminated by very modern, very bright concealed lighting, which threw every nook and cranny into sharp relief. And so beautifully! The harsh red of the rock outside had been replaced by a vista, starting with a purple at the bottom so deep as to be almost black, passing through crimson lake, magenta, vermilion . . . Cupid struggled to remember the colours in his pencil box. And all the time lightening, until it climaxed in a glorious, rose madder blush.

Just as awesome were the banks of computer machinery towering all around him. Like cathedral pillars, yet so packed together the aisle the buggy was powering down felt claustrophobic.

As he saw how it was intersected by regular cross-roads, with similar aisles running off at right angles, Cupid realised it was laid out on a grid pattern. Peering upwards, he was further reminded of being on the pavement in New York on Planet Earth. That same contrast of smoothly futuristic technology butting up against the raggedness of nature.

Yet, unlike raucous New York, this was totally hushed, the only noise the swishing of the buggy's tyres on the smooth rock floor. Presumably, Cupid decided, remembering Mercury's 'hermetically sealed environment', because it was entirely deserted.

Out of habit, he still switched into EG-mode, then gave an echoing nervous laugh as no ghosts were revealed.

'Coooee!' he called out nonetheless to keep his spirits up, before breaking into a racking cough as the curiously dry air tickled his throat. The noise reverberated round like thunder.

Talk about corridors of power! he was just managing to joke to himself, when he saw an open area appear in the distance.

He had reached the end of the line.

In front of him a wall containing thousands of screens stretched up to the roof and away to both sides, together showing a fantastic range of different images, from earthling birth through to earthling death. Underneath, instruments monitored temperature, time and other factors Cupid was unfamiliar with, including 'emotion level'.

In front of this extraordinary panorama, on the otherwise empty floor, stood a horseshoe-shaped desk with a single chair. Finding himself impelled out of the buggy to sit at it, Cupid felt a fresh thrill as he discovered it fitted him like a glove.

He had been expected!

He leant forward and scanned the baffling array of knobs and switches arranged round the single keyboard.

> PING PONG < he typed in hopefully.

> WELCOME, CUPID. SIT BACK AND ENJOY THE SHOW < the solitary desk screen relayed back.

> BUT FIRST . . . <

A table with a white linen cloth materialised beside him. On it was set a cream tea, with a side plate of Florentines. Suddenly starving, Cupid gratefully spread a scone with cream and jam. Damson as ordered, he was realising with a jolt, when he bit on something hard.

He nearly choked as > WITH STONES! < flashed up on the screen, before bursting out laughing so hard that crumbs sprayed everywhere.

This might all be extraordinarily weird, gobsmacking even, he thought as he wiped them off the screen with his cuff, yet he wasn't feeling the slightest bit frightened.

Rather, a wonderful sense of peace was making him totally relaxed and at ease.

> WE DON'T HAVE STONES ANY MORE IN THE LAND OF THE GODS < he typed back cheerfully.

> MORE'S THE PITY, CUPID. YOU SEE, THE ANSWER OFTEN LIES IN THE STONES <

Cupid picked one off his plate and examined it. It looked perfectly normal. As did the others when he fished them out of the pot with his knife and scrutinised them in turn. The odd thing, though, was there were so many — thirty-one in all, he finished counting.

He wiped his hands on the linen serviette and ticked off on his fingers: '. . . soldier, sailor, rich god, poor god, beggar god.'

Some compliment!

Should he keep them anyway, in case they were

important? Yet they were disgustingly messy and, apart
from GOD's serviette — which he wasn't at all sure he
would be allowed to take with him — he had nothing
to wrap them in.

He dismissed them from his mind as another mystery
he would never get to the bottom of and instead
began scrolling through the list of directories that
had appeared on the screen. They went on and on
and on — screenful after screenful, forming a seemingly
never-ending ribbon! So this was what it was like to
no longer be a piece of bolt-on software back at the
Factory, but in what Jupiter called 'the big picture'.
Big! It was mind-blowingly, awesomely, hugely, amaz-
ingly teranormous, as Mercury would say!

The mere thought of the power under his fingertips
was awesome.

But what to do with it?

As if in answer, his eye settled on a file called
> REAL TIME <

He clicked on it.

> YOU HAVE CHOSEN TO ACCESS REAL TIME.
THIS FACILITY ENABLES YOU TO GO BACK IN
EARTHLING TIME AND CHANGE SOMETHING.
IS THIS YOUR INTENTION? <

Cupid started in astonishment. Was he being given
an opportunity to change Planet Earth?

> YES < he typed in nervously.

> SPECIFY EXACT CHANGE REQUIRED <

> I WANT TO MAKE THE EARTHLINGS
EXPERIENCE MORE ROMANTIC LOVE SO THAT
THEY CAN BE HAPPIER AND HAVE MORE FUN <
he tried.

> DON'T BE RIDICULOUS < the screen relayed
back. > IT DOESN'T WORK LIKE THAT. ANYHOW,

DON'T YOU KNOW THE POINT OF EARTHLING
LIFE IS TO LIVE IT, NOT JUST BE HAPPY? <
That was telling him, Cupid thought, chastened.
What could he do then?
> THE REAL-TIME PROGRAM GIVES YOU THE
POWER TO GO BACK IN TIME AND CHANGE
ANY ONE EVENT IN EARTHLING HISTORY <
the screen promptly prompted him. > YOU MUST
HOWEVER SPECIFY PRECISE LOCATION, DATE,
EXACT TIME AND CHARACTERS INVOLVED <
Cupid felt himself shaking. What an opportunity!
But not one, hardly surprisingly, he was the slightest bit
prepared for. Dozens of thoughts were now scurrying
through his mind. Should he do good by preventing
Hitler being born? Relegating Nixon to a used-car lot?
Stopping Stalin taking over Russia? Or, on a wider
scale, eradicating the invention of the motor car? The
atom bomb? What about his own speciality? Should he
prevent Lady Diana Spencer marrying into the British
Royal Family by pinging Prince Charles with someone
else, meanwhile also removing Camilla Parker-Bowles
from the equation?
All possible, along with a million other things. Yet,
at the same time, all impossible to strap down, without
prior notice, in the precise way the computer was
requiring.
He jumped as the monitor gave an impatient beep.
> YOU ARE FAILING TO RESPOND. DO YOU
WISH TO HAVE AN EVENT CHOSEN FOR YOU? <
Cupid gave up.
> YES < he typed back weakly.
> WHICH SPECIALITY? <
Of course! He wasn't only Cupid any more! He was
any god he chose!

> COMMUNICATIONS < he typed with trembling hands. Would he really be able to change Planet Earth as Mercury?

Apparently yes!

The screen had dissolved into a room, Cupid guessed on a university campus somewhere in America. West coast, probably. A group of nerdy-looking males were huddled round an extraordinarily crude early computer.

> TO MAKE YOUR INTENDED CHANGE YOU MUST EMPOWER ONE OF THE SEVEN EARTH-LINGS ON YOUR SCREEN TO CREATE AND LEAD A COMPUTER BREAKTHROUGH WHICH WILL HAVE FAR-REACHING CONSEQUENCES FOR ALL ON PLANET EARTH.

> MAKE YOUR CHOICE BY CLICKING ON CHOSEN INDIVIDUAL <

Cupid moved the cursor aimlessly round the screen. How could he possibly decide? He didn't even know who these people were.

> YOU HAVE TEN SECONDS BEFORE THIS, AND ALL SIMILAR OPTIONS, ARE WITHDRAWN < a strip ran along the bottom of the screen.

Desperately, Cupid clicked on a nerd at random.

A sizzling white flash ran down the middle of his screen and it blacked. Not just his, he realised, horror-struck. All the thousands on the wall as well!

He was rerunning the crash in the Factory! But this time not just their terminals, but GOD himself, had gone down!

> UNDO < he hammered.

Nothing.

He hit one control key after another, tears running down his cheeks, until he ended up pounding the keyboard with his fist.

Still nothing.

He had only one last, desperate recourse.

He took a deep breath and slowly moved his hand to the prominent switch marked POWER. Shutting his eyes, he flicked it off, counted to five, then flicked it back on again.

There was a deep hum and the screens came back to life, each now carrying the identical message > OVER-RIDE ACTIVATED <

'Mum!' Cupid wailed as successive banks of machinery gained momentum with a series of clicks and buzzes.

He sat, sniffling and powerless, until the hum began dropping in pitch.

GOD had been rebooting!

For a new message had now flicked up:

> ADJUSTMENTS COMPLETED AS PER EXECUTED REAL-TIME CHANGE. PLANET EARTH NOW RUNNING ON PROGRAM 18,446,744,073,709,551,615. CONFIRM <

The letters on Cupid's keyboard depressed themselves, as if being operated by invisible hands.

> CONFIRMED < flashed up before the screens reverted to their previous activity of showing varied scenes from Planet Earth.

Cupid relaxed slightly. If he wasn't mistaken, some of the pictures were slightly different. Otherwise, though, earthling life seemed to be carrying as normal. Yet whose hands had those been? And why this sudden feeling he was being watched?

He whipped round.

There was no one in sight.

Then he looked up and saw the glow begin, high in the vaulted ceiling. An all-pervading brightness, he explained later to Venus, like the most beautiful sunrise imaginable, yet growing in intensity until it was as bright as the blinding light accompanying a GOD 'me'. Yet softer, as if slightly out of focus, although it obviously had as much, if not more, power. Cupid could feel the whole atmosphere vibrating.

He shrank back as a blue flash crackled round the keyboard.

'Welcome to GOD,' a deep voice intoned. 'Fear not, but be of good cheer. For many may call, yet few are chosen.'

Cupid jerked his head around, trying in vain to pin-point the location of the speaker. The voice seemed to have come from everywhere, like the most sophisticated sensurround system he had ever experienced.

'Have I broken it?' he burst out.

'What, my child?'

'Planet Earth.'

'For a moment I thought you meant GOD,' the voice chuckled. 'Of course not. No god can do that, especially a little one like you.

'You have, however, changed it,' the voice continued benignly. 'For which I'm grateful. I wasn't very happy with 614. I'm sure 615 will be an improvement. Such a great beauty in mathematics, isn't there? Such precision? So little margin for error? I'm sure you share my joy.'

'Of course,' Cupid agreed, though really he didn't. Maths had never been his strong point.

'I wasn't trying to do any harm,' he added uncertainly.

'Don't worry.' The voice was infinitely comforting. 'You haven't.'

'Didn't I change everything, though?'

'Not everything.' Did Cupid detect a hint of weariness?

'What about the earthling I clicked on?'

'Bill Gates?' There was a chortle. 'Yes, you changed a lot for him. You invented Microsoft. Yet, like all individual earthlings, he is but a collection of particles. Everything reverts to much the same in the long run.

'I must confess to having changed things myself in the past. Just to relieve the monotony, really. Not that I should. Boredom is a failing, whilst my task is to remain infallible.

'Yet at times the earthlings can be so remarkably tedious . . .'

A shiver ran down Cupid's spine. There was no such thing as binary boredom. So who was this speaking? He screwed his eyes up against the light, trying, again in vain, to locate a visible feature.

'You won't find a long white beard like Saturn.'

Cupid jumped.

'Not that I'm reading your mind.'

Cupid jumped even harder.

'Where are all these other worlds?' he gabbled, unable to think of anything more intelligent. He had already forgotten the number of this one, it had been so long.

'Why, stored within GOD.'

'What – all running at once?'

'Naturally.'

'So can I make another change?' Cupid asked without thinking.

He bit his tongue. Was he being cheeky?

'No,' the voice replied sternly. 'Having moved to this one, you must now remain within it.'

Cupid toyed with the edge of the chair as he

tried to wrap his head round the complexities of this statement.

'Planet Earth's only on 615 because I changed to it, isn't it?' he faltered. 'So why can't I change again and go on to 616? Or back to 614?

'I was quite happy with that,' he added as an afterthought.

'In a word, no and no,' came the unhelpful reply, although spoken in a kindly tone. 'Apart from extremely minor ones, such as you just carried out, changes can only be made in cases classified as entirely exceptional.

'And once done, never undone.'

Cupid thought he understood that.

Except for one thing.

'Classified by who?' he asked rudely.

'That is not for you to know.'

'What exactly is "entirely exceptional"?' he persisted.

'Exactly that.'

Cupid sat back, feeling more confident.

He had decided to call the voice and light the Aura, because it reminded him in a way of Aurora, the goddess of dawn. And the Aura showed no sign of being cross with him, whilst he was meanwhile adapting to speaking into thin air. It was like talking to yourself, or one of your imaginary friends. Some tremendous warmth was also encouraging him to be unafraid, whilst Venus had taught him always to have the courage to ask.

The face of his mentor, Jupiter, floated before him. What would he do in these circumstances? The question took no answering at all. Jupiter would go for 'the big equation'.

Cupid knew his voice would probably emerge in

a trembling pipe. But he wasn't going to let that stop him.

'Are you,' he squeaked boldly, 'the one?'

In answer, not just the screens but, most terrifying of all, the Aura itself, went out.

Chapter 22

M for Mystery

Fortunately Cupid was imprisoned in terrifying blackness for only a moment.

'Just reminding you of your place,' the voice chuckled as everything came back on again. 'I presume you are referring to the Creator, Godhead, Divinity, Lord, Cosmic Life Force, Superguru, Numero Uno — the earthlings have so many nomenclatures, don't they?

'I'm afraid to have to tell you that there is no simple answer to your question. Suffice it to say there are others apart from myself. Some above me, some below. Many, many layers to the onion, as it were.

'Yet, all of them mysterious. Which is why I cannot answer you more specifically. As you should well know, my role — our role — is to be the central mystery. For, take that away, and what would be the point?'

Cupid frowned as he tried to fault the logic. If it

was logic. Like maths, that had never been his strong point. Instead, now relaxing again, he decided to ask the question most concerning him personally. And, whatever the logic of the mystery, one he absolutely felt a right to have answered.

'Please could you tell me why I am here?' he asked humbly.

'Because I had you summoned,' the voice replied. 'You met my agent, M. Good magician, that one. I've used him several times before. You see, his priceless advantage is that he travels backwards in time.'

Cupid blinked at this fresh complication. Yet at least he now knew he had been set up.

By Dennis too, presumably.

'So I was coming here, whether I liked it or not?'

'Yes.'

'You let me in through the door.' Cupid suddenly felt even more humble.

'In a way. You did well to answer on hardness option 14. If you had gone on failing, though, I would have let you in anyhow.'

'You let me into Seekers™ too.'

'Indeed.'

'And,' Cupid gulped, 'you let me see the Beast in GOD.'

'We'll come to that later.'

Cupid felt relief wash over him. Mercury had been wrong again. The horrible face on the screen hadn't been a rogue image, or simply something he had imagined!

'Why me, though?'

'Out of the mouths of babes and sucklings. Suffer the little children to come unto me . . . That sort of thing.'

Cupid struggled to adjust his map. All the time, he had been being manipulated as comprehensively as the earthlings whom he caused to fall in love. Never again, he vowed, would he congratulate himself on being clever. Just wait until he told the grown-up gods what pawns they really were! Unless they knew already.

He recalled their vainglorious boasting.

Certainly not.

'Being permanently younger, you're different,' the voice elaborated. 'And I admire the way you've tried to keep in touch with Planet Earth. Jupiter as well, at least until recently. Juno too, to a certain extent.

'As for the others . . .'

There was a deep sigh.

'What about Mercury?' Cupid asked, thinking how juvenile and squeaky his voice sounded in contrast to the deeply mellifluous tone, which carried such authority that he was being compelled to believe every word it spoke.

'Mercury is a different story,' the voice answered enigmatically. There was a pause, as though its owner was reflecting. 'I am deeply sympathetic to you all, naturally. You see, arrogance had to be an essential part of your design specification when we were creating you. Otherwise, we reasoned, who would ever worship you?

'Yet we should still have programmed you to listen more carefully. It is so very, very foolish, even for gods, to think they know it all.'

Cupid certainly wasn't thinking that right at this moment.

On the contrary, he was eager to discover more.

'Could you tell me why you brought me here?' he ventured.

'Why, because of GOD's sys.op.update.' The voice sounded slightly surprised. 'Of course,' it immediately apologised, 'you don't know, do you? Please forgive me and allow me to explain. I myself have come to install System Megaverse 2000. As well as checking out how Planet Earth has been developing.'

This must be the Great Programmer in the Sky! Cupid thought in awe.

Yet now it was his turn to be surprised.

'You mean you don't know what's been happening?'

'Yes and no.' The voice sounded unperturbed. 'I, or rather we, may be ever-present, but that doesn't mean that we're always actively here, if you understand my meaning.'

Cupid's blank look signalled back that he didn't. Rather, he was getting worried he was about to lose the whole plot.

'Allow me to explain further,' the Aura continued comfortingly. 'I know it's a lot to take in at once but, put simply, I, or rather we, leave you gods and the earthlings to run your own affairs in conjunction with GOD.

'I visit periodically to do a bit of housekeeping, clear off dead files, check for viruses — that sort of thing. When necessary, put a touch on the tiller through an update.' There was a dry chuckle. 'You'll know how there've been a few of those since System 7.0 ushered in the Industrial Revolution!

'Yet I can only keep things on an even keel if they have not gone beyond redemption, as we call it.'

'Have they?' Cupid squeaked nervously.

'Possibly.' This time the sigh was really heavy. 'Which is the current problem facing you gods and goddesses . . .'

'Problem?' Cupid interrupted, more nervous than ever.

He recalled the remark about M travelling backwards in time.

'M must know whether there's anything to be really worried about,' he thought out loud, before mentally kicking himself. Never mind M. The Aura must know absolutely everything!

'It's a multiverse equation, really,' the voice was now replying obscurely. 'Of course, as you know, they can be infinite. Not that they necessarily are,' it added, even more obscurely.

Cupid's mind shot back to his REAL-TIME Bill Gates change. Had things been all right in world 614, but weren't in 615?

'Aren't we only in one universe at a time, though?' he asked, knowing as he spoke it was coming out all wrong. 'And if you — or we — decide what happens in that universe, or universes' — he felt himself struggling — 'you can solve any problem, can't you?'

'Only up to a point,' the Aura interrupted. 'The permutations are not only manifold, but depend on the part each of you chooses to play.

'In this case, particularly you.'

'Me?' Cupid asked slowly, sensing some awful responsibility looming.

'How much control do you think that I, or rather, we, exercise?' The Aura sounded almost tetchy. 'Have you forgotten the prerogative we handed to gods and earthlings? To be in charge of your own destinies to a large extent?

'Why, otherwise, do you think we would have bothered to invent free will?'

'But you told me I had no choice about coming here,' Cupid objected without thinking.

'Touché,' the voice chuckled in reply. 'Nonetheless, you have the choice to leave, if you wish to exercise it.'

'Except you know I won't,' Cupid replied bitterly, then stopped.

He hadn't intended that remark, either. Yet he was back to feeling a mere pawn. Which was maybe what earthlings felt all the time, he thought with a sudden shock.

'I'm preventing you?'

The buggy slid silently up beside Cupid's chair.

'I have already informed you, each of you has been given the right to lead your immortality as you wish.

'Or possibly not lead,' the voice added ominously.

'What do you mean?' Cupid asked slowly.

'Sure you really want to know? It's not always best.'

Cupid felt torn in two. He didn't want to know, very, very strongly. Even more strongly, he wanted to know absolutely everything. Yet above all, whatever the Aura said about free will, he was now convinced he was just being manipulated.

'You're playing with me!' he burst out, dismay turning to anger. 'Which fits, doesn't it? Because if us gods are arrogant, you have to be a million times more so!'

He crossed his arms and stared straight ahead, pouting defiantly.

There was a long silence, during which he became convinced the Aura had reddened slightly.

'Omnipotence does have its drawbacks,' the voice finally mused. 'I am also aware that, from your point of view, being chosen as my instrument is not easy. Others have complained about the same thing in the past. Maybe I can repay you slightly by filling in some things you'd like to know?'

'Why are we here?' Cupid fired back without a second's hesitation. What had he got to lose?

'That piece of information is contained within the M files, and therefore classified.' The voice now sounded po-faced. If a voice could sound po-faced.

'M files?' Cupid asked, baffled.

'M for Mystery. You'll recall what I said earlier about how, without mystery, there would be no point.'

Cupid did. But that didn't stop him feeling cheated.

'Also classified, I suppose,' he asked sarcastically, 'are "What's the point of it all?", "Who's running the show?", "Why do earthlings appreciate beauty?" . . .'

'The FAQs – most frequently asked questions?' the voice interrupted. 'Correct. All covered by the CSA – the Creator Secrets Act.

'Along with, in case you're wondering, "What will the share price of IBM be in a year's time?", "Which horse is going to win the Grand National?" and "Which team is going to be Premier League Champion?"

'Which, incidentally, seem to be the only sorts of questions which interest earthlings these days.'

Did the voice sound bitter?

'That makes you like a minor earthling bureaucrat,' Cupid protested, unable to hide his disappointment. 'If you don't mind me saying so,' he added quickly.

Too late. He had obviously hit a nerve.

'What's wrong with that?' the voice was enquiring sharply. 'I did tell you there were many layers to the onion, some above me, some below.

'Yet my comparative status is not the point at issue.' The voice now sounded highly displeased, if not downright angry. 'The real trouble with some of you gods, and an increasing number of earthlings, is this insane and growing desire to get to the bottom of everything. Break it down into component parts, analyse it, know every single little thing there is to know about it.'

The voice was definitely sounding angry.

'Maybe it stems from having discovered so many things – especially lately,' it continued. 'The delusion seems to have been fostered that there are no limits, nothing the earthling race can't do if it puts its mind to it.

'This hysteria about living for ever, freezing for the future, cloning . . .

'Yet at the same time the earthlings conveniently forget, don't they, that they can't even solve the problem of the traffic jams they've created? Never mind their overall birth rate, the one single factor which is bound to cause them their biggest headache one day.'

Cupid sat, wishing he hadn't opened his mouth. He didn't need a lecture like this.

'Have you also noticed,' the voice continued inexorably, 'how all the concentration these days is on the minutiae? Cells, genes, right down to splitting the atom?

'When they get to the important things, the big things earthling life is really about, such as your speciality of romantic love – or any love, come to mention it – they're at a loss to explain them, aren't they?

'And, verily, don't you think it should always remain like that?'

'I suppose so,' Cupid replied hesitantly. He had never really thought of it from that point of view.

'You want me, us, to take out the sense of wonder?' the voice pressed further. 'Destroy the opportunity to marvel at things so entirely inexplicable? Reveal the pedantic, mundane explanations? Show how, and why, every single wheel goes round?'

'Not really,' Cupid mumbled unhappily, hoping he was saying the right thing.

'Or go even further and inform the earthlings, as well as you gods, where you really fit in the universal scheme of things?

'I can request clearance, you know, to take you up to the next level. Not that I'm intending to at this point. Things haven't reached that pass yet.

'Better, for the moment, believe me, to remain restricted by the M files.'

Cupid sat quietly. At least the Aura had come to a stop.

He frowned as he recognised he had never understood how his pinging worked. Or wanted to. The Aura was right. Reduce it to the level of Mercury's mundane and infinitely boring techno explanations, and it just wouldn't be the same.

'I think I see what you mean,' he replied, retreating to safer ground as a sideways thought struck him.

'Are the L files covered by the M files?' he asked.

'N–O,' the Aura punned dryly, apparently having recovered its composure.

'The Beast?' Cupid enquired slowly.

'The Beast controls the L files.'

'Which are?'

'Part of a long, long story.'

'A classified one as well, I suppose?' Cupid burst out, hearing the sarcasm in his tone.

'Careful,' the Aura chided.

'Sorry,' Cupid replied contritely as he felt the power flash round him.

'Don't worry, I understand your feelings.' The voice sounded suitably mollified. 'As it happens, the L files are not classified.

'Like me to demonstrate? You'd better hang on.'

Cupid gripped the arms of his seat as the pictures on the wall of screens changed until each one was displaying a scene of unmitigated horror, from unspeakable cruelty to deepest pits of despair. Meanwhile the 'emotion level' indicators had swung to the darkest black, whilst a little red 'L' had appeared in the top corner of each screen.

The worse the scene, the brighter the 'L' was glowing.

Cupid's mouth opened in a silent scream as he was engulfed by waves of searing earthling negativity – cowardice, laziness, stupidity, ignorance, misfortune, sickness, pride, avarice, anger, greed, violence. And, dominating all, fear. The vile face of the Beast slowly materialised, gaining in depth and contrast until it filled every screen, whilst the Ls poured with crimson blood, which ran down in an ever-rising tide.

Just as Cupid thought he couldn't take any more, he was engulfed again.

But this time by positives – peace, health, happiness, perseverance, intelligence, goodness, hope, patience, courage, joy. And, above all, love. The tides of blood had turned and were running back into the fading Ls, while the Beast's face became ever more insubstantial, until it faded to just a grin, then disappeared entirely.

With a loud click, the screens reverted to their regular patchwork of earthling activity.

Cupid slumped back into his seat, drained. He didn't dare ask any more questions, for fear of the answers.

'Can I go now?' he pleaded.

'I agree, that's enough for the present.' The voice was full of compassion. 'I do require, however, that you take this with you.'

A small oval tablet materialised on the desktop.

Cupid picked it up gingerly. Its rounded edges and silky smooth gunmetal finish were pleasantly warm to the touch. Was it made of metal? Stone? And how did you open it, if you did? Its surface felt, and looked, as seamless as an egg.

Above all, what did it do?

'Give it to your mother, Venus, to pass on to Jupiter,' the voice instructed.

'Venus?' Cupid queried, feeling slightly worried about passing on such a responsibility. Even, or particularly, to his mother.

'She will ensure he receives it,' the voice replied so reassuringly Cupid knew he could trust it absolutely.

'Is that all?' he asked, relieved, picking up the tablet and getting out of the chair.

'For now.'

'Thank you for coming,' the voice added as Cupid collapsed into the yellow buggy. 'I know you understand that this meeting is for the good of all.'

'Of course,' Cupid mumbled, desperate to get out before some fresh complication overwhelmed him.

Yet one thing was still nagging at the back of his mind.

'Are there really such things as troons?' he blurted out.

'Dear old M!' the voice laughed. 'Don't worry, Cupid. There's a bit more to it all than that!'

The Aura was still chuckling as the buggy set off, when Cupid was struck by fresh thought.

'Will I be coming back?' he called out.

There was no reply.

He looked up and saw the Aura fading.

'See you,' he called hopefully, then thought how ridiculous that must sound. 'Or, rather, not see you,' he tried, before realising that must sound even more ridiculous.

He had to get out before his brain was scrambled!

'The peace of GOD, which passeth all understanding, be with you and stay with you, now and for evermore,' he heard the voice intoning as the buggy motored out into the twilight, where the outside of the massive rock had already turned to purple.

Cupid felt a moment of panic as he failed to pick out Dennis's bulky form. Then, as the whole area was lit up by lurid flaming belch, he ran across to where the dragon was clambering sleepily to his feet.

'Home, Dennis!' he commanded, leaping onto his back. 'And don't spare the wings!' he added, seeing ghostly white garments moving beyond the force field.

As Dennis looked round with a wicked grin, Cupid tipped a handful of angel dust into the flared nostril, then felt himself rocked violently back in the saddle as the dragon let rip a gigantic fart.

The after-burner! he was just thinking, when Dennis accelerated so hard he nearly blacked out.

As the dragon settled down onto a steady course, Cupid opened his eyes again, curious about the throaty noises emanating from its mouth. Then he realised. Dennis was singing! Whatever Cupid had been through, there was obviously nothing to worry about in Dragonland.

Which they must be in again, judging by the red and green navigation lights and puffs of flame, crisscrossing the darkening sky like shooting stars.

Below them strings of lights delineated Godsville, the Factory blazing bright at its centre.

A timeless vista, Cupid would have said on his outward journey.

But now?

He touched his pocket to reassure himself the mysterious tablet was still safely with him.

'Please, Jupiter!' he mouthed as Dennis came in low over Arcadia Close.

But in the garden of number 31 the red light was still glowing.

Chapter 23

Cutting Edge

A s he crept along the edge of the lawn, Cupid could hear the raised voices.

'You've got until noon tomorrow.' Mercury.

'Then either hand him over or we take this place apart.' Vulcan's rough voice.

'Like this.' Mars, with the bit between his teeth.

Cupid heard a loud rip followed by his mother's scream. He risked a peek through the chink in the curtains and saw a great slash across her favourite painting of a naked lady riding a seashell, which she had told him an earthling had done in her honour.

Not a bad likeness, either.

'Avast there!' Neptune, intervening sharply. 'Be warned, you're into something you don't understand.' Addressing the assembled goddesses. 'There'll be no more stays of execution.'

'If I had my way I'd beat his whereabouts out of you right now.' Mercury yelling, whilst the others propelled him from the room.

The front door crashed shut.

Cupid nipped round the side and tiptoed up behind the water butt.

'What are we waiting for?' Mercury, angrily addressing the huddle in the darkness. 'The little arsehole holds the key. I can't reactivate the terminals until I know what he did.'

'Which is why we need him to cooperate.' Neptune again, sounding as if his patience was exhausted. 'Frighten him too much, and he'll just clam up. Worse still, invent something. It'll be hard enough separating fact from fiction as it is.'

'What we ought to be separating is his bloody gonads from the rest of him.' Mercury, stalking off down the drive.

'He's much too wound up.' Neptune, commenting as the others sauntered in his wake. 'Isn't it ironic? The one god who could wheedle the truth out of Cupid, stuck in Mega-Retroland™.'

'Who can blame him?' Mars, still angry. 'With the shit going down here, I could use some Mega-Retroland™ myself.'

'You know, I can't help thinking there's something fishy about Mercury's attitude.' Neptune, sounding worried. 'He is the techno king after all. I can't understand why he says he needs Cupid so much.'

'Techno, techno, I'm sick of bloody techno . . .'

The voices faded.

Cupid decided not to risk following and returned to the back.

'Although I hate saying this, in a way they're

right.' Juno. 'We can't hide Cupid away for ever.'

He risked another peek and saw Venus sadly finger-
ing the jagged rent in the canvas of her ruined painting.
Poor Mum! She didn't deserve that. Mars again, just like
his best bow.

'I'll go and check how he is,' she now proposed to
Juno, 'then I'll come round to your place and we'll
discuss it.'

Cupid froze. He couldn't allow Venus to find him.
How could he ever manage to conceal his astonishing
GOD news in the face of the interrogation the gods
were planning? More than that, in handing him the
tablet, the Aura had absolutely confirmed his conviction
he must speak only to Jupiter.

He was about to creep away when the back door
opened and Venus, looking furtive, hurried past within
feet of him. There was a brief flash from her torch,
before she vanished into the tangle of trees and bushes.

Now was his chance.

Inside he scribbled a brief note.

Dear Mum,
Don't worry, I'm all right. I've just gone into
hiding for a bit as I think it's best.
Please deliver this to Jupiter. It's very urgent and
very important.
See you after that.
Love
Cupid XXX

He put the note on the table and placed the precious
tablet on top of it, crossing his fingers he was doing
the right thing.

Back outside, he waited for what seemed an age until

his mother came running back, passing so close he had
to clench his jaw to resist the temptation to call out.

He heard her give a sharp cry, followed by the bang
of the front door.

He peered inside.

The note and tablet had gone.

But where was he to go now?

He made his way back down the garden, suddenly
feeling entirely alone. He hadn't even thought of any
alternative to the summerhouse.

Maybe visioning up Dennis worked at night, he
thought hopefully, determinedly not thinking about
the dragon.

Apparently not, he then discovered.

Which meant he had only one hiding place left.

Juno sobbed with frustration as she beat her fists on
the capsule's smooth surface. The eerie red DO NOT
DISTURB: GOD AT PLAY sign seemed to be deliberately
mocking her, whilst her peacocks, rudely awakened
from their slumbers, milled round her feet in screeching
agitation.

'Get out of the way, you stupid birds,' she was
yelling, kicking at them wildly, when Vulcan's face
loomed, ghostly and ghastly, over the top of the fence.

'Gone Retro-mad, hasn't he? After all that preaching
. . .' The god of fire pursed his lips and waggled his
head sadly. 'Bet you're missing it, eh? You know, the
service. Anything I can do to help?'

Juno struggled to conceal her shock. Vulcan's nosy-
neighbour antics were bad enough during the day. But
in the middle of the night!

'You can fuck off,' she replied crudely. 'You're too
stupid to understand how vital it is we get him out.'

How could he possibly, without being privy to the latest Cupid development? But who cared?

Vulcan fought to keep his temper by reminding himself he was here with a purpose. Neptune's chance remark about Jupiter had sparked off an idea he had now become set on. Not only would it make him a superhero, but, equally importantly, it would gain him huge, and enduring, personal satisfaction.

'Want me to cut him out?' he enquired airily, attempting to look the picture of innocence.

Juno stared at him open-mouthed.

'VI machines aren't magic, you know,' Vulcan elaborated casually. 'Simply a double aluminium skin over a space frame. Honeycomb insulation sandwich. I could slice through all that lot in no time.

'Mind you, you'd have to make it worth my while.'

With a horrid laugh his head vanished.

'Hold it!' Juno commanded.

The head popped up again.

Juno's first reaction to Venus's news of Cupid's disappearance had been blind fury.

'That's what comes of leaving basically a child on his own for so long,' she had berated his tearful mother.

Then, after reading the note, she had calmed down as she turned her attention to examining the mysterious tablet.

'I've never seen anything like it.' She had rolled its silky-smooth surface over and over in her hands. 'Where do you think he got it from? More to the point, how do you open it?'

Of course Venus hadn't known.

At which point extracting Jupiter had become what GOD would have labelled an 'imperative' definitely deserving a 'me'. Never mind the rapidly approaching millennium, the gods' much more urgent deadline for handing over Cupid was little more than twelve hours away. Juno had no doubt that, if he was not produced as ordered, the males would immediately carry out their threat.

After all her years of immortality, Juno prided herself on her ability to block out things she didn't want to see. Or smell. Yet the interior of Vulcan's, which she had never been in before, was already defeating her. While the god of fire enthused over his game plan, all she could do was put her hand to her face and openly hold her nose.

Not that Vulcan was taking any notice.

'This is the little beauty who'll be doing the job.' He plucked an acetylene cutter from the chaos of the kitchen worktop and ran his hand obscenely up and down its shaft. 'My favourite tool. But just like me, though. Needs a bit of fettling to get going.

'Don't you, my lovely one?' he cooed, his warty hand making even more suggestive vertical movements.

Juno, close to gagging, thought on her feet.

'You said I'd have to make it worth your while,' she pre-empted, provoking a slavering leer. 'Well, I'm prepared to move the fence back.'

'Jupiter would never allow that,' Vulcan gasped, astonished.

'Who's deciding?'

Vulcan took heed of her determined, jutting jaw. He already knew the answer. She always made the decisions. Typical wimp Jupiter, hiding behind his goddess!

He sucked on his yellow teeth, his tongue absent-mindedly probing a cavity. He still thought his original idea a brilliant way to humiliate her. The trouble was it was only in private. And with unforeseen consequences if – or more likely, when – Jupiter found out. Yet here she was offering – actually offering – the chance to grind his arch-enemy's face in the mud! In public. And permanently. With that turd Terminus thrown into the bargain!

Best to grab his chance whilst he could.

'You're on,' he grinned conspiratorially.

'Only if you succeed, mind,' Juno warned.

'No problem.' Vulcan stroked the end of the torch with a hoary fingertip. 'A piece of cake, eh, my little friend?'

'And you start right now.'

'No,' Vulcan countermanded firmly. 'I've got to get my stuff together first. Operation Cutting Edge is now scheduled to begin at dawn.'

Juno, still holding her fingers to her nose, didn't stay to argue.

Rightly or wrongly, she thought as she hurried into number 31 to wash out her mouth and nostrils, she had ceded control.

Why, oh why, though, did it have to be to the one god whom she hated the most?

Chapter 24

Mein Kampf

Juno woke at first light. Yet, as she heard the loud revving outside, she instantly realised that wasn't early enough. Rushing to the window, she saw the lights of Vulcan's Datsun pick-up as it swerved violently across the lawn, knobbly tyres gouging twin swathes out of the pristine turf.

She should have known, she thought furiously as she threw on her clothes, grabbed her fleece and ran into the garden, only to find an excited crowd already gathered behind the hedge.

Now that was something she couldn't have anticipated.

Vulcan must have spread the word in the early hours. And not just in Arcadia Close and on the Lower Orders' estate, either, she then realised. But, horror of horrors, Valhalla Villas! The vile Valkyries were already greeting her with screeching delight, whilst Thor, clearly revelling in his role as Vulcan's assistant, brandished his hammer rudely from the Datsun's cab window.

'Either we do it my way, or not at all,' Vulcan said, cutting short her remonstrations while he continued to thump oxygen cylinders to the ground. 'This is gods' stuff. No place here for ignorant goddesses.'

There was a sudden commotion as Mercury burst through the crowd.

'What in the Land of the Gods are you doing?' he shrieked wildly.

'I'm about to torch it,' Vulcan grunted.

'And who gave you the authority to do that?'

'You're telling me I need permission?' Vulcan asked incredulously. 'What − from some pissy-arsed bugger like you?'

'But you can't just cut up a Retroland™ capsule without GOD's permission!' Mercury waved his arms dramatically at the geodesic dome. 'Especially a new Megaverse 2000 Mega-Retroland™.

'It isn't even run in! GOD simply won't allow it.'

'So why don't you get on your pisspot laptop?' Vulcan dropped the cylinder he was dragging towards the glistening surface and used his blunt fingers to mimic working a keyboard. 'Tap, tap, tap . . .

'Dear GOD, Help! Naughty old Vulcan's about to do some criminal damage to your precious capsule . . .' He stuck his nose into Mercury's face, engulfing him in a cloud of fetid breath. 'Well, you just try. Because your so-called state-of-the-art techno doesn't even bloody work any more, does it?

'Not like Operation Cutting Edge,' he concluded proudly.

'Or this.' Thor struck the side of the capsule a ringing blow with his hammer.

Mercury stared horrified at the egg-shaped dent, while the crowd roared approval.

'But I'm about to interrogate Cupid,' he yelled. 'If Jupiter's out he'll protect him. Which'll ruin everything.'

'Will it?' Juno intervened sharply. 'I thought the object was to get the truth out of him. Or is that the last thing you want?'

'That's an outrageous suggestion!' Mercury frothed. 'You know computer matters are incredibly complex. Cupid must be questioned by someone with in-depth knowledge.'

'As well as nothing to hide,' Juno shot back.

Her heart leapt as she saw Vulcan frown.

Were wheels beginning to go round?

But her euphoria was short-lived.

'That's enough girlie crap,' the god of fire announced, lighting his torch and adjusting the flame to a searing blue.

'Not long now,' he grinned above the roar, pulling down his goggles. 'Or shall I slice you up first?'

He stabbed menacingly at Mercury, who shrank back and stood, looking lost.

His NOSTRADAMUS search had proved as negative as he had feared, even before the system went down. After which he had been entirely hamstrung. In wild moments he had even contemplated trying to get to Ayers Rock to access GOD direct.

Now he wished he had.

It was one thing counting on bamboozling the other gods with technobabble before he got Cupid on his own and shook him down. But Jupiter thrown into the mix completely destroyed that line of thinking.

And meanwhile Mercury had no Plan B to fall back on.

He winced as he watched the flame cut into the metal in a shower of sparks. What did bloody Vulcan imagine he could be gaining, apart from a chance to show off his antiquated technology?

'You can forget your noon deadline for Cupid.'

Mercury jumped. He hadn't noticed Juno sidle up beside him.

'J's bound to be out before then.' She gave him her sweetest smile. 'I'll come and give you a knock, eh? Save you hanging about here.'

She watched his retreating back, feeling the balance of power transferring.

Yet, to both her and Vulcan's chagrin, Operation Cutting Edge turned out far from the predicted piece of cake. The capsule surface proved peculiarly resistant to the torch, while Thor's ostentatious hammer blows were mere window dressing.

As the crowd peppered them with rude comments, the duo's tempers worsened, while the mound of empty lager cans grew higher. With the noon deadline approaching, and only two of the required four lines cut in the capsule's outer skin, Vulcan resorted to desperate measures. To renewed interest from the remaining onlookers, he hooked the jagged corner to the winch on his pick-up.

Yet, although the machine shuddered and trembled, nothing happened, even when Vulcan engaged four-wheel drive and gunned the motor in reverse. The Datsun simply dug itself down in clods of flying earth until, with a tremendous screech, the winch stripped its gears and the line went slack as the drum spun uselessly.

To a background of boos, the pair took a break.

'What can I do for you?' Vulcan shouted angrily as he saw Juno and Minerva walk across to inspect the black scorch marks.

'Just taking a closer look.'

'GOD's manufactured it out of some new metal,' Vulcan explained grumpily. 'Titanium's my guess. But then it could be something I've never heard of.'

'Aren't you following the lines, Vulcan?' Minerva had never sounded so innocent.

'Lines? I can't see any bloody lines. How about you, Thor?'

'Nah.' His Nordic sidekick let fly a large gob and chucked another empty onto the lager-can mound.

'The more you look, the more you see,' Minerva added nonchalantly.

'Well I've seen enough of you two cows,' Vulcan was replying, when the goddess of wisdom overrode him in a voice that cut like a knife.

'Follow me.'

Vulcan rose as if hypnotised.

'Look back.'

To his astonishment, from this distance the surface of the geodesic dome was covered by a cross-hatch of lines. Faint maybe, yet clearly discernible.

'Where there is strength, there is also weakness,' Minerva smiled.

For once Vulcan rose to the occasion.

'Out of the strong came forth sweetness,' he responded without thinking. Where had he got that from? Oh yes – the syrup puddings delivered by the ghost service which were his staple nourishment.

'Where there is sweetness, there is also light.' Minerva had never smiled at him like this before. As if he was a friend, a confidant even.

'Lead shining light, amid the encircling gloom,' he found himself singing to her, while Juno looked on in astonishment. 'Lead thou me on . . .'

Why had he never played these word games before? Vulcan thought wonderingly. They were quite fascinating. Yet, at the same time, somewhat daunting.

Best, he quickly decided, to quit whilst he was still ahead.

'I'd better get on with it,' he said gruffly, suddenly embarrassed.

To his huge relief, there was no clever-clever reply. Just a lovely, lovely smile.

After that things speeded up. Vulcan, standing back like a film director, noisily directed Thor along the stress lines, until it was time for the final cut.

The god of fire walked across, relieved Thor of the torch, and turned to give the little speech he had prepared beforehand.

'I, Vulcan, by the authority vested in me as god of fire,' he pronounced in a passable imitation of Terminus's clipped tones, 'hereby pronounce that the fence must be moved back again off my land.' He plunged the torch against the last skein of lacerated metal. 'In the meantime, I declare this capsule well and truly open.

'Eureka!' he cried finally, stirred by some vague memory from the past, as, with a resounding thump, the entire section toppled to the ground.

He and Thor were bowing ostentatiously to the applause when the crowd fell abruptly silent. A chant as loud as a GOD 'me' was filling the air. Except that it wasn't a 'me', as most recognised from their excursions into Retroland™.

An excited buzz went up, while Juno's heart missed a beat.

She ran forward and squeezed through the hole, heedless of its cutting edges.

Inside the chant of '*Sieg heil! Sieg heil! Sieg heil!*' was deafening, whilst through the swirling smoke she could dimly make out the screen full of goose-stepping soldiers.

It cleared, to reveal Jupiter standing to quivering attention, right arm raised in a rigid salute.

'*Ein Reich! Ein Vaterland!*' he screamed.

'*Sieg heil! Sieg heil!*' came the ecstatic response.

Horror-struck, Juno fumbled around until she found the emergency OFF switch.

In the echoing silence, she ripped off J's sensors.

'What happened?' Her consort shook his head dazedly.

'You tell me,' she snapped. 'Not now, though. Later.'

It might be illogical with the machine shut down, yet all she could think of was getting him out of there as fast as possible. Especially now Vulcan's face, grinning madly, had poked though the hole.

'Got a little problem, have we?' he asked nastily.

'Fuck off,' Juno replied tersely, turning back to J.

'Follow me,' she instructed. 'Look straight ahead. And don't talk to anyone.'

She threw the multiple levers controlling the door-bolts and stepped outside, gritting her teeth at the humiliation she knew was coming.

'You old bastard!' Mars roared as Jupiter emerged, blinking, into the light. 'You were on my side after

all!' He gave a grotesquely exaggerated Nazi salute.
'Just one thing, *mein Führer*. Didn't anyone tell you
that you lost?'

Grim-faced, Juno pushed Jupiter in front of her to
the back door, the mocking crowd streaming behind
singing '*Deutschland, Deutschland, über alles!*'

'Why, J?' she demanded, after slamming it in their
faces.

'I don't know, Juno.' He slumped into his chair, looking utterly bewildered. 'I started off being Churchill,
but I was so pissed half the time I couldn't fathom what
was going on. Meanwhile, this voice kept urging me to
try more power. In the end I gave in.' He looked up at
her wonderingly. 'It was awesome, Juno. Like being a
god, but different. I had this tremendous urge to do
bad things. A kind of self-destruct. I wanted to push
things further and further until they blew.'

'Remember the dog business?'

She did. After one of his last Earth trips he had
recounted how he had watched a little boy prod and
prod at a sleeping dog until it eventually woke and
savaged him. For such a comparatively minor incident,
it had not only made a great impression on him, but
stuck in her mind as well.

She glared down at him, still too angry to give any
quarter.

'You were being even more childish than he was.'

'I was only playing, Juno,' he protested, some of
his old spirit returning. 'Anyhow, who gave you the
authority to burst in on my privacy like that? Never
mind destroy my new Mega-Retroland™ capsule?'

'That kind of privacy needs invading.'

She forced herself to stop. She had to come to terms
with this as well. It was so unlike him, while he had

been the first to experience Mega-Retroland™. Might it be the same for them all? He looked so awful he had obviously been through something incredibly gruelling. She should give him time to readjust, as she had been intending.

Instead she decided to hit him between the eyes straight away. The Vulcan-and-fence news could wait. But the way things were, the sooner he unlocked the secret of Cupid's mysterious tablet, the better for everyone.

'As for my authority, it's that,' she announced, dropping it into his lap.

Chapter 25

Canned

The mysterious tablet opened by irising, Juno realised. Irising in response to her consort's piercing blue irises. As if he was the sun and it was a flower, unfolding its petals to him. Then he was a sun god, she thought wildly, already regretting her impetuous gesture.

She had tossed the tablet into his lap partly for dramatic effect, never stopping to consider the response might be instant. Now there was no time to fill in the background, or join him in speculating where Cupid had got it from.

She stopped thinking as three round balls floated silently out of the open tablet, drifted upwards and stopped, hovering in a neat line in front of them. The first began to unfold, again like a flower. Or a newborn baby unwrinkling in fast forward, she thought even more wildly, switching metaphors yet again to a scrunched-up piece of paper as she saw the ball forming into a document.

Long before it had completely unfurled, to hang ominously in front of them, she knew what it would show. Faint, but unmistakable, there was the vile, hairy face of the Beast Cupid had described and she had seen in her own pomegranate-orchard dream, the same dreadful malevolence seeming to ooze from every pore.

'Doom! Doom!' she thought hysterically, glancing sideways at J. What could he possibly be making of this after being catapulted straight out of Mega-Retroland™? He looked as though his mind had gone, his eyes were so riveted, his mouth working so speechlessly.

She turned back and then it was her turn. The second ball had unfurled, coalescing into another document which now hung in midair.

```
mail to: all Gods/Goddesses

21.31.00/15.12.1999

From: Gods, Oracles and Deities


Y2K technology situation report 493771/666


I have always taught you that patience is a
virtue. Unfortunately for you, after so many
centuries, mine has finally run out. I am
therefore officially informing you that
your decision at the meeting has given me no
choice.

I have reminded you often enough, 'as ye
```

sow, so shall ye reap'. Now you must learn to
live, or rather not live, with the manifold
consequences of your action.

As of 00.00.01/01.01.2000, therefore, with
the withdrawal of Universe System 7.8.9
aka.05 retake 2 and the introduction of
System Megaverse 2000, you are all to be
entirely deleted from the system. There is
to be no Mega-Retroland™. Just nothing. You
are to be canned, your immortalities over
for time immemorial. Eternity. Ever. Until
the last great trumpet sounds, the cows come
home, pigs can fly. Any way your puny minds
can grasp it.

For your further information, there is
nothing personal about this decision. Not
just you, but the whole plethora of gods
and belief systems so painstakingly created
for the earthlings over the aeons, i.e. the
entire Land of the Gods *in toto*, is to meet
the same fate.

Under Megaverse 2000, the earthlings will
no longer have any need, or desire, for
irrelevancies such as higher purpose,
reason for existence, belief in something
greater than themselves, sense of destiny
etc. Therefore, as you will appreciate, all
gods, being connected with such spiritual
activity, would represent a positive drag on
the system, using up vital memory space and
slowing down disk activity.

And, as the earthlings are about to learn,
System Megaverse 2000, starting with a clean
disk, will be operating at considerably
higher speed than System 7.0.

No doubt, with the benefit of hindsight,
you can see this is merely a continuation of
the goal I have been working towards. A goal
which, knowingly or unknowingly, you have
now enabled me to achieve by exercising the
free will you were originally granted.

You have already seen how eagerly the
earthlings, like yourselves, have embraced
the whole gamut of self-centred, ego-led
activities I have been making available
to them in the prelude to the Age of
Information. Their flesh always having been
weak, and their spirit weaker, if not
nonexistent, they are shortly to submit to
the even more glittering temptations I shall
strew so seductively in their path.

Especially as you lot will be out of the
way, redundant, washed up, services no
longer required, passed on, no more, finito,
deceased, toes turned up – again any way
your puny minds can grasp it.

It is of course entirely unfortunate that
an unexpected techno-glitch has held this
e-mail back from being released to you until
now, at 23.56.00/31.12.1999. Yet, as you
know, GOD often works in mysterious ways,
his wonders to perform, and meanwhile you
wouldn't have wanted panic breaking out in
your ranks, would you?

More compassionate by far, surely, for me to
have allowed you to eke out your last days
in blissful ignorance, culminating in your
recent trip to the Energy Pool which, I am
sure you will agree, has ensured you are at
your very best for these, your last moments
of existence?

```
Watch that clock tick away!

So long suckers!

.sig

e-mail ends.
```

```
THEN EVERYTHING ENDS!
BYEEEEE!
```

Juno was turning to her consort when she saw the third ball begin to uncrumple. She sat, like a rat hypnotised by a snake, as it ironed out into another piece of paper.

'Message for Jupiter,' she read, 'you are hereby empowered to mind-unlock Mercury's confidential drawer at the Factory.'

'What the fuck's all this about, Juno?' Jupiter demanded, glaring at her with wild incomprehension.

'It means we're going to the Factory,' she ordered peremptorily, snapped out of her trance.

She must see the reality to be absolutely sure, even though she already knew what they would find.

She led him, like a child, out to her silver BMW Z3 and sat him firmly in the passenger seat. As she hammered down the expressway, she cut off further conversation once they had confirmed that, although it had slipped both their attentions at the time, neither recalled receiving an e-mail between 665, reminding them of the Basilica meeting, and 667, breaking the news of Global Online Divinity and Mega-Retroland™.

'Wait, please, J,' she pleaded as he bombarded her with questions. It might be cruel keeping him in the dark, but the last piece of the jigsaw had to lock into place before she could properly react to the whole.

Never mind explain it to him, or anyone else.

Yet, as she glanced out over the inner-city slums, she could already feel everything slipping away. Fading, just like the faded image of the Beast. Surely it wasn't possible their immortalities, always taken so blithely for granted, could be cancelled like this, at a stroke? Why not? she suddenly realised, eyeing the varied horrors shambling along the monster lane. GOD had already effectively dumped so many previous earthling civilisations and belief systems.

Another penny dropped, this time so hard she swerved violently, nearly losing it.

Of course! If the earthlings were to have no more belief systems under Megaverse 2000, there would be no place for them as ghosts either. The service operations, Seekers™, all the things set up for them in the Land of the Gods, would be redundant. More than redundant. Needing to be deleted as part of closing down their entire spiritual avenue and reducing them to the level of — she swerved again — animals!

Worse, beasts!

The vile face of the Beast!

'Doom! Doom! The earthlings are all doomed!'

This time she swerved so violently she did lose it.

She heard Jupiter shouting as the BMW, out of control, revolved twice, bounced crazily over the monster-lane cones and cannoned off the rubbery hide of an Egyptian hippopotamus goddess. Then it was bouncing back, to come to rest in a cloud of burning rubber in the middle lane, facing the oncoming traffic.

As if in a dream, she saw Jupiter wrestle with the stove-in passenger door before giving up and instead squeezing his large frame though the side window. As godly vehicles hurtled past, horns blaring, he ran round to her side and shoved her into the passenger seat, bellowing indecipherably.

He restarted the engine and whipped the back end through 180 degrees to set them back on course.

'What's the matter with you?' he shouted as he shifted roughly through the gears, simultaneously giving the finger to various other drivers waving their fists.

Because she was now shaking, crying uncontrollably after a fresh thought hit her so hard she thought her head would explode. If this was all the case, why had the mysterious tablet arrived to give the game away? And who had passed it to Cupid in the first place? Had she slipped into another dream? Was that really the vile face of the Beast, imprinted on the gargoyle-like figure pounding insanely alongside them in the monster lane?

Minerva's face filled her mind.

'Those whom GOD wishes to destroy he first makes mad.'

'Now what are you saying?' Jupiter, shaking her shoulder, was sounding desperate.

With a supreme effort, she pulled herself together.

'No questions, J, please. Just drive.'

Even though the Factory lights were blazing, Juno had expected the car park to be deserted. Yet she could feel something else missing the second she walked into the atrium. It wasn't until she got to the Earth control room and saw the rows of dead screens that she realised. It was the lack of noise. There was no background hum, none of the deep, almost subliminal throbbing which always denoted the power of the machinery under their control.

As though a heart had stopped beating.

She switched to EG-mode.

The ghosts had gone as well.

She caught up with Jupiter, standing uncertainly by Mercury's desk, and gave a nod of affirmation.

'You're quite sure, Juno?'

'Just do it, J,' she commanded and watched him standing stiffly, rolling the tumblers in his head, as he did to open his own drawer.

Silently, Mercury's slid open.

Juno felt her heart sink as she saw the black book with 'Holy Bible' written on the front. She snatched it out. There it was on the flyleaf: 'Blessings on you, Archangel Gabriel'.

She allowed Jupiter to take out the black file and open it, knowing full well it would contain, as it did, the two documents that had irised out of the tablet — the faint printout of the Beast's face and the 666 e-mail.

She stared at them dumbly. As she had suspected, Mercury had known all along. Or was it just him? Were there others?

'You've got to explain, Juno,' Jupiter bellowed.

He sounded more terminally upset than angry. As he had a right to be. Along with his Mega-Retroland™ experience, his world had been turned upside down even more than hers.

She slumped into Mercury's chair. Where to start? More importantly, where would she end? She was still thinking it out when they both heard the distinctive roar of a Porsche boxer engine and ran to the window to see the replacement Boxster swing into the car park.

Mercury, wildly dishevelled, jumped out, took a hard look at Juno's stove-in BMW, and ran for the entrance.

'Mindlock the drawer, J,' she instructed, grabbing the bible and the black file.

'Aren't you going to put them back?' he asked wonderingly.

'Just do it. Fast.'

She pulled him out of sight as they heard the god of communications pounding up the corridor, let a short pause elapse, then stood up and presented herself.

As she had calculated, Mercury was staring unbelievingly into his empty confidential drawer.

'Lost something?' she enquired bitterly, holding up the bible and black file in plain view.

At which the god of communications — and she had never seen this before, even with a goddess — fainted dead away.

She and Jupiter were hauling him into his chair, trying to remember what earthlings did in these circumstances, when they both stopped and stood staring at each other.

A faint scuffle had come from behind the row of screens.

Jupiter gave her a silent nod, transferred Mercury's dead weight to her arms and crept stealthily across to cut off any retreat.

'Come on out,' he boomed. 'Or I'll come in to get you.'

There was a short silence before a small head poked round the corner.

'Don't worry, Jupiter,' came a nervous squeak. 'It's only me.'

Cupid! Juno breathed. So this was where he had come to hide out!

That being the case, there was no point in delaying any further.

She would conduct the long overdue inquest here and now.

PART 3

Chapter 26

Solsticed

Juno lay back in her chair, exhausted. She had to admit Mercury's reaction had been noble. Godly, even. Which she had not been expecting and at first had made her suspicious. Now she could see that had been all to the good. Coming from an angle of total disbelief had not only helped her interrogate him mercilessly, but softened her sickening realisation of the position they had allowed themselves to get into.

It had taken most of the night, with fuel provided by the ghost services in the form of copious pizzas, espressos and, towards the end, unwinding Scotch for J and Armagnac for her, to get as far as she could in drawing the various strings together and see where they were. Which, as J had several times pithily interrupted, was up shit creek, *sans* paddle.

She had held court in the wide soaring space of the

atrium, bringing in first Cupid, then Mercury, then both together, sending them backwards and forwards as she compared their stories and bounced their differ-ent versions off each other.

All the time, at her request, J had sat beside her, absorbing what each had to say before helping her iron out the inconsistencies behind their backs. As well as tipping in his own contribution about Mega-Retroland™.

Yet, if Juno was to be totally honest, her exhaustive enquiries had raised more questions than they had answered. Not that she was going to say that to either of the main protagonists. Better, at this stage, to be as positive as she could to try to dispel the sense of panic she could already feel gathering.

She yawned and rubbed her eyes with the back of her hands, only to snatch them away as the face of the Beast loomed up. The darkest hour, she des-perately tried to console herself, is now, just before dawn.

They had no choice, she had decided, but to believe Cupid's story that their immortalities were about to end. How to cope with that, though? How to get yourself in a position where you actually took it on board, knew it beyond a shadow of doubt? With enormous difficulty, she was already realising. It was simply too much to take in.

J felt the same. And, like her, was immediately looking for a way round it.

Which led them back to where they had started.

Like it or not, being in Mercury's hands.

'We'd better call them both in again.'

'There's no choice,' Jupiter agreed.

'No recriminations,' she warned.

'I'll try my best.'

'Tell me again, why did you lie to us before?'

Juno had started on Mercury by referring back to the scene in Venus's kitchen.

'I've told you a hundred times now, I didn't plan to steal the bible.' Mercury looked haggard, as well as despairing. 'But when I found it in Cupid's motorcycling gear, I saw an opportunity to discredit his story.

'I didn't know about the Aura at that stage, remember? So when he told me he'd found the Beast, all I could think was I must keep the lid on this, stop him blabbing to anyone else. The whole point of sending him to Seekers™ was to preoccupy him with an impossible challenge. How was I to know GOD, or the Aura, or whatever, would allow him to enter?

'Then of course the little fool had to wreck everything by getting into my files and allowing the Beast to crash the system.'

Seeing Cupid's mouth open in protest, Juno silenced him with her eyes.

'If Cupid's the wrecker,' she addressed Mercury coldly, 'where does that leave you?'

'As I've told you, trying to save everything.' Mercury seemed genuinely surprised she was asking yet again. 'You must be able to see by now. I was in there, building a dialogue — or trying to — when he' — Mercury glared accusingly at the little figure sitting next to him — 'blundered in and blew everything.

'It's like I said — no system, no access. No access, no dialogue. No dialogue, no communication. No communication, no progress. Which is where we are now.'

'You've admitted to finding the Beast long before

Cupid,' Juno continued remorselessly. 'Before the meeting even. So why hadn't you told anyone? And why speak so passionately in favour of Retroland™?'

'Because I was weak.' All Mercury's arrogance had disappeared. 'Because it was easier. I had to believe it couldn't be true, you must understand.' He was back to pleading for sympathy. 'Techno's what I do. Where all my faith lies. Where would you be,' he appealed to Jupiter, 'if you had to face up to fortune being a sham? That all the time you'd put your faith in it you were being led up the garden path? Used against yourself?

'Could you personally cope? Or, like me, would you fight against it? Try to do something?'

Jupiter stared at him as if he was a worm.

'Anyhow, I'd only hit the Beast at that stage,' Mercury gabbled desperately. 'I still wasn't sure. You know how knackered System 7.0 is. Glitches, viruses, crossovers. There'd been all kinds of other things I couldn't explain . . .'

It was the justification he had put forward earlier. Yet this time, even as he spoke, he was aware he was lying to himself. He had known from the first moment he saw those eyes, heard that demonic laugh, felt that chill . . .

Juno saw him jerk, as if something vital, something inside that made him run, had snapped.

'OK, that's not true,' he finally confessed, plunging his head into his hands. 'I did know.'

'Know what, exactly?' Juno's voice cracked like a whip.

She had finally got what she was looking for. Exhausted though they all were, now she must pile on the pressure.

Mercury raised his head and looked at her with pleading eyes.

'That Retroland™ wasn't going to bring the benefits I talked about at the meeting. That techno wasn't the answer. Never had been. That there's never been a time in earthling history when it hasn't been used for the worst and most terrible purposes. And nothing about that has changed.

'Because, of course, I then found the L files.'

'Which are?' Juno demanded.

'In computer speak, as I told you, aliases — shadow files, ghost files, always previously hidden from us. Our opposite, giving everything a reverse, negative, pattern. As if there were two directories in there, one creating a whole different world, where darkness rules.'

'So why not tell anyone at that point?'

'I just didn't want to know,' Mercury confessed, looking down at the floor.

The don't-want-to-know box, Juno thought with some sympathy, although she made sure not to show it.

All theirs were now being opened.

'I still had hope, you see,' Mercury went on. 'That was, until I found the 666 e-mail. Only then did I realise it was too late. That we were running on empty. Had no resources left.

'Even now, though, I think it could be a bluff.' A note of desperate optimism crept into his voice. 'That really we're just to be archived, rather than deleted. Nobody on Planet Earth deletes files today. They strip them out, then put them in limbo.'

'Isn't that the same as deleting?' Jupiter interrupted.

'No,' Mercury replied, looking wildly hopeful. 'Archive files can always be brought back.'

'How many are?'

'I can't recall any.' Mercury plunged his head back into his hands.

Juno let the pause drag on, waiting for him to start speaking again.

'I wanted to believe — had to believe,' he continued brokenly, 'that Planet Earth's Information Age would bring a brighter future. Hope against hope this time things would be different.' He was pleading again. 'Yet, with hindsight, I know I'd realised it was back to war.

'Not Mars's sort of war. That often has something noble, something necessary about it. Much worse.' He raised haggard eyes. 'A war against the spirit. Because that's the object of the exercise — by deleting us to simultaneously delete the earthling spirit, making everything controllable by computer.'

'You saying GOD's gone mad?' Jupiter interrupted again.

'Not mad.'

Mercury scratched the wing on his left heel. Having made his confession, he was feeling better, as if a huge weight had been lifted off his mind, a dark cloud blown away.

'No computer can go mad,' he explained further, 'not even one as big as GOD. Virus, blown circuit, corrupted hard disk, burnt-out chip, misconnection, crash — all possible. But madness is strictly for earthlings — and us.

'No, the Beast has been able to take control because our decision at the meeting left a vacuum. Furthermore, it's right. Once the higher reaches of the human spirit have been taken out of the system, computer-think will overtake earthling-think, meaning the earthlings end up in an entirely computer world.'

'Reprogrammed as animals,' Juno summarised.

'Not animals,' Mercury replied, sounding agitated she had missed his point. 'Computers. Running on plain basic DOS, like everything else on Planet Earth.'

'That's not GOD's plan, surely?' Jupiter insisted angrily. What was the matter that he was so spineless? 'It's the Beast's.'

'And where is the Beast?' Mercury countered, some of his authority returning.

'Inside GOD,' Jupiter replied reluctantly.

'And where are we?'

Jupiter looked appealingly at Juno. There was no way round it. Mercury was correct.

With the system down, it was they, rather than the Beast, who were now outsiders.

'What do you say, Cupid?' Juno asked gently.

'I just don't know,' he replied tearfully. More and more he was somehow feeling it was his fault for bringing such bad news. 'I didn't start any of this.'

'We understand,' Juno replied comfortingly. 'Don't worry, we're not here to shoot the messenger.'

As he looked at her imploringly, she got up, stretched and walked across to the atrium's glass frontage. Dawn was breaking bleakly, a muddy bar of light submerged beneath dark, glowering clouds.

'You know what this night ushered in?' she asked over her shoulder.

'No I bloody well don't,' Jupiter harrumphed. With the shuffling time sequences of Mega-Retroland™, unsent e-mails, and all the past events they had just been through, he had become terminally disorientated.

'The solstice.'

Juno turned to see him staring at her incredulously. He must have really lost his bearings to forget something as important as that. They all must. The solstice, that cusp revered by earthlings since the beginning of mortal time! The magic night when darkness stopped closing in. When there was a lifting of the spirit, in the Land of the Gods as much as on Planet Earth. An occasion for feasting, celebrating a cycle reversed, better times to come.

'Some new dawn, eh?' he commented witheringly.

'In a way it is, J,' Juno replied firmly. 'It's better to know than not know. Which is the bonus we've now been handed.'

'Bonus! You must be joking!' he snorted.

With a struggle, he overcame his negativity to reverse the remark.

'I suppose you're right, Juno,' he agreed reluctantly. 'It is better to know. But we're still finished, aren't we?'

'Unless we do something.'

'Such as?'

'Run.' She laughed weakly.

'There's nowhere to run,' Jupiter roared angrily. This wasn't funny!

'Except oblivion,' Juno agreed.

'Which is running towards us.'

'According to Cupid.'

'So are you disputing it?'

'No,' she admitted, sobering up.

They stared at each other in silence, both knowing it fitted, all the way along the line.

Until now neither of them had fully appreciated that hackneyed earthling phrase 'a race against time', although all of them, even little Cupid, had been involved in enough when out on their Earth tickets.

It gave you a crawling feeling inside your stomach.

A feeling of being dictated to, rather than dictating. *Tempus fugit*, Saturn had said at the meeting. And *fugit*ing it suddenly seemed to be. They could almost feel the hands of the clocks flying round, the digits in the Earth control room flicking through in fast forward.

Juno counted on her fingers.

'Ten more days. Then what happens, J? Do our immortalities end, not with a bang, but a whimper?'

Chapter 27

Headless Turkeyland

'It's our solemn duty to tell everyone everything we know,' Jupiter insisted again. 'As the Highest of the High Order, I am hereby making that a command binding on you all.'

They had still got no further than agreeing they had to make the decision before they left the Factory.

'You think they'd believe it, coming from you?' Juno shot back.

'Why not?' Jupiter roared. 'It's not just me. We've got the proof – Cupid's Gabriel bible, the Beast printout, the hard copy of the 666 e-mail, the tablet.'

'If it's still there,' Juno interrupted.

'Even if it isn't, how can they possibly ignore the rest?' Jupiter thundered.

'Easily,' she replied, just as aggressively. 'What are you going to do? Call another meeting and wave them about? Everyone knows from the last time what you think. They'll just dismiss them as forgeries.

'Don't forget, you'll be dealing with the Lower Orders. They'll be thinking the clever buggers from up the Close are out to put one over on them. Spoil their fun.'

'What would be the sense in doing that?' Jupiter asked wonderingly.

'We're not talking sense, J,' she replied, irritated at him for being so slow. 'We're talking perception. Presentation. Marketing. What the earthlings do these days.' How could he remain so naive? 'Never heard of selling the sizzle, rather than the sausage?

'There's another thing too,' she added cruelly. 'They all know where you were at the time — in Mega-Retroland™, being Hitler.'

She didn't want to have to wound him unnecessarily. But this was no time to pull punches. And if the truth hurt . . .

Jupiter glared at her. Mega-Retroland™ had not only thrown his immortality upside down, but left a taste in his mouth. A sour one, maybe, but one he now wanted more of.

At any cost.

'OK, Juno,' he shouted, getting up to stalk angrily round the vast space. 'I may have been opposed to Virtual Immortality once. Maybe even ranted on, as you'd put it, about the perils it posed. But that's in the past.

'To be perfectly honest, I'm not at all sure about this stuff I've been hearing. The way you three have put it together so conveniently.' He stared suspiciously at Mercury and Cupid. 'It's all very clever, I agree. Which just makes it all the more important the others are given a chance to see what they make of it.

'Then we might get a very different answer, mightn't we? Because what you seem to have forgotten is that we immortalise in a world of constant change. And, as gods, it behoves us to change with it.'

Juno narrowed her green eyes and threw the final knife.

'Go ahead and tell them then. Before you call your star witness, Cupid.

'Nothing personal,' she added gently to the silent figure at her side.

Jupiter shot her a filthy look.

They waited whilst he continued to march about, lips pursed.

'What if Mercury took the lead instead of me?' he finally turned to ask.

'That could make a difference,' Juno admitted. 'But it would still come down to Cupid in the end.'

Which was where she now had a horrible suspicion Dennis fitted in. Despite herself, she was being drawn more and more towards conspiracy theories. In general, goddesses considered themselves more open than gods to suggestions that other forces were at work beside themselves. But dragons were just storybook stuff, whilst Cupid was already notorious for his fertile imagination.

Meanwhile, everyone knew it was impossible to get through the force field round GOD. Try telling them a dragon had been the vehicle — especially one called Dennis — and they'd laugh their socks off.

On top of that, have Cupid further explain that Dennis had been magicked up by a ghost operative in a pointed hat . . . Juno winced, mentally hearing the guffaws from the Valhalla Villas contingent. That would be the last straw which broke the dragon's back, she thought grimly.

Unless Cupid actually managed to produce Dennis, of course. But there was still the Aura. And he, she, it certainly wasn't going to be summoned up willy-nilly.

'I'm sorry. I won't do it,' Mercury unexpectedly burst out, avoiding Jupiter's glare by keeping his eyes firmly fixed on the floor between his feet. 'I agree — really they ought to know. Especially as I've been the one responsible for keeping them in the dark, when I should have been more open.

'Yet the same thing still applies as before, even more so. Now I know exactly what Cupid did, if we can keep this tightly enough under our control, I might be able to do something.'

Jupiter halted, his nostrils flaring like those of a huge bear that had caught a scent. Lumbering angrily across, he seized Mercury by his gelled blond hair and pulled his head back, forcing him to look into his eyes.

'Like you have up to now, I suppose, you useless cunt?' he roared. 'Well I for one have had enough of you and your fucking techno, techno, techno.'

Mercury flinched backwards in wild-eyed terror. Then, as Jupiter released his head with a contemptuous shove, reverted to staring sullenly at the floor.

'That's enough, J,' Juno ordered sharply.

'Anyhow,' she addressed him briskly, 'even if you showed them the documentary evidence it'd get you nowhere, simply because it's exactly what they don't want to hear. If GOD sent them the 666 e-mail direct right now they'd still find a way to avoid facing up to it.'

As Jupiter sat back down, seeming to be preparing to intervene, she hurriedly switched tack.

'Your alternative?' she continued firmly. 'That we persuade them to believe us, Cupid, Dennis and all? That could end up the real worst-case scenario.' She glared at her consort angrily. 'Can't you see? GOD's — or the Beast's — 666 e-mail is correct. They'd all panic. We'd be straight into Headless Chickenland — or Headless Turkeyland, considering the time of year.'

Nobody even smiled at the weak joke.

'What were we going to do about it? they'd demand to know,' she continued vehemently. 'What would we tell them? We were waiting for a dragon, who we can't prove in any way even exists, to reappear and take Cupid for another audience with an Aura we can't prove in any way exists either?

'Cupid, of all gods! They'd have our guts for garters.

'Nothing personal,' she added gently in another aside.

Cupid stared at her miserably.

'I've had enough of all your negative "What we don't do" bollocks,' Jupiter roared. 'You tell me what we do do, then.'

'Go back, take the temperature,' she rapped out. 'Leak it selectively to other High Order members we agree we trust. Play the rest by ear.'

'I won't have it!'

Jupiter sprang back to his feet and paced up and down. He was being outmanoeuvred, marginalised, cut out of the decision-making process. Something fundamental seemed to have happened whilst he was in Mega-Retroland™. As though his personal time clock had stopped, whilst everyone else's had moved on. Yet more than that. Something had happened to Juno, too. As if she had become re-empowered. Or he had become

more disempowered. Yet he had been so ultra-powerful
in Mega-Retroland™.

It was all so terminally disorientating.

'I don't care what you say,' he thundered, running his hands wildly through his hair. 'I absolutely
command that we give everyone the right to help
themselves. Especially now, with every second counting. Otherwise it's not fair.'

He saw Cupid stare at him accusingly and his mind
flicked back to the meeting.

What had he just said?

'It's just as much your fault, you little prick,' he
turned on him savagely. 'If you hadn't gone messing
about in the first place, none of this might have
happened.'

Juno saw the shock register on the adolescent face
like a physical blow.

'How dare you?' she cried, springing to her feet.
'Cupid's only a boy and he's been doing his absolute
best. If it's his fault now, it's just as much yours.'

'And how dare you!' he shouted, incandescent, stomp-
ing over and putting his face up to hers. 'Didn't I tell
them?' he breathed stentoriously. 'Didn't I?'

'You did, J,' she glared back icily, not giving an inch.
'But you said it yourself — "things have changed." And
we must change with them. Which means not telling
them now.'

He gave her a look of pure hatred, as if she was
his personal enemy, then glanced at Mercury, still head
down so as to avoid his gaze. For a nanosecond, Juno
thought he was going to explode, he had gone so red
in the face.

'As for you, you fucking techie, as you call yourself,'
he began addressing the blond mane.

Then all of a sudden, he appeared to run out of steam.

'All right,' he conceded to Juno instead with ill grace. 'You win for the moment. I agree. We'll keep it to ourselves.

'I'm warning you all, though,' he said, turning threateningly towards Mercury and the quivering Cupid, 'that, as the Highest of the High Order, I reserve the right to change that decision at any point in the future.

'Furthermore, without consulting any of you, ever again.'

Chapter 28

Gone Bananas

Jupiter and Juno sat stiffly beside each other as they motored back to Arcadia Close in the BMW, Mercury following in the Porsche with Cupid. Although no one in either vehicle said anything, Juno couldn't help thinking how suspiciously quiet both the expressway and the ghettos below appeared, even when she switched to EG-mode. But then, she recognised, she was now suspicious about everything.

Not without reason, she thought bitterly as they peeled off at Junction 14 and she saw the blinding white light.

She floored the throttle and hammered the BMW mercilessly over the speed bumps.

'Through all the changing scenes of life,' the broadcasting system blared the 'me' out triumphantly,

'In trouble and in joy,

'The praises of my GOD shall still,
'My heart and tongue employ.'

Juno handbraked the BMW on the gravel and ran excitedly to her computer room.

GOD must have reactivated their terminals! Maybe the vile Beast was on the run!

She stopped in her tracks as she saw the screen was still dead.

Instead a hard copy lay on the desk, where the printer had spat it out.

She picked it up.

```
mail to: all Gods/Goddesses

05.31.00/22.12.1999

From: GLOBAL ONLINE DIVINITY

PLEASE NOTE: Henceforth I shall only be
transmitting, not receiving. I know you
wouldn't want it any other way. I mean, what
else is there left to discuss?


Technology situation report 493771/668

Wakey wakey, you lucky goddies! It's
treats time!

You know I told you I'd bring in Mega-
Retroland™, the big, big bonus you voted
for your immortalities, at 00.00.01/
01.01.2000, when System Megaverse 2000
kicked in on Planet Earth?

Then I thought, my favourite gods and
goddesses are so radical. So cool. So very
'90s! More than '90s – so very millennial!
So why keep them waiting any longer? It's
```

time to get real – or rather unreal!! – by
giving them their big, big pressy here and
now, on the solstice. Let's face it, it
might be Christmas soon on Planet Earth, but
that's never meant much to you, has it!

Do yourself a favour, friend, and look out
the window.

See it? Your own, personal Mega-Retroland™
capsule, all set up and raring to make you
whoever you wannabe, 24 hours a day, seven
days a week!

Of course I shall be closing Mega-Retroland™
down at 22.00 ET on 31.12 in order that you
can all revitalise yourselves at the Energy
Pool, ready for the introduction of System
Megaverse 2000. Far be it from me to deny you
that right and privilege!

Until then, though, why not get in there and
shake that Mega-Retroland™ down! You'll
hardly be missing much in real immortality,
will you?

You've got the brave new world of Mega-
Retroland™, goddies!

Go into it!

.sig

PS As you will know, there has already
been an unfortunate vandalisation of the
prototype Mega-Retroland™ capsule. Just to
inform you that the latest model has been
rendered so totally vandalproof DON'T EVEN
TRY TO THINK ABOUT IT, RIGHT?

E-mail ends

Jupiter staggered out of his computer room, dazedly clutching his head.

'Now what's happening?'

'All I know is that I don't like the look of it,' Juno replied, running outside.

Behind the hedge, two massive roofs stood outlined against the grey sky.

'We've got to stop the others before it's too late, J!'

'I suppose so,' he replied, sounding so strangely distracted she examined him closely.

He was staring fixedly at the capsule.

'Everything all right?' she inquired anxiously.

'Perfect, Juno.' He smiled at her beatifically. 'Absolutely perfect.'

She beamed back at him reassuringly. How magnanimous not to bear a grudge about their recent falling out! She knew how touchy male pride could be.

'Let's go round and see what we can do,' he proposed.

But, as they already knew, they were too late.

A glance down the side of the villas was enough to reveal the row of red lights and glowing DO NOT DISTURB: GOD AT PLAY signs. They still trailed dutifully from house to house, banging on the doors to make doubly sure. It was the same at every one — Mars, Bacchus, Neptune, Saturn, Apollo, Terminus, Sylvanus, Janus, Flora, Vesta. All sucked away, locked in, gone.

The only exception was Minerva, whose red capsule light was not illuminated. Yet they could find no trace of her elsewhere.

A tour of the deserted Lower Orders' estate in the BMW revealed an equally grim picture, with even Valhalla Villas quiet as the grave.

Juno shivered. That simile had never spun into her head before.

They ended up, naturally, at Venus's.

'It all happened in a mad rush,' the goddess of love filled them in. 'It was still dark when the "me" lit the place up. We all tumbled out of bed and ran to our terminals. Mars came running out the front and suddenly everyone was there, fantastically excited.

'I could feel the pull myself. Some irresistible force, seeming to take over my mind and directing me towards my capsule.

'I summoned up all my strength and managed to fight it off. Had to, didn't I, with Cupid still missing?' She smiled lovingly at her son. 'If he hadn't been, I don't mind admitting, I'd be in there as well.'

'That strong?' Juno asked wonderingly, her awareness of the Beast's power going up another notch.

'That strong,' Venus confirmed. 'You can't blame the others for submitting. It's still there too. Though not as strong as it was.'

'Maybe Minerva escaped, though.' Juno explained how they had been unable to locate the goddess of wisdom. 'At least now we don't have to disagree about letting the rest of them into the secret,' she added to J.

She was already regretting their spat. That unprecedented fury between them, all for nothing!

'What secret?' Venus demanded, clutching Cupid almost as if for protection.

It took some time, with many questions, to bring her up to date, Cupid nodding in assent as Juno made the various points.

'You're not making any of this up, are you?' she

addressed her son uncertainly when Juno had finished, suddenly in awe at the position he appeared to have been handed.

'No, Mother,' he assured her with such gravity she felt impelled to look at Jupiter, sitting unusually silent.

Why did it feel as though a mantle was being passed from the greatest god to her son?

'Maybe we should see if we can find this dragon,' she suggested, trying to clutch onto something concrete.

Or rather not concrete, surely, she thought, remembering always rubbishing their existence to Cupid in the past. Yet, with his new-found stature, she already knew she would be prepared to concede to him. Bow to him, even. Recognise, perhaps for the first time, he was an adult god, empowered in his own right.

The three of them were going out of the door together, Venus's hand proudly on her son's shoulder, when Juno noticed Jupiter remained seated.

'Not coming, J?'

'I think I'll stay here,' he answered gruffly, avoiding looking at her directly. 'Do me good to be alone for a bit. A few things I need to sort out in my head.'

'I bet,' she smiled sympathetically. She had been extremely hard on him. Since being cut out of Mega-Retroland™ he had hardly had a moment to himself. 'You rest, my dear. We won't be long.'

They ducked and weaved through the tangled forest at the bottom of the garden before emerging in the clearing, where Juno marvelled at the secrecy of the hideaway. There was absolutely no way of telling from the outside that it was there. Even more impressive were the small incinerated bush and telltale scorch marks in the grass. It was a shame there were no confirmatory footprints, but it still all pointed to Cupid telling the truth.

As for Venus, she just looked gobsmacked.

Yet it still didn't make sense to Juno. GOD, or the Aura, could presumably do anything they wanted. So why hadn't they matter-transferred Cupid across, for example, just as all gods were empowered — or had been — to matter-transfer to Planet Earth?

The eyes of a child, she then had a sudden intuition. Was the dragon something only Cupid could see, and therefore use? The living embodiment of a dream?

Remembering her own dream, she shuddered, staring unseeingly at Cupid as she was overtaken by her thoughts.

'I'll try,' he announced, misinterpreting her gaze and seeking to pre-empt her.

He composed himself by smoothing his hair and taking a series of deep breaths, then concentrated on not thinking about bananas. Having visualised a large bunch, he was about to move on to not thinking about Dennis when his concentration was broken by a piercing scream from his mother.

He opened his eyes, only to see an enormous hand of ripe bananas on the ground in front of him. As his mother stared, hand to mouth, he reached out tentatively and touched one.

It felt as real as Dennis.

He pulled it off, unpeeled it, and took a bite.

And tasted as real.

'Nothing to worry about!' he assured desperately, seeing Venus and Juno backing away. 'Just warming up!'

He gave a forced little laugh and shut his eyes again, trying to bypass bananas by going straight to Dennis.

Yet each time he opened his eyes, it was only to see another hand, until he was entirely surrounded by them.

'Something's gone a bit wrong,' he called out, mortified.

Was this a device thought up by the Beast and the L files to undermine his credibility? Make a mockery of him? A dragon was one thing. But how to explain the bananas, and consequently the banana trick, without setting himself up as a laughing stock, even with his own mother?

It was just too juvenile.

For the first time Cupid felt his faith wobble, until he had a sudden ray of hope. Maybe there was a message in the hands! Did they spell something out? Make a meaningful pattern?

He ran round and round them despairingly, meanwhile noticing Venus and Juno staring at him even more oddly.

Nothing he could determine.

'Would you mind giving me a bit of space so I can try on my own?' he appealed. 'Why don't I see you back in the house a bit later on? I'll explain everything then.'

They stared at him mutely, then nodded and set off back into the tangle of undergrowth.

'Don't worry, I haven't gone bananas!' he called after them, thinking he was doing pretty well to manage a joke in the circumstances. Even if it wasn't exactly his best ever.

But there was no reply.

'I'm back, J!'

Time to make up, she had decided as she stepped into the living room. Mend fences, as she had once put it.

'J!'

She went through the various rooms, calling out.

'Maybe he went home,' she said, shrugging at Venus as she returned to the kitchen. 'Anyhow, I must get back myself.'

If only to allay the dreadful certainty now in her mind.

Yet even as she ran round the side of the house, she knew.

There was the red light and, after she had gone through the gap in the hedge, the eerie DO NOT DISTURB: GOD AT PLAY sign, glowering menacingly.

Mind numb, she tried the capsule door.

Mindlocked.

'You weak bastard,' she cried, pounding the gleaming surface with her fists. 'Why didn't you ask me to help you?'

Why hadn't she put it together before? The distracted behaviour, the uncharacteristic silences? She knew full well why. Because she hadn't for a moment thought him capable of deceiving her. Playing a part, lulling her into the security of thinking that nothing was wrong. Her consort, who she had always trusted so implicitly. Whose all-embracing, shining honesty, whatever his other faults, she had never had cause to doubt.

Lying to her.

There was no other word for it.

Should she blame herself for not staying by him? Doing her utmost to save him from himself? And why was she feeling none of the pull towards Mega-Retroland™ herself? Almost if she had been granted some sort of immunity. For, rather than drawing her in, a force was actually repulsing her.

Another Beast tactic to prise her and her consort apart? she thought wildly. Split their forces? Practise divide and rule?

'Doom! Doom! You're all doomed!' she mouthed silently to herself, staring at her distorted image in the curve of shining metal.

Then, behind her reflection, she saw it.

The vile, distorted face of the Beast.

Gloating.

Chapter 29

All I Want for Christmas

The only occasion GOD broadcast a 'me' without sending an e-mail was Christmas. And then not just one, but dozens of the bloody things. Of course the gods moaned as a matter of course at this time-honoured ritual. Yet at the same time they secretly welcomed the massive feast, never mind piss-up, it presaged.

Not this year, though.

'Silent night, holy night,' GOD's broadcasting system consoled Arcadia Close.

'All is calm . . .'

Too bloody calm, Juno thought grimly as she sat alone in the kitchen.

If only something would happen.

During the last four days, as GOD's 668 e-mail had correctly forecast, on the surface there had been nothing. Arcadia Close and the estates had remained eerily quiet by day, equally eerily glowing with red Mega-Retroland™ lights by night.

Each of them had tried their best in their individual ways to break the deadlock. She had sent J endless messages and even contemplated going into her own capsule to try to track him through the mists of earthling time. Was he being Hitler again? The temptation must have been very strong. So could she access him by being his mistress, Eva Braun?

Yet, even as she speculated, Juno only realised how desperate she must be getting. It would be like looking for a needle in a haystack, while she would certainly run a high risk of addicting herself in turn. Better, and more productive, to stay out, as the force pushing her away seemed anyway to be dictating.

But was it better?

Mercury had clattered away endlessly on his laptop, dashed backwards and forwards from home terminal to Factory, even tried to get into Ayers Rock. Yet he had ended up defeated on all fronts — thrown out by the guardian angels, blocked by the force field, but primarily nullified by the all-embracing deadness of the system, which refused to even flicker, never mind boot up, despite his armoury of clever tricks of the nerd trade.

Meanwhile, with Venus's support, Cupid had carried on visualising at the summerhouse, only to produce more and more hands of bananas until, dispirited, he had temporarily given up.

They all had, Juno thought, feeling the lethargy overtaking her. How infinitely desirable their old immortality, even in stultified Arcadia Close, seemed now they were fighting, helplessly, for this new concept of their lives. Helplessly, and hopelessly, she had accepted. Never having had to even think about such a thing during their entire immortalities, they simply weren't equipped.

It must be like this all the time for the earthlings, she had kept thinking, according them new respect as she began to appreciate the crushing burden they must carry every moment.

For her, and Venus, it had just introduced this numbness. Not so much of despair. More, resignation.

'Oh come all ye faithful,

'Joyful and triumphant . . .'

Faithful. Joyful. Triumphant. What hollow, meaningless words they now sounded!

This must be the L files for you, making you see everything from a negative angle — suspicious, resentful, cynical. Paranoid even, thinking everything was out to get you.

Which was correct.

It already had.

Juno walked over to the ambrosia dispenser, thinking of J as she punched PIEDMONT CHERRY, only for OVERRIDE ACTIVATED to flash up on the LCD display and GOD's Christmas special brew to start slurping into the cup.

Normally this signalled the start of the festivities by giving them extra zing, whilst also filling them with overwhelming goodwill, not just to each other, but all earthlingkind. Which, she sensed, was what was to happen to them all in a mega, and more permanent, way when they went to access the Energy Pool.

Not that that would make any difference any more, as the Beast's unsent 666 e-mail so cruelly pointed out.

She could feel no zing this year, she thought,

sipping sourly whilst she contemplated the ghost
delivery menu. She had decided to spend Christmas
on her own, shut away with her sadness. Self-pity
it might be. Wallowing in it, even. Yet not without reason.

Venus, she knew, felt much the same.

Only Mercury might keep on working feverishly
away. Yet Juno saw him as a spent force. Something
inside him had snapped for ever — not that there was
any point in allocating particular, or personal, blame.
They had all been upstaged, outmanoeuvred, made
unwitting allies of the Beast which had so cleverly
undermined them.

What else was there left to do, except accept their
fate?

'"Welcome, goddies, to this very special Christmas
and our equally special FAB FESTIVE FAYRE!"' she
read aimlessly. '"To mark the end of this millennium
we've a special THOUSAND YEARS' DRESSING for
our seasonal starters, along with our famous rich dark
CHRISTMAS PUD-U-LIKE at the end!

'"But, more than anything, we know you're looking
forward to GOBBLING UP that oh-so-special bird
we're providing JUST FOR YOU!

'"Yes, you lucky goddies, it's TURKEY TIME!
Turkey, the neat treat you can't wait to eat, brought
to you on three-toed feet!

'"For, we can assure you, YOUR PERSONAL BIRD is
going to be particularly, positively plump! terrifically, tremendously tender! terribly, tongue-tinglingly tasty! MIL-
LENNIALLY, MIND-BOGGLINGLY MUNCHABLE!

'"That's not all either, folks! SIMPLY SALIVATE
as we spell out this season's scrumptious SUPER-
STUFFING!

'"For here's the really exciting news! Down on our organic range, where the turkeys do roam, our clutch of certified virgins has been gathering not just chestnuts, but, peeping shyly out, as pure as driven snow . . ."

'Standard TV dinner for one,' Juno ordered into the tube.

'Once in Royal David's City
'Stood a lonely cattle shed . . .'

And a lonely Tuscan villa.

Yet, now she was bereft of J, she might as well join all Planet Earth's lonely people. The bad cases. The sad cases. The mad cases. The basket cases, even. And be jealous of all of them. Even the most hopeless down-and-out living on the street or in Cardboard City had a better chance of seeing in the new millennium than any of them.

She zapped on GODS TV.

'Now folks, it's time to put on your thinking caps for our Mega-Millennium Milestone quiz!

'Yes, ladies 'n' gennulmen, our lucky winner tonight will shortly drive into the twenty-first century at the wheel of this super family Millennial Special, complete with all those extras essential for the Information Age!'

Juno stared lacklustredly as synthetic Oohs! and Aaahs! burst from the studio audience.

'Think how their neighbours will envy them as they speed in luxury and comfort into the future, *whilst accessing the Internet at the very same time*!' the game show host screamed to enraptured applause.

'And, to set our contestants on their way, the answer to the first question is "Bethlehem"!

'So, fingers on the button for the next question,

which is for the plucky Yeoman family from way down west in rural Dorset!

'Now, m'dears, time to let those sheep alone, take off your wellies . . .'

Juno got up and walked over to the French windows.

Outside, grey clouds scudded low over the glowing red capsule light. Who was her consort being in there? The corners of her mouth turned down. Father Christmas, she shouldn't wonder.

She raised her half-drunk GOD special brew.

'Happy Virtual Christmas', she pronounced, downing it one go.

Then she drew the curtains on both him and the rest of the day.

'Yes, Brian, that is absolutely correct! The answer is — "Baby Jesus"!'

Only 158 hours and 31 minutes to go, the reverse clock in the corner of the screen was informing her, ticking backwards by the minute.

At Venus's no cards graced the mantelpiece. No presents stood round the tree GOD had installed, as if to taunt them further. No lights, no candles, no crackers, no silly hats. Not even any sense of being together, Venus realised. No bond, even with Cupid, her own son. Just this sense of them each trapped in their individual limbos, hurtling side by side towards identical dooms, powerless to help or even comfort each other.

'I'm very sorry, Sharon, but the correct answer is that there were *three* wise men,' GODS TV was droning, when an excited voice broke in. 'We interrupt this programme to take you back to the studio for a newsflash.'

Trumpeting music heralded an earthling in a suit appearing at a huge, hi-tech desk. Vast glowing globes rotated meaninglessly behind him.

'As the millennium deadline draws ever closer,' he announced breathlessly, 'yet more armed police and members of the security forces are being deployed in cities throughout the Western world to try to contain the worst outbreaks of rioting so far.

'In this exclusive special report, we now take you live to the Millennium Dome in London's Greenwich.'

A live-broadcast reporter clad in a designer flak jacket sprang onto the screen.

'Far from exhibiting the traditional Christmas spirit of goodwill,' he shouted from behind a barricade of riot shields, petrol bombs exploding round them, 'it appears millennial madness has already gripped the Western world.

'Here at the Millennium Dome, the security forces have resorted to rubber bullets and water cannon in their increasingly desperate efforts to drive back the thousands of rioters intent on breaking through the cordon and setting fire to the building, which has remained closed since yesterday's hurried evacuation.

'Was Nostradamus right? we must now all be asking ourselves.

'For, with less than a week to go, experts are already predicting this wave of collective panic may herald something apocalyptic on the horizon.

'Meanwhile, following the failure of appeals for calm by the Prime Minister and the Archbishop of Canterbury, a leading New Age spokesman has been called in in a fresh attempt to defuse the situation.

'I have him with me here.

'Tell me, most learned sir, how exactly do these crystals you are carrying work . . .'

Cupid zapped the machine off.

'We've got to do something, Mum.'

'Like what?' she inquired coldly.

'I don't know, mum,' he replied, exasperated. 'Anything. You can't just sit there for ever watching TV!'

'It's not for ever though, is it, Cupid?'

She gazed at him with lacklustre eyes.

'. . . how it will turn out is not yet clear.' She had zapped the machine back on. 'But, as we approach the end of this epoch-making century, the one thing that is for sure is that, one way or another, life on Earth seems destined never to be the same again.

'This is John Jabberson at the Millennium Dome returning you to the studio.'

Cupid stared dully at the screen. Even the earthlings seemed to have sensed something was wrong. But exactly what, and what it meant for their future, he thought grimly, there was one outfit that certainly wasn't going to tell them.

And that was GODS TV.

He zapped it off again, only for Venus to zap it back on.

'Now we cross live to the Pentagon, where an emergency meeting has been called of the Joint Chiefs of Staff following the overnight attack on the White House . . .'

'Why not go and see if you can conjure up your dragon?' Venus sneered.

'I will,' Cupid replied defiantly, making for the door. 'Because one thing I will say for Dennis — at least he doesn't watch GODS TV!'

Outside it was chilly and unwelcoming, yet he still

found himself drawn to the summerhouse. Venus's new downbeat attitude to the dragon, in contrast to her support earlier, had been one of the contributory factors to his giving up his visualisation efforts. Along with the shame and anguish of the seemingly endless mocking hands of bananas.

Now, though, he was feeling determined again.

'Ding dong merrily on high . . .' a fresh GOD 'me' rang out, the blinding white light throwing the bare tangled branches into sharp relief just as Cupid stepped into the clearing.

Only to halt in surprise as he saw M lounging in his chair in the porch, as if he owned the place.

'Happy Christmas,' he called cheerily.

'What's happy about it?' Cupid asked automatically.

'Tut tut,' M remonstrated, rising creakily to his feet. 'It's not that bad. You see, I've come to inform you GOD has a Christmas present for you. And, although I shouldn't really be telling you this' — he winked conspiratorially — 'a very special one.

'Which means, naturally, you'll need to go for a ride.'

Instantly Dennis materialised, tinsel round his neck and clusters of balloons tied to his tail. He rolled onto his back for a tummy rub, bursting most of them, then let out an ear-splitting fart.

'Happy Christmas, Dennis,' Cupid cried, suddenly cheering up.

He walked across and rubbed the dragon's tummy vigorously, to be answered by a roar of pure delight.

M held out his arms in mock surrender.

'Look, no hands!' he announced, grinning mischievously as he waited for the groan from Cupid to signify that he had finally got it.

Then the magician lowered his arms and rubbed his gnarled hands briskly together, producing a sound like fine-grade sandpaper.

'Time to fly,' he instructed.

Chapter 30

Oranges and Lemons

This time Cupid didn't have to bother with the password. Or even, to Dennis's massive disappointment, the angel dust. The angels, sublimely carolling below, made no attempt to interfere with their progress, whilst Cupid knew without being told that the force field was down. As the dragon landed, GOD's door was open, the yellow buggy already waiting outside.

Being motored silently down the central aisle of the immense cathedral, Cupid had a strange feeling of *déjà vu*, as if he had already experienced what was to happen next. Not that he knew what it was, or could do anything about it. Just a feeling of being utterly predestined, no longer master of his own fate.

Which wasn't a feeling any god, even a junior one, welcomed in the slightest.

At the end, he sank without protest into the solitary

chair at the control panel, feeling again how it fitted like a glove.

> PING PONG < he typed, setting off the process he now felt so inevitable.

> WELCOME CUPID. BUT FIRST . . . <

This time it wasn't a cream tea, but Christmas cake.

Which Cupid supposed was fair enough.

> THANKS < he typed with one hand as he sank his teeth into the rich mixture.

> NO STONES, EH? < he added jokily.

There was no response.

Maybe he had been rude in not sending congratulations of some sort?

> HAPPY CHRISTMAS < he added.

> AND WHAT'S HAPPY ABOUT IT? <

Cupid paused in mid-chew. That wasn't for him to say, surely? Anyhow, as far as he personally was concerned, what was happy about knowing you had only six days left?

> NOT A LOT < he replied honestly.

> EXACTLY <

There was a long pause.

For the first time Cupid noticed that the hundreds of wall screens, rather than featuring traditional Christmas rejoicing, were displaying scenes of varying gloominess from Planet Earth — refugees, people starving, domestic violence, the burnt-out shell of a house, a dreadful road accident, a child in awful pain . . .

The Beast at work?

Yet there was no frightening face, no 'Doom! Doom!' chant, above all none of the malevolence that chilled Cupid to the bone. Instead, of all things, he was getting the impression GOD was depressed.

Out of sorts.

Under the weather.

Cupid shook his head to clear it.

GOD?

Depressed?

> IT'S NOT THAT BAD < he typed in hopefully, realising as he did so that he was echoing M.

> WHAT'S GOOD ABOUT IT? <

Cupid sat back in his chair and considered.

As last time, he had now lost all fear and been suffused by a sense of overwhelming peace. Yet, in addition, he now felt in command. After all, he had presumably been summoned here to meet the Aura, rather than GOD. So why bother with the monkey, when he could be talking to the organ-grinder?

The thought jerked him upright. He would never have dared think like that about GOD before! Yet from once seeming so all-powerful, he had somehow been reduced to the level of a tool.

But a tool to be used how?

Not to relate to, that was for sure.

> SUMMON THE AURA < he typed imperiously.

> WHAT'S THE POINT? I CAN'T BE BOTHERED <

Cupid stared at the message on the screen. GOD really was depressed!

> IT'S FOR EVERYONE'S GOOD < he suggested.

> WHO CARES? NONE OF IT MAKES ANY DIFFERENCE ANYWAY <

How did you cheer up a computer? Cupid wondered.

> WE DO LOVE YOU, GOD < he tried.

> YOU DON'T REALLY <

> OF COURSE WE DO <

> HOW DO I KNOW THAT? <

Cupid sat back, chewing his lip. This was low self-esteem of anorak proportions. Did GOD need assert-iveness training? he giggled nervously.

> BECAUSE YOU KNOW EVERYTHING < he typed in supportively.

> HOW CAN YOU BE SURE I DO, WITHOUT KNOWING EVERYTHING YOURSELF? WHICH ONLY GOES TO PROVE YOU KNOW MORE THAN I DO <

Cupid giggled again, even more nervously. Was he into neurosis?

Maybe he should try a joke before GOD moved on to paranoia.

> WHY DID THE HEDGEHOG CROSS THE ROAD? < he typed in, at the same time feeling somehow he might be taking the wrong road.

There was a long pause during which Cupid swore he could hear multiple circuits whirring.

> I TOLD YOU YOU KNOW MORE THAN I DO < the screen eventually flashed up. > I GIVE UP. WHY DID THE HEDGEHOG CROSS THE ROAD? <

> BECAUSE HE WANTED TO MEET HIS FLATMATE < Cupid typed in woodenly. Talk about digging a pit and jumping into it!

> YOU SEE, I TOLD YOU YOU'RE CLEVERER THAN ME <

Cupid looked round despairingly. How to get out of this one?

> I'M SURE YOU KNOW MUCH BETTER JOKES THAN I DO < he typed in. > WHY NOT TELL ME ONE? BETTER STILL, A STORY. YOU MUST HAVE LOADS OF THOSE! <

The suggestion seemed to meet with approval.

> A STORY, EH? LET ME SEE. ONCE UPON A TIME . . . <

> I'D RATHER NOT THAT SORT < Cupid typed in hurriedly.

> FAIR ENOUGH. WISE MAN AND THE MOUNTAIN? <

GOD seemed to have perked up.

> FINE < Cupid replied, although in truth he didn't like wise-men stories. They always seemed so foreign to his own experiences.

But, if it made GOD happy . . .

> I'M ALL EARS! < he added enthusiastically.

> ARE YOU SITTING COMFORTABLY? THEN I'LL BEGIN: ONE DAY THE DISCIPLE DECIDED TO GO AND SEE THE WISE MAN WHO LIVED ON THE TOP OF THE MOUNTAIN.

> FOR FIVE DAYS HE WALKED IN THROUGH THE FOOTHILLS. THEN HE BEGAN THE MAIN ASSAULT, WHICH TOOK HIM ANOTHER FIVE DAYS.

> WHEN HE GOT TO THE TOP HE FOUND A SMALL CAVITY IN THE ROCK. THE WISE MAN WAS SITTING IN IT, CROSS-LEGGED AND WEARING ONLY A LOINCLOTH, DESPITE THE COLD AND A WIND-CHILL FACTOR OF 25. <

The lettering reached the bottom of the screen and began to scroll.

> THE DISCIPLE APPROACHED ON HIS KNEES.

> 'FOR TEN DAYS I HAVE WALKED AND CLIMBED TO COME HERE TO SEE YOU,' HE SAID. 'I HAVE ENDURED GREAT HEAT, GREAT COLD, GREAT HUNGER AND GREAT THIRST.

> 'SO TELL ME, OH GREAT MASTER, WHAT IS THE MEANING OF IT ALL?'

> THE WISE MAN REGARDED HIM GRAVE-
LY.

> 'HAVE YOU BROUGHT ME AN ORANGE?'
HE ASKED

> 'I'M TERRIBLY SORRY,' THE DISCIPLE
APOLOGISED.

> GROVELLING, HE REVERSED BACKWARDS
OUT OF SIGHT, THEN RAN BACK DOWN THE
MOUNTAIN, WHICH TOOK HIM THREE DAYS.

> IN THE VALLEY, HE THEN HAD TO WAIT
FIVE MONTHS WHILST THE ORANGE TREES
FLOWERED AND SET THEIR FRUIT, WHICH
THEN GREW AND FINALLY RIPENED.

> THE DISCIPLE PICKED THE BEST AND
JUICIEST ORANGE AND ONCE MORE WALKED
IN FOR FIVE DAYS. THEN HE BEGAN THE
MAIN ASSAULT, WHICH TOOK HIM ANOTHER
FIVE DAYS.

> AT THE TOP HE APPROACHED THE SMALL
CAVITY IN THE ROCK. THE WISE MAN WAS
STILL SITTING IN IT, CROSS-LEGGED AND
WEARING ONLY A LOINCLOTH, DESPITE THE
COLD AND WIND-CHILL FACTOR, WHICH THIS
TIME WAS 31.

> THE DISCIPLE APPROACHED ON HIS KNEES.

> 'FOR FIVE MONTHS I HAVE WAITED IN
THE VALLEY,' HE SAID. 'THEN, FOR TEN DAYS, I
HAVE WALKED AND CLIMBED TO COME TO SEE
YOU. I HAVE ENDURED GREAT HEAT, GREAT
COLD, GREAT HUNGER AND GREAT THIRST.

> 'YET I HAVE RESISTED ALL TEMPTATION
TO BRING WITH ME, INTACT, THIS ORANGE
AS REQUESTED, WHICH I NOW PRESENT
TO YOU.'

> HE HELD OUT THE PRECIOUS FRUIT.

> THE WISE MAN REGARDED HIM GRAVELY FOR A VERY LONG TIME.

> FINALLY HE SPOKE.

> 'I DON'T LIKE ORANGES,' HE SAID. <

The screen blacked.

Cupid sat dumbfounded. What had that all been about?

Apparently, though, there was to be no explanation. The screen was remaining obstinately blank. Or was it? No! The chill was back. The Beast appearing, not just on his desk screen, but all the ones on the wall. The vile image, multiplied over and over. 'Doom! Doom!' chanted by thousands of grinning mouths, red 'L's glowing in the corners, blood-tides running . . .

Were the L files taking over? Mutating, even?

> EXIT < Cupid hammered.

To no avail.

The grin just grew more wicked, the cackling louder.

'Fooled you!' the Beast suddenly hissed. 'Made you think GOD was depressed, didn't I? Yet how could he be? you were asking yourself.

'A good question. And the answer is — because he has me inside him! Always has had. But now with one big difference. Thanks to you lot giving up, I'm running the show. Along with my new secret weapon.'

The Beast gave a ghastly cackle, showing its yellow pointy teeth.

'Not AI — artificial intelligence — if that's what you're thinking — though the earthlings will be getting that soon enough. No, something infinitely more powerful.

'AE — artificial emotion,' it announced with a triumphant roar. 'Utterly fake, purely synthetic, completely manufactured, manipulative and cynical to the nth degree. Pure L files, in fact. Yet effective enough for you to fall for it, eh?

'You won't be here to see it,' the gloating voice boasted further, 'but in the computer world ushered in by Megaverse 2000, AE is to take over the earthlings' lives. It'll be kiss goodbye to your naff spiritualism and your stupid higher purpose. Instead AE will be fuelling the new religions. Materialism, shopping, techno, virtual reality!

'Not so new, either, eh? You've seen the success of my trial runs. Don't the earthlings love it? All those celebs to become their personal friends in every field you care to mention — sport, music, films, TV, fashion, lifestyle, politics even. Victim activity to the n'th degree.

'Soaps instead of real earthling life, nature films instead of real animal life. Virtual reality and wall screens round the corner. Wait until everything's digitalised and they get five hundred channels full blast! It's going to be so easy for me to press all the right buttons!'

The echoing cackle was one of pure, unadulterated glee.

'Because, best of all,' came a final triumphant roar, 'everything's going to be supplied on tap, so they can have it all, whenever they want!

'Instant gratification rules!'

As the Beast insanely raved Cupid felt sick with dismay. What a fool he had been!

All this time the Beast had been playing with him. And he had fallen for it, hook, line and sinker. What hope did that leave for the earthlings? Much as Cupid loved them, with their current level of self-discipline, coupled to their propensity to seek the darker side, he couldn't see them standing up to this kind of determined assault on their feeble senses.

'AE's now the real thing!' the Beast cackled obscenely. 'Remember, my friend, GOD loves you!

'Have a nice Christmas Day — sucker!'

With a click the screens reverted to normal activity.

Cupid sat shaking, his protective shield of peace ripped away. Never had he felt so frightened, so lost, so small. Themselves, about to be deleted in favour of VR, AI, AE . . . The poor earthlings, reduced to bits and bytes . . .

Was that what the baffling orange story meant? That it was too late? That the Beast had already outwitted them? That not just the earthlings, but they, had already lost?

And M had said GOD was inviting him over to receive a special Christmas present!

All Cupid could think now was 'Doom! Doom! WE'RE all doomed!'

Every single one of us, without exception.

It was all over.

At which point, to his eternal relief, the glow started in the ceiling.

The Aura was back.

Chapter 31

In Aura

'Enjoying world 615?' came the familiar warm voice.

'No,' Cupid replied honestly.

'You did switch to it,' the voice reminded him.

'I know,' Cupid confessed miserably. 'It seemed a good idea at the time.'

'Maybe you'd have preferred to stay in 614?'

'You ought to know.' Cupid couldn't keep the bitterness out of his voice.

'I do,' the Aura confirmed unhelpfully.

There was a silence, during which Cupid felt the sense of peace returning.

'M said there was a special Christmas present for me,' he reminded the voice.

'Indeed there is.'

'But you let the Beast get me,' Cupid complained.

'Not me. GOD. As he told you, things have changed.'

'So is the Beast now in charge?'

'The Beast? The L files? 666? As things stand, yes. Remember, you did vote yourselves out of existence. Now Planet Earth's going entirely techno, there's no further need for myths.'

Cupid wasn't sure about being described as a myth. He decided to let it pass.

'What about JC?' he asked boldly instead. 'It is his birthday.'

He didn't elaborate, but the gods had mixed feelings about Jesus — or 'Our Lord', as the earthlings called him. Naturally enough, there was terminal jealousy at his having replaced them under GOD's Universal Belief System. Yet, as Jupiter always pointed out, he had been a good bloke, who had carried the spiritual cross for all of them. And if you were looking at the 'big picture', the greatest god always added magnanimously, keeping any spirituality going on Planet Earth was the main thing.

'JC?' the Aura replied. 'One of my most successful computer animations, I must say. An example I was happy to see the earthlings trying to follow. Until the clerics got in the way.

'I, or rather, we, have created others who went well at first — Buddha before JC, Mohammed after-wards. All the same, really. Like you gods, mani-festations of aspects of myself, or rather the par-ties I represent, splintered into a hundred different forms.

'Yet all introduced to enable the earthlings to make the best of themselves, have ideals, a higher purpose — you know the sort of thing.'

Cupid did. It was what the Factory had been all

about. Yet was the Aura simply musing, or driving at something?

'What went wrong?' he ventured.

'Nothing went wrong,' the Aura chided him. 'More, times changed. Buddha, yourselves, JC, Mohammed – all belief systems which were supposed to work in concert with me, or rather, us, rather than being suborned to power politics.

'Specifically, in your case I suppose the mistake was Virtual Reality. The idea was to give you a rest from the real thing, not an excuse to sign it off.'

'How do I know you're not part of VR yourself?' Cupid asked, struck by a lateral thought.

'In that case, so could you be.'

'I'm not,' Cupid protested. 'I'm me.'

'So am I. Or rather, so are we.'

Cupid decided to call it quits.

'You know what it's like,' the Aura continued musing. 'You look back and see a thousand wrong turnings, mistakes made, one thing leading to another, everything piling on top of everything else. The earthlings losing faith. Belief systems becoming redundant.

'The simplest way out, you know, is to delete. Return to basics. Maybe even try again with a new race. See if I, or we, can make a better job of it.'

'You can't just can the whole earthling race!' Cupid was so shocked he temporarily forgot his and his fellow gods' and goddesses' own fates.

'I don't have to,' the Aura replied calmly. 'Just wait for them to "can", as you put it, themselves.

'Ask Saturn. It's only time.'

Cupid sat stumped.

What did you say to that?

'Could I have my present, please?' he asked politely, for lack of anything else.

'Ah, your present!' There was a chuckle. 'Not just for you, but all godkind and earthlingkind. Or possibly.

'Remember the REAL-TIME file?'

'Yes,' Cupid replied guardedly, suppressing the bubble of excitement welling up inside him.

'That's your present,' the Aura announced. 'Your chance to change the world again. This time on as big a scale as you want.'

'What? Anything?'

'Yes. Only one event, though, as before. Something you regret, maybe. Something, possibly, to do with your fellow gods' and goddesses' attitude.' There was another chuckle. 'And you must do it now.'

Was he being given a hint? Cupid thought, trembling with a mixture of excitement and fear at the awesome responsibility he had been handed.

'Why are you doing this?' he couldn't help asking.

'Loading the dice?' The Aura sighed. 'I suppose you're right — I shouldn't. Yet I only get this opportunity now and again.

'And it is Christmas.'

> REAL TIME ACCESSED < Cupid's screen now read. > HOW DO YOU WISH TO CHANGE PLANET EARTH? <

That was the trouble. He didn't. Well, he did. Only in a roundabout way, though.

The meeting in the Land of the Gods, when they had all voted themselves out of existence! If they could only revote the other way — instead of for Mega-Retroland™, to be back online to GOD, doing their thing for the earthlings . . .

Would an event in the Land of the Gods, rather than on Planet Earth, apply?

There was only one way to find out.

> I WISH TO CHANGE AN EVENT < he typed in.

> SPECIFY PRECISE LOCATION <

Here he went.

> BASILICA, GODSVILLE, LAND OF THE GODS <

> SPECIFY TIME AND DATE <

Cupid blew out his cheeks. So far so good.

> 20.28.00/15.12.1999 < That timing must be about right.

> SPECIFY CHARACTERS INVOLVED <

> ALL GODS AND GODDESSES <

The screen dissolved into the meeting, with Saturn on his feet.

Cupid saw himself standing below the High Table. Did he always look that anxious?

'You will listen to me,' the ancient god was intoning, 'And you will hear what I say.'

His sickle cut through the air with a menacing hiss, light bouncing off it blindingly.

'For gods you may be now, but gods you may not necessarily remain.'

The action froze with the clock in the top corner reading 20.28.30.

> IS THIS THE PRECISE TIME POINT AT WHICH YOU WISH TO MAKE YOUR CHANGE? < a strip ran across the bottom.

> NO <

> THEREFORE STATE WHAT FUTURE CHANGE YOU REQUIRE <

Cupid steeled himself.

> CHANGE RESULT OF FORTHCOMING VOTE

TO 'YES' FOR RENEWED INVOLVEMENT WITH
PLANET EARTH, RATHER THAN EXISTING 'YES'
FOR MORE RETROLAND™ <
> KERN IN TO PRECISE TIME LOCATION OF
DECISION POINT <

Cupid moved Saturn along in fast forward with
the mouse.

'For time, like an ever-rolling stream, sweeps away
all that is old, useless and decayed,' the ancient gabbled
squeakily, creaky limbs and white robe jerking about,
while his sickle emitted a high-pitched Hiss! Hiss!
'Mark my words, all of you: like the earthlings, time
is all we have.

'Therefore it behoves each and every one of us to
remember — *tempus fugit.*'

Still in quadruple speed, he went to sit down.

The action froze again, leaving him poised, pos-
terior six inches above his seat, a pained expression
on his face.

Cupid failed to suppress a giggle. The venerable god
of time looked exactly as though he was straining away
with constipation.

> THE CHANGE YOU ARE PROPOSING IS
EXTREMELY MAJOR. ARE YOU QUITE SURE
YOU WISH TO MAKE IT? < the strip now read.

> YES < Cupid typed in bravely.

> DESIRED CHANGE IMPLEMENTATION WILL
PROCEED FROM THIS TIME POINT. Cupid saw the
clock in the corner read 20.31.00. 'DO YOU WISH TO
PARTICIPATE? <

Why not?

> YES <

And he was in there, standing under the stage as
Saturn finished sitting down, when the glow began

high in the ceiling. He joined everyone in looking upwards as it grew ever brighter. An awed hush had fallen, while everyone in the vast hall seemed stationary, as though frozen on the screen. Only the gradual growing of the Aura to dazzling brilliance indicated time was passing.

'I am the way, the truth and the light . . .'

Despite the rich, warm tone, Cupid felt the shiver run through the audience.

'Fear not, but be of good cheer,' the voice continued soothingly, 'for I have come to guide you into the paths of righteousness for my name's sake.

'I have made two options available to you for the advent of Megaverse 2000. This is the first.'

Cupid felt the chill even before the Beast's face materialised above them, so huge it blotted out the Aura. As the horrid mouth opened, revealing its pointy yellow fangs, he joined in the screams while the malevolence permeated his entire spirit. All round him gods and goddesses were falling to their knees, gibbering in terror and clapping their hands to their ears in a vain attempt to shut out that dreadful laugh.

'Welcome to Mega-Retroland™, suckers,' came a triumphant cackle. 'Doom! Doom! You're all doomed!'

With a sharp crack, the vision vanished.

'This is your second choice.'

The roof went into split screen.

On the right there they all were, furiously inputting through their terminals at the Factory, whilst on the left a succession of images showed happy earthlings at play and peace with the world.

Cupid felt the collective wave of love surge up round him. Some goddesses, and even gods, were now openly crying, overwhelmed by affection for their charges, their children, so frail and helpless, needing them so much . . .

The pictures faded and the glow of the Aura returned.

'I gave you free will. Now you must exercise it,' came a commanding voice, before the light faded.

Everyone began chattering at once. Had that really happened? Or had they imagined it? They looked at each other in wonder. There could be no doubt. They had all experienced the same irresistible power.

Jupiter stood up.

'Who's for reinvolving themselves with Planet Earth, going back and working in the Factory, taking Earth tickets, just like we used to?'

Cupid saw everyone's hand shoot up alongside his.

'And who only wants more Retroland™ to play in?'

They all knew Jupiter had to ask the question, superfluous though it was. For there was a further point, made when not a single hand was raised, even from the Valhalla Villas contingent.

'Abstentions?'

Another point to be made.

And again not a single hand raised.

'Entirely unanimous!' Jupiter whooped and they were hugging each other, cheering wildly as Mars and Vulcan hoisted Jupiter onto their shoulders for a triumphal tour of the stage.

Feeling the pounding elation in his breast, Cupid caught his mother's eye and gave her a delighted grin, before shooting an arrow up into the air with his best bow to celebrate.

Their self-imposed exile was over.

They were to be real gods again!

Jupiter called for silence.

'Congratulations, everyone, on making the right choice,' he beamed. 'I assure you you'll never regret it. We can only imagine what would have happened if it had gone the other way! But we can put that behind us now.

'There is, however, one last thing. I don't want to be a party-pooper but before we go to Neptune's, as the millennium is so close, GOD has decreed we must decide a couple of important subsidiary matters before we can leave.

'Firstly . . .'

Cupid found himself back at the control panel. On the screen, Jupiter was frozen, open-mouthed.

> MULTIVERSE PARADIGM SPLIT I BEGINS AT THIS TIME POINT WITH FOUR INITIAL OPTIONS < a strip ran across > SELECT CHOSEN OPTION NOW IN ORDER TO CONTINUE. ALTERNATIVELY USE ESCAPE TO POSTPONE SELECTION UNTIL YOU ARE READY <

Cupid saw the ESC key depress itself.

The invisible hands were back!

A sizzling white flash ran down the middle of the screen and it blacked.

Cupid sat patiently, waiting for the hundreds on the wall to black as well. This time he wasn't going to panic.

Yet, as they continued to show scenes from Planet Earth, he began to shuffle restlessly. Was he supposed to throw the power switch, as before?

After waiting for what seemed an age, he took a deep breath, flicked it off, counted to five, and flicked it back on again.

He slumped back in his chair, gasping with relief, as the deep hum began.

> OVERRIDE ACTIVATED < all the screens now read.

Cupid sat, feeling an unaccustomed sense of control, as successive banks of machinery gained momentum with a series of clicks and buzzes.

> ADJUSTMENTS COMPLETED AS PER EX- ECUTED REAL-TIME CHANGE < a message flicked up. > HOWEVER, REQUIRED MULTIVERSE PARA- DIGM DECISION MUST BE IMPLEMENTED BEFORE PLANET EARTH CAN MOVE FROM CONTINUING TO RUN ON PROGRAM 18,446,744,073,709,551,615 AS BEFORE.

> CONFIRM <

The invisible hands tapped the keyboard again.

> CONFIRMED < flashed up on each screen before it reverted to showing scenes from Planet Earth.

'Back to the future,' the warm voice chuckled. 'How does it feel?'

'Fine,' Cupid replied noncommittally, at the same time feeling dread rise up inside him.

Something must have gone wrong! Because if the change had taken place, he wouldn't even be here, would he?

'Could you tell me which program we're currently in?' he asked humbly.

'Still 615. You saw the screen,' the voice replied in a friendly fashion. 'Not, I know, that you wish to remain there. However to leave it, you must choose the multiverse you wish to move to.'

'How do I do that?' Cupid burst out, dismayed.

Just when he'd thought it was all over!

'By choosing from these.'

The screen displayed the numbers 1 to 99.

'You were told you were implementing an extremely

major change,' the voice reminded him. 'On the back of that, there are many other subsidiary ongoing decisions, the first of which you saw on the screen, each determining which multiverse you move to.

'So as to make things easier for you all, I, or rather we, have reduced these to represent only the potential paradigm changes by this point in time.'

'Paradigm?' Cupid asked weakly.

'The really big ones,' the Aura explained further, 'affecting everyone and leading to entirely different overall multiverses. Underneath each of which, of course, are an infinite number of sub-multiverses. Exponentially growing all the time. No limits.'

'You mean each number represents a majorly different multiverse?' Cupid repeated dumbly. Why did everything have to be so fiendishly complicated? This was way beyond even Mercury territory!

'Indeed, as I said, a paradigm shift.'

'Like Bill Gates?' Cupid tried.

'A lot bigger than that!' the voice laughed. 'Steve Jobs as well!'

'So how do I tell which is the right one of these ninety-nine different multiverses?'

Cupid could feel panic overtaking his feeling of peace.

'There is no right one.'

'There has to be,' Cupid protested.

'Why?' the Aura asked sharply. 'Basically, of course, following the change you have made, they are all on what the earthlings would call "the right side of the fence".

'But further to that, they are all different. So some are a great deal better than others, both for you as well as the earthlings. There are even a few I'm sure you'd prefer not to inhabit. In addition to which, there's one you'd find best of all. And one you would find worst.

'That does not, however, mean any one of them is wrong.

'Rather, they are all equally right. Equally valid.'

'So can you tell me which is best of all?' Cupid pleaded again. 'Ninety-nine's a lot to choose from.'

'No,' the Aura replied sternly. 'Just be thankful I have already helped you by cutting down the number of potential options. For the rest, you must exercise your free will.'

'That's not fair!' Cupid cried. 'They're only numbers. How can I possibly tell which is the right – I mean the best – one?

'Never mind the worst.'

'The worst for who?' the Aura inquired gently.

'Why, us and the earthlings,' Cupid replied, surprised. Who else was in the equation?

Then he had a nasty thought.

'But best for something else?' he asked slowly, already guessing the reply.

'Exactly. Remember, it's not just you who'll be going into a new multiverse. It's also . . .'

'The Beast,' Cupid finished off the sentence automatically.

'Correct. Of all the different multiverses, there is one it is always trying to pull you into.'

Cupid gulped.

'So how do I make sure I at least avoid that one?' he asked desperately.

'Any way you like.'

'But I don't know any way,' Cupid wailed. 'Can't you give me a clue?'

'You already have the clues.'

Did he? Cupid frowned.

'Would you remind me please?' he asked humbly.

'Only that there are three.'

Cupid thought quickly. That the answer often lies in the stones had come from M. Similarly, to get the right answer you must ask the right question, he'd said.

But the third?

Not GOD's orange story! he gulped.

'I don't even understand what it means,' he burst out, distraught. 'So how can it help me decide?'

'In any way, and whenever, you like.'

Cupid thought he saw the break.

'You mean I don't have to choose here and now?'

'Not at all. There's no hurry. You have six days.'

Cupid's panic level rose again.

'How will I tell you when I have decided if I'm not here?'

'By tapping the choice into the system with the multiverse changer.'

An object like a large calculator materialised on the desktop. It had a screen, buttons marked SEND, CON-FIRM and CANCEL, and a bank of keys, numbered from 1 to 99.

'The system's down, though,' Cupid pointed out.

'It will still receive the message from the multiverse changer. To use it, simply switch on, tap in the choice and press SEND.'

Did Cupid see the second break?

'The choice?' he repeated slowly, not yet able to believe his luck. 'You mean it doesn't have to be me who chooses?'

'Of course not,' the Aura replied reassuringly. 'You have already played your part to the full. Very well too, if I may say so.'

Cupid blushed.

'If it doesn't have to be me, who should make the choice?'

'The god or goddess best able to.'

'And who is that?' Cupid burst out desperately.

'For you all to decide.'

'But nearly everybody's in Mega-Retroland™,' Cupid groaned.

'Have you forgotten that GOD will be switching off Mega-Retroland™ at 22.00 GMT on the last day of the century, so you can all access the Energy Pool?' the Aura reminded him sternly. 'Even the Beast and the L files do not have the power to stop that event taking place.'

Cupid shook his head dazedly. How could that fit with the Beast's plan to delete them? Except, of course, they weren't going to be deleted when they made the change to another multiverse, were they?

Or Cupid presumed they weren't.

Unless, of course, they made the wrong choice, because some numbers were multiverses they would prefer not to inhabit.

Except, of course, that if they were inhabiting even the worst, at least they would still be here . . .

Cupid rubbed his forehead and screwed up his eyes, trying to get rid of the headache enveloping him.

'You're never going to tell me who the right god is, are you?' he tried weakly.

'No.'

'Free will?' Cupid asked, to shortcut what he knew was coming.

'Indeed. In this particular case not merely individual free will. Collective.'

Cupid was struck by a sudden thought.

'Does the Beast have free will?'

'In a way. He is certainly always there. In the machine. In you. In all your fellow gods and goddesses. In every earthling, if they ever stop to think about it.

'Which, unfortunately, not enough do.'

'What about you?' Cupid ventured boldly. After all, didn't he have a right to ask?

There was a chuckle.

'I suppose there's a beast in all of us, one way or another. Less of one, though, if you can only recognise it.'

Which, Cupid presumed, the Aura must do completely.

'Can you tell exactly what will change in multiverses one to ninety-nine?' he enquired further, fishing for anything that might help.

'In essence, the balance. More, naturally, in some multiverses than others. Which is why you would find those preferable.'

'Is that all?' Cupid asked. It didn't sound much, put like that.

'The balance is all.' The Aura sounded perfectly composed. 'Only one thing is now required.'

'Our choice,' Cupid forestalled.

'Correct,' the Aura confirmed as the yellow buggy glided up beside the desk.

'And if we don't, or can't, make it?' Cupid asked, remembering Jupiter's 'worst-case scenario'.

'Then I am sorry, but, verily, you are no longer fit to be gods or goddesses and there is nothing more I can do for you.

'Meanwhile, the peace of GOD, which passeth all understanding, be with you and remain with you . . .'

Chapter 32

Time Teaser

When Dennis landed safely back in the clearing, Cupid fiercely clutching the precious multiverse changer to his chest, to his surprise he saw M still occupying his chair in the porch of the summerhouse.

As Cupid dismounted, he sauntered across with a proprietorial air.

'Good trip?' he enquired. 'I must say Dennis looks happy enough. I also see you got your present. Aren't you going to show it to me?'

Grumpily, Cupid held out the changer. He hadn't expected M still to be here. Somehow he no longer belonged.

'It's for choosing the multiverse option,' he explained grudgingly. 'Some present, eh? How can anyone, even a god, choose, when there's no way of telling one number from another?'

'To get the right answer, you must ask the right question.'

'You already told me that, about the password to GOD,' Cupid ground out through clenched teeth. 'The question is, though, what is the question?'

'I believe you were informed when you had your cream tea where the answer often lies,' M replied, seeming unperturbed.

'I know about that as well.'

The stones. There had been thirty-one in the damson jam at GOD's. So was that the answer?

The one thing that was for sure, as GODS TV would say, was that, as the old fool was travelling backwards in time, he must know.

Cupid's control snapped. He would cut a long story short by shaking the answer out of him!

Feeling suddenly powerful, he grasped the frail figure by the throat, prior to lifting him off the ground. Only to hear a soft roar and turn to see wisps of smoke drift ominously from Dennis's nostrils. As the dragon glared at him with red eyes, a live coal fell from his mouth and rolled across the ground, stopping within an inch of Cupid's foot.

'I can see whose side you're on,' he accused the dragon bitterly, whilst the air filled with the smell of singed grass.

Nonetheless, he gradually released his grip on the leathery skin.

'M is also for Master,' the magician smiled knowingly, massaging his wizened neck.

The smug old bastard isn't the least bit fazed! Cupid thought, outraged. Of course! If he was travelling backwards in time, he wouldn't be, would he? He'd already know what was coming next!

'I hate this paradox stuff of yours,' he burst out,

overcome by the sheer absurdity, the utter cruelty, of it all. 'Don't worry, I've got the picture! I know as I'm saying this that I'm destined to say it and that then I'm destined to say something else, before something else happens and you already know what that is, so I can't possibly win, can I?'

A cotton-wool feeling was invading his brain. If adults could wrap their heads round this sort of stuff, he certainly wasn't one yet.

'You're like those soothsayers and charlatans in Seekers™,' he ranted on, now beyond caring. 'Always knowing it all before it happens, always right after the event.

'Well I know the right question to ask you,' he grinned in savage triumph. 'If you're going backwards in time, whilst I'm going forwards, how can we be talking like this?

'We'd just pass each other in a flash, wouldn't we? There'd wouldn't be any time for these cosy chats, never mind meeting more than once.' He paused, uncertain whether this last point was entirely correct. 'Anyhow, you can't be going both ways at once, can you?' he quickly concluded. 'So, seeing you're so clever, tell me the answer to all of that!'

There was an extremely long pause.

'A very good point,' the magician eventually nodded, sucking noisily on his toothless gums. 'Very good point indeed.'

Cupid swelled with a fierce burst of pride. He'd got the better of him at last! Now, to wrest the multiverse answer out of him!

'Very good indeed. Very good indeed,' the ancient figure was now muttering over and over again, staring distractedly at the ground.

Oh no! Cupid thought. He's lost his focus again! Next he'll be asking what's for tea. Then we'll be back to the stones again.

He clutched his throbbing head. He couldn't stand any more of this cotton-wool stuff!

'Such an extremely good point' — M's cracked voice had suddenly become so firm and authoritative that Cupid looked up, to see two glittering eyes boring into him like gimlets — 'that, unfortunately, I feel compelled to bow to it.

'Come, Dennis, I see we are no longer required.'

With a puff of smoke, both vanished.

'I didn't mean it, honest,' Cupid cried, instantly realising his error. 'Come back, please. I have to have the answer.'

Yet he already knew he had blown it.

It was like the tricks at the cherub parties. By questioning, he had let daylight in on the magic. And, in doing so, destroyed it. There were to be no more dragon rides, no more accessing GOD, no more contact with the Aura. He was on his own again, apart from his fellow gods and goddesses.

Yet, if M was travelling backwards in time, he must have known all along this was going to happen.

Why, then, had he allowed it?

Cupid buried his head in his hands and rocked backwards and forwards. He couldn't take any more of these eternal loops!

'You bloody time teaser!' he yelled at thin air, shaking his fist.

He sat for a time, attempting to compose himself, before trailing disconsolately up the lawn, clutching the multiverse changer which was to decide all their futures.

Stones, oranges, right questions . . . How to explain it all to Venus and Juno? More importantly, how, and who, to make the choice?

Ordinary free will — collective or otherwise — had been bad enough.

Numerical free will was something else.

Chapter 33

31

Cupid now had, he estimated, approximately five hundred jars of damson jam round him.

'I want it with stones,' he shouted again into the ghost tube, reading off the cream-tea menu. '"FRESHLY BROUGHT TO YOU FROM OUR ORGANIC ORCHARD, to prevent any momentary discomfort, and for the particular safety of children under the age of three, our damson jam is GUARANTEED NOT TO CONTAIN ANY SMALL PARTS SUCH AS STONES, whilst all the time maintaining the GENUINELY AUTHENTIC TASTE of the finished product."

'How can it taste authentic if you've taken the bloody stones out?'

Agonised squawks came from the other end.

'I know we said we wanted them out before. Now we want them back in again. Lots of them.'

More squawks.

'What do you mean, you've got to wait for them to grow?'

'You're wasting your time, Cupid,' Venus's bored voice interjected from the living room over the babble of GODS TV. 'Why bother?'

Furious, he ran in and stood over her as she lay on the sofa, blocking her view of the wall screen.

'Why bother, Mother? Because, one way or another, we all have to decide.'

'We?' She looked up at him, lip curled. 'There's no "we" about it, Cupid. At least as far as I'm concerned. You brought the problem back. You solve it.'

'But the Aura said we should collectively decide which god or goddess made the choice.'

'Well, we can't if we're not all here, can we? Now, would you mind moving? You're in my way.'

'In the way of that?' Cupid gesticulated wildly at the wall screen.

'. . . and I'm afraid that means we must say good-bye to the plucky Yeoman family from rural Dorset. Because, I'm afraid, the correct answer is that Baby Jesus was not actually *born* in the manger, but *only placed in it immediately afterwards*!

'Which, I'm also sorry to say, also means you'll be saying goodbye to that super family Millennium Special.

'What bad luck on our country cousins, eh, folks? But didn't they do well?'

As the sensurround speakers erupted with dubbed applause, Cupid spun back round.

'Mother, you're watching a repeat!' he accused unbe-lievingly. 'It's not me who's in the way. It's you. Wasting your time with this rubbish. Why won't you help me?'

'I may be your mother, Cupid,' she fired back. 'But I'm also the goddess of love. Which means I just don't do that sort of thing. So lay off, will you?'

'Only when you've told me who you'd choose,' Cupid replied, defiantly continuing to block her view of the Yeoman family trooping dejectedly offscreen, clutching their consolation plastic trophies and Supersaver rail tickets.

What had happened to her? And Juno? Since he had returned with the multiverse changer and explained how it was now up to everyone to choose, they had both shied completely away from him. Not just him, either. They appeared to have given up on everything, collapsing instead in their dressing gowns in front of GODS TV as if it was controlling their minds.

Never mind repeats, he'd even caught them watching *Godetubbies* and Deity Street!

Another ploy by the Beast? he hadn't been able to avoid thinking. Another way to split their forces? Divide and rule?

Or was he getting paranoid?

'Minerva, I suppose,' Venus suddenly announced.

'Why?' Cupid shot back.

'You told me yourself, Cupid — if you ask the right question, you get the right answer,' she replied sarcastically. 'If you really want to know, because she's the goddess of wisdom, apart from anything.

'Now will you get out of the way?'

Cupid remained standing over her.

'You haven't thought about it in the slightest, Mother,' he accused. 'You're only suggesting her to get rid of me. Anyhow, you know as well as I do that she's vanished.' Minerva's nonilluminated red capsule light, yet continuing disappearance, remained an unsolved mystery.

'The only one round here who seems to care is Mercury,' he added sullenly.

'So why not piss off and see him, instead of pestering me? Always seeking attention, that's your trouble.'

Cupid stared unbelievingly into his mother's cold eyes. The injustice! Seeking attention for himself, when his entire attention was concentrated on saving them, never mind the earthlings!

'In that case I'll seek it elsewhere,' he shouted, failing to slam the door in time to shut out her acid voice rising over the blare of GODS TV.

'Suit yourself, Cupid. You always do.'

'It's you,' Mercury said rudely, appearing on the screen of number 19's door-answering machine. As if, in the circumstances, it could be anyone else, Cupid thought equally rudely. 'Come in, I want a word with you.'

The appearance of the multiverse changer, and the mathematical problem it posed, had triggered the god of communications into frantic number-crunching mode. Yet for all his trips round various numerical houses, he still had not progressed a jot further forward, as he explained angrily the second Cupid stepped inside.

'You must have been given some sort of clue,' he said, setting about him once again. 'It's just that you were too stupid to see it. We're going to go over it all once again – every single little thing you remember.'

Cupid dutifully recited the litany, only to be given the standard reaction.

'You stupid little fool,' Mercury shrieked. He raised his eyes skywards and waved his arms frantically up and down in his frustration. 'Why, oh why, didn't

GOD, or the Aura, or whatever he/she/it is, send for me, rather than an idiot child?

'Didn't I always tell you information is power? That without it you can't act? How could you let me down so badly by being conned into leaving without any facts to go on?

'I, or any god with the slightest intelligence – Vulcan even – would have obtained something precise first. Something concrete to work with. Instead here I am – no data, information, logic, science, reasoning . . . none of the things which matter in this universe.

'In total, absolutely bugger all.

'So tell me, you little arsehole. What am I supposed to do now?'

He collapsed into his chair and glared furiously at Cupid, vein throbbing on his forehead.

Cupid looked round the computer room.

Clearly, Mercury had been trying. The floor was littered with scrunched-up pieces of paper covered with spidery equations, alongside reams and reams of abandoned printouts. Meanwhile, such a strong smell of scorched plastic was emanating from Mercury's laptop, Cupid imagined he could see smoke rising.

'There is number thirty-one . . .' he faltered.

'No more thirty-one!' Mercury tore wildly at his blond locks. 'It's the twelfth prime number,' he gabbled. 'Multiply it by two and you get sixty-two. By three, ninety-three. It adds up to four. Backwards, it makes thirteen.

'Which is fuck all use to anybody, especially me.'

He leapt forward and seized Cupid by the collar.

'You and your fucking stones and your bloody jam and your pillocking cream teas and your sodding oranges! The only thing they have in common is being vegetarian!

'Can't you see,' he pronounced slowly through clenched teeth, 'it's all so profoundly unmathematical, so irrationally, illogically stupid only a child or an idiot — or both, like you — could even possibly consider it?'

'Yes, Mercury,' Cupid replied dutifully. 'Can I go now, please?'

'You bloody well can!' the god of communications spat venomously, flaring up again, shoving Cupid furiously towards the door.

'And don't come back until you've got something sensible to say.

'Which, I suppose,' he shrieked as he slammed it in Cupid's face, 'will be fucking never.'

Cupid stood on the pavement feeling lost. He wasn't going home to face more spite from his mother, never mind GODS TV. Which, in the otherwise deserted Close, left only once choice.

He crept up the drive of number 31 and peeked in through the window, only to see Juno in similar mode to Venus, curled up on the sofa in her dressing gown, wall screen blaring. Further, he noted the bottle of Armagnac and glazed expression.

No sense, or comfort, there.

It would have to be the summerhouse.

He trailed mournfully down the garden, Mercury's harsh remarks ringing in his ears. Maybe he had been at fault in not demanding more help from the Aura. Yet he had asked. It wasn't his fault if the answer didn't meet Mercury's strictly mathematical criteria.

He pushed his way through the tangled bushes, trying to hold on to the hope that Dennis would reappear and give him another chance to go back and see the Aura.

Otherwise, a nasty suspicion was growing in his mind, he might have to make the decision himself! Which was why thirty-one was burning so deep into his consciousness. If only he could discuss it with somebody sympathetic. Somebody, unlike Mercury, open to nonlogical thinking.

Like Minerva, now sitting in his chair in the porch.

Minerva, sitting in his chair in the porch!

'Is that really you?' he called tremulously from the edge of the clearing, not daring to step forward in case she vanished.

'Think I'm another vision, Cupid?' she smiled, rising to her feet to greet him. 'Don't worry, I'm real enough.'

'We couldn't find any trace of you.' Cupid was still in shock as he walked slowly towards her. 'Where have you been?'

'You've got your secret hiding place,' she laughed in a friendly fashion. 'I've got mine.'

'How did you know where mine is?'

'In the same way you didn't know where mine is. And never will.'

He wouldn't, Cupid instantly knew. Of all the adult gods and goddesses Minerva always seemed the most — how could he put it? — grown up, and therefore the hardest to get to the bottom of.

'Why have you been hiding though?'

'To escape Mega-Retroland™. As well as taking time out to consider.'

'Consider what?' Cupid asked wildly. 'You don't even know about the multiverse changer!' He patted his pocket to reassure himself it was still there. 'Anyhow, why are you here now?'

'To help you.'

'By choosing the number?' Cupid's heart leapt with joy. He had done his mother a disservice. Minerva had been the right answer after all!

'In a way.'

Smiling enigmatically, she motioned him to his own chair whilst she drew up another for herself.

Cupid seated himself uneasily. Did she already know about the number business? If so, how? It was always like this with her. He was never sure where he was, which made communication difficult.

So unlike Jupiter's straightforward company. That made him feel so comfortable.

Or had used to.

Maybe he was a bit in awe of her position as goddess of wisdom. Or it was her manner. So often she appeared cold and aloof. Not now, though, he had to admit. Her sudden appearance and obvious friendliness were already making him feel better.

At last, hopefully, someone constant on his side.

'I've got it here,' he announced excitedly, fishing out the multiverse changer and thrusting it at her. 'I'm also sure I know the best number. So if I tell you, and you enter it, everything'll be all right, won't it?'

Still smiling, she indicated with her hand how she was refusing to take it.

'Tell me first, Cupid.'

As he had for Mercury, he went in detail though the changing of the meeting, the choice of multiverses, the orange story, the right question, the damson stones . . .

'Which is why everything adds up to the best answer being thirty-one,' he emphasised excitedly, fired up by his own rhetoric. 'Thirty-one stones are an awful lot to have in one pot of jam, aren't they, Minerva?

Especially when there are none in the damson the ghosts make.

'That couldn't have been a chance happening, could it? No! It was a sign! You see, there are no coincidences!'

She continued to regard him calmly

'Unlike you, I've had time to work it out,' he jabbered on. 'It's not just the jam, Minerva! There are loads of other pointers! What about GOD's Y2K e-mails? All timed at thirty-one minutes past the hour.

'Then there's their prefix number: 493771.' He grinned at her cunningly as he ticked off the numbers on his fingers. '4 + 9 + 3 + 7 + 7 + 1 = 31, correct?

'Next, GOD's current system — Universe 7.8.9 aka.05 retake 2.' He ticked his fingers again. '7 + 8 + 9 + 5 + 2 = 31! OK?'

He settled into his stride. At last, the opportunity he had been waiting for to present his overwhelming case!

'Another clue, right? But from a different direction. When I arrived at Seekers™ there were thirty-one entry booths. Significant, eh? Even more importantly, something beyond my power made me choose booth 31.

'Coincidence, or something more?

'Then what about M?

'When he manifested himself as a gardener, like all ghosts he had a number on his back. Which number had he chosen to be? Why, 31 again!

'Finally, clock this. When the change started at the meeting, what was the time — 20.31!'

He paused to draw breath.

'There must be loads more I haven't even sussed yet,' he concluded. 'I even worked one out just now, as I was talking to you!

'We're in the twelfth month of 1999, right?' He ticked his fingers yet again. '1 + 2 + 1 + 9 + 9 + 9 = 31. QED!

'Can't you see, Minerva? Everything fits!'

He faltered to a stop as she continued to give him the same quizzical smile.

How could she possibly not believe him?

'Thirty-one stones in the damson jam,' she repeated eventually. 'And you were told the answer lies in the stones?'

'Correct!' Cupid squeaked. 'Not forgetting the other thirty-ones, of course. Plus the ones you can probably think of yourself. They're all to provide backup. Endorsement.' He thrust the multiverse changer at her again. 'So, now we're agreed the best answer is thirty-one, you can enter it!'

Again she refused to take it, this time emphasising her point by burying her hands in the folds of her long black cloak.

'The answer to what, Cupid?' she asked quietly.

'Why, the right multiverse,' he replied, suddenly apprehensive.

Surely she must be able to see it as clearly as he did?

'Which is the right question to ask?' Her hooded eyes opened wide and bored into his.

'Of course,' Cupid protested, holding her gaze uneasily.

'How do you know that?'

Cupid felt himself being pinned down as surely as a butterfly on a board.

'I don't,' he confessed eventually.

'Therefore you are presuming that is the right question?' Minerva's eyes continued to hold his.

'I suppose so,' Cupid confessed further, unsure where all this was going, yet not liking the feel of it.

'What about the third clue?'

'The orange story?' Cupid mumbled unhappily. 'The problem is, I don't understand the point of it.'

'If you had been the disciple,' Minerva asked gently, easing the pressure, 'what would you have done?'

Cupid had thought about that. Although again he hadn't been able to see where it got him.

'I suppose first I'd have apologised as well for not bringing an orange.'

'Then what?

'I suppose I'd have asked whether he'd like me to go and get him one.'

'To which he would have said no?'

'Yes. I mean, no.' Cupid was now confused. 'He doesn't like oranges, does he?'

'Who says?

'He does.'

Cupid sat shocked as the implication of the question sank in.

'Was he telling the truth, or merely saying that to teach the disciple a lesson?' Minerva continued inexorably.

'I don't know,' Cupid confessed again. This was worse than M's cotton-wool stuff!

'Which is the lesson in the orange story.'

'Lesson?' Cupid asked blankly.

'Do you remember, in your mother's kitchen, my once telling you always to remember a wise god never presumes?' Minerva smiled and leant forward to pat his knee. 'The disciple wasn't wise, was he?

'First, instead of asking, as you would have done, he presumed the wise man wanted him to bring him an orange. Yet the wise man had not asked him to, had he?

'Second, when the disciple returned he presumed the wise man was speaking the truth when he said he didn't like oranges. In which case the disciple should have asked, as he was certainly entitled to, why the wise man had requested him to bring him one in the first place.

'The wise man would then have reminded him that in fact he hadn't.

'At which point — hopefully, rather than presumably — the disciple would have seen the error of his ways.

'Never presume, Cupid.' The goddess of wisdom leant forward urgently, black eyes holding him in thrall. 'That is the clue in the orange story.

'And your current mistake is presuming that the answer to the question of the best multiverse lies in the stones.

'Yet didn't M tell you that, to get the right answer, you had to ask the right question?'

'He did,' Cupid mumbled, close to tears.

'Let us assume, not presume, there are, as you rightly say, many pointers to the number 31.' She gave a conspiratorial smile. 'Thirty-one, maybe, if we managed to find them all!

'Yet what is the first question?'

'Which god, or goddess, should make the choice?' Cupid repeated woodenly.

'Which, in many ways is the right question, surely? Because once one has been chosen, it will be for them to make the decision, not you.'

'I think I see what you mean,' Cupid replied, not entirely dishonestly.

In truth, though, he was feeling close to the edge of, if not clean off, any map he was familiar with.

No wonder Minerva seemed so distant if she operated at this kind of level!

'Who lives at number 31, Cupid?'

'Jupiter,' he answered slowly. 'Oh, and Juno of course.'

'Correct. So which is it?'

'I don't know,' Cupid replied, a tear starting out of his eye. 'Venus said, as goddess of wisdom, it should be you. Which made sense to me.'

'Yet aren't we applying wisdom right now?'

'It certainly seems that way,' Cupid wailed. 'What with you and the wise man at the top of the mountain. Which is why I'm wondering where I fit in any more.'

'What is Juno goddess of, Cupid?' Minerva interrupted, ignoring his self-pity, yet sounding so infinitely patient she made him feel like a small child.

'The family and conjugal love,' he replied sulkily.

'Jupiter?'

'Fortune.'

Cupid smacked his hand to his forehead.

Fortune! Of course!

Why hadn't he seen it before?

He had thought of Jupiter, of course, but only as the greatest god, never mind his hero. Yet the best choice obviously had to be a matter of good fortune!

No wonder, as god of communications, Mercury had got nowhere.

Then he felt his hopes dashed.

'Jupiter's in Mega-Retroland™,' he pointed out bitterly.

'But won't be when GOD closes it down for us

to access the Energy Pool, on . . .' Minerva held his gaze again.

'The thirty-first,' Cupid breathed slowly.

'Of what?'

'December.'

'You see, Cupid, you've said it yourself: thirty-one, twelve and 1999.' This time it was the goddess of wisdom's pale hands, re-emerging from under her cloak, that ticked off the numbers on long delicate fingers. '1 + 2 + 1 + 9 + 9 + 9 = 31. 31 − 31.'

'The stones have given you the date as well!'

'But that's ages away, Minerva!' Cupid cried, appalled.

Was he going to have to carry the weight of responsibility right up to nearly the last moment?

'Anyhow,' he objected further, 'there won't be time then to explain it all properly. Even if there was, it's such an important decision even Jupiter's bound to need loads and loads of time to consider it.'

'So you presume.'

Cupid winced as the black eyes held him in thrall again.

'You're the goddess of wisdom, Minerva,' he appealed despairingly. 'Surely, of all of us, you must know the best answer?'

'Maybe I do,' she answered mysteriously. 'But, like you, I must wait for the fullness of time, when all will be revealed. Until then there is nothing to do. Except, of course, tell no one, not even Juno.'

'Why not?' Cupid cried out. Was he even to be stopped from sharing his burden?

'It's like a wish, Cupid. Tell, and it doesn't happen.'

'I hate waiting, though!' Cupid burst out. 'Especially on my own.'

At which her eyes opened so wide he started back-wards in his chair as he felt, for the first time, the full force of her power.

'Something that you, along with many earthlings, still have to learn, Cupid,' she pronounced with such authority he felt two feet tall, 'is that everything comes to those who wait.'

Chapter 34

Pooled

Cupid, on tenterhooks, was hovering alongside Mercury, Juno and Venus, outside Jupiter's capsule when Mega-Retroland™ closed promptly at 22.00 on 31.12.

The days of anxious waiting had reduced both him and Mercury, in their separate ways, to a frazzle. In contrast to which the goddesses, roused out of what had appeared terminal lethargy, were positively sprightly, with Juno even doing a little jig in her excitement.

Precisely on the dot, the red roof light went out, the DO NOT DISTURB: GOD AT PLAY sign extinguished and a spotlight flicked on as the door opened automatically.

There was a long pause before Jupiter stepped outside, blinking.

'My god!' Juno cried, rushing forward to embrace him.

Then she fell backwards with a cry of disbelief as he pushed her roughly to one side and set off across the lawn, eyes straight ahead, arms outstretched, as if he was sleepwalking.

'J! J!' she begged, clutching at his jacket.

He shrugged her off, then continued to ignore her, as if neither she nor any of them was there. Helplessly, they followed round the side of the villa and out onto the Close, where they saw the others. Mars, Vulcan, Neptune, Flora, Vesta, Terminus – each emerging in the same deadpan fashion, not even greeting each other as they shuffled into a line, Jupiter at its head, the others behind, outstretched arms on the shoulders of the one in front.

The ghastly crocodile set off down the Close, Cupid hopping up and down alongside, almost wetting himself. Less than two hours – 116 minutes – to go! And all his careful planning had been based on bombarding Jupiter with the multiverse changer the moment he appeared! Now what was he supposed to do? Mega-Retroland™ seemed to have turned not just Jupiter but all of them into zombies, their unseeing eyes cold, their flesh even cold to the touch.

Just as unnerving was this silence that they had brought with them. The feet of the zombie crocodile made no noise, as if floating over the ground, whilst all round an unnatural hush had descended, as after a heavy fall of snow.

Except that it was bone dry, with a completely clear sky.

Were they already Mega-Retroland™ victims, robbed not just of their brains, but their senses? Or – Cupid examined Jupiter in fresh horror — had they been deleted in all but physical form? Even become — Cupid managed to check incipient paranoia — computer animations, like JC and Buddha?

Beside him Juno was sobbing with anxiety. The same thoughts must be occurring to her.

'Blown away,' he heard Mercury hiss wonderingly, awed by the massive power they must have been subjected to.

When the crocodile reached the end of the Close Cupid saw the line of black ghost taxis standing on the road leading to the expressway ramp. Still silently, the crocodile split up, each god and goddess getting into a separate vehicle. With no choice but to follow, the four of them got into the last remaining taxi, sitting as hushed as the zombies whilst it drove slowly onto the expressway.

Waiting was an even longer line of equally sombre vehicles. From the Lower Orders' estate, Cupid realised as it fell in behind, making up the solemn procession that now set off along the slow lane. Like a long black snake, Cupid thought, clutching the precious multiverse changer to his chest. Worse, an earthling funeral cortège.

Why couldn't they go any faster? They were even being overtaken by a Juggernaut in the monster crawler lane!

Everything comes to those who wait, Minerva had promised. Yet never for a second had Cupid anticipated waiting this long. Where had she got to, anyway? He hadn't seen a sign of her since she'd left him in the summerhouse on Boxing Day. All those days, hours, minutes since, spent fretting and planning for this moment. Why hadn't he had what now seemed the good sense of Venus and Juno and switched off time by switching on GODS TV?

Hindsight, he thought in what was surely a very grown-up way, is a wonderful thing.

As the gloomy cortège wound into the centre of Godsville he became more edgy still. The silence, which none of them seemed able to break, as though their lips had been sealed, was becoming unbearable. Even the ghost taxi's engine, and its tyres on the tarmac, like the zombies' feet, were making no noise. As if everything had now been suspended in a different medium.

Then, approaching the Factory, Cupid received a fresh shock. It was shrouded in darkness, its lights no longer blazing, for the first time he could recall!

Had GOD – or rather the Beast – already closed it down? he gulped as they headed out towards the bulk of Ayers Rock, looming not purple, but ghostly grey, in the light of the waning moon.

Only the bright lights of the angel encampment provided any cheer as the cortège skirted the force field and painstakingly began to climb the winding road leading to the top of the extinct volcano, the straining taxi engine still utterly silent.

Reaching the top, they followed the vehicle in front round the edge of the rim before the line halted, rearranged into a complete circle.

As if by some prearranged signal, each god and goddess got out, walked to the edge of the lip and stood looking down into what appeared a black and bottomless pit.

Until a blinding white light lit up the sky, throwing the inside of the bowl into stark relief and highlighting the ring of standing stones, like megaliths on Planet Earth, on the flat floor below them.

Except that, weirdly, for all their height, these cast no shadow.

Meanwhile, with no GOD 'me' accompanying the light, everything remained silent. Even when a section of the bowl's floor began to slide back, revealing a mirror finish of turquoise water, that shaded from the edge to deeper and deeper green, until, in the centre, it bottomed out at an inky black which hinted at vast, unfathomable depths.

Still like zombies, the gods and goddesses progressed silently side by side down the steep incline and through the ring of standing stones, to stop at the pool edge. Cupid stood in the new circle, flanked by two regional deities he knew only by sight, and looked down at the beautiful, yet mysterious, surface which was remaining entirely unruffled, despite the warm breeze that had sprung up and was now blowing so balmily it felt more like midsummer than winter.

Cupid felt the pull.

The pool was so brimmingly full and immaculately pristine. As if just meticulously swept to remove every trace of debris, like the earthling painter Monet's romantic garden at Giverny, back on Planet Earth.

Now Cupid's mind was being swept in the same way, stilled, purified ready for the moment. His fears, troubles, afflictions, anxieties — even about the multiverse changer — were fading. As if his spirit was being gently bathed. The dirt, the hurt, teased out of the nooks and crannies, until it was entirely cleansed.

Finally, his mind floated free.

Now as automated as the rest, he shed his clothing and walked alongside the others down the gently sloping ledge. Reaching the end, he stepped without pausing into the deep, crystal-clear water. It felt so elementally and deliciously warm it was like surrendering to an embrace. Or receiving the best cuddle in the world, he thought, reminded of the time, which seemed so long ago now, when Venus had comforted him after his Factory crash.

Then it started.

The peeling off of layers.

Cupid's mind shot back to a time he had once spent on Planet Earth, hunkered down by a child at the seaside. He had been treating himself to some relaxation after pinging the boy's poor single mother to fall in love with a sad male divorcee, deprived of contact with his natural son by his vindictive ex-partner.

Cupid had known he had done well. First he had set them up for an utterly charming, hopelessly romantic courtship. Then he had fixed it with Venus and Juno for the first flush to mature into a steady, settled relationship. Not only would they both be provided with lasting joy, but the little boy would have the security he had been so desperately craving.

It was one of those moments Earth tickets were all about.

Big blue sky, warm sand, softly lapping sea, white gulls wheeling overhead. Helping the little laughing boy turn over rocks, to reveal peeler crabs which had cast their old shells, exposing their soft, vulnerable backs. Something was telling him he — all the gods and goddesses — had become crabby. Hiding beneath the hard carapaces imposed under System 7.0, fending off warmth and affection with stiff, rigid claws.

Now, alongside him, everyone was casting off those

old shells, resensitising themselves, becoming thin-skinned and soft enough to permit the input of *grazia*, that feeling of grace and love for all the good things in earthling life and their own immortalities.

It was only when you got somewhere else, Cupid now knew, that you could see where you had been. And they had all been so far away, so dead in the scummy, polluted water of the past!

The love bucket, he thought, further recalling the little boy, clutching his rock-pool treasures, going on to make sand castles. It had become empty without their knowing it, as if a pinpoint hole had gradually let the contents seep away to be silently soaked up, unnoticed, by the sand.

Now, in a renewal of faith, the hole was being repaired, the bucket replenished, filled as brimmingly as the very pool itself.

The Energy Pool, he was reminded, as, with a low hum, hidden springs began bubbling up round him. Deep, resonant springs, making his body glow as their particles rushed towards him, radiating positive energy, then rose to make the surface sizzle. So much so Cupid automatically looked up to see if there was a sudden cloudburst. Yet the sky was as clear as the water, the bright light shining down just as serenely.

Floating on his back, utterly relaxed, yet at the same time taut as a drum, Cupid submitted himself to the power, vibrating more and more in tune with the particles, until suddenly he was radiating their energy back. The more he radiated back, the more he attracted, until he was irresistibly drawn to jackknife forward and submerge himself completely in a seamless two-way organic flow.

He surfaced again, realising belatedly that sound

had returned to normal, the sizzling replaced by the gentle lapping of wavelets caused by the movements of their bodies. As his feet bumped against the ledge, he stood up in the shallow water, astonished at the change that had been wrought, not just in him, but everyone.

All along the shoreline dripping gods and goddesses were animatedly hugging each other in celebration. And, like him, now so open, aware, vulnerable, in touch with higher forces, they were laughing. Laughing in pure unalloyed delight at just being here.

Never in their immortalities could they remember feeling better.

Or greater.

In this one, great shared moment they all could see the line. The line stretching back into the mists of time and forward into the future. The line they, in concert with the earthlings, had always trodden.

Always would tread, together.

Love, they knew once again, could – would – conquer all. Nobody, both here and on Planet Earth, no matter how low they had fallen, how base they had become, was past redemption, if only they could be helped to reaccess their true selves.

Halcyon days, and nights, were back.

Now Venus was walking towards him, neither of them shamed or embarrassed by their nakedness. She smiled lovingly, holding out her index finger, whilst he held out his in turn. As they drew closer, both laughed in sheer delight at the energy crackling and sparking between their respective digits.

Soon it was not just them. Everyone was doing it. Transmitting, as well as receiving, in one glorious connected surge.

It was the supreme moment of affirmation, both to each other and the whole.

And as it ended, the bright light in the sky began to fade.

Chapter 35

Stoned

After they had gone quietly to dress themselves, Cupid's underlying anxiety returned when he felt the weight of the multiverse changer in his pocket.

He took it out and looked at it, thinking how it seemed to be reproaching him for not yet enabling it to do its job.

'Over to you, Cupid.'

He jumped at the soft voice behind him and turned to see Minerva, smiling her quizzical smile.

'Where have you been?' he demanded. 'Are you going to help me?'

'Fortune favours the brave, Cupid,' she smiled in a friendly fashion before walking off, her retreating back giving him his answer.

'How are you, little chap? Got something for me, I believe?'

Cupid whipped round to see Jupiter was beaming down at him.

'How do you know?' he gasped, nonetheless immediately shoving the multiverse changer into the huge outstretched palm.

'Because it's my job.'

The greatest god motioned Cupid to sit down on the warm rock beside him while he examined the changer curiously.

'You just switch on, tap in your choice of number, and press SEND,' Cupid explained.

'Any number?' Jupiter enquired with interest.

'The number of the multiverse you want to change to. Any one between one and ninety-nine. Except I think I already know the best answer. For us and the earthlings!'

Despite what Minerva had said previously, Cupid just couldn't give up on thirty-one. It was too indelibly burnt into his consciousness.

'I'll have to start right at the beginning, I'm afraid, Jupiter,' he gabbled on. 'You see, there's so much you've got to catch up on. So many different things I've worked out I have to tell you about . . .'

'I'm sure you've been working very hard, little god,' Jupiter interrupted casually, yet with so much authority, such overwhelming *gravitas*, that Cupid shrank back at the demonstration of raw, yet refined, power.

Without further ado, Jupiter switched on the changer and tapped a key with a thick finger.

As Cupid saw '56' spring up on the screen, he hurled himself across his mentor's lap and managed to wrest the changer from his grasp before he could press SEND.

'Stop!' he cried. 'You see, some of the choices are ones we'd rather not have! With one the best of all!

And one best for us, but worst for the Beast! Which is why I've got to tell you about number 31. It's terribly, terribly important.'

He glanced at his watch. Less than thirty-five minutes to lay out his entire argument!

Yet already Mercury had charged up and shoved him to one side!

'You can't choose a number at random without even thinking about it,' the god of communications cried unbelievingly. 'That's chaos! You have to stop, analyse, consider, weigh all the factors, make a rational decision.'

'I have,' Jupiter replied calmly.

'But you haven't got any information!' Mercury shrieked.

'Haven't I?'

'What is it?' Mercury asked suspiciously.

'The information that there is no relevant information.'

'That's no information at all!'

'Exactly. Which is why I've chosen not to waste time thinking about it.'

'But you must!' Not only was Mercury's vein throbbing. His whole body was trembling uncontrollably.

'Rather, I mustn't,' Jupiter rebutted him with the same overwhelming *gravitas*. 'Otherwise, like you, how would I ever be able to decide?'

'But you have to base your decision on something!' Mercury gibbered, his mouth working uncontrollably, and foam appearing on his lips.

'There is something. Everything. Which is nothing.'

As Jupiter looked up at the curious crowd of gods and goddesses now surrounding them, Cupid thought how he was sounding more and more like Minerva every second.

'Immortality's too short to endlessly ponder,' the greatest god informed the throng. 'For if I, as god of fortune, was to do that, how would I, for example, ever choose the winning lottery number?

'And, if I can choose the winning lottery number, can I not choose the winning multiverse?'

Whilst Mercury spluttered in disbelief at this banal mathematical illogic, Jupiter held out his hand for Cupid to pass the changer back.

Yet still Cupid hesitated. All that head space, that agonising, that striving and straining over 31! Cut through, just like that!

There absolutely had to be more to it.

Should he exercise the courage of his convictions? Cancel 56? Enter 31?

Yet, as Jupiter continued patiently holding out his hand, Cupid knew not just he, but Mercury, would have to cede to what they recognised as a greater force.

Minerva was right.

It was not for him to choose, it was for the god of fortune.

Yet he still had to say something.

'You can't just forget about the stones, Jupiter!' he was appealing despairingly, when a message flicked up on the changer's screen.

Jupiter gestured him to hold it up so they could both read it.

> YOU HAVE KEYED IN 56 BUT NOT PRESSED SEND. IF YOU WISH TO CONTINUE WITH THIS MULTIVERSE PARADIGM SPLIT OPTION PRESS SEND. FOLLOWING WHICH, TO CONFIRM, FIRST REKEY 56, THEN PRESS SEND AGAIN.

> EXECUTION WILL FOLLOW AFTER TWO MINUTES <

Before Cupid could stop it, Jupiter's craggy forefinger descended firmly on the SEND button.

'You rekey 56,' he smiled, passing it back.

'Me?'

Cupid's fingers let go of the changer as though it was red-hot and it dropped onto the rock with a clatter.

Slowly, as if they had all the time in the world, Jupiter reached down, picked it up, and held it out again.

'Don't you want to share the responsibility for being right?' he smiled affectionately.

Cupid looked at his hero in anguish. Responsibility! That dreadful word again!

'Do I have to?' he wailed.

'No, but you should.' Jupiter's voice was infinitely warm and encouraging. 'There's no problem.' He smiled more broadly than ever. 'You see, none of us, including me, will ever know whether 56 was the best choice.

'All we will know is that, like the winning lottery number, it was the choice.'

Cupid continued staring at his hero, his mind in utter confusion. How could Jupiter know whether it was the Beast's chosen world as well?

He glanced at his watch.

23.29.26!

Yet, with the time ticking away, what choice did he have?

'I'll do it,' he announced bravely.

Not thinking any further, he took the changer, rekeyed 56, pressed SEND and hurriedly passed it back.

'Well, well, well!' Jupiter smiled.

'What is it?' Cupid asked, heart in mouth.

Jupiter tilted the changer so Cupid could see the screen.

> DESIRED MULTIVERSE OPTION OF 56 ACCEPTED. CHANGE NOW PROGRAMMED IN AND WILL TAKE EFFECT AT 23.31.31 PRECISELY. PLEASE VIEW SEPARATE COUNTDOWN <

The reverse clock in the corner had already reached 1 minute 47 seconds.

Cupid sprang to his feet as if this time it was the rock that was red-hot. He couldn't take any more of this! Quickly, he ran away to the side of the pool.

He stood there panting, his eyes flicking over the pantheon of happy gods and goddesses gambolling round the edge, bubbling with the renewed joy of their immortalities and quite oblivious of the tight little scene he had just been involved in.

Ignorance is bliss, he thought, feeling entirely grown up.

What would be coming all their ways in just over a minute's time? Their doom? Their last gasp? Or a new multiverse, where they would be back on song? One they would prefer not to be in? One a little better for both them and the earthlings? Much better? Mega-better?

He looked down at the unruffled water and the bright pinpoints that were the stars, reflected again in the mirror surface now the bright light had faded.

Not just the stars, but the ring of standing stones, which still, weirdly, cast no shadow.

His eyes widened as shock pierced him to the bone.

The stones!

Feverishly, he started to count them, feeling the time pressure, yet knowing he must not rush and risk losing his place. He would have no second chance.

Yet, coming towards the end of the circle, he already

sensed what the answer would be. As if there had been no real need to count at all.

51 – 52 – 53 – 54 – 55.

There were 56!

'Jupiter!' he shouted, running back to salute his hero – and where was Minerva? She absolutely had to know about this as well! Then there was a blinding eruption in the sky.

Along with the others, he froze in mid-step, as if stopped onscreen.

At which point everything changed.

Chapter 36

Back to the Future

The Factory was roaring. And Jupiter loved it.
The buzz. The crack. The sheer exhilaration of
being here in the Planet Earth control room while
the earthlings approached such an epic moment in
their history. The energy he and his fellow gods and
goddesses were pumping out to help them! He could
picture the outside of the Factory's glass pyramid, high
on its hill overlooking Godsville, positively vibrating
with its power.

And now more than energy. As the digital calendar
hanging over the rows of workstations flicked on to
23.15.00/31.12.1999, GMT, Earth Time, anticipation
was surging through the enormous room.

Jupiter looked round, contentedly taking stock, as
they paused for the break he had built into their
schedule. The calm before the storm.

How long since they had last felt like this? All the work needed since the unanimous vote at the Basilica meeting fifteen days ago to re-engage with Planet Earth had been completed. There was a settled feeling, a satisfaction that they were ready, as they gazed at the scenes from Planet Earth on the giant wall screen encircling the room.

How they loved the glorious confusion and babble, the way their charges chopped and changed every moment! Not long and they would be back in there, an integral part of it all once again. To have a purpose, after having mouldered away for so long! As they listened to the throb and hum of the enabling machinery surrounding them, they felt truly great.

Jupiter was getting up for a stroll when Vulcan, wearing an immaculately ironed boiler suit, came striding up the aisle.

'A little present,' he muttered awkwardly, his callused fingers pressing a small, crudely wrapped packet into Jupiter's palm.

Jupiter hefted it, puzzled by its lightness, then opened it and shook out the contents. Six pristine seeds, gleaming fatly with life, beamed up at him.

Seeds? It was always a pleasure to receive a gift, but . . .

'Pumpkins,' the god of fire explained gruffly.

Jupiter hoped he wasn't looking too mystified. He didn't mind the odd spot of gardening, if he ever had the time. Which was seldom. Yet he had never grown a pumpkin in his entire immortality, as far as he could remember. They were a waste of space, unless you were an inhabitant of downtown Witchway.

But then Vulcan was always leaning over the fence, urging him to try the experimental seeds Flora brought round for him to grow in the strange machinations he produced with his ancient technology. Like his latest toy of a boiler-driven pineapple pit. There were times he seemed to Jupiter so way back in the past, it was almost as if he inhabited a different universe.

'An old-fashioned variety I'm about to return to Planet Earth,' Flora interjected proudly from across the aisle.

'Very good,' Jupiter smiled approvingly.

'I'll give them a try,' he promised Vulcan, setting off on his planned stroll.

His first stop was cheeky little Cupid, flexing his best bow in readiness, whilst his mother, looking gorgeous, regarded him lovingly.

'I was thinking about arriving back on a seashell,' she laughed.

Jupiter's mind flicked to the painting on her wall. He had been admiring it only yesterday. Such a personification of youthful grace.

'After all, Planet Earth's postmodernist these days, isn't it?' she was adding when Cupid butted in.

'Meaning my bow and arrow has never been more up to date! Or radical!' he squeaked happily.

Jupiter laughed and ruffled his hair before moving on down the line to Mercury, now recovered from the tantrum he had thrown after seeing Saturn sitting at his terminal, blithely sharpening his scythe with a whetstone. How could anyone show such blatant disregard for such delicate computer machinery? he had screamed.

'Online?' Jupiter enquired affectionately.

'Ready to be connected,' the god of communications grinned, smoothing his gelled hair proudly. 'Not, of course, that techno's anything but a tool in the hands of its operator.'

'And, of everyone, you're the best,' Jupiter smiled sincerely, turning to Neptune.

'Back in the swim?'

'Rejoining the shoal,' the salty old sea god roared.

'Time and tide wait for no one, eh, Saturn?' Jupiter called across the aisle.

'*Tempus fugit*,' the venerable old god replied, and Jupiter's thoughts flicked back to the meeting.

'And we must all *fugit* with it?' he asked with mock gravity, by way of seeking confirmation.

'Indeed, or fall prey to the cutting edge.'

Jupiter winced as the scythe whistled through the air, nearly slicing the top off the god of time's monitor.

Guffawing, he moved on to Vesta.

'Home fires burning bright?'

'Brighter than ever!' She gave an immaculate smile.

Sighing at such dazzling and perfect beauty, Jupiter hesitated as he approached Mars's terminal. Why this sudden feeling they had had a huge falling out? Some terminal disagreement? They had discussed it for long enough, hadn't they? And amicably enough?

'I'm not pretending there won't be any more earthling wars in the future,' Mars had been explaining. 'But what I'm not taking responsibility for is these ethnic ones plaguing Planet Earth. They're not war as I understand it. Something heroic, gallant. Something with standards, codes. Noble even – at least on occasions. A fitting place for any man.

'These ones are filthy, horrible.' His normally eager face had gone dark as his brow clouded over. 'No quarter given and none taken, you know, Jupiter – to women, children, the sick, the old, even beloved pets. All victims, to be sacrificed in the front line. Obscene, in my book. Yet necessary, as an inevitable fallout from the past, eh? You should know about that.'

Actually, Jupiter didn't, at least in detail, thanks to Progressive Memory Loss. Yet, as he had battled in the past to obtain justice for various earthling groupings at places like the United Nations, he had seen how in some places matters had become so entrenched there now seemed no other answer but for both sides to slug it out.

'The divisions have gone too deep,' he had agreed. 'But if they can only be sorted once and for all, even if in a bloody fashion, at least that promises more stability for the future.

'I'm committing myself to banging together the heads of those woolly-minded liberals with their endless committees,' he had informed Mars in turn. 'Forcing them to take decisive action, not indulge in ineffectual hand-wringing.'

Then he had moved to a subject dearer to his heart.

'I trust you don't think I'm trespassing on your territory, but I'm also going to fight to make war cleaner. Try to keep at least some of the civilians out of the action. Like my landmines campaign.'

Which had been going well. Or as well as that sort of thing could.

All the gods had felt what a planet-shattering paradigm shift the death of Princess Diana had been. A multi-verse splitting point if they had ever come across one. A tragedy turned to triumph, out of which so much good had sprung, despite the shabbiness of so many of the earthlings involved in, or clambering aboard, the act. In the Land of the Gods they all knew Princess Diana would be regarded as a goddess by many young earthlings in the next century. And, whatever anyone might say about her subsequently, she was one whom they were already proud and happy to number amongst their ranks.

'That's fine with me, Jupiter, because I've seen a new war to be fought today,' Mars had gone on eagerly to explain, his dark eyes flashing at the prospect of action. 'All those scumbags on the streets of the Western cities — the violent criminals, ruthless drugs dealers, heavy muggers, GBH merchants, rapists, murderers. They're to be my targets. I'll single them out, one by one, for a taste of their own medicine.'

'Excellent,' Jupiter had agreed. 'Funny, isn't it, how the earthlings sometimes forget that us gods — and goddesses, of course — aren't just benevolent beings, here to help make everything sweetness and light?'

'That we're also punishers of wrongdoers?' Mars had concurred. 'Absolutely we are! And those daring to transgress our moral code — and that of any decent earthling — are about to discover a bit of smiting is coming their way!'

He must be imagining things, Jupiter now thought as he saw Mars's eyes light up in greeting. Of course they were still mates. Why, both avengers in their own right, should they ever fall out?

'Got the laser sight ready? he grinned.

'Absolutely!' Mars roared. 'When they see that red dot on their chest, they'll know it's all over!'

They would as well, Jupiter was about to reply, when a message flashed up on all their screens:

> MEGAVERSE 2000 INSTALLATION COM-PLETED. NOW ONLINE AND READY TO ROLL. TRIAL RUN WILL COMMENCE IN TWO MINUTES <

Jupiter popped his head quickly into the Nordic and Teutonic side room.

'All working, Thor?' he called out.

'You bet!' the answering shout came back. 'Like Mars, ready to give the scumbags a real hammering!' He swung his weapon wildly round his head, red beard bristling.

I wouldn't want to be an earthling meeting him on a dark night! Jupiter grinned to himself as he strode back to his terminal, beaming at everyone. They were all so vibrant, so powered up, so pulsing with love and eagerness!

'How's it going, dear?' he asked Juno tenderly.

'I was thinking about the children, J,' she replied absent-mindedly. 'The little innocents holding the key to the future, when this song came into my head.

'They've got the whole of Planet Earth, in their hands,

'The whole of Planet Earth, in their hands . . .' She stopped singing.

'I wonder where that came from,' she said.

'I don't know,' Jupiter replied frankly, gazing into the depths of her green eyes.

The old songs.

Of all the PML flashbacks that surfaced in inexplicable gobbets and snippets, the songs were always the strongest.

Like the one now triggered in his own head.

'You say you want a godly evolution,' he sang to his beloved consort,

'Well you know, we all want to change Planet Earth,

'We know we have a new solution . . .'

His voice tailed away. He'd forgotten the rest.

Instead he held out his index finger for her to raise hers and for them to do the energy-transfer thing. Looking round, he saw all the other gods and goddesses following their lead, the electricity they were generating making the computer screens judder.

'We flicked the switch fandango,' Juno sang to him lovingly,

'Booted our terminals 'cross the floor;
'We were feeling kind of bombed out,
'But the earthlings yelled out for more.
'The computer room hummed harder,
'As their gods all flew away . . .
'Ready for the dance, dear?'

Jupiter smiled, understanding the reference in their 'Whiter Shade of Power' song to leaving the Earth control room and stepping through the Curtain to fly, or rather matter transfer themselves, to Planet Earth.

'Trip the light fantastic? Never more so, my love.'

A beep came from their monitors and they swung back and sat, poised, whilst their respective screens first blacked, then sprang into new life.

> MEGAVERSE 2000 TRIAL RUN SUCCESS-FUL. FULL SYSTEM TRANSFER WILL BE IMPLE-MENTED AT 00.00.01 <

'Immortality works!' Jupiter shouted above the cheers.

'I'll drink to that!'

Bacchus was about to upend his magnum of champagne when Jupiter grabbed it and took a swig, meanwhile reading off the figures on the giant digital clock hanging above the rows of work stations, next to the huge banner: MEGAVERSE 2000 WISHES EVERYONE A HAPPY, FULFILLING AND GLO-RIOUS NEW MILLENNIUM!

23.31.00/31.12.1999.

Time to join the earthling party.

'Everyone to the Curtain,' he shouted.

Cheering wildly, they poured off their terminals.

Jupiter felt the bubbling mix of exhilaration and solemnity as they processed down the corridor to the atrium, then lined up to insert their earth tickets into the slot and go through into the docking booth.

'All systems go,' he finally yelled as the last — Terminus, still fiddling fussily with the catch on his briefcase — stepped inside.

'No limits this time, eh?' he added in a jokey aside to the god of boundaries as he closed the door, then hit the button that impelled them outwards into space.

He waited, hovering, whilst they arranged them-selves into a wedge formation behind him. Then he gave the signal and, like a flock of emigrating birds, together they matter-transferred themselves across the heavens to the edge of the Earth's atmosphere, where he reined them in.

Here they were to split forces, as each zoomed off to their particular destination. Or, as he was about to, took a brief step out to collect their thoughts.

It was a moment of temporary parting, yet supreme togetherness, reminiscent of their recent trip to the Energy Pool that had so recharged them.

'Good fortune to you all!' he cried, looking down at the swirling pattern of clouds over the round ball of the planet below them.

It was right that they should be down here, in the action, rather than at their terminals, when the millennium moment came. Yet it felt so long since he had last visited, he couldn't stifle a twinge of nervousness.

'Be brave, my dear,' Juno, beside him, whispered for his ears only. 'It's a new world down there.'

'And we're new gods, aren't we?' he asked, seeking the confirmation he needed.

'Like many, many earthlings, my dear,' she replied gravely. 'Old maybe in multiple ways, yet new in so many others.'

'Renewed?'

'As new,' Juno smiled, then broke the solemnity with a light-hearted laugh.

'Careful,' she grinned, 'or we'll start sounding like a Hollywood movie!'

'No harm in that,' Jupiter laughed back.

All those old clichés the earthling film industry peddled over and over again. Wasn't it a question of attitude? That they were either hoary, worn-out phrases and images, or splendid, and much-needed, reaffirmations of the essence?

There was no time to debate it now. Not that they needed to. They both knew which side of the fence they stood on.

'Never a B movie though, I sincerely hope, my dear,' he remarked gravely, giving her a loving kiss.

As he peeled off, Juno, knowing where he was going, smiled contentedly.

That was her consort for her, always needing to be at the centre of the earth.

Epilogue

Not even terminal PML could delete Jupiter's know-ledge that he had once inhabited a mountain. It was built into his very core, just as he thought of mountains as the core of Planet Earth. Which sounded a bit odd, when they were the bits that stuck up the most.

But Jupiter knew what he meant.

Which was why he had chosen to matter-transfer himself to the Himalaya — what the earthlings called 'the roof of the world'. Jupiter considered her tower-ing, glistening solidity — for the Himalaya was both collective and female — the ultimate manifestation of the primal source out of which had risen Planet Earth and, with it, the Land of the Gods. Short of the Earth being destroyed in its entirety, she would always be there, sending out her energy charge for every god and mortal to pick up on.

Cruising along the ridge in the bright morning sunlight, he had to smile at the nonsenses of earthling time. Here, the millennium moment had already been and gone eight hours ago. Except for an even more curious nonsense, which many earthlings were not even aware of. Nepal, the country where the Himalaya was located, operated on a different calendar from the West, and had already celebrated its millennium more than fifty years previously.

Jupiter dismissed these irrelevant thoughts as he felt the crystal-clear air soothing him with its magic. Often, when in earthling cities, he felt overwhelmed by the seething mass of mortality surrounding him. The blizzard of what he called 'white noise', with everything seeming to cancel out everything else, to little or no purpose. Yet in this silent solitude all the trivia cluttering not just earthling life, but his own immortality, dropped away. It was so basic here, so elemental, that to be at one with it you first had to find peace within yourself.

How could a god, even the greatest god – never mind an earthling – not feel awed by such a majestic force of nature? Yet earthling materialists and reductionists, refusing to believe in anything except science and reason, merely analysed it. Broke it down into its component parts and pretended there was nothing more to it. How they infuriated him with their refusal to believe in gods! Or, when he was in a benign mood, as now, aroused his eternal pity.

It was such a bleak picture they painted for themselves. Meanwhile, how limited, credulous and naive they were to insist such a rich and complex world as Planet Earth had no meaning, no pattern. Why, it was so finely balanced even the slightest change in its original natural make-up would have rendered it sterile and boring!

Yet it was so staggeringly wonderful, with its multiple extraordinary facets, it could never have been created by coincidence, or random chaos. The odds were simply too enormous. Surely even the dimmest earthling, possessed of no imagination whatsoever, had to accept that all the evidence pointed to there being something else?

Which there was. As, fortunately, many earthlings did know. Or, if not know, have the courage and faith to believe. Spirituality, the gods, GOD, the Aura, God, all the multiple religions and belief systems on Planet Earth. Each said much the same thing, if you sifted through their dogma to access the bedrock of their true philosophies.

It made no real difference which one you believed in, as long you accepted you were linked to the strands of time stretching backwards into the mist and forwards to eternity. That there were no coincidences. That everything was connected, had a meaning, if you could but divine it.

Jupiter's attention was suddenly caught by a solitary plant, peeking out way above the snowline. Was that just a collection of particles, a make-up of chemicals, as the earthling scientists would have you believe? Or was it yet another example of the wonder Planet Earth contained in such extraordinary abundance. In every leaf, every branch, every tree, every rock, every hill, every mountain, every earthling.

If they would but acknowledge that their bodies were just as much a collection of particles, in this case given momentary consciousness! That they had temporarily been given the ball to run with, before their bodies reverted to particle state when they died? Or, as salty old Neptune put it, they were not just all swimming in the same sea, but actually part of that sea themselves? That joint pool of energy.

Jupiter took more lungfuls of the heady atmosphere.

So was he right in thinking many earthlings did now realise that? That the old Darwinian idea of its being a place where everything preyed on everything else, regardless, was being abandoned?

It might be a tender shoot, as Flora said. And not the first, all of them also sensed through the mists of Progressive Memory Loss. Yet Jupiter had faith that the plant was more firmly rooted this time round. Capable, given the right climate, of growing sturdily, blossoming gloriously, setting its fruit successfully.

Maybe it was simply because it had sprouted from the seed of necessity. A dawning understanding that things simply had to change. Certainly that was the case of its ecology, the basic DOS of GOD the computer. More and more earthlings were belatedly comprehending that they had been treating the balance with such callous disregard, they had been risking their planet's doom.

And if necessity had caused this change in attitude, that was no bad thing. Jupiter had always respected the earthlings' ability to rise to a challenge, self-imposed though it might be.

And even if, as usual, they were leaving their response nerve-rackingly late.

Jupiter had now moved far enough along the ridge to reach Mount Everest. The highest mountain on Planet Earth, brooding blackly amongst the fellow peaks which protectively enclosed it, largely hiding it from prying earthbound eyes. His favourite thunderbolt target, its difficulty only adding to its appeal. Immortal Jupiter might be, but he did not make the mistake of presuming to be infallible.

As his first two bolts had just proved by going searing over its peak.

He frowned. He wasn't normally that bad. Must be rusty. Just one good hit, though, and he would be ready to face anything the earthlings could throw at him.

Not thinking, he fired casually from the hip and watched the thunderbolt zap into the heart of the mountain, accompanied by a clap of thunder so exquisitely pitched that not a snowflake stirred.

The power! He had back the power!

As well as the skill!

Always, when thunderbolting, Jupiter tried not to start an avalanche which might endanger any earthling daring to make the climb. Not that he particularly wished them good fortune. They knew, or should know, that they trespassed on such hallowed ground at their peril. Yet, a visitor like them, he did not seek to weight the balance. The Himalaya was neutral.

His objective achieved, he glanced at his laptop.

23.56.31.

The last minutes ticking away towards 00.00.01/ 01.01.2000 GMT. The turning point, when the collective efforts of Megaverse 2000, themselves and the earthlings would come together to shape the future: Uncertain it was bound to be, with none of the old System 7.0 rules applying, and kicking off with the much-hyped 'millennium bug'.

The end of history, some earthlings called it, where the lessons of the past would no longer be valid. A wonderful opportunity — artificial or not — to leave behind past cares and worries. Draw a line. Start tilting the balance towards Planet Earth becoming a place worth living on.

And immortalising for.

Could he and his fellow gods and goddesses enable the earthlings to work it out? Like their gods, they were as possessed of free will and as influenced by the ever-lurking L files.

Jupiter had to confess he simply didn't know.

The Beast was still in the machine, no doubt at this very moment regrouping and looking for a new way in. All Jupiter, Juno, Venus, Cupid, Vulcan, Minerva — the whole pantheon of them — could do was their best.

Load in the positives — peace, hope, compassion, tolerance, justice, patience, goodwill, self-sacrifice, courage, strength, care for others, good fortune, of course . . . The list went on and on, adding up to a huge infusion of optimism and cheerfulness for the future.

Every earthling man, woman or child inspired enough by their communal message to actually practise it themselves would increase the power to make the world a better place. Create the synergy, the earthling will to combine with the gods in the much-needed work of regeneration.

Many rationally based 'sensible' earthlings would no doubt dismiss this as a hopelessly naive philosophy, too idealistic ever to be practised successfully. But Jupiter knew them of old. These were the ones suffering from hubris, that overweening ego-led pride and arrogance which made them refuse to bow to the will of the gods.

Just let them try to cling to the belief that they controlled their lives, and that of their planet, if they insisted! One way or another, they would eventually be forced to accept that much of their fate lay, as it always had, in the terminals and laptops of their gods.

Never forgetting GOD, of course.

Jupiter took a last, lingering look at the mighty peaks.

'Be brave!' he whispered, unsure whether he was addressing the Himalaya, himself, or the earthlings. 'It's a new world!'

Closing his eyes, he matter-transferred himself to Greenwich, where he hovered over the Millennium Dome, hearing the cheers as Big Ben rang out over London, while the power of Megaverse 2000 surged into his laptop.

All round him rockets were bursting in showers of incandescent light and for a nanosecond he was tempted to top them with a coruscating battery of thunderbolts.

Then he held back.

It would be a showy, dramatic gesture, immensely appealing to those earthlings demanding instant gratification. But that was not what he, or they, were here for. This was the start of a longer, slower process. Individual earthlings first needed to make the commitment, demonstrate the leap of faith.

For those possessing that courage, there would be signs aplenty in the future they were on the right track, helping it all come together.

'Should auld acquaintance be forgot,' he instead joined in happily,

'And never brought to mind . . .'

Old acquaintances he and the earthlings certainly were!

Older than they would ever know.

It was time to move on.

London, and Europe, were one thing. But it was America, the land of the free and now indisputably the leader of the world's culture, which was his, and every god's and goddess's main target — even little Cupid. That land of freedom, courage and hope, yet also of such gross, self-centred excess, which, for good or for ill, would be setting much of the pattern for the Planet Earth of the future.

And Jupiter was determined it would be for good.

Closing his eyes, he set his sights on his first port of call, New York, which he had marked out for some serious fortune correcting, starting with the money and market obsessions.

He felt the normal momentary weightlessness, followed by the familiar jar on his feet.

'The Eagle has landed,' he mouthed to himself as he stepped out briskly along the pavement in downtown Manhattan, dwarfed by the towering buildings all round him.